Th

Elizabeth Har[...]
brought up in [...]
graduation she l[...]ing driv-
ing a van, being a lifeguard and working in the
Civil Service. She has travelled extensively in
Europe and America, and lived for some years in
the Far East.

Elizabeth Harris was one of the finalists of the
1989 Ian St James Awards.

The Herb Gatherers

Elizabeth Harris

Fontana
An Imprint of HarperCollins*Publishers*

*With grateful thanks to Tim and Penny Harris,
for allowing me to make free with their cottage;
to Judy Sharpe and Charles Pailthorpe for their
professional opinions; and to the many friends
and family members who have given
encouragement and advice.*

First published in 1991 by Fontana,
an imprint of HarperCollins Publishers,
77/85 Fulham Palace Road,
Hammersmith, London W6 8JB

9 8 7 6 5 4 3 2 1

Phototypeset by Input Typesetting Ltd, London
Printed and bound in Great Britain by
HarperCollins Manufacturing, Glasgow

For my parents, with love

I

One

'That was a bit perfunctory.'

Rafe, lying half asleep with one arm across his face to block out the bright morning sun, heard Suzanna's voice as if from another world. Her complaining tone eloquently expressed her dissatisfaction, and he knew she wasn't going to content herself with that one brief sentence. He sighed. So much for his hopes of dozing away another hour and escaping the disgruntled analysis that was now the inevitable aftermath of their lovemaking.

'Sorry,' he said lightly. 'You crept up on me when I wasn't ready.' He reached for her hand, giving it a squeeze. Sometimes she could be deflected by a combination of affection and humour.

'You bloody well seemed ready enough.' Not this time, apparently; her words were angry with reproach. 'You had a hard-on like a helter-skelter, the moment I touched you!'

Yes, but that was nothing to do with you, he thought, his body throbbing faintly at the memory. I was dreaming, and you dragged me away.

'Sorry,' he said again. There wasn't anything else he could say. He wasn't surprised she was cross; it had been over too quickly for her to have got anything from it. He'd felt her hands on him, rousing, demanding hands that in some way echoed whatever it was he'd been dreaming about, and he'd turned mindlessly to take her. But not as herself, not as Suzanna; as a mere impersonal female body. Representing any woman. All women.

She was sitting on the edge of the bed, pushing her arms into the sleeves of her dressing-gown. Her hands were clenched into fists. She stood up, bending to put on her sandals. The movement revealed one of her small breasts, tanned to gold, its nipple brown and still glistening slightly from his own

11

recent sucking. He felt disappointed in himself, that he could have made love to a woman from whom he had come to feel so detached.

'Are you going to make some tea?' he asked. She looked down at him, her face expressionless. 'Will you bring me a cup?'

She turned and left the bedroom, answering neither his questions nor his placatory smile.

He listened to the flip-flop of her sandals going down the steps, heard the creak of the bathroom door sound in the stillness. Someone called from the kitchen, 'Want some breakfast?' Caroline was up, then. That'll be nice for Suzanna, he thought. She'll have someone to moan to. Someone to say consolingly, oh, poor you, typical of a man, they're all the same, only thinking of themselves. To pour out platitudes along with the tea in a militant upsurge of female solidarity.

They were old hands at solidarity, those two. He pictured them, heads together, muttering intently and exclusively. They were so damned typical of their class and their country.

They're alien to me, he thought. As alien as all this is to them.

He leapt out of bed, his irritation reaching a peak so that he could no longer lie still. He crossed to the window, flinging back the shutters to let the sun come swamping eagerly in. He stood with his eyes closed, feeling the heat like the touch of a familiar hand on his naked body. Just as he'd felt it on countless mornings, all his life. Why do I ever leave? he wondered. Why, when I have this house that stands on one of the most beautiful sites on earth, do I let the English half of me persuade me that Crete is a backwater, that *real* life only starts when you forsake the sunshine for the chilly, rational north?

He opened his eyes and leaned on the window-sill, and immediately the palliative effects of the scene before him began to work. His bedroom faced the hillside behind the house, and, other than a few goats whose bells produced an irregular and melodic tonking, not a living creature was in sight. There was a smell of herbs which brought back for an instant something he'd been dreaming about. The grass was still lush and green from the winter rains, and the wild flowers were at the peak of their brilliance. He wished he knew what they were. His grandmother had known them, all of them, reeling off their names as if they were a family of exceptionally pretty children. One unforgettable day in a spring that had gone into folklore for its profusion, she had taken him out and shown him twenty different species of orchids. On that same hillside, behind the house that used to be hers and that now belonged to him.

The tranquillity washed over him, smoothing away the tension. There were other people in the house – Suzanna and Caroline in the kitchen, Malcolm no doubt still fast asleep, Stephen probably sitting in some shady corner reading – but they were irrelevant. They didn't have the power to disturb a peace of this profundity. He had known almost immediately that it had been a mistake to invite them all out here, but he'd learned to live with it. It was going to be okay.

And anyway, in less than a week they'd all be going home.

A door opened, interrupting the quiet. A heavy-footed tread lurched along the corridor and down the stone steps, and Malcolm's loud voice said petulantly, 'I *hate* houses where you have to go downstairs to the bog!'

One of the girls made some comment, and Malcolm, shouting to make himself heard over the sound of his own urinating, replied, 'I don't care if it is a traditional Cretan house! Don't traditional Cretans ever feel it'd be nice to piss upstairs?'

Rafe resumed his communing with the silent hillside. I'm not sure I'm ready for Malcolm just yet, he thought. Why does he have to be crass all the time? Once in a while, being outrageous is entertaining. But when it goes on and on, it becomes a pain. Like Malcolm. Unfortunately, until I invited him out here I didn't *know* it went on and on. And it doesn't help that he drinks such a lot. As if he were back on one of those rugby tours he recalls with such fondness.

I'm hungry, he thought. Hungry enough to put up with Suzanna being angry with me *and* Malcolm being a prat. No reason why either of them should keep me out of my own kitchen.

He pulled on a pair of shorts and went down to breakfast.

Downstairs, it was clear that a meal of epic proportions was being prepared. Rafe sat down in a chair on the terrace, watching Caro steamroller Suzanna and Malcolm into carrying trays and laying the table. She was efficient at people-management, but he usually tried to avoid being drafted into the workforce; he was too readily annoyed by her attitude of being the only one to know how to do things *properly*. He wondered idly just how long you could drag out the first meal of the day and still call it breakfast: it was after half past ten.

'Count me out, please,' he said to her when she emerged briefly to check that Malcolm had put the salt and pepper mills on the right mat. 'I only want coffee.'

'Well, I'm not cooking lunch!' she snapped. 'It's this or go hungry.'

He forbore to say that it was her own choice to install herself in his kitchen. There were tavernas in the vicinity, nobody had to cook anything unless they really wanted to.

'Bloody hell!' Stephen said, coming out just as she was sweeping back inside; the unmistakable smell of overheating fat was wafting from the kitchen. 'What's the matter with her?'

Rafe shrugged. 'The effort of trying to organize four people who don't want to be organized, I suppose.'

'Wouldn't be in Malcolm's shoes,' Stephen remarked, pulling up a chair and sitting down beside Rafe. 'He's a brave man if he's prepared to face that every morning for the rest of his natural.'

'They're getting married, then?'

'Didn't you know? She makes enough show of sticking out

14

that damned great rock on her finger for even *you* to have spotted it!'

Rafe smiled: Stephen had been accusing him regularly and unfoundedly for years of failing to notice things. But I did know about Malcolm and Caro, he thought. Suzanna and I went to that special dinner, lovingly cooked by Caro, to celebrate the occasion of Malcolm finally bowing to pressure and asking her to marry him. Or, more likely, acceding to her demands that he marry her. His mental graph of the similar pressure applied by Suzanna on him had shown a sharp increase in steepness around that time. Whilst it irritated him greatly, part of him felt a deep sympathy for Suzanna, forced to endure Caro's triumphant jubilation day and night – the two of them shared a flat – and forced, by his lack of enthusiasm, into being the one who wasn't engaged yet.

Only she wasn't going to be. Not to him.

I shouldn't have let them push me into agreeing to this holiday, he thought wearily. They got to me when I was feeling sorry for her. I should have said no, I don't want us to go away together. Not Suzanna and me, even more so not the whole lot of us. And now she seems to have been encouraged by all this, maybe got it into her head there'll be two weddings in the autumn.

'Shit,' he muttered.

Stephen looked up from his book. 'What's the matter?'

Rafe shook his head. 'Nothing.'

Stephen stared out over the balcony rail. 'Hmm. Not the restful fortnight away from it all that you'd envisaged, is it?'

'No.' He doesn't miss anything, Rafe thought. 'Crazy to have invited them, wasn't I?'

'I don't remember that you did, exactly. I'd say it was more a case of Malcolm saying in his usual forthright way, hey, Rafe's got a house in Crete, let's all go out for a holiday, and you finding it easier to agree than to think up convincing reasons for putting us off.'

15

'I don't mind *you*,' Rafe said mildly. 'I hardly notice you're here. What *is* that you're reading?'

Stephen held out the huge book he took everywhere with him. 'Freud and Jung.' His tone was throwaway, as if such writings constituted everyone's holiday reading. 'Summary of their works on dreams and the subconscious.'

'Some summary,' Rafe remarked. 'You must have had to pay excess baggage on it.'

'It'd be worth it if I had. It's incredible – did you know that . . .'

'Stephen, shut up,' Rafe said firmly. 'I'm on holiday.'

'Eat it while it's hot.' Caro's commanding voice rang out as she and Suzanna emerged on to the terrace carrying plates piled high with food. 'Malcolm's just coming, he's washing up the grill pan.' Rafe heard Stephen give a suppressed snort. 'Where are we going today?' she asked briskly. 'Suzanna, pour the coffee. Did we decide on Agia Galini or Matala?'

Suzanna, ignoring Caro's order, was picking at her food. 'Agia Galini,' she said, a hint of rebellion in her tone. '*I* want to go there. I want to buy that brooch I saw the other night.'

'We can go to that restaurant where they do the special squid dish,' Malcolm said, joining them. 'You'll have to order it for us, Rafe – they never seem to understand when I do. It's probably so good that they save it for the locals.'

'I'm not coming with you,' Rafe said, making the decision and announcing it in the same moment. 'I'm going to see my uncle in Rethymnon.'

Suzanna gave an exaggerated sigh. 'Oh, well, I can go to Agia Galini another day. But you can get the brooch for me, Caro, if you would – you know the one, I was looking at it in the window of the shop opposite the jeep-hire place.'

'Yes, all right. They might . . .'

'Hold on,' Rafe said.

There was dead silence. He thought rapidly, do I take her, then? That wasn't my intention, although she's made it almost impossible for me not to. Then he was furious with her for backing him into a corner.

He said, with more force than he'd intended. 'I'm going on my own.'

She went white, then flushed dark pink. Wanting to mitigate the offence of humiliating her in front of everyone, he said, 'Family business. You'd be bored. Much better to stay here and have fun with the others.'

He was aware he was patronizing her, patronizing all of them. He almost added, to take away her look of outraged hurt, we'll go out to dinner later, just the two of us.

But he didn't.

'How are we going to get home?' Suzanna's angry voice demanded as they turned off the main road and drove down into Agia Galini. He glanced across at her; as usual she had laid claim to the front passenger seat. She was staring straight ahead, drumming her fingers impatiently on the dashboard. 'On the bus, I suppose?' Her words were overladen with venom.

Rafe was about to say he'd collect them, if they told him when they'd be ready. Then he thought, no. He ran back in his mind through the days of the holiday, seeing himself always smiling, agreeing to plans formulated by other people, driving them to places he'd been to a thousand times and had no wish to see again. And always, because it was his car, his country, his duty to act as host, it was he who stayed sober and sensible and rounded them all up so that they got safely home.

He said quietly. 'There are plenty of taxis. You can split the fare four ways.'

He turned off the main road and drove down into Agia Galini. As soon as the car stopped Suzanna had the door open and was stalking away. She managed, he observed, to express crossness and dissatisfaction more than adequately, even with her rear view.

'No rumpy for *you* tonight,' Malcolm said as he got out,

17

holding the door open for Caro and Stephen. 'You haven't half put your foot in it!'

Rafe had no reply.

'See you later,' he said distantly, and drove away.

Suddenly he couldn't face the drive over the mountains to Rethymnon. His uncle's company was of a very different calibre from that of the people he'd just got rid of, and Rafe knew with certainty exactly what the two of them would do. They'd have several slow drinks outside a café that faced the shore, then they'd go to the house of one of their numerous cousins for a late meal, eventually finding a pleasant corner somewhere in which to sit and pass the rest of the day in undemanding conversation.

But Rafe didn't want company of any kind. I've just manufactured a free half-day, he thought. And as it's probably the best I'm going to do for a while. I'm not going to waste it.

He turned back the way he had come and headed for home.

He woke to noisy laughter and shouting; it sounded as if about a hundred people had suddenly arrived to fracture the peace.

He was lying on a lounger on the terrace, and it was quite dark. He wondered how late it was. It didn't seem any time since he'd returned, and now here were the others coming back already and, apart from a bit of half-hearted gardening, he'd wasted his precious solitude in sleep. So many things he'd been wanting to do, too, things that the presence of other people in his house had prevented. Like playing classical music – Stephen didn't mind a bit of Beethoven, but the ears of the rest of them seemed to have self-blocking devices for anything with more than four different chords.

He'd been dreaming – he remembered fleetingly a girl, a field of corn dotted with poppies. And something had been wrong – she'd been crying. He strove to bring the images back, but they'd gone. As irrevocably as his afternoon and his privacy.

18

He got up and walked across to look down over the balcony rail.

There was a taxi in the road, and Stephen was paying the driver. Malcolm had his arms round both Caro and Suzanna, and in each hand he held bottles. Standing awkwardly by themselves were another couple. The man was wearing a brightly-coloured Hawaiian shirt with its collar outside a navy blazer; in that and his grey flannel trousers, Rafe thought, he must be sweltering. Even if he was wearing sandals over his socks. The woman wore a skimpy blouse, and shorts, very tight, out of which bulged the major part of each fleshy buttock. The small amount of surplus material was caught up in the crack of her bottom, presumably as a result of sitting in the taxi, and she was surreptitiously trying to free it.

Malcolm looked up and caught sight of him.

'Hey, Rafe!' he shouted, waving both hands and losing his balance, falling against Caro and Suzanna. 'How're you doing? We've had a great day, haven't we, girls?' He paused to give each of them a loud kiss. Then he started to laugh. 'We've got a surprise for you!' he sang.

Rafe was afraid he was going to make some remark about the extra couple. 'Come up,' he said quickly. 'And keep the noise down.'

'It's not late,' Malcolm protested, 'is it? Oh, well, perhaps it is.' He began tiptoeing, putting each foot down with exaggerated care. 'Rafe says we're too noisy,' he confided to the woman in the shorts. 'And as it's Rafe's house, we have to do what he says. That's Rafe.' He pointed upwards.

'Good evening,' Rafe said politely.

'Hello.' The woman giggled nervously. The man merely nodded. Oh, God, Rafe thought.

Malcolm was negotiating the steps, with difficulty as he was still trying to keep an arm round both Caro and Suzanna.

'For heaven's *sake*, Malcolm!' Suzanna said. 'That was my foot!' She pushed him on ahead of her, and he stumbled up the top step and over to Rafe.

19

'We thought you'd appreciate the gesture,' he said. He was grinning idiotically, his mouth loose and slightly moist. He smelled like an aniseed ball – he must have been on the ouzo, Rafe thought. He went on in an all too audible whisper, indicating the couple just coming out on to the terrace, 'I picked the most awful pair I could find!'

The strangers didn't appear to react to the insults heaped on them. Rafe wondered if they hadn't heard, or whether they were too drunk to mind. He found himself moving forward to greet them, the old hospitable habits of the house coming out in him without his conscious volition.

'Please, sit down,' he said, arranging more chairs round the table. 'And what can I get you to drink?'

'I'll have a beer,' the man said. 'A proper one. Can't stand this Greek rubbish.' He glowered at Rafe as if he'd been trying to force-feed him some ferocious local concoction.

'Coffee,' the woman whispered.

Rafe collared Stephen as he went inside. 'You can come and give me a hand,' he said. 'What the hell are you doing, letting Malcolm bring that pair back here?'

Stephen pulled himself free. 'All right, don't lose your rag! They were in the bar. I did actually say I didn't think you'd be too pleased, but you know what Malcolm's like.'

'Yes.' Rafe plugged in the kettle and reached in the fridge for a beer. 'I'm not getting you lot a drink, you can see to your own.'

'Yes, fine.' Stephen stood awkwardly, for some reason lacking his usual cool.

'What's the matter?' Rafe demanded. 'Remorse?'

'Er – no. Worse than that.' His eyes met Rafe's, and slid away. 'I – er, it wasn't my idea. They talked me into it, and actually it might be quite entertaining, they often are.'

'What are?'

'Especially if people are keen, and all of them – us – are. And I do know what I'm doing, I've often done it before. At least it might sober them up.' He looked pleadingly at Rafe.

20

'WHAT? What the hell are you talking about?'

'I'm afraid I've said I'll hold a séance.'

A séance. Part of his mind was rebelling, ducking away from sitting out on his own terrace with a load of drunks doing something so ridiculous.

But a different, stronger force seemed to be saying, yes. Oh, yes. And guiding his speech and his movements so that he walked calmly back outside with the beer and the coffee saying, 'Well, I don't suppose it'll do any harm.'

They sat expectantly round the table.

Its top was bare of glasses or cups. The drinking was over, and there was a new tension in the air that seemed to have a sobering effect: even Malcolm's face was intent and serious.

The glow-worm lights of candles in glass jars set on the terrace walls were the only illumination. Beyond their small golden circle the darkness began.

Rafe felt a shiver of fear.

He ignored it.

Stephen took a breath, and quietly asked, 'Does anybody there want to make contact?'

For a moment nothing happened.

Then, as if the spirit had been kept waiting for too long, there came a response of such violence that the wicker table creaked in torment.

A voice said nervously, 'Someone's pushing it.'

But their hands, linked by the little fingers, were all held well above the table top. And their legs remained as Stephen had ordered, away from the table's central support and tucked under their chairs.

Stephen said, his voice quiet but admirably commanding, 'I shall name each of us in turn. Please indicate yes or no by one and two movements of the table respectively.'

Rafe had the feeling that it was a crucial moment. They could plunge ahead, or right now he could say, enough. The urge to go on was strong, but he held himself back. He looked round the circle of faces, then let his eyes roam away beyond them. The night sky was brilliant with stars but moonless. Along the plain to the east distant headlights moved, tracing the routes of the roads. Clusters of lights showed where the villages lay, but it seemed that with every moment they grew less and less bright, as though the whole world were settling down to untroubled sleep.

Except the seven of them.

'Rafe?' Stephen's voice came softly from across the table.

He knew, Rafe thought. He could tell I wasn't concentrating. Does it make that much difference, then, one out of seven not totally involved?

'Okay,' he replied. His heart felt suddenly heavy, as if he had committed himself to some grave act from which there would be no turning away.

Faces, all turned fixedly to the table. Some looked frightened. Somebody coughed, the sound loud in the silent tension.

Stephen's calm voice went on. 'Is the message for Suzanna?'

The table shook twice. Suzanna said, 'Phew!', very quietly. Rafe thought he detected relief.

'Malcolm? Caroline?'

Two more negative responses.

'Is the message for me?'

Two staccato shakes.

He's disappointed, Rafe thought, studying Stephen's face. He wanted it to be for him, since it's his show. Probably thought it was going to be, he's always pretty sure of himself. He was going to save himself till last, but he couldn't bear to wait any longer.

Then Stephen asked, 'Is the message for Rafe?'

A single huge movement that seemed powerful enough to break the table in two.

As if someone – some thing – else were indeed thinking the words that Rafe seemed to hear in his head.

At last.

Even Stephen was taken aback. Suzanna shrieked and tried to pull her hands away, but Stephen and Malcolm on either side of her gripped her fingers too tightly. Rafe saw her close her eyes. Malcolm muttered something – it sounded like 'Oh, Christ!' – and then glanced quickly round to see if anyone had noticed. Caroline was looking over her shoulder into black shadows, and the wife of the couple from the bar, after having unsuccessfully tried to gain the reassurance of her husband's attention, was now sitting silently crying.

In his own mind Rafe was shouting, no! no! And against the sound, like a frantic melody played in cross-rhythm to an ominous drumbeat, other noises. Laughter. Sobbing. A discord of voices shouting in many languages. And a whisper that came with warm moist breath against his ear: Richard.

'Please!' Stephen's voice. Not quite as calm as it had been. 'May we have order?' He glared at each of them in turn, his eyes resting longest on Rafe. The force of his will was palpable; the noises in Rafe's head ceased abruptly, as if someone had commanded, Cut!

Squaring his shoulders and closing his eyes, Stephen resumed his communion with the other world. He asked most conversationally, 'Are you a man?'

Two shakes.

'Have you recently gone over?'

Two shakes.

Stephen opened his eyes, stared straight at Rafe, then closed them again.

'You knew Rafe?' he asked.

Hesitation. Two shakes, a pause, then a tiny movement that might have meant, yes. And in Rafe's head the sound of someone laughing with happiness.

'Did you live in Crete or England?'

The table gave a shudder. Stephen clicked his tongue, and corrected himself.

'I'm sorry. Did you live in Crete?'

Two shakes.

23

'England?'

One firm shake.

'South?'

One shake.

Then, in an efficiently speedy manner that underlined his experience in communicating with spirits, Stephen began to elicit from the table a place-name. Rafe listened in admiration; as long as Stephen held the spirit's attention the noises in his head stayed quiet, and he had room for emotions other than fear. He thought with detachment, no wonder mankind has been such a successful species. Here we are, feeble bodies sitting in the vast threatening night, conversing with the spirit world. And although some of us found it fairly terrifying to start with, already awe is modulating into curiosity.

'Last quarter of the alphabet?' Stephen was saying. 'S? T? T. Right, that's W-E-L-L-S-T . . .'

'Wells? In Somerset?' Malcolm suggested.

'Tunbridge Wells, in Kent?' said the man of the couple from the bar.

He sounds all right, Rafe thought, although his wife still looks scared silly. But then she looked nervous when she arrived. Not very kind of Malcolm, to have uprooted them and plunged them into this. He ought to have . . .

But just then, like someone trying to regain his attention, a voice in his head said sharply, listen!

'W-E-L-L-S-T-O-N-E,' Stephen was concluding. Rafe forced himself to concentrate on Stephen. On the others. On anything, to stop him hearing wild noises and an insistent voice that he knew with an instinct as sure as death couldn't be heard by anyone else.

'Never heard of it,' Malcolm said dismissively. 'Anyone else know it?'

There were mutters of 'No,' heads shaking in the dim light.

Wellstone, Rafe thought. It meant no more to him than to the rest of them.

Stephen was using the same method to discover the spirit's name.

'A-L-I-E-N-O-R,' he said after a few minutes. 'Strange name.'

'Foreign, probably,' Malcolm said. 'You've got tons of foreign relatives, haven't you, Rafe?'

Obligingly Stephen asked the table, 'Were you related to Rafe?'

Again, the successive yes and no signals that seemed to suggest the spirit was confused.

'Blood relation?' Stephen asked intelligently.

Two shakes.

'Related by marriage?'

Another strong yes, threatening the table's structure. But almost immediately, two shakes. Then a shudder. And right against Rafe's ear, like someone gently and erotically blowing, the sigh that said, Richard.

'She doesn't seem to know,' Malcolm said. 'Perhaps it's one of your ex-women, Rafe. Someone you promised matrimony to, in a weak moment of Saturday night fervour!' Rafe noticed even in his confusion the spiteful glance Malcolm shot at Suzanna. That remark was meant for her, he thought. Because I haven't proposed matrimony to *her*. Malcolm's a bastard. And I had to come on holiday with him before I realized.

Stephen was saying, 'I'm going to ask you how long ago you went over. Was it within the last ten years?'

Two slow shakes.

Stephen glanced at Rafe, as if trying to remember how old he was.

'Within the last forty years?'

Two shakes.

Caro gave a high-pitched giggle, a nervous sound as if her heart were not really in it. 'You're well-preserved, Rafe!' she said. 'This woman's giving your secrets away, unless you knew her in your cradle.'

Rafe hardly heard her. His attention was on the table. It

had started a constant, barely perceptible trembling, which continued even when Stephen hadn't just asked a question. Am I the only one who's noticed? he wondered anxiously. He leaned forward, staring more closely. No, he wasn't imagining it. It was like . . . He couldn't think. The movement put him vividly in mind of something, if he could only . . .

Yes. Oh, God. It was like his headmaster's hands, which had held a panicky fascination for him throughout his schooldays. Because immediately before the old man used to explode into one of his legendary and awe-inspiring rages, his hands would tremble. Just as the table was trembling now.

We've made it angry. The spirit's going to blow its top, any minute now. It – she – doesn't like our flippancy.

'Hundred years?' Stephen's voice was going on, calm, detached. In the midst of the superstitious dread creeping up on him, Rafe wanted to cry out, stop! Can't you see what's happening?

Two shakes. The trembling seemed to be easing off a little.

I don't want to know, Rafe thought wildly. The noises in his head were thunderous now, confusing him, making it difficult to be rational. Couldn't the others hear them too? We shouldn't be doing this, we shouldn't interfere in things so far beyond our understanding. A spirit that wants to talk to me. The soul of someone who's been dead a hundred years. More than a hundred years – he made himself concentrate on Stephen's questions, still eliciting negative answers, throwing them further and further back into the secret, unknowable past. Stop, Rafe pleaded mutely, there are things we should leave alone, things that if we have to face them might . . .

But he had lost the power of speech. Like the others, he sat silent and stone-still. And Stephen went on, and on.

The 'YES', when at long last it came, informed them that this female spirit, this woman who wasn't sure if she'd actually known Raphael Westover and couldn't tell them how, if at all, she'd been related to him, had been dead since the beginning of the thirteenth century.

Then several things happened at once. The wife of the bar couple leapt up, wresting her hands free, and ran half-falling to be noisily sick over the terrace wall. Stephen flung himself across the table to try to join Rafe's hand to Malcolm's and reseal the circle, but Rafe had had enough and pushed himself away and out of reach. Caroline started to laugh hysterically, and Malcolm said disgustedly, 'Jesus, that woman's thrown up all over the car!'

And with a sound that was far too similar to someone screaming under torture, the wicker table ripped apart.

Two

'We are not going on with it.'

Rafe in the sharp light of morning was adamant. The entice-
ment of the unknown that had briefly seduced him last night
was gone, annihilated by the events that had concluded the
evening.

Gone. Wasn't it?

It was difficult to conjure up the dark fear he had felt. The
day was bright with promise and the early summer sun, even
at nine in the morning, was a white-hot force that shone into
the corners and cauterized the shadows. Sounds of ordinary
human activity floated up to the terrace from the village street
below – voices talking vociferously, breaking off into sudden
laughter; a clatter of running children; the gossiping noise of
clucking hens somewhere on the hillside behind the house.
To look out over the plain provided more solid evidence of
normality in the form of mile after mile of fertile, intensely
cultivated land. And in the distance, through a cleft in the
mountains bordering the plain to the south, a glimpse of dark
navy-blue where the Libyan Sea washed between Crete and
Africa.

This was reality. Last night was aberration.

Rafe looked at Stephen, sitting across the table from him
calmly eating bread and honey, regarding him with a slight
smile on his thin lips. The two of them were on their own;
Malcolm, Caroline and Suzanna were still upstairs and the
couple from the bar had gone shakily back to their hotel by
taxi in the small hours.

Rafe thought, damn you, why are you looking at me like
that?

Stephen said in a reasonable tone, 'Not just one more
séance? It was pretty successful, you know. Most entertaining.
We all enjoyed it, didn't we?'

'Did we?'

'No.' Rafe thought, *you* enjoyed it. Everybody said afterwards, when they'd drowned their terror in Metaxa, how clever you were. How unusually gifted. You held centre-stage till they all fell into bed.

You weren't scared witless.

'No!' Rafe said loudly.

'We don't need that awful couple,' Stephen wheedled. 'Five will be quite sufficient. There's no magic number for a quorum. Nothing special about seven.'

'No.'

'Well, don't decide now.' God, you're relentless, Rafe thought. 'It may seem a more attractive proposition, tonight. When it's dark, and the spirits walk. And we've polished off the odd bottle or two.' He stretched across the table and poured himself more coffee. The kitchen table now stood on the terrace; they'd carried it out to replace the broken wicker one. 'You must admit, Rafe old chap, we gave a splendid performance.'

Rafe's head shot up.

'*I* wasn't performing! Jesus, Stephen, if you think . . .'

'No, of course I don't,' Stephen said irritably. 'Bad choice of words. I didn't mean to imply any sort of pretence. That was the real thing, all right. Incredible strength of signal. And the spirit stayed with us so long, too. Unusually long. That's why I want to have another go. Have you – er – ' He broke off.

'Have I what?'

'Ever been involved in a séance before. Got through to the other side?'

'Never.' The work of the devil, my mother would have called it, Rafe thought. And my maternal grandparents would have had masses said and bought me a dozen charms against the Evil Eye at the very suggestion that I was interested.

'I wonder,' Stephen said. 'Oh, I don't disbelieve you – ' Rafe had begun to protest – 'but, given the single-minded way in which that spirit homed in, I'd have thought she might have tried to make contact before, given half a chance. It was almost as if she was waiting for you.'

The echoing of his own thought in someone else's speech gave Rafe an unpleasant shock. He felt a slither of ice down his spine. He wanted to say, rubbish. To scoff away his unease. He looked at Stephen, and noticed that there was understanding in his expression. Rafe laughed awkwardly.

'I don't know,' he said. 'It's as if – ' He hesitated. 'I dream, here,' he plunged on, 'I always have done. This was my grandmother's house.'

Stephen nodded. 'You told me.'

'I've been coming here ever since I was a small child. My mother and I used to descend on her parents whenever she felt like returning to Crete for a holiday. Or wanted to get away from my father!' He smiled, remembering how sometimes his mother used to burst into tirades in her own tongue against the over-civilized ways of life in England with an English husband, rushing out to book herself and her son on the next flight to the more comprehensible and open-hearted south. 'This was my home, as much as England ever was,' he went on, 'and my grandparents always treated me as if my English side didn't exist. As if I were as total a mixture of their Greek and Italian blood as my mother. I always thought that was why it was.' He fell silent, random childhood scenes vivid in his mind. His mother, so demonstrative in her affection, playing with him on the beach and happily encouraging his hesitant and awkward attempts to speak Greek. His grandparents, almost overcoming him with that proud, deeply loving protectiveness that was typical of their generation and their nationality. His mother again, drawing him aside in the course of some tempestuous family celebration and saying to him quietly, tears in her eyes, 'Do not forget Papa while we are far away from him. Always remember that love takes many forms, and that although he may not make it so obvious, you are as precious to him as you are to all of us.'

He remembered. He knew he always would.

'Why what was?' Stephen prompted.

The dazzle of memories retreated as he brought his mind back to the present. 'Why the dreams only happened here.'

The dreams, he thought. My dreams, my wonderful, colourful, happy, sad, gentle, violent dreams. Like a film. So real that when I was first taken to the cinema, I said to my mother, it's like my dreams. She didn't answer, she just hugged me very tightly, and I knew she understood. Probably she had them, too. Perhaps every member of my family did that lived in this house.

Stephen's voice disturbed him. 'What were they about? The same things always?'

'Yes, more or less.' He paused, trying to put his thoughts into words. 'Different places, but always the same group of people. And as I grew older the events got increasingly complicated. In step with my growing understanding, I suppose. I used to see a woman, fair-haired and wearing a long gown. White-fair, she was, sort of Scandinavian blonde, which was strange here, amongst all these dark-haired people. Once she bent over my bed and whispered, 'You're mine, you'll always be mine,' and I cried out that I wasn't, I was my mother's, and the household woke up to see what I was shouting about.'

'And the dreams always centred around this woman?' Stephen's voice sounded different suddenly. Rafe looked at him, and his expression was uncertain. Disturbed, almost. As Rafe frowned at him, his face cleared and he put on an encouraging smile.

'No,' Rafe said, recalling the question. 'But she appeared pretty regularly, and if she hadn't been for a while I knew she'd come back sooner or later. There were other people, too. Sometimes they'd start to tell me things, as if they were reading me a bedtime story, then the things would sort of come alive, and I'd be there living it all with them.'

'What sort of things?'

'Oh, God, I can't remember! All sorts. We were on a ship once, a sailing ship. It had rows of shields along its gunwales,

31

and we were hit by a storm that blew us off course. And often I rode a horse, a great grey, and over its back it wore a decorated cloth. I went to a manor house, built of golden stone, and the fair-haired girl ran out to meet me. She was a child, at first, although even then there was something . . .' He frowned, then laughed uneasily. 'I don't know. I suppose they were pushed into womanhood earlier in those days. And an older man with her – her father, probably – said she was wilful. But he was deferential to me.' He broke off, remembering a particularly vivid dream where he'd sat on the grey horse as it wheeled in the manor house courtyard, easily mastering its restlessness, and looked down to see the girl gazing up at him, in her wide, green eyes a look of such fierce carnality that he had ached to take her there and then.

'Do you dream in England? Or any of the other places where you travel?' Stephen asked.

'Of course. Everyone dreams.'

'Don't evade the question. You know what I mean.'

He did. 'No. Nowhere else.' He wondered why he was reluctant to confess to it. 'As I can see you suspect, I only have these special dreams here.'

Stephen said, 'Ah.' He managed, Rafe thought, to put an awful lot of meaning into it.

They fell quiet. The silence extended, and Rafe found his mind returning to the long parade of nightly entertainments that had always been better than any bedtime story or late-night movie. He saw again the fair girl, the fall of her long, silky hair so real that he felt he knew what it was like to twist it in his hands. He saw her body, the round breasts pushing against the fabric of her gown and stretching it taut, making it seem about to split open. His body began to respond, desire swamping him just as it did in his dreams so that he woke so stiff and hard that it was a pain. He got up from the table, turning his back to Stephen, and went to lean against the terrace wall.

He made himself concentrate on an old woman in the street

32

below, painstakingly climbing the hill. He watched as she arrived with evident relief at her own door and disappeared into the cool gloom inside.

Gradually the excitement receded.

He didn't think it was necessary to tell Stephen of this new aspect in his dreams that had crept in as he grew to manhood. Being Stephen, and an amateur psychologist deeply in the Freudian vein, he probably knew without being told.

Eventually Stephen took in a sighing breath, letting it out slowly and noisily. Having made certain of gaining Rafe's attention, he said, 'You appreciate, of course, what's so fascinating about these dreams of yours?'

'Probably.' Rafe turned from his contemplation of the street and went to sit down again. 'Still, no doubt you're going to tell me.'

He leaned back, smiling tolerantly.

But the answer wasn't anything that he might have expected. It was something he had never realized before, and it shook him profoundly.

'When you relate them,' Stephen intoned, with a disproportionate drama that curiously had the effect of making his words even more chilling, 'you don't say, I *dreamt* I saw this, or it was *as if* I was doing that.' His eyes burned into Rafe's, deeply compelling.

'You speak as if the people and events were real.'

As if *she* were real? Stephen was quite right. How else would he speak to her, when she was indeed as real to Rafe as the people he moved with in his waking world?

But Stephen's words were disturbing. Suddenly he wanted time on his own, time to think. And here he was with a gaggle of people around him. Even now, the peace was beginning to break up as Malcolm and Caro, discussing the drama of last night, came out on to the terrace.

Rafe stood up. 'I'm going for a swim,' he said. He tried to ignore the expression on Stephen's face that said all too plainly, that shook you!

33

'Oh!' Caro looked surprised. 'But we're all going, later. Wasn't that the plan?'

Plans, plans. God, why did she always have to be making plans?

'Okay, I'll walk then. Leave you the car.' He didn't care.

'We'll come and join you, if you tell us where you'll be. Then ...'

'I don't *know* where I'll be!' He regretted the words as soon as he'd said them – her face closed into a frown, and underneath the disapproval he thought she looked hurt.

'Caro, I'm sorry,' he said. 'I'm ...' But it was impossible to explain. 'See you later.'

As he jumped down the steps Malcolm's voice floated after him.

'Not getting his leg over. That's his trouble.'

And in a strange way, Rafe thought, for once Malcolm's simplistic view of things wasn't far from the truth. Only never in a million years would someone so unimaginative comprehend that his frustrated desire was for a creature who lived only in his dreams.

He stayed out until early afternoon. At first he had just walked without much purpose, deep in his thoughts, and it had been with surprise that he'd found himself down by the sea. Nobody was about, so he stripped and swam vigorously for a long time. His appetite aroused, he walked back towards home and stopped for a huge meal at a local taverna. His bottle of retzina made his mind pleasantly muzzy; by the time he mounted the steps on to his terrace he was feeling sleepy and relaxed.

The car wasn't there, and he realized with relief that all his guests had gone out. He stood for a while on the terrace, then, obeying a whim, moved the kitchen table into the spot where the wicker one had stood last night. Pausing to think, he arranged the chairs around it.

'Suzanna, Mr Awful, Stephen,' he said, moving round the

circle and touching each chair in turn. 'Caro, Malcolm, Mrs Awful. And me.'

He sat down in his own chair. He stretched out his hands and closed his eyes. For a split second last evening came back, the darkness, the sawing of the cicadas, the strong night scent of the tobacco plants. And for less than a split second, a feeling like the clamping of a hand on his heart. And he thought the table shuddered.

His eyes flew open. The moment was gone; he was back in the brilliance of early afternoon.

No spirit reached out for him now.

He got up and went into the house. He was overwhelmingly tired. Slowly he climbed the stairs and opened the door to his room.

No, he thought, I can't sleep here. It smells of Suzanna's perfume. Her clothes are thrown all over the floor. And she hasn't made the bed.

Stephen's room, then. He won't mind.

He went along the narrow, white-painted landing. As he entered the small room, its familiar aura welcomed him inside. He began to smile. Yes. Of course.

Stephen had left it ordered. He always was well-organized, Rafe thought, remembering school days. The woven bedspread was pulled up over the tidy single bed, the modest amount of clothing still in Stephen's suitcase on a chair in the corner. The room had taken on nothing of its latest occupant's personality; Rafe easily transported himself back to the time when it had belonged to a child. Him.

He lay down. The shutters were closed against the sun, but a slight breeze blew in through the open windows. His eyes felt heavy, and he fell into a peculiar state between waking and sleep. He could still hear noises outside, but gradually they began to interweave with sounds supplied by his imagination. He thought he heard his grandmother's voice. 'Wash your hands,' she was saying, her anxious face looking lovingly at him, 'you must not soil the tablecloth because it is pure white, for your first communion.' Then she leaned towards him and he felt the touch of her lips on his forehead. A warm feeling of security flooded through him. He said softly, 'Yiá sou.'

He was seeing pictures. His mother dancing in sedate measure with his grandfather, the full skirt of her frock lifting as she moved, showing a white petticoat. A priest holding his grandmother's gnarled hands in both of his, talking to her urgently, concern in his face. Someone said in a voice of tenderness, 'Go to sleep, Raphael. It is time.'

She was there, right by his side, bending over him. Her lint-white hair was wound into long, heavy plaits threaded through and bound with silver ribbons. Her face was set with determination, but her youth made the expression touching. Young indeed she looked, yet her body was fully mature, the scarlet silk of her close-fitting gown pulled tight across her breasts. The long skirt was lifted at the sides so that folds formed across her stomach, emphasizing its slight swell and the feminine curve of her hips. She held out her arm, kneeling down beside him, and her lips parted slightly. She had a tiny mole at the corner of her mouth, above her upper lip. It looked almost like a dimple. Her eyes were wide and shining, the pupils dilated so that the irises were thin bands of colour. They were an incredible shade of sea-green, incandescent, as if her inner glow were emerging through them.

She peered into his face. 'Father beat me,' she whispered. 'They threw me in the undercroft and barred the door. But I climbed out of the high window. I hurt my ankle.' She lifted her foot, the flat leather slipper caked with mud. The flesh was swelling and discoloured. Tears formed in her eyes, and she wiped her nose with the back of her hand. Small hand, with little nails like shells. A hand that was used for only the most ladylike of purposes.

Her cheek was against his, her breath sighing against his ear. 'Oh, Richard, Richard!' His body was responding, desire for her racing through him. 'Richard, once more, oh please, once more! I cannot live without you, I am so afraid that I will lose you!'

He heard a voice say, 'Take off your gown.'

Then she was lying down with him, pulling up the scarlet gown, scrabbling at the laces down both sides that bound it so tightly against her body. His face was momentarily covered by some white cotton undergarment, then she had thrown it aside. Her flesh caressed his as her breasts pushed against his chest; he could feel the hard points of her nipples. Her hips ground into his pelvis, her hand stroked down over his belly and for a moment of ecstasy her fingers played over his penis. She threw one leg across him so that she straddled him, and he could feel her warm dampness sliding against him.

In a voice made hoarse by excitement she cried, 'Richard! Oh, Richard! Dear God, how I love you!' and the words that might have been uttered in reply were lost as her soft wet mouth came down on his.

'Damn!' a female voice shouted. Hers?

'DAMN!' more loudly. No, not hers. A part of him knew instinctively that she was being wrenched away. 'We're bloody well out of ouzo! Why didn't you *say*, Malcolm?'

He opened his eyes. In a hectic mental mix of fear and euphoria, he started the descent to reality.

Three

The room was dark. He was drenched in sweat, his clothes damp and clammy. He thought frantically, when did I get dressed? Who dressed me? Just now when she was here I . . .

Oh, God.

It had happened again.

He sat up, swinging his legs down and resting his head in his hands. His flesh retained the memory of how she'd felt when she flung herself against him, and his own pounding blood had heated him to aching fever. He recognized the feelings: he'd experienced this disorientation so many times before.

Only not for a very long time. And *never* so strongly.

She was here, he thought, there's no doubt of it. It's just not possible to dream someone so clearly, to feel them with every bit of you. She's come looking for me. The séance, that's what it is, somehow it's shown her where to find me. It's allowed her to cross back, so that she can be here in body and not just in spirit.

She says she loves me.

No. She said she loves Richard.

I want . . .

What did he want? The dream was fading, and he was no longer sure. Someone – Suzanna, he thought – was calling from downstairs. 'Rafe? Rafe? Are you there?'

I can't go on lying in hiding up here. Much as I'd like to. 'Hello,' he called back unenthusiastically.

'What are you doing? Shall I come up?' It *was* Suzanna. Her voice seemed to be getting closer; he heard the click of her heels as she walked across the house's central courtyard.

'No!' He leapt up. I don't want her to find me in here, don't want to have to explain. 'I was asleep,' he called hurriedly. 'Go out on the terrace, I'll be right with you.'

38

He shut the door behind him and stumbled down the steps to the bathroom.

'Well, I still say Rafe looks funny,' Caro persisted much later in the evening. 'You're pale even now, and you looked terrible when we got home. Didn't he?' She looked around at the others. Nobody seemed prepared to offer a view. Not surprising, Rafe thought, since Malcolm's pissed, Stephen's retired with Freud, and Suzanna's in a mood.

'Leave it, Caro,' he said. 'I'm fine.'

'I think you ought to see someone,' she said firmly. 'You must have a doctor here, haven't you? At the very least I should take your temperature. You might be sickening for something.'

'Hope it isn't anything catching,' Malcolm remarked. There was the clink of bottle on glass as he clumsily poured himself another ouzo.

'It isn't anything to joke about, Malcolm,' Caro said primly. 'Just what *would* happen if we all got ill? Hm?'

Rafe didn't know how to contain his irritation with her. All evening she'd been making remarks that had got under his skin, mainly about marriage and setting up home, and the arch glances she kept directing at him and at Suzanna, usually in quick succession, left him in no doubt that this was some rearguard action to bring him up to scratch. She would, he thought, consider it a personal triumph if he and Suzanna were engaged by the end of the holiday. 'Oh, it didn't occur to Rafe,' he could hear her saying. 'It took a few tactful moves from me to make him see what was the sensible thing to do!'

Suzanna, reading a book of Stephen's about witchcraft, was affecting not to hear.

Caro had held forth for half an hour – he'd timed her – about bathrooms. Bathrooms, for God's sake. Peach and eau-de-nil, she wanted for the colours. Malcolm was to help with the decorating, but the choice of materials was going to be hers alone. 'Malcolm's going to have a pale green bath robe,'

39

she said, 'with matching towels, of course, and I'm going to have a peach one.'

And when she was finally through with bathrooms, she'd started on about how awful he looked.

He stood up, his patience snapping.

'I'm all right,' he said. 'I'm not ill. I'm – I have things on my mind.' Caro and Suzanna looked at each other, then at him. He was aware he must seem to be acting oddly. 'I think I'll go out for a drive,' he hurried on, 'get some air. Don't wait up, any of you. I don't know how long I'll be.'

And he was off, down the steps and out to his car before anyone could say, oh, what a good idea, let's all go.

I'm not cut out for cheerful group holidays, he thought ruefully. Why did I ever imagine I was? Now they'll think . . .

He realized, with faint surprise at his detachment, that he didn't give a damn what they thought.

He drove out of the village and along the road leading across the plain. The clock on the dashboard said it was half past eleven; he had no idea where the hours of the afternoon and the evening had gone. The roads were totally deserted. He had nowhere to go.

He drove on, aimlessly, for a long time.

He had already turned for home, resigning himself to creeping back into the house and trying to settle down to sleep on the sofa, when he passed the turning to Phaestos. Without thinking, he took it. The car climbed easily up the increasingly steep slope, and as the great sleeping plain became visible spread out below, he began to feel better. It was one of his favourite places, and its magic never failed. He stopped in the car park, then walked slowly up the shallow steps to the ruins of the old palace.

The site was locked up for the night. He settled himself on a low wall that was still warm from the day's sun, closed his eyes and let his mind run free.

He tried to remember what day they were meant to be

going home. Next Thursday. And today's Saturday. Well, nearly Sunday now.

Five more days.

He groaned aloud. They'll want me to join in everything, to be cheerful and good company. Suzanna's sleeping in my bed, and I know only too well what *she* expects from me. And all I want to do is be in my house by myself so that the spirit can come back to me. With Stephen on call to organize another séance if it's necessary.

What do I say to them? How do I tell Suzanna it's over?

Too easy to go on with a relationship, he thought, because it's too difficult to say, look, it's been great, but it's over. No words to say unhurtfully, you no longer mean to me what you once meant. You no longer mean anything at all.

And it leads to this, to being stuck in a house – *my* house – with her, wishing that she was anywhere but here.

He sat ruminating for some time. Can I put up with them? Just for a few more days?

I can if I don't share a bed with Suzanna.

I'll have to tell her. It won't come as a surprise. Maybe it'll even be a relief.

He was depressed at the thought of having to say to her words that might hurt. But it'll be the truth, he thought. There won't have to be any more pretending.

It wasn't much of a conclusion. But he realized it was the best he was going to find.

He got up. He was about to return to the car when he changed his mind and instead went over to the fence that enclosed the ancient palace. He leaned his arms along the top of the wire, and straight away his mind cleared of anything but appreciation of what was in front of him.

The old smooth stones lay gleaming softly in the moonlight, taking on a silver tone now instead of their daytime gold. Then, as he'd known it would, the familiar sensation began. The conviction he'd experienced countless times that the site wasn't really a ruin but a vibrant palace in its proud prime,

41

just like it had been in the painting in his grandfather's office. And thronged with colourful, extrovert people who looked quite alien.

But they weren't alien. They were a part of his heritage, for his grandmother's ancestry was pure Cretan and every so often the machinery of genetics threw up a child who looked exactly like a character from one of the Minoan frescoes.

By some long chain in the blood, he was distantly and very tenuously connected with the people who had lived here.

He felt faintly the throb of violence that had so disturbed him as a small child, making him cry out in alarm until his grandmother had soothed the fear away. It was nothing to worry about, she'd said gently. It's over. Long gone. It has no power to hurt you.

Later he'd found out more. But he'd had to discover it for himself; his grandmother, source of all information on Crete and its history, would not tell him. 'It is not fit for a child's ears,' she would say when he badgered her with his questions, glaring at her husband in case he was tempted to supply the forbidden knowledge. But Rafe found a book in the house of a friend, a book with terrifying pictures of people leaping over huge bulls and women with bare breasts staring out provocatively at him. He read of sacrifice, of a queen's unnatural lust that resulted in the birth of a monster that ate people. And he realized what creature's blood it was that he'd seen in his mind seeping into the golden earth of Phaestos. Knew, even if it was without understanding, an ancient people's dark beliefs, some element of which had crept out of the ground to wrap itself into his own brain cells.

And having found out, he wished he'd stayed in ignorance.

But that was long ago.

He stood and absorbed the beauty and the violence. As if looking at a horror film that through repeated viewings had lost its power to terrify, he let his mind take in the whole image. Glory and carnage. A work of man that stood on its summit and reached for the wide sky, and the rumbling, secret

42

earth beneath to which it was too closely bound and which ultimately had brought it to its downfall.

His grandmother, comforting him once after a nightmare, had said to him, 'It is a part of us, we who belong here. But only a small part. Accept.' Her strong brown hand had reached inside his pyjama jacket, finding the gold chain around his neck and pulling at it until she found the triangular-armed cross that he had worn for as long as he could remember.

That she herself had given him.

She put it into his hand, closing his fingers tightly around it. 'Accept,' she said again, 'and keep your faith in Our Lord's protection, so that the powers of the dark may not overcome you.'

He thought that it was a good maxim to remember just then.

He found with relief that his mind had been deflected from Suzanna. 'The powers of the dark,' he said aloud. 'Is that what we're meddling with?'

Not sure whether the thought attracted or appalled him, he turned to walk down the path and back to his car.

Four

He woke early. Sleeping on his lumpy old sofa wasn't conducive to long restful nights. It seemed to be hours before anyone else stirred. As soon as he heard Caroline go into the kitchen to make tea, he went in to join her.

'I'll take a cup up to Suzanna,' he said.

Caro didn't answer, other than to go, 'Hmph!' They had, he thought, obviously found the time for some more female solidarity.

Suzanna was lying in bed propped up on pillows, reading a magazine. When she saw that it was he she said, without much enthusiasm, 'Oh. Hello, Rafe.'

'Morning.' He passed her the tea. 'I'm sorry I'm poor company,' he said without preamble. 'I'm not feeling too good.'

He paused to collect his thoughts and give her the speech he'd prepared through the long uncomfortable hours since dawn. But before he could get started she said coolly. 'It's all in your mind.'

Surprised, he sat down on the bed, waiting for her to enlarge. She looked at him for a moment, then turned her head away. She seemed to find it hard to meet his eyes.

'What do you mean?' he asked.

She stared down at her tea. 'You're getting peculiar,' she said baldly. 'Really strange. I'm not sure I want to be around you any more.' She laughed shortly. 'I'd never noticed how – how *foreign* you were, till we got here. In England you seem just like us. But here, you keep talking Greek to people, and you've got such a tan, and with your dark hair and your beard . . .' She trailed to a halt.

'Foreign!' he echoed, almost laughing. He leaned closer to her, trying to make her look at him. With a definite movement, she edged away.

He stood up, moving over to stand by the window. Foreign.

She meant it. And peculiar, she'd said he was that too. Was that what she really felt, that suddenly he was impossibly alien to her? He thought how ironic it would be if all the time he'd been up at Phaestos trying to work out a way of ridding himself of her, she'd been lying here in his bed dreaming up a reason for walking out on him.

'It's that bloody séance!' she shouted, making him jump. 'That's when it all came to a head! There was always something weird about you, something I couldn't reach. But spirits, Rafe! Messages from the other side! Honestly, it's a bit pathetic, isn't it? Most of us grow out of ouija boards and contacting our grannies when we're still at boarding school!'

Now she was looking at him, anger making her face red and giving her courage to say the unsayable. He thought detachedly, these are probably the most honest things she's ever said to me, and they're part of saying goodbye.

She was apparently waiting for a comment. He shrugged.

'If you feel like that, there's no point in me trying to explain,' he said. He'd had no intention of doing so, not to her. She would no more have understood than if he'd spoken in Greek. And anyway, it was private. He stood up, taking her empty cup from her. 'So, what now? Do you want to leave?'

She turned her eyes back to staring through the window at the world outside. 'Some friends of my parents have taken an apartment in Agios Nikolaos,' she said. 'I think I'll go and spend the rest of the week with them.

He wished, for the sake of the happy times they'd had, that he could have experienced an instant's regret. She's going, he thought, she's going for good.

All he felt was an overriding relief.

'Okay,' he said neutrally. 'I'll drive you up there.'

'Malcolm and Caro are going to. If you don't mind them using the car.'

He thought, it's worth it, even if I do mind. He walked towards the door.

'Rafe?'

'Yes?'

There was a strange expression on her face. Not regret – what, he asked himself, did you expect? – but a sort of kindness. Amused tolerance, almost.

She shook her head. 'Nothing.'

Nothing. He ran down the stairs, feeling happier than he had for a long time. That probably summed it up.

He dreamed on all the remaining nights of the holiday. Never so vividly as on the afternoon he'd slept on Stephen's bed, but scenes he'd lived in childhood dreams came back again and again, lively, fresh and in the brilliant colours of embroidered cloth.

And she came to him.

Sometimes she was so close that he could look into the sea-green eyes and watch the mole turn into a dimple as she smiled at him, enticing him, her sensual mouth and eager body promising a frenzy of joy that slipped from him even as he became certain that this time it would be different.

Sometimes she was no more than a faraway figure, running across distant fields and gathering flowers. Trudging through snow that reached over her knees. Hurrying furtively through a spinney and darting into a squalid and ramshackle hut. And for the first time he was aware of a sense of smell invading his dreaming brain; once the evocative smell of a wood fire, once the stench of wet dirty wool. And, repeatedly, a flower scent that he didn't know but that reminded him of cloves.

On the penultimate morning Stephen said, 'I was going to suggest another séance. But apart from the fact that I think it's unwise, I see there is no need.'

Rafe stared at him. They were eating breakfast alone; there was no sign yet of Malcolm or Caro.

'What do you mean?'

Stephen hesitated. 'I feel like a voyeur, but I'm not doing it intentionally. The fact is, I seem to be sharing your dreams.'

46

'What?'

'The girl in red silk? The meadow? The two of you, lying by the fire? Oh, don't worry – my unconscious self seems to have a reliable censoring device, I only saw you afterwards. Although it was quite obvious what you'd been up to. But I'm right, aren't I? They *are* your dreams?'

It's bizarre, Rafe thought. I'm not sure I believe him. He could have made all that up, from what I've told him before.

But he found he accepted Stephen's conclusion.

Which was even more bizarre.

'Yes,' he said. 'I'm glad I – we – have been so entertaining.'

There was a pause. Stephen seemed to be gearing himself up to add something more. 'And – I wonder if you agree?' he began hesitantly. Then he plunged on, 'It occurs to me that this – er – eager young woman in your dreams and the spirit who was so desperate to get across to you the other night might be one and the same.'

Yes. Obviously they are.

'Rafe? I'm right, aren't I?'

He pulled himself back into the moment. Stephen's eyes were on him, intent, slightly narrowed.

'Yes. You're right.'

'When did you realize?'

'There wasn't a moment of realization. She was just there, like she's always been, and I knew. It seemed obvious.'

Stephen nodded. 'Obvious to you. It's taken me days to work it out. I find it all so difficult to believe, you see, and my conscious mind's been refusing to contemplate the impossible.'

Rafe smiled. 'Why is it so unbelievable? You read Freud and Jung for pleasure, you should be an expert in the dark side of the human mind. Not to mention your vast experience as a séance-holder. You of all people shouldn't be sceptical.'

'Well, I am. Certainly I've held séances before – I've known I was psychic since I was eleven, and it's quite a social skill, believe me. Gets me invited to all sorts of places. I used to

47

hold séances at school, too, which you'd remember if you'd joined us a few times earlier. As it was, by the time you came on the scene, we were all too busy trying to notch up our first tug at a bra-strap to think about summoning spirits. Weren't we?'

'Yes!' Heady days, Rafe thought.

'But the thing is,' Stephen said, his voice suddenly serious, 'I've always been in control.' His eyes locked on to Rafe's. 'Till now.'

The words seemed to write themselves in the air above Stephen. As their meaning filtered down into Rafe's understanding, he saw the letters flame and begin to turn black. He shook his head violently, trying to dispel the images that were beginning to form on the edge of his perception.

'I don't mean to scare you, Rafe.' Stephen's calm voice brought him back. 'But this is something bigger than I can handle. I think we – or at any rate you – ought to leave.'

'We are leaving.' This is crazy. Crazy, to feel scared sitting here in the sun on my own terrace. 'Tomorrow night.'

Stephen sighed. 'I know. But I wonder if we should go sooner. Before – '

'Before what?'

'Before anything happens.'

'No.' Rafe wasn't aware that he'd meant to be so decisive. 'No. I'm not going to alter my plans. This is my house. What happens the next time I want to come here? Are you saying there's always going to be this unspecified danger?'

'I'm not saying that at all,' Stephen said forcefully. 'I'm afraid to say I think it's me – I seem to be the means by which the power is able to focus on you so strongly. It's as if – ' he paused to think, screwing up his thin face in the intensity of his need to find the right comparison ' – as if I'm a magnifying glass, increasing the sun's heat a hundredfold. And it's pinpointing right on you.'

It was not a pleasant image. Meeting Stephen's eye, Rafe saw that he hadn't intended it to be.

'I don't feel threatened.' Pursued, perhaps. Possessed, even. Not threatened.

'I think you are.'

'You'll have to live with that. I appreciate the warning, but I'm not going till tomorrow night.'

Stephen shrugged very slightly. I wash my hands of you, he seemed to say. 'Well, don't say I didn't warn you.'

Rafe smiled. 'I never say that.'

He couldn't wait for the night to come. He went through the day mechanically, going along with whatever the others wanted to do. He didn't care. They went down to Matala for an evening meal, and he half-listened as Caro outlined plans for the next day.

'. . . and then we'll go into Heraklion after lunch, and have a look round,' she was saying. 'That'll give us the morning to get packed and tidy up the house. Then we can have a late dinner in Heraklion before going for the flight. What do you think, Rafe? Rafe, you weren't paying attention!'

'Sorry. I don't mind, whatever you want.'

She was looking at him strangely. He suspected she was concerned for him, but since the night she'd annoyed him so much by saying so, she'd kept it to herself. To his relief.

'Are you okay?' Stephen asked.

'Yes.' God, he thought, if it's not one of them it's another. Go away. Just leave me alone.

At last, to bed. Alone, eyes closed, silence all around him as the house settled for the night. His body relaxed, on the verge of sleep.

But then he began to tense. To shiver. And in the dark a haziness of snowflakes aiming at his eyes as he rushed head-long, passing either side to disappear into nothing. The sound of galloping hooves, and a rush of cold, cold wind.

He was racing, running for his life. Men after him, wanting his blood – for an instant he saw them, swords drawn, arrows

49

to the bow-string, mouthing words he didn't understand but that he knew meant danger, mortal danger. For him. The skin of his back aching with the tension of clenching against assault. How would an arrowhead feel? Like the heat of the sun, magnified a hundredfold? Run! Run! The horse's silver flanks covered in blood, spurs digging in. Blood running down the cloth. White cloth, embroidered with a coat of arms.

Galloping on, alone. Then, from out of the swirl to his left, somebody flying to intercept him. A bay mare driven beyond her endurance, stumbling and foaming as again and again she fell down on to knees already broken. The girl on her back sitting astride, woollen gown and white underskirt flung high out of the way, bare thighs mottled and blue with cold, little leather slippers held on to her feet by a mess of mud and half-melted snow. Her mouth open in torment, screaming at him, her hands imploring, the fingers curled into talons that would claw at him, pull him back to her, hook into him and never let him go.

'You're mine!' wailed the voice of desperation on the icy air. Swirling white muffled sight and hearing, but then it cleared and she was closer, closer, running now over the snow, the steaming mare collapsed on the ground abandoned, froth all around the mouth, heaving sides still at last in the rigour of approaching death. Little slippered feet seemed to skim over the frozen ground, little bare hands reached out. But their tips were brilliant jewel-red. Bloody, like an eagle's claws as they rip into living flesh.

He cried out.

She stopped dead.

Her hands dropped to her sides. The blood dripped more swiftly; her own blood, her nails torn to nothing, the ends of her fingers mauled from some awful punishment.

'I climbed down the wall,' she said. Her face was streaked with tears, lines of black filth against the fine cream skin. 'I could not let you go without saying farewell. Will you not tell me where you go? For how long?'

Slowly she dropped to her knees in the snow. Head bowed, he heard her say, 'Richard, my love.' Then she raised her eyes to his. 'Oh, my lord, I entreat you!'

So young. His heart turned over in pity. He opened his arms to her, and her face lit with joy. She scrambled to her feet, leaping towards him. The wrecked hands twined around his neck, icy, slippery, bleeding on his skin. Dear God, was her very blood cold, too?

Then she was pushing herself against him, surprisingly strong, and he sank with her to the ground. She covered him with her body, legs opening to clench his thighs between her knees, hands fumbling at the front of her clothing, ripping at the fine wool and the soft undergarment, heavy breasts falling out to hang like some unimaginable white fruit that was ice-cold and veined with blue.

The bloody claws touched his lips, and he tasted salt. He shouted in horrified protest, but heard no sound. Tried to shout again, then the gelid nipple was inside his mouth and the fleshy fruit covering his face was stopping his breath, and so cold, cold, cold . . .

He opened his eyes.

Stephen was shaking him, holding him by the shoulders, rocking him vigorously backwards and forwards, blood vessels in his neck standing out alarmingly with effort.

'Breathe, breathe, damn you!' His hand slapped Rafe's face hard, once, twice. 'Come back! COME BACK!'

With a great shuddering moan, Rafe drew air into his lungs. His ribs seemed to have been bound: it was as if he had to use his muscles to break out of a corset of iron. Or of ice.

Stephen collapsed on to the floor, panting loudly.

After a time, he lifted himself up on one elbow.

'I think I'll say it for you,' he gasped. 'I warned you!'

51

II

Five

Rafe returned to London with the fervent hope that he would never dream again. He was shocked by what had happened. He was also embarrassed, every time he recalled Caro's and Malcolm's incredulous faces peering into his bedroom at Stephen collapsed on the floor and himself sprawled across the bed. Malcolm had started on some crude remark but Caro stopped him.

'Shut up, Malcolm,' she said firmly. 'We're going back to bed.' As she turned to follow him she glanced once more at Rafe. And he saw with dismay that what had once been kindly concern was now more like abhorrence.

Now he threw himself into his work. Before the holiday, he had completed the research for the script he was writing for the American radio network that bought many of his pieces on European life. The notes lay waiting for him on his desk, and the compulsion to mould the material was enough to distract him from the events of the recent past. For a time, he was content each morning to get up, hurry off to his office and put in a dedicated and satisfactory day's work before coming wearily home in the evening.

For a time.

But, like an addict drawn back irrespective of his own will to whatever poison is ultimately going to kill him, images from his night world began to beckon. They were subtle and clever, though, these spirits, he realized. For as long as his state of shock lasted, his sleep was undisturbed by anything but the most mundane dreams. As if the spirit knew she'd gone too far. But as the need for her reawoke in him, insidiously she began to creep back. But cunningly, so cunningly – with the whisper of silk as a figure on the edge of sight twitched her skirt. The lightest touch of a soft moist mouth on his. The scent of cloves.

And racing to the forefront of his mind came the obsession to bring her back.

How? I can't go back to Crete, I've got far too much work to do to take any more time off. And anyway, would it be the same without the presence of Stephen?

Stephen's here. He said he was the focusing agent. Then maybe we don't need to be in Crete.

They met in a pub one weekday lunchtime.

'No,' Stephen said. 'NO.'

'But I haven't explained what . . .'

'You don't need to. I know very well what you're after.' Stephen leaned closer, talking more quietly but with tense emphasis. 'I *will not* be a party to it. You could have died, that night. If I hadn't heard you shout – and I might tell you that in itself was enough to shake me rigid – I don't like to think what could have happened.'

'Nothing would have happened.' Rafe felt awkward. He wished he didn't have to involve anyone else.

'You didn't see yourself,' Stephen said softly. 'You'd stopped breathing. You were lying across the bed with your eyes wide open. And although the night was hot, the hottest we'd had, you were stone-cold.' He looked down at the glass in his hand, as if he could no longer meet Rafe's eyes. 'To be honest, I thought you were dead.'

An instant of memory flashed through Rafe's mind. Icy pressure on his mouth. The panic of not being able to draw breath. But then the moment was gone.

'It wouldn't be the same here. I never dream so vividly anywhere except Crete, and nothing like that's ever happened before. It'd be all right.'

'How can you tell?'

'I can control it.'

Stephen laughed harshly. 'You can? That sounds to me like hubris. Watch it, Rafe, I can sense Nemesis gathering herself.'

'Well *you* take charge then. Hold another séance.'

56

'No fear! And with whom, do you suppose? Suzanna's stayed on in Agios Nikolaos with the son of the friends of the parents. And Caro and Malcolm, in case you've forgotten, were there the night you tried to step across to the other side. And for the whole of our last day in Crete and the journey home treated you as warily as if you'd just grown horns and a tail.'

He hadn't forgotten. He thought also of how he'd called Malcolm the previous morning, wanting the phone number of one of Malcolm's friends. Only when Malcolm's secretary said, 'Mr Westover for you,' Malcolm, never aware of how his voice carried, replied in a stage whisper, 'Oh, shit! Tell him I'm out.'

'Perhaps you've got a point,' he admitted.

'Dead right I have! You won't be seeing them for a while, mark my words. They'll keep their distance. And they *certainly* won't want to sit round a table summoning spirits with a maniac. They've probably spread the word to everyone else, too – Malcolm's incapable of keeping a good tale to himself, especially if the telling of it allows him to slander one of his friends.'

Rafe felt unreasonably angry. Watching Stephen's face taking on an expression of supreme superciliousness, suddenly he wanted to feel Stephen's flesh split under his knuckles. The sensation was alarming in its strength, and in the fact of its having no precedent. He liked Stephen, they'd been friends on and off for years. He'd occasionally felt mildly irritated with him, yes, but that was all. And this feeling was close to hatred. In amazement he stared down at his right arm: obeying a command that he was not aware of sending, the muscles were bulging thickly as the hand clenched into a fist.

He turned hastily away. But Stephen had noticed, was pushing himself backwards off his bar stool.

'Christ, Rafe!' he said. And walked hurriedly out of the pub.

57

I'm on my own, then, Rafe thought, going home that evening. In a way he was relieved, although he regretted not having run after Stephen to try to explain. But now nobody else need know, and there was a sense of liberation in that. Nobody to criticize, nobody to imply with such absurd exaggeration, you're risking your life. But without the aid of Stephen as procurer, how was it going to be possible to re-enter the dream world?

The problem lay dormant in his mind for several days. His work continued to preoccupy him, and he was pushing hard to meet his deadline. Then out of the blue one morning, when he was sitting at his desk totally absorbed in painting a convincing word-picture of Easter in a Cretan mountain village, he thought he heard a voice say, 'Wellstone.'

Everything else flew out of his head.

Wellstone. He saw the seven of them again, sitting round the wicker table. Heard Stephen's calm voice spelling out the letters. Wellstone, in the south of England. God, why didn't I think of it before?

He leapt up from his desk and ran out to the general office, digging through the great pile of reference books that over flowed the corner table.

'A map!' he shouted at the nearest of the bemused people sitting staring at him. 'Large-scale, with a detailed gazeteer. What's happened to all the sodding maps?' He banged his hand on the table.

'What about this?' Someone was holding out a big green book. The cover said, Ordnance Survey Road Atlas of Great Britain.

He snatched it, driving back towards his office. At the last moment he remembered to say, 'Thank you.' As he closed the door behind him he heard indulgent laughter; his staff were remarkably tolerant.

He opened the atlas to the gazeteer. To the W's, right at the back.

Wellington, Wellow, Wells, Wellsborough, Wells-next-the-Sea.

Wellstone.

Seeing the name in print, an actuality, made his heart jolt.

He flicked back to find the page, running his finger across the grid lines until he was in the right square.

And there it was. A tiny dot with tiny writing. Wellstone. In the middle of the country, below the North Downs.

He left the office early. His quest had taken him over, and there was no room in his mind for anything else. He stopped at a stationer's shop, where he bought the relevant large-scale map. Back in his flat he spread it out on the floor. It showed fields and rights of way, villages and small towns with unfamiliar names. All of this was there, he thought, less than thirty miles away, and I had no idea of its existence.

Wellstone was two lines of houses on either side of a road that led from one unheard-of village to another. A stream ran at right angles to the road, forming a rough cross with arms of blue and brown. Green dotted lines marked footpaths, meandering with the apparent aimlessness of birds' footprints in the snow.

Wellstone. I've found it.

He sat back on his heels, triumph flooding him.

Now I know what to do next. And I'll do it alone.

Damn you, Stephen. I don't need you.

He left London on Friday afternoon. The nearest place to Wellstone that had accommodation was a small village with two pubs and a tea-room, all made uncomfortable by the July crowds visiting the village's elegant Tudor stately home. One of the pubs was able to offer him a single room.

He had planned to drive out to Wellstone that evening. But now that he was so close, he was aware of a slight loss of nerve. What was going to happen? What was he expecting? The possibilities, if he allowed himself to dwell on them, tended to become alarming. He ate early, then went into the bar to spend a couple of hours over several pints of beer. He got into conversation with a group of other men, and listening to their talk of local matters proved an effective antidote to his own thoughts. He went up to bed late, and his sleep was peaceful and so totally lacking in dreams that he awoke with a feeling of disappointment.

It isn't necessarily significant, though, he thought as he packed his bag. Maybe I have to be right there, in Wellstone, before anything can reach me. Maybe I'm still too far away for it – her – to get through.

Maybe she doesn't know I'm coming.

He set out mid-morning. He had learned the route perfectly, and as each small landmark was passed he nodded slightly, mentally ticking them off.

Wellstone. A modern road sign, on a big luminous board. Out here in the middle of fields and woodland unchanged for centuries it would look incongruously bright, reflecting headlights at night.

There were two or three cars parked outside houses, and in an immaculate front garden he saw a man and a woman on their knees by a colourful border. There was a pillar-box attached to a telegraph post. And a barking dog that hurled itself against a wire fence as he drove slowly past. A red-tiled cottage with a wide-based chimney stack, disproportionately large as if it accommodated a vast inglenook fireplace. By the gate a large board advertised 'HERBS – everything for the cottage garden.' A Land-Rover stood in the narrow drive, edged in beside a pretty rockery.

And that was all there was to Wellstone.

He wasn't sure what he had expected. A village green, with an ancient oak and a pond? A crouching stone church dating from Norman times? Something, anything, more than this. With a demolishing sense of disappointment he thought, now where the hell do I go from here?

He parked the car at the side of the road, a few yards past the last house. He stood in the lane, and everything felt totally normal; it was just a quiet country road where a few houses were built for no apparent reason other than that, possibly, once upon a time a little community had grown up at this spot where a track forded a stream.

Nobody called out to him from inside his mind. He closed his eyes, willing some sort of a sign, but there was nothing.

He sighed, opening his eyes again and looking around him. The bridge across the stream was about twenty yards on down the road. He walked along to it. Thick greenery overgrew the slow summer water, some fat-leaved plant that had bright pink flowers.

Mallow.

Now how, he wondered, did I know that?

Further on, up the slope that led on from the bridge, a signpost pointed left across a field of barley. It said 'Public Footpath', and in the distance he could see the top of a church tower. It was probably the way that people from Wellstone had gone to church, for as long as the hamlet and the church had existed. Did they still? Did they still walk across the field, never mind go to church?

He pushed at the gate, which was off its bottom hinge. It leaned, rather than closed. The path went in a straight line through the barley, green in the middle of gold, just like its colour on the map. The barley was patterned with other feathery green patches, where longer-strawed wild oats grew. It seemed to him that the field was only just cultivated, on the edge of turning back to its natural state.

He reached the summit of a slight rise, and stopped to pick a couple of ox-eye daisies. Day's eye. Again, a thought that seemed to come from nowhere. And when did he last pick flowers, for God's sake? He shook his head, letting himself be cooled by the breeze that blew across the field and bent the grain. The footpath led straight on. But he found himself drawn to the left, where a wide dark group of trees stood shoulder to shoulder, hunched in towards each other. The

61

barley grew sparsely here, and he eased his way through the few yards that separated him from the margin of the field.

The ground fell sheer away in front of him, as if a quarry had been dug here. Or a deep, wide ditch. But it was a long time ago; the slopes were thickly covered in dense bramble now, and both saplings and mature trees grew. It was a strange sight, in the middle of a quiet field.

He walked on, keeping the drop to his left. He seemed to be following the circumference of a rough circle.

Then, dropping down to a marshy spot where the slope had levelled out, he came across the suggestion of a gap in the trees. If it had once been an entrance it wasn't now, but overgrown with nettle and bramble, and hazel trees that pushed out their branches as if swishing curtains across a window.

He thought, I'm going in.

Kicking down nettles as tall as himself, trying to hold out of his way stems of bramble as thick as hawsers, he had the eerie feeling that this entrance was deliberately difficult. It was a doorway, from something he knew into something that he both feared and greatly desired.

Then he was through, into sunlight again after green gloom. He turned to look at the spot where he'd just emerged, wanting to make sure he'd be able to find it again; he had the illogical feeling that something wanted to imprison him here. Already the branches had snapped back together, and for a moment he couldn't see any marks of his passage. Then, with a sense of relief that surprised him with its enormity, he saw three stamped-down nettles. He took out his penknife and notched the slim trunks of two of the saplings he had just pushed past.

He had the unpleasant feeling that someone was laughing at him.

He turned his back on the entrance and walked out into a forgotten piece of ground.

Untangling himself from wiry threads of bindweed that still

clung to him from the hedge, he climbed the slight slope into the middle of the enclosure. It was hot, with the sun beating down. He realized with a finger of alarm that the wind in the field outside wasn't blowing here. The air was totally still.

He reached the higher ground of the centre. Slowly, he turned in a complete circle, looking all around.

He felt utterly alone.

He could still see the place where he'd come in, down there through the stands of rose-bay willow herb and summer-high grasses that reached to his shoulders. Now he was in the midst of even taller growths, rampant here where no man's hand had subdued them for a long tally of years. The thick, purple-blotched stems of some giant white-flowered plant grew everywhere, sprouting bulbous buds that gave the impression of being about to burst open to emit God knew what.

Grasses heavy with seeds moved against the light, making it difficult to focus his eyes. His mind wandered, and he began to see shapes that weren't there. Shushing sounds came to him, quiet buzzings of flies and bees that seemed to say, hush, hush, go to sleep. Which was strange, when in all that place there was not the slightest movement of any living thing. A scent rose from the ground, of sappy stems crushed by his feet, of the rich patient earth lying unused but for ever potent. On the edge of sight he thought he saw a woman, bending down to gather flowers. But when he turned his head to look, she wasn't there. Sun on the greenery gave off a smell that was the essence of growth and fertility. And within it, the merest whisper that tantalized and wouldn't come out and allow itself to be identified, something that smelt like cloves.

Around the borders of the enclosure the trees moved, stirred by a wind he couldn't feel. He was alone, apart, encircled in this sheltered, isolated place. What happened outside couldn't affect him here.

His eyes were heavy, his mind soft and receptive. He smiled, knowing that this was hallucination but with no will to oppose the trance that was falling on him. He made a great effort to direct his thoughts, trying to conjure up pictures of a girl with lint-white hair, of a body that was made up of sumptuous curves, of breasts that swung heavily against his face. Just for an instant, it seemed that some other power took up the impetus, began to provide the illusion . . .

Then in the faraway world he had left behind a power saw started up. It was distant, but its faint, raucous hum was sufficient in the stillness to startle a pigeon, which got out of the far side of the hedge with a cracking of its wings that fractured the magic like a clumsy hand irrevocably smashing glass.

He cried out in protest, 'No!' knowing he had been on the way, that only a little while longer would have seen him across into the world that was waiting for him.

Or brought that other world to him.

Then as the dream retreated and his own mind raced in to fill the vacuum, he started to tremble.

He sank down among the nightmare vegetation, feeling a powerful tension in him as if opposing forces were pulling him two ways. Then it was gone, and he was sitting sweaty and shaking in an overgrown, forgotten meadow.

He retained only a confused memory of getting back to his car, a stumbling progress that left his face and hands scratched and bloody from the long barbs of bramble and dog-rose. He must have run flat out through the barley; when he finally made the lane, his throat was raw with panting.

Sitting in the car he inspected his face in the rear-view mirror. His eyes appeared slightly red, the lids puffy. His skin was flushed, and a long scratch ran down his cheek to disappear into his beard. The wound was bleeding profusely, the trickles of scarlet glistening against the dark hairs. He wiped his hand across his face, blurring the blood streaks into something marginally less alarming.

The urge to get away was overpowering. Shaking, he

started the engine and drove very slowly until he came to a pub.

'This is when I say, "Been in a fight?" ', the landlord remarked as he served Rafe with a second measure of brandy, 'and you reply, "yes, but you should see the other fellow." ' He grinned, apparently waiting for an answering pleasantry.

Rafe had momentarily forgotten his vagabond appearance in the relief of being with real people and with his hand round a glass of five-star cognac.

'Oh,' he said lamely. 'Right.' He wiped again at his face, and winced. The scratch felt sore and inflamed. 'I got lost, walking across the fields over there,' he waved vaguely. 'Ferocious brambles you grow around here.'

'You ought to put something on that,' the landlord said. 'Your face looks nasty.'

Rafe smiled at the ambiguity, them immediately straightened out the expression because smiling hurt.

'I will.' He realized there was a danger of being talked at; the pub was quiet, and the only other customer here in the public bar was an old man dozing in a sunny corner. He didn't want conversation. He wanted to think. He drained his brandy and stood up. 'In fact I will right now. Good afternoon.'

'Post Office and general store up the road has TCP,' came the landlord's voice after him. 'They're usually open Saturdays, for the ice-creams, see.'

The small shop a few doors up from the pub was full of children choosing sweets. When they had gone Rafe went inside and, grateful for the gloom that allowed him to keep his face in shadow, bought a small bottle of disinfectant.

Getting into the car, he was overcome with tiredness. The drive back to London was a daunting prospect. He slapped some neat TCP on to his cheek, and the intensity of the stinging brought tears to his eyes.

I am, he thought after the tears cleared and he was eventually able to drive off, probably lucky only to be needing TCP.

Six

It was November before he went back to Wellstone.

The late summer and early autumn had taken him to Rome, where he had combined work with pleasure by staying with some of his Italian relatives while he researched a series of three pieces on Vatican power-struggles. His mother's father had had many brothers and sisters, and every one of them had married and produced children; the Italian side of Rafe's family was impressively vast.

For a few weeks it was pure pleasure to be with them. He was involved with their triumphs, their disasters and even their arguments that could escalate to plate-throwing in the blink of an eye. No matter that it was months since he'd come to see them, their affection towards him, and even more so the way they carried on exactly as they would have done had he not been there, let him know without a doubt that he was a part of them, that he belonged with them. He knew how much they had all loved his mother. The Little Foreigner, all the aunts and uncles used to call her, he remembered, because she was the daughter of the brother who'd gone to Crete and come back with a Cretan wife. And they'd loved Gianna even more, if that were possible, because of it.

They persuade me I'm all Italian, Rafe thought, trying to get to sleep one night after gorging himself far too well on his Aunt Lucina's cooking and his Uncle Giovanni's wine. ('Eat! Eat!' Aunt Lucina had kept saying. 'You are too thin, Raphael! And the face, aaah! And so gaunt!') They have drawn a veil over my one Greek grandparent and my two English ones. I'm Gianna's son, that's all that matters, and the love they would still be showering on her had she lived comes instead to me.

In some ways, it was a relief when, after kissing twenty-two relations farewell at Rome airport, he finally left them all behind.

He returned to London in time to attend Malcolm and Caro's wedding. Stephen was best man; Malcolm said somewhat apologetically, 'We weren't sure you'd be back in time. Caro said the best man had to be here for all the rehearsals. Actually we've already had two, while you were still away. So . . .'

Rafe told him not to worry. 'I'd be a lousy best man. No good at speeches. You're better off with Stephen.'

He was quite surprised that he'd even been invited. Perhaps they'd forgotten about the summer.

Suzanna was Caro's chief bridesmaid. Rafe noticed her turn to smile at a man sitting in the third pew. Perhaps he was the son of the friends of the parents.

Not that it had anything to do with him.

At the reception, Stephen joined him at the bar. 'Large whisky and water,' he said to the barman. 'God, I hate all this.' He brushed a disparaging hand over his grey morning coat. 'Pink carnations. Pink and white striped marquee. Pink and white icing on the cake. She'll probably have bloody Malcolm painted pink and white.'

'No need, he already is,' Rafe said. The drink, the heat inside the marquee and the occasion had combined to bring out magenta patches on Malcolm's fair skin.

Stephen barked a laugh. 'Look at him now,' he said, 'chatting up all the old ladies. Not at all his style, one would have thought.'

'He's making a special effort. Nice, for Caro's sake, since they all seem to be her old ladies. You can almost forgive him for being such a prat.'

Stephen caught the barman's eye and ordered a couple more drinks. 'Anyway, how are you? Haven't seen you for months.'

'I've been in Italy. Working.'

'Ah.' Stephen hesitated. 'No more dreams?'

67

'Not – No. No more dreams.'

Stephen thumped him on the shoulder. 'Good. Glad to hear it. Doesn't do to meddle, you know. I've felt bad, being the one who started it all with that séance. I'm relieved to know you've done the sensible thing. All a load of nonsense, really.'

'Yes.'

Then the drinks arrived, and they went on to talk of other things.

The next day he went back to Wellstone.

He knew exactly where he wanted to go, this time. It had all been planned, and stored in his head awaiting this moment; it was almost as if part of him had never left. He parked in the same place as before, then put on boots and walked quickly down over the stone bridge and up to the gate. The barley field was now bare brown earth, ploughed since the harvest in a pattern of ridges that wandered, not quite straight, away into the distance.

The footpath was hard to distinguish, but since the field didn't appear to have been sown it wasn't important to keep to it. He headed for the top of the slope, then turned left towards the enclosure.

The entrance bristled as discouragingly as it had done in high summer. Although all the green was dead and gone, the bare branches seemed to be trying to make up the deficit in the barrier with an extra display of prickle and spike. He put his arms up to protect his face, pushed, and gradually the thicket parted and grudgingly let him through.

He looked around him. Dead stalks were everywhere – the remains of the tall, white-flowered plants. Some had been battered down by wind and rain, but some still stood erect. He made his way between them to the centre of the meadow.

And slowly, as he stood in the silence, the same feelings began to overcome him. The sense that he was in a place apart. The uncanny suspicion that things affecting the rest of the world had no relevance here. The soft, sleep-inducing sound, although this time it was more like the faint rustling of dead leaves than the buzzing of insects.

And, entering his head and pervading all his mind, the smells.

Earth, dormant, waiting in its power for reawakening. Dead greenery, rotting, going back into the soil from where it had come. The faint November smell of woodsmoke. Whispering past, the scent of something reminiscent of cloves.

Down in the bottom corner of the enclosure, where the presence of willows suggested that a stream ran, a mist was forming. It was steadily filling up the dip in the ground with milky white. He watched as the mist swirled nearer, its movement hypnotic. And why was it swirling like that? There was no wind. The air was still and moist, as if rain were imminent.

He began to feel drowsy. His body was heavy, and he sank down on to a mat of dead grass and thick stalks.

He closed his eyes, smiling. This time, he thought. This time.

There came the sound of a horse blowing down its nostrils, somewhere very near.

He opened his eyes. The mist was still there, and, even as he watched, from out of it a shape began to form, white like the substance from which it grew. It became clearer, detaching itself from its birth medium and making straight for him.

Then the horse snorted again, and trotted up the slope kicking its hind legs.

As if from a distance Rafe looked down on himself, no longer lying in a wild dead meadow but standing in a paved courtyard. The pale stone walls of a large manor house rose up behind him, and on either side of the courtyard were beds of flowers and herbs, divided into tidy geometric shapes by low hedges. Not November there, wherever it was, for they were gaudy with colours, pink, mauve, red, white. And, under a full summer sun, the scent was glorious: the rich, spicy smell of carnations. Like cloves.

Beside him stood the horse. It was huge, a grey with the lines of a shire. But he was lighter, somehow more flexible. The large, prominent eyes, full of intelligence, seemed to take in everything. The neck was graceful and arched above a short muscular back. The legs were strong and lean, with a great deal of feather over the solid feet. As if sensing admiration the horse was dancing, stroking the ground and drawing sparks from the stones of the courtyard. Then he stopped, went back on to his quarters and pawed the air with his huge hooves.

There was a glint of metal from the heavy shoes. They looked like weapons, and wielded with that strength . . .

The horse came down on to all four feet, the harness jingling. He blew at Rafe, his warm mealy breath like a caress. He pushed his nose into Rafe's chest, and Rafe reached up to pat the creamy neck.

The horse nudged him harder, and Rafe almost lost his footing. He seemed to trip over his own feet; there was something unusual about his boots.

They were spurred.

He pushed the horse's head aside, patting the withers that were level with his face. He started to move away, towards the house. He thought someone was beckoning. A man. Lined, craggy face, grizzled hair. He looked vaguely familiar, and for some reason he was associated with danger . . .

The horse nudged Rafe in the small of his back, and he fell on one knee.

In that moment the picture flashed into his head of the same man, wielding a sword, and he knew where he'd seen him before.

Run. Run!

The horse was between him and the entrance. Damn it, then I'll break out another way.

He ran, swerving and weaving across the meadow. No longer a courtyard. He thought he heard the drumming of huge hooves behind him. Reaching a copse of hawthorn, ash and oak saplings, he dodged behind the trunk of the biggest tree and turned.

The horse, the manor house and the man had gone, and so had the mist.

He didn't stay for another look. Pushing his way through the trees and the undergrowth, his sense of direction deserting him, his only aim was to get away. As soon as the ground was clear enough he began to run again. And kept on running.

He was among old hop-poles, long disused. Then the ground fell into a ditch, where a stream wound sluggish and muddy. He gathered himself for a last effort and jumped, landing on the far side with a jolt that took away all his remaining wind.

After a while, breathing more evenly, he started walking.

The yellow arrows marking the footpath seemed to have petered out. Or more likely, he thought, I've missed one and now, several fields away from where I ought to be, I'll never find the marks or the footpath again. How do farmers round here react to trespassers?

His head was reeling from what had just happened. And without the map, which he had carelessly left in the car, he was half afraid he would plunge through some hedge or over some stream and find himself back in that same meadow.

Where he had seen the manor house that wasn't really there.

He told himself doggedly that he wasn't lost, that he knew roughly where he was going. If he kept turning left he'd complete the circle and return to Wellstone at the opposite end from where he'd left the car. Closing the gate he'd been leaning on while he got his breath back, he strode out determinedly along the margin of the next field.

The small collection of houses came into view as he reached the top of another slight rise. He made himself ignore his huge relief, instead thinking lightly, I have a marvellous sense

71

of direction. A true natural, me. I have no use for ley-lines and lodestones. There's that house where the barking dog lives, and beyond it will be the one with the big chimney where they sell herb plants. Then, a few yards down the road, my car.

The nature of the soil changed as he went down the slope towards the hamlet. Water lay on the surface, where a vein of yellow clay was visible underlying the thin topsoil. Heavy mud clung to his boots, and he had to stop several times to bang his feet against fence-posts, dislodging great clumps of yellowish soil. Then the composition changed again, and, going down into a dip where there was a gap in the fence, it was like squelching through unset concrete.

He heard the sound of a hard-working engine. A battered Land-Rover was coming along the track from the left, parallel to the Wellstone houses. As he watched, it turned in towards the houses, and he saw it was pulling a trailer piled high with manure.

The driver was obviously aware of the difficulty Rafe could see coming. The track led through the gap in the fence, where the soft churned mud had been compressed and displaced to form a steep-sided trough. The Land-Rover squared up for the attack, then accelerated towards the opening.

Neat driving, he thought appreciatively, thinking at first that the Land-Rover was going to make it. But the combination of the overloaded trailer and the quagmire was too much; with a visible shudder the trailer settled down into the mud and stayed there.

He ran down the hill to offer his help, thinking in a corner of his mind that trespassers weren't such a bad thing after all. But as he reached the gateway the Land-Rover began to move, backwards then forwards in a gentle rocking motion that gradually got its wheels on to less churned mud. You've played before, Rafe said silently to the unseen driver. He went to lean his weight against the back of the Land-Rover, but in the instant that he did so the driver, perhaps feeling himself on firm ground, put his foot down. All four wheels slipped for a second, sending up arcs of mud, but then they gripped. The trailer flew past Rafe with an alarming bounce that liberated most of the top layer of manure and dropped it down on top of him.

'SHIT!' he shouted appropriately, brushing wildly at the clods of coagulated straw and dung scattered all over his shoulders and chest.

The Land-Rover stopped well away from the gateway, a head appearing through its open window.

And a female voice said anxiously, 'Oh, GOD!'

She was out of the Land-Rover and running back towards him. A slight figure. Or did she just seem so inside the large and tatty waxed jacket she was wearing?

'Oh, Christ,' she shouted, 'are you all right?'

She slipped in the mud and cannoned into him. He caught her by the shoulders to steady her, looking down into her anxious face.

'Did I hit you? Are you hurt?' she panted, her eyes going over him apparently searching for blood and gore.

'No, I'm okay. You just gave me a shower-bath of cow-shit.'

She stopped scanning him for mortal wounds and looked up into his face. Her eyes under the peak of the big cloth cap were sea-green.

He caught his breath, feeling his heart pound suddenly.

She seemed to think he was angry, and leapt on to the defensive.

'Well, it was a stupid place to stand, right in the bloody gateway! I could have crushed you with the trailer.' She turned away to glance at the thick wooden gatepost, wound with strands of barbed wire. She shuddered slightly. 'And anyway,' she went on briskly, as if distracting her thoughts from visions of what might have happened, 'it's not cow-shit. Not fresh, at least. It's well-rotted manure.'

'Is there a difference?' He removed his eyes from her with

73

an effort and went back to brushing himself. 'And I wasn't *standing* there, I was coming to help you.'

'Oh!' A rosy flush of embarrassment coloured her face. Lowering her head she began to help with the brushing-down, her hands in large thickly-padded gloves bashing against him.

She reached up to pick a piece of straw off his collar. She said, 'You *are* hurt. There's a cut on your cheek – there must have been a sharp stone in among the shit.'

She took off her right glove. Her hand was small, and square and dirty. Nails like little shells, he thought, except for the filth around them. Dirty shells. He felt her fingers touch his cheek, and closed his eyes in an effort to deal with the effect it was having.

'Come on,' she said authoritatively. 'Come down to the house. I'll bathe it for you. And I don't suppose your tetanus injection is up to date?' He shook his head. He couldn't remember having had a shot since he was seven and his cousin's dog had bitten him. 'Well, we'd better get you one, just in case.'

She led the way back to the Land-Rover and opened the passenger door for him. She drove carefully down the field, as if intent on showing him that she *could* drive smoothly and safely if she wanted to. They went through a gateway in a hedge and came out on to a paved drive, on either side of which were small outhouses, a glasshouse, and row upon row of narrow flowerbeds.

He realized where they were.

'You're the herb person,' he said.

She smiled. 'To put it mildly. I'm the horticulturist, who just about scrapes a living working herself into the ground running a herb farm and selling the produce to anyone who'll relieve her of it.' She was looking over her shoulder, backing the trailer into a space between two beds which both had deep trenches dug along them.

'This is all yours? Just you?'

'Well, I do all the work.'

'It must keep you busy,' he said politely. He was thinking, God, she must work non-stop. The image of her hands came into his mind. Little hands. And their touch on his cut cheek had been gentle.

'Come into the house,' she said.

She jumped down steps through a rockery. He had an impression of a profusion of small plants, neatly arranged, and in the corner some sort of miniature tree whose branches drooped down like a weeping willow. Crossing a patio, she opened the back door of the house and went into a small scullery, out of which led two other doors. There were racks on the floor, holding pairs of muddy wellingtons and leather walking boots. On the wall were pegs hung with jackets and coats. One of the doors was open, on to a big kitchen where work-tops were ranged around a large sink and an Aga. In the middle of the floor stood a solid wooden table. The room was tidy, but he felt straight away that this was the lived-in, worked-in, warm and welcoming heart of the house.

He bumped into her backside; she'd stopped on the threshold to bend down and remove her boots. He did the same. He muttered, 'Sorry.'

She walked in socked feet across the kitchen to move a kettle on to the hot plate of the stove. Then she ran warm water from the tap into a bowl, reaching into a cupboard for a glass bottle of some green liquid.

'Sit down,' she said, pulling out a chair by the table for him. Then she called loudly, 'Sem!'

Husband. God, she's got a husband.

It hadn't even occurred to him that she'd be married.

Footsteps sounded above, and he heard the tread of somebody coming downstairs. A door opened in the next room, which appeared to be a sitting-room. Then, ambling into the kitchen, stooping from long practice at exactly the right place to avoid banging his head on the low lintel, came a tall, greyish and obviously elderly man.

'My father, Spencer Gurney,' she said. 'I'm Nell Gurney.'

No husband. Rafe felt a huge relief.

'Raphael Westover,' he said.

The man advanced into the room. Rafe stood up to shake the hand he was holding out.

'Raphael,' he said. 'What an unusual name. Oh, sit down, don't let me disturb you. After the archangel, is it?'

He had a gentle face, with a kindly expression that suggested someone who expected to like people and to find them congenial. And it seemed unusual, that a man summoned into his own kitchen to find his daughter with a stranger should start with such an apparently irrelevant question. Me, now, Rafe thought, I'd be wanting to demand, who are you? Where did *you* spring from?'

He felt like a honoured guest. He was drawn towards the man's warmth.

'My mother was half Italian,' he said. 'Half Greek, also. But when I was ready for baptism we were in Italy. And my father – he was English – was several thousand miles away, so any say he might have had was overruled by the weight of the Italian relations. I was born on 24th October, which is, as all good Catholics know, the feast-day of St Raphael.'

'Are you a Roman Catholic?' the man asked.

Rafe smiled. 'People more often ask if I'm Jewish.' He looked at the old man closely; so often he got the feeling that much hung on his reply to such questions. But the lined, eager face held nothing but an intense curiosity. No, not that – more a keenness to know.

He wondered briefly at his own willingness to be so forthcoming. But then he thought, why not?

'No, I'm not,' he said. 'For all that I was christened in a long white lace robe with bell, book and candle. I last went to Mass when I was eighteen and still had no choice. Even then I wasn't listening.'

The old man sat down beside him at the table. 'It interests me, this business of being brought up in a religion,' he said,

76

obviously winding up for a full-scale discussion. 'I sometimes think that . . .'

'Sem, would you please make the tea?' his daughter interrupted. 'I hit this poor man with a trailer-load of manure, and I've brought him in to look after him.'

'Oh, Lord, why didn't you say?' Sem was out of his chair, preparing to leap into action. 'Is it serious? Should we . . .'

'He's not hurt,' Nell said. 'Not badly, anyway. Just a cut cheek.'

'Oh, dear, I am sorry,' Sem said, looking worriedly at Rafe. 'Yes, I can see. Nell, dear, you must bathe it for him.'

Nell, a bowl of steaming, herbal-smelling water in her hands, smiled.

'Yes. That's just what I had in mind.'

Rafe caught her eye. She smiled very sweetly, just at him, and he smiled back.

Sem moved out of her way and ambled over to the Aga, humming quietly. Brahms, Rafe thought. There was a quiet clink of china as he got out mugs and plates.

Nell perched on the table beside Rafe and wrung out a piece of cotton wool in the hot water. A sharp smell rose up with the steam, reminding Rafe of green young pines. She leaned towards him and tentatively began dabbing.

'Well, that's funny,' she said, her eyes studying his face. 'This new cut begins just exactly where an old one ends – you'll have one scar now, right down your face, except the bottom bit won't show because it runs through your beard.' Her eyes met his.

'I'll still have one good side,' he remarked, holding the look. Her face was still overshadowed by the cap, which she hadn't yet removed.

'Oh, I didn't mean it'd be a real scar,' she said hurriedly. 'This isn't a serious wound, not like that earlier one must have been.'

He wanted to tell her. To say, that wasn't a serious wound either. It was just a scratch, which I did on a bramble in your

77

field out there. But it ulcerated and refused to heal, and it's left that damned great scar.

But he just said quietly, 'No. Good.'

'I'll drive you round to the doctor,' Nell said, 'in a minute. When I've cleaned this thoroughly. You really should have that tetanus shot. I'm sure she'll do it for you straight away, even though today's Sunday.'

Rafe had forgotten it was Sunday. He hoped he wasn't interrupting their day of rest. But then Nell hadn't been resting, she'd been carting loads of dung about the place.

'Milk and sugar?' Sem asked, putting a blue and white teapot and three mugs on the table.

'Yes, please,' Rafe said.

Nell finished her bathing. He watched her at the sink, washing her hands and rinsing the bowl. The cut was stinging, which might be expected. But it was also throbbing with a bone-deep ache, just like the earlier one had done. He thought, with a chill of apprehension, it's going to be the same. And he knew without even having to think about it that all the nice, plausible reasons he'd come up with the last time for having a mild scratch turn into a festering sore just weren't going to work a second time.

Sem came to sit down again, carrying a cake on a plate.

'Would you like a slice?' he asked. 'I made it myself. It's seed cake – caraway seed. I love the taste, it reminds me of gripe-water. I became addicted to that when Nell was a baby.'

Rafe, who wasn't in the least hungry, found himself saying, yes, please. Sem cut him a piece, then watched happily as he started to eat. It was delicious.

'You have a light hand,' Rafe said. 'And I agree with you about the taste.'

Sem looked pleased. 'Have another cup of tea,' he offered.

His kind-hearted smile would have countered bigger demons than Rafe was facing. Suddenly things didn't seem quite so bad.

Nell drove him to the doctor's house, where a young

woman doctor whom Nell introduced simply as Rosemary said no, she didn't mind, and yes, it certainly was important to have an injection straight away. They interrupted her in the middle of a film on television, but she said disarmingly that it didn't matter, she'd been dozing and missed most of it anyway. Rafe, unused to such informality in his few dealings with the medical profession, felt he'd strayed into another era.

On the way back to Wellstone he asked Nell if she'd have dinner with him.

She frowned. She was in the middle of negotiating the Land-Rover round a right-angle bend, and he didn't know if it was a frown of concentration or of annoyance at his question.

She said, 'No. I can't. I'm busy.'

She wasn't being very encouraging. But the desire to see her again was too strong for diplomacy. If I go away now, he thought, what then?

I don't want to go away.

'What about tomorrow? Will you be busy then?'

They were almost back at her cottage. He could see his car, further down the road. He had an awful feeling of time running out.

She said, 'No. I'm free tomorrow.'

'So will you have dinner with me tomorrow?'

She pulled up in the entrance to her drive, turning to look at him. And she said, 'Yes, please.'

Seven

He was in the midst of an uncannily still throng.

The grey beneath him strained to move, great feathered feet tiptoeing in tiny dance steps, ears pricked towards the unknown ahead, big strong body trembling with excitement. To either side the line of mounted knights stretched as far as he could see, and in front of them were rank upon rank of bowmen. On the extreme right, although distance made him think it might be illusion, he thought he saw the indigo of the sea.

It was so hot. The sky was colourless with heat, its white brilliance hurting the eyes. The last trace of moisture had long gone, along with the dawn and the dew, and now the air was desert-dry. The least movement by man or horse set up puffs of yellow dust that gritted in the mouth and invaded beneath the eyelids.

Like a wave breaking along the length of a wide shore, the line began to move. From the west, where the vast army met the sea, a forward impetus began that rippled ever faster, accelerating towards him until he knew he was going to be enveloped and swept along. And with the surge came an incredible noise. Men shouting, their war-cries in many languages massing to a deafening human sound. And above it in counterpoint, the harsh percussion of a million plates of armour clashing together as the knights charged. Below, like the alarmed heartbeat of the earth itself, boomed the bass drum of an uncountable number of great hooves striking again and again against the sand.

He was flying, his mouth open, and he distinguished his own youthful voice yelling with the multitude. Figures to either side had become no more than vague shapes of fast-moving dust; like a ship in fog, he dared not change direction and had no choice but to press on forwards. The lance under his arm seemed to weigh a ton. The muscles of his shoulder and back strained as he tried to keep its point up.

Then there were smaller, nimble horses intruding among the ranks, weaving and leaping, the dark men astride them seeming to grow centaur-like out of their flesh. But their presumptuous courage gained them nothing; against the juggernaut attack, they were as useless as a child's waving fist. He saw horses and men fall, still welded together, everywhere he looked. Saw heads in strange hooped helmets crushed squarely by huge round iron-shod hooves. Saw fragile chestnut and bay legs shatter like kindling, ivory bone and crimson blood introducing vibrant colour into the dead dust. Felt the slightest of jolts as the grey rode down a brown man screaming his agony as he tried to crawl away.

Sick, he shut his eyes.

The sudden impact against his shoulder came with unbelievable force, winding him and flinging him into the air. Then he was down in the sand, whooping for air and instead drawing in great mouthfuls of gritty, abrasive dust. He tried to cover his face with his hands, the movement sending a sudden pain through his shoulder so that he looked down at himself in alarm. Crimson, spreading right over his chest. Oh, sweet Jesus, I'm wounded, I'm mortally struck!

He put a trembling hand to himself, his fingers going into the liquid mess . . .

And coming away quite dry.

It was silk, scarlet silk, sewn on the white of his surcoat in the shape of a cross.

A dust-cloud swirled right before him, revealing itself, as the storm settled slightly, to be a mounted knight. He held the snorting grey by the rein.

'Get up, man!' he shouted. 'You can do no good lying down there!'

Get up. Climb up into that odd chair-shaped saddle. So high, and the sand in my eye is beginning to hurt. Itching, prickling, making my head ache . . .

81

He was trying to mount, and he didn't seem to be able to work out how to do so with a lance under one arm. There must be a place to rest it, on the saddle. But he couldn't see, his eye hurt. No! Don't rub it, not with a mailed glove on your hand, it'll scratch the flesh. But I must, I can't stand it . . .

He was crouched under his duvet, his fist pressed into the socket of his left eye which itched unbearably. He rolled over on to his back, and very slowly the night world receded.

He arrived in Wellstone early. Impatient, he'd left too soon and then driven too fast. Light shone out from the windows of the cottage, and he went up to knock on the front door.

Sem's face appeared at the window, incongruously framed by flowered curtains.

'Round the back,' he mouthed. 'Where you came yesterday.'

Rafe retraced his steps and walked along the side of the house, past the broad chimney-breast. He sensed heat from it; it was warm to the touch. Turning another corner, he saw Sem opening the back door.

'We sealed up the front entrance several years ago, when the winter was especially severe,' Sem said. Rafe wondered if he ever wasted time on 'hello', or whether the next topic for discussion was always too pressing. 'It must have increased the discomfort of medieval homes so very much, having the door open straight into the living quarters. One wonders that their ingenuity didn't come up with a better arrangement. But then no doubt they were used to being cold, damp and thoroughly miserable.' He firmly closed the back door and the scullery door, then stood smiling at Rafe, rubbing his hands together. 'What will you have? Nell's in the bath, she was held up because someone she had to see kept her waiting more than half an hour. So rude, don't you think? Sherry? Whisky? Gin?' He had turned his back to Rafe and was rummaging through a collection of bottles at the back of a worktop. 'How's the face?'

Rafe debated which question to answer first.

'I'll have a gin and tonic, please.'

'Grand!' Sem poured several fingers of gin into two enormous cut-glass tumblers, reaching into the fridge for tonic. 'Oh, look, we seem to have a lemon. *And* it's sound. Dear Nell, sometimes she forgets what she's stowed away in there and we discover the most interesting fungal growths. My fault, not hers.' He turned to fix Rafe with an earnest look. 'I'm meant to look after the commissariat, but I fear I've never quite got the hang of it.'

'Other than the seed cake.'

'Ha!' Sem looked pleased. 'I'm glad you liked it. I'd offer you some more, but we polished if off at tea-time. Here you are.' He handed Rafe a glass. 'Happy days!'

'Yes. Cheers.' The drink was generously strong.

'Come and sit by the fire.' Sem led the way through to the living-room, where a log fire drew the eye and the flesh. 'There,' he nodded towards a chesterfield upholstered in worn chintz, and as Rafe sat down he lowered himself into a battered leather arm-chair on the other side of the hearth. He smiled indulgently at Rafe, then said expectantly, 'Well?'

Rafe ran back over the battery of questions, looking for the most obvious candidate for immediate answer. Unsuccessfully. He shook his head, grinning, and said, 'Sorry. Well what?'

Sem leaned forward, jerking his head slightly. so that his spectacles, which had been resting in defiance of gravity just above his eyebrows, fell neatly on to the bridge of his nose.

'Dear me, it doesn't look any better,' he said worriedly, staring at Rafe's cheek. 'Is it painful?'

'A little.' Rafe had been trying not to think about it. The scratch was worse than the previous one, and today its edges seemed to be curling apart, as if there were some deep infection. The eyelid above the wound was swollen. And his eye hurt.

83

'Nell shall give you some of her camomile stuff,' Sem said. 'Marvellous for inflammation – the Greeks use it for pink-eye. You know, in children.' He tutted. 'Of course, *you'd* know. Makes their lids gum up. Conjunctivitis, I suppose it is. Nell makes all sorts of herbal concoctions – she's acquiring quite a name for herself. She has the National Health quite worried.'

'I'm sorry I'm early.' Rafe shot in his conversational opener while Sem's chuckling was momentarily stopping him from talking. 'And I wasn't sure where Nell would like to go for dinner – can you suggest anywhere?'

Sem seemed flattered to be asked, and frowned as he concentrated on a thorough answer. 'Well, there's The Rose and Crown, up on the main road,' he began, 'although I imagine one would have needed to book. And since I'm not sure whether Nell was planning to *dress*, possibly if you had no objections, one of our local pubs might suit? There's The Star, in the village, or The White Bear up the road in the other direction. I know Nell likes that one.'

'Right. That'd be fine.' Rafe wondered whether to ask the old man to join them. In the face of his warm welcome, it seemed discourteous not to. 'Would you . . .'

Sem spoke at the same time. 'I'm expecting the Lord of the Manor this evening,' he said. 'He's not really, he just lives in a rather pretentious Victorian Gothic pile in the village. But he quite likes it when I call him My Lord. We play chess, every Monday. D'you play?' Rafe nodded. 'We must have a game, one of these evenings.' Sem's smile was like a comradely embrace. 'And bridge – the vicar joins us whenever he can, but we're frequently stuck for a fourth.'

'You seem to have a lively community.'

'Lively! Oh, I don't think one could call us *that*. We're all elderly, round here,' he said with a sigh, flinging himself back in his chair. 'Not senile,' his eyes flashed a direct glance at Rafe, who hadn't remotely imagined that they were, 'but far, far too old to be any fun for my Nell. She buries herself here, you know,' he leaned forward again confidingly, 'and she seems happy. And of course, it's marvellous for me, having her delightful company. But I do think that perhaps life is passing her by.'

He hesitated, eyeing Rafe intently as if assessing his quality. Apparently finding it good.

'She's had great sorrows, you know,' he said, lowering his voice. 'Usual sort of things. Men letting her down. Now she lives for her herbs and her gardening and devotes her loving heart to me.' He fell silent, gazing absently into the fire. After a few moments he recovered himself with a start. 'Oh, good grief,' he said, 'hark at me! Whatever must you be thinking?' Too late, he seemed to realize that what he'd been saying might not be suitable for the ears of a stranger. Especially, Rafe thought, one who's just arrived to take his Nell out to dinner. 'Please, ignore my remarks. I . . .'

A door closed overhead. Rafe leapt to his feet, feeling guilty because he and Sem had been talking about her. Because now he had the advantage over her, knowing more about her than she did about him. Even if the knowledge had come to him uninvited.

A door opened in the wall behind him. It gave on to a staircase, and on the bottom step stood Nell.

She wasn't wearing her cloth cap tonight. Rafe thought her hair was still slightly damp, but even half-dry it was an extraordinary colour. White-blonde, darkening through every subtle gradation until underneath it looked almost black. It was straight and heavy, hanging glossily to her shoulders.

'Hello,' he said quietly. She smiled, appearing slightly self-conscious. He felt he was discomfiting her by staring so obviously. 'You look prettier without the cap,' he added.

Her smile deepened. 'So do you without manure all over you. Sorry I wasn't ready, but you were very prompt.'

'I was early. You father gave me a drink. We – er,' he glanced at Sem, who seemed to have forgotten his somewhat tactless remarks and was looking with pride at Nell, 'we've been talking.'

85

'*He's* been talking, more like, if I know Sem.' She returned Sem's look, smiling lovingly at him. 'See you later,' she said, moving across to stand by his chair. She rested her hand on his shoulder. 'Enjoy your chess – give My Lord what for, he's beaten you two weeks running.'

'Unfair!' Sem protested. 'I had a touch of back trouble, and he took advantage of my weakened state.'

Nell leaned down to kiss his forehead. 'All guns blazing tonight, then.'

'Quite. No quarter given.' Sem stood up, holding out his hand to Rafe. 'Bon appetit!'

'Good night,' Rafe said, and followed Nell out through the kitchen and into the darkness.

He took Sem's advice and suggested that they eat at a pub. She directed him to one a mile or so away. As they sat together at the bar over the first drink, he was glad he hadn't swept her off to anywhere more up-market. He thought of Sem's remark about her not planning to *dress*. Maybe he'd known she couldn't even if she'd wanted to: her clothes, although of good quality and meticulously clean, were old and worn. Her blue pullover had a small darn on the neck – he thought fleetingly of his Cousin Seraphina, who the last time he'd seen her had been wearing a soft green cashmere sweater exactly the colour of Nell's eyes – and her black skirt was shiny from repeated pressing. Something about her touched him, creating a response in him that made him want to cherish her. He looked at her hands. Little hands. The nails were clean tonight, but red and rough from the scrubbing she must have given them.

'The pizza's very good here,' she said, breaking in on his thoughts. 'Oh! That's probably the last thing you want.'

'I like pizza.' He watched her creamy skin grow pink, wishing he didn't have this unwanted power to make her feel awkward.

'I meant, being part Italian, you must chomp your way

86

through mountains of it.' She seemed to feel the need for an explanation.

'I still like it. Is that what you're going to have?' She nodded. 'Then I'll have it too.'

'You don't – this isn't – '

'What?'

'Is this okay? The pub, I mean. It's a bit rustic, I'm afraid, probably not at all what you're used to. Big restaurants, I mean. With head waiters and wine lists. I hope you weren't wanting to – ' She trailed off.

He hadn't been aware of giving such an impression of sophistication. Why does she think that? he wondered. He went to rub at his eye, and the light glinted on the heavy gold signet ring on his little finger.

And he saw himself through her eyes. Expensive clothes. Fast car.

He reached out and took hold of her hand, and she didn't pull away. After a moment she raised her eyes to look at him. He said impulsively, 'Nell, it's fine. Anywhere would be. It's the company, not the place.'

Her lips moved as if she were repeating his words. Then, disbelief leaving her face, her expression softened. And she didn't look awkward any more.

'These are my herbs,' she said over the pizza, pointing with her fork to sprinklings of green.

'What are they?' He was enjoying the evening more with every minute since she'd relaxed and started enjoying it too.

'Basil and oregano. You don't really need both, actually I prefer one or the other.' She leaned across the table to whisper. 'But it's a bit of a novelty for the kitchen staff here. All one of him.'

She had a mole on her upper lip, at the corner of her mouth. Or was it a dimple? For a moment another presence flashed through his mind, and he felt dizzy.

87

She was frowning, staring at him. 'Are you all right? You've gone pale. Perhaps it's the herbs.'

He shook his head, trying to smile. 'I'm fine.'

She was still staring. 'I don't like to mention it, especially while we're eating,' she said doubtfully, 'but that cut on your cheek looks horrible. And it's spread, hasn't it? I'm sure it didn't go right *into* your eyelid, yesterday.'

He put down his fork, unable to eat any more. 'Yes. It's spread.'

She looked puzzled. 'But it wasn't that bad. Just a scratch, really. And I bathed it, and we got you an injection. What else could we have done?'

She looked stricken, as though some oversight on her part had been responsible. No, he thought. Don't think that.

'Nothing,' he said. 'There wouldn't have been any point.'

He met her eyes. He had no idea how to tell her what was in his mind, no words with which to express his dark suspicions. You couldn't sit in a peaceful country pub and suddenly start talking about spirits and fields where you saw things that weren't there.

But her face was full of concern, and he was worn out with the ceaseless chasing around his head of his fears and his feeble attempts at explaining them away. The basic human urge to communicate to another sympathetic being his fear and his need was overwhelming. He wanted to say, help me.

He hadn't spoken, but still she seemed to hear. Her eyes widened. He thought in panic, stupid! STUPID! What the hell is she thinking, having some near stranger sit staring at her in supplication? Just when she'd got easy with me and we were beginning to feel happy together.

I've blown it.

He pushed his plate away and reached for his wine glass. He could no longer look at her.

He felt the touch of her hand on his arm. Her fingers slid down his sleeve until they rested on the skin of his wrist. Then they tightened, a warm, reassuring pressure.

'I'm not sure I understand exactly,' she said softly, 'and I'm not sure I want to. I think – I get the feeling you're in danger. Something's menacing you.' Her expression faltered. He looked up at her, and she flinched slightly. Then determination came back. She stuck out her chin. 'I don't know what's brought you here, nor why it is that you've been attacked. But if you want me to help you, I will.'

His first reaction was a rush of relief, not so much because she'd so staunchly offered her help but more because she'd taken him seriously. She'd believed in his fear. But then the relief abated, and he thought, why is that good? Oh, God, how much better if she'd calmly provided the final unequivocable reasonable explanation. Some strong chemical dressing was sprayed on that field by mistake, she could have said. Infected cuts like yours are ten a penny round here.

Only she hadn't. She said he'd been attacked.

Attacked. The word rang out in his head.

And, he wondered, what of her? What if I drag her into danger with me so that she gets attacked too?

He wanted to have her by him. On his side. But it was only fair to warn her. 'You don't know what you're taking on,' he said.

She sighed. Her hand slipped round so that she was clasping his. She shook it gently, as if they were sealing a bargain.

She said, 'Oh yes I do.'

Nell was glad that the next day was mild. The air first thing was soft and misty, and looking out through the open back door as she drank her tea, she felt a strong sense of urgency pulling at her to get out of the silent house and start digging.

'Nothing like hard physical work, when you've just been mentally coshed,' she muttered. Digging was conducive to thinking, she'd always found. And she couldn't remember a time in her life when she'd had a more pressing need to do *that*. She finished the tea and rinsed the cup, putting Sem's mug ready for when he came down later. She took her socks from the top of the Aga, then went into the scullery to put on her boots and stepped out into the morning.

For a while, as she concentrated on getting into a rhythm, the sheer effort occupied her. Then, as the spade bit again and again into the crumbly earth, digging the rich black manure into next season's beds, the action became automatic.

And her thoughts sprang to life.

Raphael's coming. Later on. He said, I'll try to get down in daylight. We'll go for a walk.

We'll go to the Magic Meadow. I know we will. He's – aware of something. I feel it as strongly as if he's already told me. I've seen it in other people, that knowledge of *Her*. Elderly people – that nice old boy who grew the lovely lilies. And the woman who used to clean for My Lord. But they never would talk about it, and I was too shy to ask. They didn't want to think about it, because it was inexplicable. They shut it away in their minds and pretended it – whatever it was – never happened.

And *She's* battened on to him now. She's made him come, and her malice is directed at him. That's why the cut on his face won't heal. But why him? Why Raphael?

Rafe. He said, my friends call me Rafe. Pity, really. I love saying Raphael. Like poetry. Makes me think of Raphael the painter, and beautiful faces of suffering and ecstasy. Raphael was Italian. I think. But Rafe's only a bit Italian. And here, in England, he acts and dresses just like an Englishman. Quite an affluent one. Except you'd guess he might be part foreign because of his dark eyes. So dark, sometimes you can't see where the pupil ends and the iris begins. And now that cut, down his face.

She jumped out of the bed to shovel over another load of manure.

Stop thinking about him like that. He's charming and courteous, but that's because he's that sort of age. Older men do have better manners, they're not trying to prove something all the time, and they're at ease with themselves. He is, anyway. Makes me feel easy, too. Well, after a while with him. How old is he? Forty at least. Old enough to say things like, it's the company, not the place, without sounding as if he's doing it for effect.

Stop it. It's just him, it doesn't mean anything.

She dug her spade in too deep, and lost her rhythm.

Damn. That'll teach me.

She tried to keep her mind on what she was doing, making a plan in her head of what she'd plant, seeing the green shoots appearing in the dark soil and the pattern they would make with their different colours and shapes.

But, unable to withstand the competition, slowly the image faded.

He said, we won't start talking now, because if we do we'll talk all night and I have to go back to London. And while I was realizing that I was right and he *has* experienced something, part of me was being bowled over at the thought of spending all night with him.

But I'm not thinking about that. Am I?

He said, I'll try to get down in daylight. What does that mean? Afternoon, some time in the afternoon. About tea-time. Sem's made a fruit cake, and we can have toast. Will he stay to supper? I'd better get down to the village and get something, just in case. He wouldn't want to share shepherd's pie or fish fingers with Sem and me, he's a man of the world. And the thought of him seems to make me more nervous than his actuality.

He drove me home very slowly. He didn't know the road, of course. Then he saw me up to the door, and when I offered him coffee or a drink he said, no, I'd better get back. And I felt like some silly teenager, wondering what the form was, whether he'd expect to kiss me good night, and I couldn't decide if the prospect alarmed or delighted me. Still can't now, so maybe it's just as well he only kissed me on the cheek.

And that was just being friendly. It didn't mean anything.

Continentals do it all the time, the men kiss each other like that too. It's a bit like us shaking hands.

Her own hands inside the thick gloves felt slippery with sweat. Coming to the end of her row, she stuck the spade fiercely into the yielding soil and stomped off up to the house.

'You're late for your coffee,' Sem said, greeting her with a smile as she stood taking off her boots. 'Would you like something to eat?'

She could smell garlic, and the mouth-watering aroma of frying onions.

'Wouldn't mind a few biscuits.' She went to give his spare frame a hug as he stood at the stove, nuzzling into his tweedy jacket and breathing in the essence of him, the scents of soap, wood smoke, and a sort of leathery smell that must, she'd decided, have permeated him thoroughly from the hours he spent in his old chair. 'What are you cooking?'

'Beef bourguignon. I thought we ought to have something nice, in case anyone comes for dinner.' He glanced at her. 'Such as your friend Raphael.'

She felt herself blush. Sem had turned back to his stirring, and what she could see of his face looked only mildly interested.

'Oh – yes, he's coming this afternoon, actually. And he might stay, I suppose.'

'Did you have a pleasant evening?'

'Lovely. He – he's very keen on this part of the country. He . . .' She didn't know how to go on. She sensed that Sem saw every new acquaintance as a prospective partner for her – oh, no, she thought hastily, not that. Not in that awful pairing-off way. He just wants me to be happy. She wanted to say about Rafe, he's not interested in me, he's been brought here by Her. By that spirit in the Magic Meadow. But she'd never been able to talk about that subject with Sem.

'Not surprising,' Sem said. She started, then remembered.

'No,' she agreed. 'Lots to see, round here. We like it, don't we?'

'We do indeed.' The milk was coming to the boil, and he made her coffee. 'Biscuits.' He put the tin in front of her as she sat at the table. 'You've earned them, you've done a lot this morning.' He looked at her, and she recognized in his expression the familiar ruefulness, that she had to work so hard. That he didn't do enough to help her. That it was she who had to do the digging.

She reached for his hand and pressed it to her cheek, touched as she so often was by all that was him, epitomized in those long, artistic, impractical fingers and the old parchment skin with the brown spots of age.

'Dear old Sem,' she said. 'And thank you for doing the bourguignon – I was dreading offering him a third of our beans on toast.'

His face relaxed. 'Perhaps we could really push the boat out and have some wine,' he suggested. 'I've still got two bottles of that claret My Lord gave me for my birthday – we'll put them out to warm, shall we?'

She worked on through the day, stopping briefly for sandwiches at lunchtime and then digging on, conscious that it was mid-November and that any day now could bring a frost that hardened the ground and shut it up like a stone prison till the spring. Hurrying to finish the last few feet, she heard footsteps. It'd be Sem, bringing her a cup of tea.

She turned to look. It wasn't Sem. It was Rafe.

'I'm early again,' he said. 'Sorry.'

I must look really awful, she thought, he thinks I couldn't possibly have intended to greet him like this.

'I wasn't sure when you'd be here,' she said. 'I wanted to finish. It's late, for digging-in manure.'

'Half past three,' he said.

'No, I didn't mean late in the day. I meant late in the year.'

'Oh. I see.' He was trying not to laugh, his face warm with amusement that seemed to well up from deep inside. 'Can I help?'

93

She studied him. He was wearing an expensive-looking sheepskin coat over beige cord trousers and a dark-brown roll-necked sweater. And look at his shoes, she thought. I expect they're Italian and hand-made and cost millions of lire. How's he going to dig in those?

He noticed her looking. 'I've brought my boots, for walking. I could put them on and give you a hand.'

'It's okay, thanks. I've only got this corner to do. I'll be finished in a minute.' She wished he'd go back to the house; she hated the thought of him watching her work. Of his unease, like Sem's, because she was digging and he was standing by. She turned her back on him and dug fast and furiously to the end of the row.

She was sure he'd gone. But he hadn't. As she straightened up he took the spade from her, bending down to clean it with tufts of grass.

'Oily rag?' he asked. She pointed to the shed, wanting to laugh. Solemnly he walked through the door, carrying her spade across his hands like some ceremonial badge of office. A moment later he emerged, brushing his palms together.

'I'll fetch my boots,' he said. 'Are you ready?'

She was going to protest, suggest tea, anything to postpone what was coming. She hadn't adjusted – one minute she'd been busy with good old mother earth, then suddenly he was there, and she was still feeling his shock-waves.

He was watching her, his head slightly on one side, his dark eyes lightened by the weak sunshine. The cut on his face looked angry. She felt a surge of compassion, that he should be driven to come here, that he should be hurt. Her discomfiture vanished.

'I'll get a coat. It'll be cooler walking than digging.'

They set off across the fields. In step, neither of them bothering to name their destination.

'Your father's asleep,' Rafe said. 'In front of the fire.'

'He's not asleep, he's "closing his eyes".'

'He's asleep. Unless closing his eyes involves closing his ears as well. I said hello, Sem, twice.'

'He's seventy-eight.' Her remark sounded inconsequential to her. But Rafe said gently, as if understanding why she seemed on the defensive, 'Then he's the right age for sleeping by the fire.'

They stopped talking as the slope of the ground increased. Then they were back on the level, walking through a thin copse of oak, ash and larch.

Rafe said without preamble, 'Did you lose your mother?'

Her first reaction was indignation. To ask that, out of the blue! Then the echo of his voice sounded in her head, and she heard kindness, not curiosity. Continental ways again, she thought. Perhaps they are right and we are too reserved.

'Sort of,' she said. 'She left us, when I was five.'

It was stark. She wondered how he would react. After a moment he said, 'How could she do that?'

The last of her resentment fled. Stupidly, she felt she was near to tears. She shook her head. I'll tell you, she wanted to say, but not now. She stared at him in mute appeal, and he nodded slowly. 'I know,' he said quietly. 'I know what it's like.' Then he took her hand.

'Here,' he said. He still had hold of her hand, and she thought she could feel him shaking slightly. They were standing on the edge of the thick undergrowth that fenced in the old field.

'The Magic Meadow,' she whispered. It always made her want to whisper, had done since she first discovered it as a little child and didn't dare go in. 'I knew we'd come here.'

He was pushing ahead, elbowing aside the branches. She noticed he had his hands up, covering his face. She forced her way through after him, following him a little way up the rough ground on the other side. Then he stopped, and turned to her.

He didn't seem to know what to say. Then, almost laughing at himself, perhaps at the whole situation, he said, 'Last time

I came here I was chased by an enormous white horse. In a dream, I suppose it was. Or perhaps a trance. I ran away, and you almost mowed me down with your trailer.'

The horse. Was that where it had all begun for him, with the horse?

'You came here by chance, then?'

'No!' He looked surprised. 'No. I was told the name. In a séance. When I was in Crete early in the summer. A spirit spelt out the name Wellstone. And a woman's name. Alienor.'

Alienor. Is that Her name? I never thought of Her having a name.

He was staring down into the far corner of the meadow where the willows were. She had the strange feeling he was drawing away from her.

'And that made you come to investigate?' she asked. Stay with me, she thought, please. I don't like it here.

'Hm?' He turned back to face her. 'Oh. No, not that alone. I don't think it would have affected me so much, by itself. But it was the last piece of the puzzle.' He dropped his head, studying his boots as he kicked at the broken-down grasses. 'I've dreamed, since I was young. I used to see people and places, but the images were random, and had no particular form. Except that there was a woman, always the same woman. But since the séance the dreams have been changing. I seem to be – it's as if I'm living someone else's life. And she's still there. The dream woman. She's the one who came to me in the séance.' He hooked his foot under a clump of rotting weeds and kicked it viciously high in the air. 'She's been dead since the thirteenth century. And she's manipulating me. Compelling me to do what she wants.'

She felt a chill run through her. Compelling him. Yes. She knew about that compulsion. Even now, standing in this place with him, she was only here because some force she didn't understand made its appeal too strong for her to resist. Her. It was Her.

She looked at him. I know how he feels, she thought.

Embarrassed, because telling another person, putting it into words, makes it all seem so absurd. And afraid, because, standing here in this haunting and lonely place, it's all too real.

She wanted more than anything to help him.

'She's powerful, here,' she began. 'Her spirit's been sensed in other places nearby, but her strength is concentrated here. There was a manor house, ages ago. Not that there's any real proof – nobody's done any excavations or anything – but Sem has an aerial photograph, and you can see quite clearly the outlines of a big building. And it was moated – that's plain. There, and there,' she pointed to where the ancient ditches were most marked, 'and the stream that probably supplied the water still runs.'

'A manor house,' he echoed. 'Yes. I've seen it. It stood there,' he pointed, 'and at the side of the courtyard there were flowerbeds.'

He sounded distant. Not at all like himself.

She felt a tingling at the back of her neck as the hairs stood up on end.

He was turning around, looking in every direction. Slowly, as if imprinting each image. He seemed to be listening.

'I don't hear it today,' he said. 'I wonder why? Is it because you're here?'

'Hear what?' She couldn't control the trembling of her voice.

'The noise. The whispering noise. In the summer it sounded like bees. The other day it was like rustling leaves. It made me feel – not sleepy exactly. More as if I was going into a trance.'

It was enough.

God, oh, God, I can't stay in here any longer. *She's* here, She's watching us.

Right now, starting to enchant us.

'Come on.' She grabbed his sleeve. 'Oh, come on! Hurry!'

'Why? I just said I couldn't hear it.'

'It doesn't matter!' It was hard to talk and run at the same time, when she was having to pull him to make him run too. 'Rafe, *come on!*'

He was resisting. 'Wait. There, is that it? Yes!' Now he was pulling at her, holding her shoulders so that she was forced to stop, forced to turn to look back at him.

And beyond him.

She shut her eyes in terror. She'd seen it once, never, never would she risk it again, no matter what. Nothing else mattered, nothing was so imperative as getting away. Let him stay if he wanted to, she was off.

She twisted herself out of his grasp, but, stumbling, opened her eyes instinctively to save herself.

And caught sight of his face. Of his eyes, vague and unfocused, slowly turning up in his head. Of his expression, vacant in an unnatural way as if someone were wiping away all his personality, preparing a blank canvas on which to start anew.

Of the cut on his face, once more open, seeping scarlet blood.

Nothing else mattered?

He mattered.

She pulled at him again, using all her strength, then let go with one hand to slap him as hard as she could across his bleeding cheek.

'Come back!' she screamed. 'Rafe, *come back!*'

His eyes snapped back into focus. Somehow she had got through to him. He said, or she thought he did, 'Stephen.' Then he started to lean towards her, pushing his body forwards as if wading through deep water, forcing himself against a resistance that was almost too much. Feeling her back crack with strain she pulled again and again, and at last they began to move.

Five yards to the hedge. Four. Three. He stopped moving, then with a great lunge that knocked her over, he was past her, pushing frantically through the shadow of the gap they'd made when they came in. She threw herself after him, and they fell together on to the bare brown earth on the other side.

She lay against him, his arms crushing her to him. She could feel his heart beating wildly, hear the sobbing of his breath. After a moment she twisted round so that she could look at him. He opened his eyes. Slowly, he smiled at her.

She said, her voice still shaking from the horror, 'She almost got you, that time.'

His eyes widened. Then he said thoughtfully, 'Is that what you think too? That – she – is trying to . . .'

'To get you across to the other side. Yes, that's exactly what I think. Who else does? This Stephen person, whoever he is?'

'Yes. It was he who held the séance. You made me remember him, when it was all happening. You said "Come back", like he did. You think it's risky, too, then.'

'*Risky!*' She almost laughed. 'Oh, yes, I think it's risky. I've lived here most of my life and believe me I know.' She didn't want to go on. Not there, when only a hedge separated them from Her domain. She got to her feet, brushing off dead leaves and mud. 'Come on. We'll go home. Then I'll tell you all I know, and hope it'll be enough to put you off coming back.'

She started off across the field, then realized he wasn't with her. A thrill of fear went through her.

She turned.

But it was all right. He was still on the safe side of the hedge. He was standing quite motionless, looking at her, an almost wistful expression on his face.

She said nervously, 'What? What is it?'

Slowly he climbed up to stand before her. He put his hands up to take hold of her face, gently drawing her close. Then he bent his head and kissed her.

She felt she had been lifted right out of the present. In no time his tentative kiss accelerated to desire, although at his or her own instigation she had no idea. His mouth was warm and firm on hers, and the strength of his big body was an antidote to her fear. She clung to him and his arms went round her, making her feel safe. So safe. She wanted it to go on and on, to lead wherever it would, but too soon he broke away.

He stood silent, cradling her head to his chest.

He said, after some time, 'I think you saved my life just then.' She started to protest, but he laid his finger to her lips. 'But apart from that, not even all the horrors there may or may not be in your Magic Meadow could put me off coming back. Not now.'

He put his hands on her shoulders, pushing her away slightly so he could look into her face. 'Do you understand what I mean?' he asked, shaking her gently.

She couldn't speak. Hardly knew what she'd say if she could. She nodded.

He took hold of her hand. 'Okay.'

And side by side they set off across the winter-stark fields for the comfort of home.

Eight

He was still holding her hand when they got back to the cottage. She was glad of it; her knees were shaking, and all the way home she'd been surreptitiously leaning against him. It's reaction, she told herself. And not only to what happened in the Magic Meadow, although heaven knows that was enough to make anyone shake.

It's also reaction to what happened afterwards.

She couldn't think when she'd ever been kissed like that, with such a potent and sudden surge of passion. It had taken her completely by surprise. Even more so had her own eager response.

Sem waved through the kitchen window as they passed. Rafe dropped her hand, and stood back to let her go first into the house. She felt a sense of abandonment at the loss of his touch.

She found it hard to unlace her boots, with hands that still shook.

'The kettle's boiling,' Sem announced cheerily. 'I'll make tea, shall I? No doubt you're ready, after your walk. Is it cold out?'

It was as well Sem was used to having the majority of his questions treated as rhetorical; she didn't think she could answer, not without arousing his concern. Or at least his interest. Rafe said, 'Getting cold, yes.'

'Mmm.' Sem was occupied with warming the pot. 'Dead time of the year, isn't it? No wonder the pagans invented a good heartening celebration of the winter solstice. We all might crawl away into our beds and sleep till spring, were it not for our December carousings. I always think it so canny of the early Christians, don't you,' he fixed Rafe with his interlocutory stare, as if defying him to stop paying attention

101

if he dared, 'to have grafted Christmas on to a date already firmly established as a festival?'

'Yes,' Rafe replied. 'But then the Church has never lacked clever administrators to . . .'

She crept away, out of the kitchen and up the stairs. She didn't want to hear any more. She was trying very hard to censor out the rebel thought that said, how can he *do* that? How can he stand there talking so calmly to Sem as if nothing's happened? She went into the bathroom, locking the door and sinking down on the closed lid of the lavatory to bury her face in her hands.

Sounds reached her from the room below; they must have moved into the living-room. She heard a faint clink of tea cups, and Rafe's deep voice occasionally interrupting her father's lighter tenor. Not often. She smiled faintly. Sem loved someone new to talk to. And Rafe didn't seem to mind. Perhaps he even enjoyed it – Sem was after all far from dull. Just a bit insistent.

She thought, I ought to go down. They'll wonder what I'm doing. If they can spare a thought from their bloody discussion.

Oh, no. Sorry, I didn't mean that. I'm being stupid.

She stood up, moving over to the basin to look at herself in the mirror.

Oh, God!

Her face was flushed, her eyes brilliant under wild hair. She reached for a brush, attacking her tangles, pulling fiercely at the burrs and the twigs.

She started to smile. I look like someone who's just been rolled in the hay. Which I almost am, except it's the wrong season for hay.

She took some deep breaths, then opened the door and went downstairs.

She stood washing up the tea things. She felt vaguely unhappy – apart from a brief locking of his eyes on hers and a faint smile, Rafe had greeted her as if she were still the tentative

102

new friend she had been before this afternoon. Before that tremendous kiss outside the Magic Meadow.

Sem was there, of course, and Rafe was fully occupied in a discussion of the ways in which religions did or did not capitalize on their power over people. But all the same . . .

She finished the dishes and hung up the tea-towel. Sem's bourguignon was fragrantly simmering in the slow oven. She wondered how she was going to fill the time until dinner. Until well after dinner, probably, because Sem never went to bed very early. The last thing she wanted to do was to discuss theology or politics. She wanted to talk to Rafe. Alone.

She became aware that the voices had stopped. Then she heard Sem say, 'They open at six. It's five to – why don't you and Nell go and have a drink? Supper won't be till half past seven, at the earliest.'

Dear Sem. Darling, diplomatic Sem.

'Oh. Okay, then. But wouldn't you like to come too?'

Don't, Rafe! Don't say that, not when Sem's set it up for us! Oh, please . . .

'No, far too cold for me, thanks all the same. Besides, I want to watch the news. Switch on the television on your way out, will you?'

Sounds of movement. Then the door opened, and Rafe was with her. He closed the door behind him.

Now?

He smiled at her. She'd noticed that he had a special smile for some occasions, one that crinkled his eyes and put deep creases in his face. And disguised his cut cheek.

'Did you hear?' he asked.

She nodded. Silly to pretend otherwise, when her flaming face must give it away.

'Come on, then. I'll drive you to the pub.'

They sat in a corner, the only customers apart from a trio of six o'clock stalwarts talking quietly up at the bar.

She couldn't look at him, too afraid that her appeal would

show. Hold my hand. Do something to let me know I didn't imagine it.

He said softly, 'I'm sorry about earlier. I didn't mean to take advantage of you like that.'

That's even worse. *I'm* not sorry. Oh, how can he be?

She didn't know how to respond. She said, fairly brusquely, 'You want to know about *Her*. I'll tell you.'

'Oh!' He sounded surprised. Then he said, 'Yes. Please.'

'I can't tell you much. Only that I think you're right, there *is* an unquiet spirit in that meadow, and she's young. And spiteful. Have you noticed all the rowans?' He shook his head, looking blank. 'Oh, well, perhaps you wouldn't recognize one unless it had a label. They're also known as mountain ash. They have lovely scarlet berries in the autumn.' She glanced at him, but light didn't appear to be dawning. 'Anyway, there's hundreds round here. Dozens at least. They're a traditional antidote to witches, so you can draw your own conclusions about why they were planted. People used rowan wood in their houses, too, for things like chimney cross-beams.'

'The pub,' he said suddenly. 'This pub is called The Well-stone Rowans.'

'Well, now you know why. It was built well after Her time, though. It's thought She dates from the time when the old manor was there, which must be before 1400 because the church records go back as far as then, and at that date the manor was, as they so quaintly wrote it, "in decaye and abandonéd by ye Squiere's familye." And as far as we can tell, nobody's lived there since.'

She stopped, and took a long drink of her lager.

'Why do you say she's spiteful?'

She looked up at him. 'Spiteful's putting it mildly. If you want to know what I really think, she's evil. You won't get a dog to go into that meadow, nor a horse.' He started to protest. 'Not a real horse, I mean! You were dreaming. There couldn't really have been a huge white horse on the loose or else we'd

104

have known about it. They're valuable, horses. They're not just left to roam around over other people's land.'

He nodded slowly. 'A dream horse. Yes.'

'You agree, then. No horse. Good.' I've got to convince him, she thought. He's got to know how dangerous it is. 'And once one of the village children was taking his cat and its kittens up to church,' she hurried on, 'you know, to one of those special services they have sometimes, for kids to have their pets blessed. The child took a short cut over the fields. Brave chap, he didn't let local tradition bother him. Or perhaps he was just showing off. Anyway, he got to where the footpath is at its nearest point to the Magic Meadow, then the cat started screeching and yowling, and although it meant leaving her kittens she was off, and the boy didn't see her again till the next day.'

He looked sceptical. 'Are you sure that's not just a good tale?'

'Yes.' She felt cross. She added decisively, 'The vicar saw it happen.'

'Oh.'

He didn't sound pleased to have such incontestable proof. With a flash of insight she realized something. She said urgently, 'You don't want to think of Her as evil! Do you?'

His eyes shot to meet hers. She thought he was going to deny it, but he said nothing. Then he said quietly, 'No. You're quite right. I don't.'

'She is!' The words came out over-loud in her excitement. One of the men at the bar glanced at her. She leaned closer to Rafe, dropping to a whisper. 'Honestly, I know it! But if She's brought you here with some purpose in mind for you, then it stands to reason she'd make herself appear attractive to you. Don't you *see*?'

He didn't answer. Wouldn't look at her. She felt desperate.

'Rafe, if you saw her as simply evil, as something horrible like others do – oh, yes, people do sense things, I know they

105

do, although nobody will ever *say* – then you'd run a mile. Wouldn't you?'

He sighed. Then said, 'Perhaps.' He paused, and she thought he looked slightly uncomfortable. 'But I meant what I said earlier.'

Her mind raced to remember. What had he said earlier? So many things. He seemed to be waiting for her to reply. She didn't know what to say.

'About running a mile,' he said patiently. 'I won't. As I said, in case you've forgotten, nothing could put me off coming back now.'

It seemed to be taking her a long time to understand. They'd been talking about Her, hadn't they? And how he had to realize the peril? Surely he wasn't going off at a tangent and referring to *that*, was he? To that wonderful moment when he'd kissed her?

He was looking into her face. 'Nell?'

She was, she realized, sitting with her mouth open. She shut it. For a second time in a matter of hours, she felt incapable of speech.

He didn't seem to mind. He moved closer to her, leaning his shoulder against hers.

'Another thing,' he began, 'and I warn you it may . . .'

She stared into his eyes. Something new flashed into his expression, something very tender. He shook his head. 'Never mind. Another time.' He leaned away slightly to free his arm, which he put around her. She edged closer, into that aura of safety and warmth that she'd found that afternoon when they clung together outside the meadow.

It attracted her irresistibly.

After a while he said in a slightly different voice, 'You call it the Magic Meadow, so you're familiar enough with it to have a special name. And you said, "I've lived here all my life, and I know".'

'Yes,' she said cagily.

'What do you know? Did something happen, when you were little?'

She thought, oh, I wish you hadn't asked. The events of the afternoon, resurrecting as they had done to full-blooded life all the inadequately-buried fears she'd carried for years, were too recent for comfort. But I have to tell him, she thought. For his sake, he must know the danger.

'Oh, something happened, all right,' she began. 'I was five, and Sem and I had just come here from Cambridge, after my mother left. He was always busy with his notes and his research and his writing. He's a palaeoanthropologist, or at least a retired one now – ' she thought she heard Rafe draw in his breath to speak, but apparently he changed his mind – 'and I used to have to amuse myself while he was working. I liked to go off across the fields behind the cottage, and one day when I'd ventured further than usual I heard the sound of running water.'

She realized she was gabbling. She made herself speak more slowly.

'I found a little brook, and it had flowers growing in it, big pink flowers. I thought they looked like the ones in my Flower Fairies book, so I went closer. There was a wooden bridge, and I was going to cross over it.' She could see it all, and the scene had lost none of its power to scare her. 'Nearly twenty-five years ago,' she said, trying to laugh, 'and I remember every little thing.'

He hugged her closer. 'Go on. If you can.'

She could. Just.

'Something warned me off. A – a feeling, perhaps, an instinct for danger like animals have. I was plain terrified. I didn't wait to find out what it was – I ran. But the uncanny thing was, I kept thinking about it. And I kept going back to stand on the bridge, as if I was daring myself – or someone else was daring me – to cross over. And then one day I did.'

She hesitated. It was still difficult to think of it. She plunged on.

107

'I thought it was so pretty, at first. There was a heat haze, and a smell of scent. Carnations, or cloves. I lay down on the ground, under some things that I thought were enormous stalks of cow-parsley. At first I liked them, only after a while, looking at them, I saw that they weren't really very nice. The stems were so coarse, and ugly, and they had dull purple blotches on them like rotten things. I found out later that they were hemlock. Then it was as if I was very tired – you know, like when you know you should stay awake but you can't keep your eyes open?'

He nodded. 'Yes. Then what happened?'

'*She* came.'

'Yes,' he said again. His voice was only a murmur. 'She came. Alienor. So beautiful. Wonderful.'

She looked at him out of the corner of her eye. He was staring into the distance, a slight smile on his face.

Whatever image is he seeing? she wondered frantically. Oh, God, can't he tell. Doesn't he realize it's enchantment?

'She wasn't beautiful and wonderful!' she hissed. 'Her face was pale and lined, with great grey rings under her eyes, and she looked sick. And she scared me, she scared me so much – she said, "I have to die, and now I'll lose him." And then she threw back her head and howled, like an animal, and she wailed, "He's mine! He'll always be mine!" And she started to scream, and I thought she was a mad lady, and I was so frightened I wet myself. I got up to run away, and I was so worried about how I was going to find clean knickers and wash out the wet ones without Sem knowing. But then I suddenly thought, that's nothing. There's a mad lady in the meadow. And then I must have fled for home, because the next thing I remember was bursting into Sem's study and throwing myself into his arms.

Rafe didn't speak for some time. But eventually he said very softly, 'She scared you. She frightened a lonely little girl.'

And the emotion in his voice, the way she felt his lips brush against her hair as he spoke, made her realize.

108

At last, thank God, he's got the message.

'Did you ever tell Sem?' he asked, in something more like his normal tone.

'No. I couldn't. I think when you're a child you feel sort of contaminated by awful things, and you're afraid they're partly your fault. So you don't tell anyone.'

'Did she ever appear to you again?'

Here is it, she thought. The question I've most dreaded. That I knew he'd ask.

She said, 'Yes.'

'Tell me.'

And she knew she must.

'It was when I was much older, not a little girl any more. I'd avoided going there for years. But I wanted to test myself, to see if I was still afraid. I was seventeen. I'd just . . . well, never mind.' Briefly she thought of him, of her first lover. Whom she'd thought so marvellous, to whom she'd willingly surrendered her virginity only to discover a week later that he was using his conquest of her as a sort of testimonial in his pursuit for someone else. Someone older and far, far more sophisticated.

No. Don't dwell on that.

'I wasn't very happy,' she continued. 'In the sort of mood when you'll do anything to stop you thinking about something that's upsetting you. And trying out my courage in the Magic Meadow seemed a good distraction. Only it wasn't, because I had no more guts than I'd had at five. I didn't even stay for a proper look. As soon as I saw – the moment it happened, I ran for my life.'

'What was it?'

'Rafe, I don't know. It was winter, and the ground was feet-deep in snow. In the meadow, it was untrodden. Imagine that, not even the tracks of birds or wild animals. It was foggy, and as I stood there the air seemed to be full of blizzard. And I thought there was a shape forming, out of the snowflakes, and it looked like hands, claws . . .'

She stopped abruptly. Given such an opening, the memory had come thundering back in its full power. She saw again the far corner of the meadow, where an unnatural swirl of white had taken nightmare form and pursued her. Heard again the howling on the ice-cold air, felt again the agony in her ankles as again and again in her frenzy to get away her racing feet landed on uneven ground and twisted under her.

She felt sweat break out on her body and across her forehead.

'Sorry,' she whispered. Even for you, she thought, I can't go on any further. 'But of course I wasn't really in a fit state to judge,' she added, trying to sound sensible and down-to-earth, 'and anyway I went down with flu the next day, so I was probably slightly delirious.'

There was a silence between them for a long time. Eventually, almost as if he agreed with her feeble attempt to ascribe the unimaginable to a nice, normal, everyday cause, he said, 'I expect that was it.'

She felt an illogical sense of let-down. But then, belying his words, he stood up and added, 'I think I'd like a brandy. I'll get you one too.'

She said, 'I don't like brandy.'

He caught her eye. He smiled very slightly. 'Then I'll have two.' He turned his back and walked up to the bar.

Neither of us knows what to say next, she thought when he had returned. She watched him. He was staring into the distance, swirling his brandy round in the glass. What do you talk about after that? The weather? Good books? She looked beyond him, through the gap between the curtains into the darkness outside. Weird world. To some of us. And yet others walk through it without so much as a twinge of the supernatural. Do I envy them?

She noticed Rafe absently rub at his face, putting his hand over his eye.

Yes. I think probably I do.

He must have been thinking along the same lines. He said, 'Do you know what I'd like?'

She shook her head. 'No. What?'

He reached out for her hand. 'I'd like to pretend for a while that we're just two people, who have met under absolutely normal circumstances – on a train, perhaps, or in a pub like this one – and we like each other, and now we're going to have a happy dinner together, and talk about nothing more alarming than whether we'll have another glass of wine or not.'

She didn't like to say that she thought that was impossible. You could always hope.

'All right. Then we'd better go home and have a go at Sem's bourguignon.'

As they left, the landlord called out, 'Good night, Nell. See you both again,' as if they had indeed been just another couple.

Perhaps, she thought, it's a good omen.

She had to concede, after only a little time, that it was proving an accurate portent. Arriving back at the cottage, they were greeted by appetizing smells, a blazing fire, and curtains drawn against the darkness. Shutting out the night and all that was out there in it.

Sem had laid the table, with the heavy white damask cloth and the best wine glasses that were relics of their Cambridge days. And he'd put new candles in the silver candelabra. She felt a rush of love for him, that he'd contributed to the mood she wanted so much to achieve.

'Come and have a drink,' he said, pushing her and Rafe gently towards the fireplace, 'the meal's ready when we are, but there's no hurry.' He stopped to pick up a jug of mulled wine standing on the hearth. 'I thought this was just the thing for tonight.'

'Not My Lord's claret!' she exclaimed.

'Good grief, no!' Sem was filling three pewter mugs. 'I

111

wouldn't dare, he'd never speak to me again. This is supermarket Bulgarian. Cheers!'

Rafe took the mug Sem was holding out to him and tasted. 'That's good,' he said. He drank again. 'Cinnamon?'

'Yes!' Sem said, topping up his mug. 'And nutmeg, a squeeze of lemon, and brown sugar. Plus a dash of cooking brandy.'

He's looking relaxed, Nell thought, watching Rafe's expression as he sampled another quarter-pint of wine. Not surprising, really. Nothing like drink for removing the sharp corners from things.

'Sit down,' Sem banged the cushions on the sofa, 'by the fire.'

She hurriedly caught hold of his arm. 'Sem, don't do that, you're advertising how dusty everything is.'

'Can't avoid dust, in a five-hundred-year-old house. Rafe doesn't mind. Do you, Rafe?'

'Not in the least.'

She glanced at him. He was leaning back against the plumped cushions, totally at ease. He saw her looking, and smiled. 'Come and sit by me, Nell.'

'Little Nell,' Sem said indulgently, his eyes following her as she crossed the room and sat down beside Rafe. 'I used to call her that when she was small. She hates it.'

Oh, heavens, she thought. He'll have the baby albums out in a minute, bare buttocks and all.

'But it's appropriate, all the same,' Rafe said. 'Fragile, perhaps, rather than little. Although I've rarely seen anyone wield a spade so well.'

'She has green fingers, too.' Sem settled back comfortably in his chair, looking from one to the other of them as they sat side-by-side on the sofa. 'She's full of talents, you know, Rafe.'

Nell, hating being the centre of attention, squirmed slightly. Rafe glanced at her. Just as Sem began on some comment about how she'd built the rockery, he interposed smoothly, 'And what did you do, Sem, before you retired?'

Thanks, Nell thought. Thanks for getting the spotlight off me.

'I was a palaeoanthropologist,' Sem intoned.

'Ah, yes. Nell mentioned it, when we were in the pub. I didn't quite catch what she said.' He caught her eye and grinned.

'The study of fossil man,' Sem supplied. 'Examining our ancient forebears in toto, just as you would, say, an aboriginal species still existing today, or, at the other extreme, a . . .'

Nell knew this was one subject on which he really could be boring. 'The lads in the pub call him Fred Flintstone,' she interrupted. 'Which of course makes me Pebbles.'

Rafe seemed to take the hint, again introducing a diversionary tactic. She felt that he was listening in to her thoughts, picking up effortlessly what was in her mind.

It was an odd feeling.

Strangely exciting.

'Nell said you lived in Cambridge,' he said. 'It's a lovely city, isn't it?'

'Beautiful,' Sem agreed. 'I had many happy years there, before I met my wife.' Nell thought, he doesn't realize how poignant that is. 'At a May Ball, you know,' he was saying. 'Can't think what I was doing there. Not my sort of thing, at all. Just goes to show.' He got up, reaching for the mulled wine. 'Some more?' Rafe held out his mug, and Sem poured him a meagre, thick trickle.

'Oh, dear. That appears to be it!' He peered into the jug in surprise, as if he'd expected it miraculously to go on filling itself up in defiance of their inroads.

'What about your bourguignon, Sem?' She thought she should steer him away from emotive things like empty jugs and memories of May Balls. 'It must be just about perfect, by now.'

'Yes! Of course.' He took their empty mugs from them. 'I'll go and stir in the soured cream and check on the rice. You come and get the salad out, Nell, and Rafe, you can pour the claret. I've opened it, it's by the Aga.'

Rafe caught her round the waist as she followed Sem into the kitchen.

'I'm plastered,' he whispered in her ear. 'Have you got a reliable alarm clock?'

She said as scathingly as she could, 'I *am* a reliable alarm clock.'

'Good. In that case I'll stay the night.'

Now we're all plastered, she thought drowsily later. Well, mellow, at any rate. They were still sitting round the table, and there was nothing left either of the bourguignon or the large steamed pudding that had followed it. The two claret bottles had been joined in the bin by one of Liebfraumilch, all as empty as the mulled wine jug. Sem was standing leaning against the Aga, where he had gone to make the coffee. But that had been half an hour ago, since when he'd been discussing with Rafe the comparative merits of Italy and Greece from the viewpoint of the antiquarian. The idea of coffee seemed to have drifted irretrievably from his head.

She got up and elbowed him gently out of the way. Rafe doesn't do too badly, either, in the conversational stakes, she thought as she put coffee beans in the grinder. She laughed to herself, as she switched it on, at their reaction to its ghastly racket; instead of letting it interrupt them, they merely raised their voices.

'We'll have some congnac with it!' Sem shouted happily. She heard Rafe mutter something, which she thought might have been, 'Jesus!' She smiled in sympathy. I know how he feels.

She started to clear the table, but Sem stopped her.

'Sit down by Rafe, Nell.' He pushed her back into the chair. 'If I don't feel like doing this tonight, I shall do it in the morning. But either way it's not your job.'

She wished she didn't keep feeling so emotional about

114

everything. It was all rapidly getting too much, and there was the bloody brandy to go yet.

Rafe was watching her, his head on one side.

'Just like two ordinary people,' he said quietly. He put out a hand to ruffled her hair. 'Two inebriated ordinary people.'

Some time later, Sem announced he was going to bed. Rafe stood up to say good night, and Sem patted him affectionately on the shoulder.

'You're not planning to drive back to wherever it is tonight, are you?' Sem asked.

'Not very wholeheartedly, no.'

'Good. The sofa's quite large enough to be comfortable. It's often served as a bed before and we've had no complaints. Have we, Nell?'

'Not so far.'

'I expect I shall see you in the morning, Rafe. Good night, Nell dear.' She went to give him a kiss, and for a moment he stood looking lovingly down at her. 'Bless you,' he said quietly. 'Lovely evening.' They heard him close the staircase door behind him, and then his steady tread going upstairs.

Rafe took her hand and led her through to the living-room, where he sank down on to the sofa. She went to sit beside him, tentatively perching on the edge. He started to laugh softly.

'What?' she asked.

'Your father. He's so –'

'Garrulous? Boozy?'

'No! Yes – garrulous, but the subject matter's very interesting.'

'Palaeoanthropology isn't, unless you're a devotee.'

'You neatly steered us off that. But everything else was. And he's not boozy, he's generous.'

'He likes to have someone to drink with. And to talk with.'

'Suits me, any time. It was a terrific evening. Wasn't it?'

He was beginning to smile at her in that special way again. She started to feel special in response.

'Yes. It was. I'm glad you were here.'

'Me too. Come here,' he patted the sofa beside him, sending up more dust. 'Sorry.'

'Don't worry. You just can't get reliable domestics nowadays.'

He laughed. Then after a moment he said, 'You were going to tell me about your mother.'

Oh God, she thought. So I was. I'd forgotten. We've had such fun, the three of us, it drove most of what happened earlier out of my mind.

He wants to hear about my mother. Well, so he shall. Now's probably a good time to talk about her, when I'm a bit pissed.

She said, 'Okay.'

There was a long pause.

'That *is* fascinating,' he remarked.

'All right!' She'd been wondering where to begin. 'It takes me a while to get started.'

'Yes, I'm sure. I didn't mean to be flippant. Just nosey.'

She slid across on to the cushion from which he'd banged out the dust. Immediately he put his arm round her. What a nice position, she thought, for talking about my mother. Cuddly and secure. And she was neither.

'I don't remember very much about her,' she said. 'Only inconsequential things, like her buying us both new dresses one day and spending ages trying to make my hair curl so it looked extra-nice. She always looked good – she had black hair, and very blue eyes. And once she made herself a caftan from some terribly expensive peacock-blue brocade stuff, and she let me have the left-over bits to make a dress for my doll. Only the material frayed, and no matter how I tried I couldn't make anything of it.' Funny, to remember that. An echo fluttered in her mind of the frustrated anger she had felt when, despite her best efforts, the lovely brocade had gradually

116

turned into a dirty scrap fit for nothing but the dustbin. 'She used to tell me I was pretty,' she hurried on, wanting to think of happier things, 'and once I said, poor Mummy, you're not a bit like me so you can't be pretty, and she got quite cross. But she *was* pretty. She was glorious. Sem used to just sit looking at her, as if he couldn't believe she was real.'

She thought suddenly of how she'd surprised him one day when she was about ten, running into his study to tell him she'd found a toad under the hedge, and found him staring at a photo. He'd pushed it under his blotter, but she'd seen who it was.

'What was her name?' Rafe asked, as the silenced extended.

'Phyllida. Nice, isn't it?'

'Mm.'

'She was much younger than him. He used to say, "Phyllida and I are spring and autumn," and once someone said, "Spring and winter, more like!", and it upset me because I could see he was only pretending to find it funny. Which he had to do, because my mother thought it was hilarious.' She stopped. She saw again Sem's face, felt again the enormous pain of seeing someone she loved being hurt. Perhaps these recollections weren't such a good idea after all. Drink tends to make you maudlin – it brought your vulnerably tender feelings too near the surface.

Rafe stroked her shoulder, as if he knew what she was thinking. 'He had you as a consolation,' he said. 'No matter how unhappy she made him, she gave him you. And it's very plain how he feels about you.'

Another precarious bubble of emotion came close to popping. 'She hadn't really had enough fun,' she said quickly. Anything was better than dwelling on *that* remark. 'I expect that was the trouble. She was twenty-two when they married, and Sem was forty-one. She was too young, and he was too old.'

She stopped. She had the sudden awful feeling that she'd put her foot right in it. Up to the thigh. Rafe must be as old

117

as Sem was then, she thought frantically, and if he's not married either he'll think . . .

'It's okay,' he said. He sounded as if he found it funny, not rude. 'And actually I'm forty-two. To help you avoid another faux-pas. And I'm not married.'

'Oh.' Now she felt totally disconcerted. And very embarrassed. He laughed out loud.

'Go on. I'm not laughing at what you're telling me. But I'm sure you already know that.'

'Yes. I do.'

'Good.'

'She went off with the bass player in a rock band,' she said, taking a run at it because it was better if she got it out fast, 'right into the heart of the Swinging Sixties. They were called the Ancient Mariners, and they played at some event in the town, in Rag Week, I think it was. Anyway, she went along to hear them, and presumably got swept off her feet by this rocker. She went on the road with him. For a while she sent letters – well, postcards to me, of places like Birmingham and Salford. And Exeter – she sent me one from there. Sem used to let me look for the towns in his big atlas.'

She felt a kiss on the top of her head. It was easier than she'd thought, telling Rafe. 'It must have been hard for you,' he said. 'For both of you.'

'Not for me, really. I didn't know she'd gone for good at first – I don't suppose Sem did, either – and by the time I realized she wasn't coming back, I'd got used to living with just Sem. But, looking back, he must have gone through hell. Not that he ever let on to me.'

'Does he ever talk about her?'

'No. Aunt Dorothy did, though. She was his sister – she's dead now, she was seven years older than Sem – and she held forthright opinions about most things. When I was thirteen she invited me to stay with her, mainly because she'd decided the time had come for me to know the truth about my mother.

118

Who, according to her, had been a cross between Lucrezia Borgia and a high-class whore.'

'And how did you feel about that?'

She laughed shortly. 'I couldn't summon much reaction at all, much to Aunt Dorothy's disgust. My mother was such a dim and distant figure by then, it all seemed irrelevant. When Aunt Dorothy pushed me into making some comment, all I said was, "It must have been absolutely dreadful for Sem." And I'm not sure, but when she was nodding her agreement, I think she had tears in her eyes.'

Poor old Aunt Dorothy, she thought, picturing her. She wasn't such a bad old girl. And she did think the world of Sem.

'We got on much better, after that,' she went on. 'I expect she reckoned I'd proved myself by showing so clearly whose side I was on. She told me quite a lot about it all. Phyllida had apparently always been something of a dilettante, and I think that, once he was over the shock, Sem started to look on the whole thing as inevitable. Aunt Dorothy said he used to try to minimize the hurt. "A decade with me and my fossils, then off with the Ancient Mariners," he used to say. "From the sublime to the ridiculous." And he would add, Aunt Dorothy said, that an unbiased observer might have difficulty deciding which was which.'

She realized that at some point Rafe had put both arms round her. And somehow she had turned so that she was lying along the sofa, leaning against his chest. She felt woozy, and drowsy, and, after so long a re-living of events that had happened years ago, not quite sure where then ended and now began.

It was a comfortable feeling.

She felt his lips against her hair. 'What happened to Phyllida?' he asked.

'God knows. The letters stopped, and the cards, and after a while I didn't bother about looking out for the postman. Sem and I moved down here, and we threw ourselves into country living. I loved it – I had a pony, and made friends, and people all seemed much more approachable than they had done in Cambridge.' He started to laugh. 'Oh, I'm sure there were approachable people there,' she said, laughing with him, 'it was just that I never met any. They were all dons, and professors, and fellows, or at the very least post-graduates.'

'You can't have known that! You were far too small.'

'Perhaps. But there's nobody like a child for ferreting out who's unapproachable and who isn't.'

'Okay.' There was a pause. Then he said, 'So it worked out all right for you both, in the end?'

She smiled. Really, it does take some getting used to, the way he so unreservedly asks anything he wants to know. 'Damned continentals,' she murmured.

'What did you say?'

'Sorry. It's the booze. Making me think out loud a bit too loudly. Yes, it worked out fine. For me, anyway. And I didn't really notice if Sem was minding or not. He seemed to be happy. Only sometimes, I think things reminded him. Like watching the Boat Race on TV – one year there was a very close finish, and when we'd stopped jumping up and down and yelling for Cambridge, he said, "I don't remember such an exciting race for years. Not since the first one I watched with your mother." And then his face changed, and he got up and left the room. And once out of the blue someone who didn't know sent a Christmas card addressed to them both. "To Sem and Phyllida." It had been forwarded from the Cambridge address. When he'd seen, he put it straight back in the envelope. Then he went for a long walk by himself.' She sighed. 'Funny, life. Isn't it?'

'Not very.'

'No.'

He was right. It wasn't. She felt a great understanding in him, a sympathy that reached out and wrapped her close. As if he perceived much more than she'd been able to put into words.

It was very quiet. The fire was dying, and she didn't have the energy to mend it. Rafe beneath her lay relaxed, one hand behind his head, one around her waist and resting on her thigh. She wondered why she was content to lie here next to him, almost fraternally, when only a few hours ago he had started a blaze in her that she'd found very hard to put out. Even now, the embers were there.

She turned in towards him, nestling her face into his sweater. His heartbeat was slow and steady, and for a moment she remembered lying against him earlier, outside the Magic Meadow, and the wild fury with which it had raced then. The passion between them started at that moment, ignited perhaps by what had happened in the meadow, and it almost seemed to her that it belonged there. It felt wrong to rekindle it now, in the peace of the evening.

But does that mean it'll always be like that? With the flame between us tarnished because of being associated with . . . with . . . She didn't want to admit to the possibility, even to herself. She shook her head.

'What is it?' he asked, taking her jaw in his hand and moving her head so that he could look into her face. His eyes were hooded; he looked sleepy.

'I don't really know.' Even less could she admit it to him. 'I'm confused.'

'So am I. It's been quite a day.' He opened his eyes wider, with an apparent effort. 'I want – there's a lot I have to tell you. About earlier. Only I can't, now. Tonight you're an ordinary woman, and I'm not going to spoil that by – well, I'm not.'

She had no idea what he was trying to say. Trying not to say, more like. She had the unpleasant suspicion that his thoughts ran on the same lines as her own.

She didn't want to dwell on it. She wished something would happen to distract her.

She wished very much that he would kiss her again.

And after a moment he did.

But it was different; this time he was gentle, his lips and his tongue exploring her with a slow, deliberate thoroughness. While it didn't send her blood-temperature soaring straight out of the top of the thermometer, all the same it began to arouse her. He's not so overpowering, now, she thought muzzily. Not so tyrannical. It's as if this time it's for both of us, not just for him. Her arms went round him, pulling herself closer to him. She felt his hand go up under her shirt, his fingers sliding inside her bra to touch her skin, to rub rhythmically at her nipple. Her body was eager, her mind already leaping far ahead of the present moment, picturing what was to come. She felt for the lower edge of his sweater, fumbling, more hasty than he and awkward in her urgency. She touched his skin, her hands running over him, feeling the hair on his muscular chest.

He took his mouth from hers and she heard him sigh. Her eyes came reluctantly open.

He was looking down at her, his dark eyes too shadowed in the dim light for her to read their expression. He stroked her hair, pushing it away from her face.

'Nell,' he said. 'Oh, Nell. It *is* possible. You don't know how good it feels.'

'What? What are you talking about?'

'Nothing. It's all right. It's much more than all right.' She studied him, moving slightly so that the light from the dying fire fell on his face. He looked happy, so very happy. And, for some reason, relieved.

'*What?*' she said again. But he was laughing, and so full of joy, and she was too far gone to push it.

She bent her head towards him so that she could kiss him. 'Never mind,' she said tolerantly. 'I expect it'll keep.'

'I'm praying that it will. Or one just like it.'

She smothered a laugh. 'Bed, then?'

'Yes. Soon.'

'Amen to that.'

She stood up, and staggered slightly. 'There's a blanket and more dusty old cushions in that chest.' She pointed. 'They smell of cedarwood, because it's a cedarwood chest, but it's good if you've got a cold.'

He was lying down, stretching out along the sofa. She fetched a blanket for him.

'Aren't you going to get undressed?'

'Not until you've gone to bed. I don't want to put temptation in your way, with Sem asleep upstairs.'

'Huh! Don't worry, I'm off.' She bent to kiss him once more. 'Good night. Sweet dreams.' The old benediction was out before she could stop it.

He looked up at her. His face was in the light, and she had no trouble reading his expression now. She saw desire, so clearly that her body gave a throbbing response.

She also saw affection.

'Sweet dreams, Nell.'

Going up the stairs she thought, mine will be. I do hope the same can be said for his.

Nine

She was awake early; she knew even without looking at the clock that it wasn't long after five. It was still totally dark.

The house felt cold, and she wanted to burrow under her duvet and go back to sleep. I can't, she thought. I ought to get up soon, to see what time he has to go. He might sleep right on, and be late for work.

She wondered what he did, trying to picture him in a bank or managing a shop. No. He doesn't seem to fit into anything like that. And he has a subtle air of wealth. That car. An Alfa Romeo, he said it was when I asked on the way to the pub. And he goes abroad a lot, doesn't he? So he must do a job that involves travel. It can't all be the holidays, unless by happy chance I've stumbled on an itinerant millionaire.

From downstairs she heard an unmistakably masculine cough, followed by the creaking of the pantry door, quickly curtailed. It didn't sound like Sem, it sounded like someone trying to find their way round a strange kitchen without waking the household. She smiled. And not being too successful.

She got out of bed, putting jeans and a thick sweater on over her nightshirt. No time to wash, he might even now be bolting his cup of tea and writing her a brief note of valediction. Nice evening. See you, some time.

She wondered if the habits of chronic insecurity and undervaluing of herself would persist throughout her life. It just shows, she thought, how thoroughly a couple of bad experiences can undermine you.

She ran silently down the stairs, avoiding the ones that squeaked without even having to think about it.

Rafe was drinking tea, leaning in Sem's pose against the Aga. He was fully dressed, his coat collar turned up. And there was no sign of a note.

'Good morning,' he said quietly. His face had lit up at her entrance. She thought, fighting down the pleasure that such a reaction in him was trying to give her, he's relieved he hasn't got the embarrassment of having to wake me up to ask where the bread's kept.

'Hello.' She felt shy with him. It was slightly shocking, having his large and dynamic presence intrude on the dark early morning. She usually had the place to herself at this time of day.

But now he was here. And she welcomed him. She asked, 'Have you got time for some breakfast?'

'I've got time. I only got up because I was so damned cold.'

'Were you? Oh, Lord, I'm sorry. I should have told you, there are heaps more blankets in the chest.'

She turned away from him, busying herself getting things haphazardly out of cupboards. She felt mortified by her huge failure as a hostess. How awful, that he should have been so cold that it woke him.

He said, 'I should have had the sense to look.'

'No, no, it was . . .' She moved to get milk from the fridge and stepped on his foot. She felt him wince. She wished she could begin this morning all over again.

'Bacon and eggs?' she asked. 'Toast? Porridge?'

'Porridge would be marvellous. Just that, please. It's a bit early for anything else.'

She glanced at the clock. Five twenty-five.

'Quite.'

She was aware of him watching her. Thank goodness porridge is easy, she thought. Any idiot can make it, even when only half their brain's functioning properly.

'Here,' she said after five minutes' simmering had resulted in a satisfactorily creamy texture. 'Sit down.' She put huge steaming bowls down at opposite sides of the table. 'Salt or sugar? Milk?'

'Sugar, please. And milk.'

He ate silently for some moments. Then he said, 'That's

125

better.' He reached across the table to take her hand. 'I'll have to go in a minute. I think I'll go home to shower and change before I go to work, and the traffic will be building up.'

'Oh. Yes, of course.'

She scraped up the last of her porridge, leaping up to put her bowl in the sink. 'Have you finished?'

He got up and came to stand beside her. 'Yes. Thanks, it was just what I needed.' He smiled. 'No doubt cold is something you have to get used to. I expect my blood's thin, from living too much of my life in the heat.'

She was looking out through the window. A severe overnight frost had covered everything in crisp white. She went to the coat-rack in the scullery, fetching her cap and a scarf. She handed them to him.

'You haven't seen anything yet. I think you'd better have these.'

His face fell. 'Oh, God. As bad as that?'

She nodded. 'Come on. I'll help you.' She picked up the windscreen scraper, shoving her feet into her boots, and led the way outside.

She heard him gasp as the sharp air hit him. He said something, but she couldn't make it out. It didn't sound English. It's the cold, she thought, it's making him pine for the south. Thin blood, indeed.

His car was covered in a hard icing of white.

'Isn't it pretty?' she remarked. He didn't answer. She heard faintly some more quiet, foreign mutterings. She set to work on his windscreen while he began the daunting task of starting the car.

'There!' he said triumphantly. The engine was roaring on full choke, and above it soared a female voice, brought to life on the cassette he must have left in last night.

'Well done. If the engine didn't wake half of Kent, the soprano should have done the trick.'

126

He leaned down hastily to push in the choke and turn down the volume. 'Sorry. Actually she's a mezzo-soprano.'

'What is it?'

'*Il Barbiere di Siviglia*.' The woman was replaced by a man. 'Oh, good. I'll have the *Largo al Factotum* to see me on to the M25.'

'No doubt you'll join in. All Italian men sing, don't they?'

'Yes. But most of them sing tenor.'

She laughed suddenly, remembering. 'Yes! Sem came up through Italy in the war, with the Eighth Army. He said everywhere people wanted to give concerts for them, and it was always *Madam Butterfly* and a short, fat, sweaty tenor in a jacket with straining buttons.'

He grinned. 'I've got to go. I'm off to America next week. Monday morning.' He hesitated.

She wanted to ask, why? For how long? What will you be doing?

When will I see you?

She said, 'Perhaps you'd like to come down on Saturday.'

He reached out through the open car door to pull her close. He was wearing her cloth cap. She thought how well it suited him, making him look quite English and contradicting the foreign mutterings and *Il Barbiere di Siviglia*. His hands on her face pulled back her panicky, fugitive thoughts despite herself.

He kissed her, his lips cold against hers. 'I'll be here.'

She watched as he drove away. Before the silence that he left behind him could desolate her, she ran back into the house.

'Rafe's coming down on Saturday,' she said later to Sem. The ground was much too hard for her to think of doing anything outside, and she was sitting at the kitchen table mapping out imaginary gardens. She bent to her task, concentrating on drawing a brick wall containing a raised bed of Madonna lilies, irises and gillyflowers.

'Oh, good. What will you do?'

She shot up her head to stare at him, sitting across the table from her, polishing shoes. 'What do you mean, what will *we* do?'

'I'm going to Cambridge, aren't I? For my dinner with the Fellows.'

Oh, Lord. I forgot all about it. Oh, damn and blast. Rafe'll think I did it on purpose. She glanced again at Sem. *He* probably will, too.

'So you are. I wish you'd said.'

'I didn't think I needed to,' Sem replied mildly. 'Only yesterday we were discussing which train I'd catch.'

She regretted her sharp tone. Sem was excited about his weekend; she thought it probably gratified him that the College went on inviting him, that retirement and long absence from Cambridge hadn't cast him far out into obscurity.

'Yes, you're right,' she said. 'It slipped my mind, that's all. I'm glad you reminded me, we should air your new pyjamas if you're going to take them. I'm sure your bedroom cupboard's damp.'

'All right, dear. If you think so.' He was frowning, clearly thinking of something else. She thought, it's okay. Bless him, he doesn't pollute his mind entertaining suspicious thoughts about other people and their deviousness. The implications of Rafe and me being alone here, and of me possibly having set it up, won't even have occurred to him.

She went back to her drawing, humming. Sem said, '*Barber of Seville*. I didn't know you could hum Rossini.'

The cold weather continued for the rest of the week. Typical, she thought. When it's wet and rainy, every day wreathed in clouds so thick that sunshine is just a memory, you long for a nice, steady, high-pressure system to anchor itself firmly right over you. Then when you're desperate to get on with some hard work to stop yourself thinking, one comes along and does *just that*. And these bright, frosty days make digging impossible, the ground's like a pavement. Sod's law.

She went outside and walked irritably up and down between her neat beds. She'd tidied her shed, swept out her glasshouse, cleaned every piece of equipment she could think of and done some long-postponed maintenance on the Land-Rover. And it was only Friday morning.

I'll have a go on the house. Nothing too obvious. Just the living-room, and the kitchen. And my room, perhaps.

Stop it. *Stop* that.

She ran back into the house, banging the kitchen door behind her so hard that the key fell out of the lock.

'We're in plenty of time, there's no need to hurry.' Sem said. She slowed down; there were still some frosty patches on the roads. Possibly he was justified in sounding slightly apprehensive.

'No, okay. Have you got everything?'

'Yes. Thank you for pressing my dinner jacket.'

'That's all right. It's right back in fashion, wide lapels and double-breasted. You'll look great!'

He sighed happily. 'I *am* looking forward to it all.' Then he added, 'Although I'm sorry to miss Rafe. Give him my regards, won't you?'

The heavy moth in her stomach had been having a well-earned nap. It woke up, and as if making up for lost time began to flutter about with a dedication that bordered on the malicious. She said briefly, 'I will.'

They reached the station.

'Don't wait, Nell dear.' Sem climbed down carefully from the cab, reaching back for his overnight bag. He put his hand to her cheek. For a moment she thought he was about to add something more, but all he said was, 'Look after yourself.'

'You too.' He looked old, his tall, spare frame appearing to shrink inside his overcoat. Her heart turned over. But then it was very cold. Enough to make anybody shrink. 'You shouldn't

129

stand about out here,' she said hurriedly. 'Go and find a nice warm waiting-room till your train comes.'

He chuckled. 'That would be a find indeed.'

'Give me a ring when you know what time you'll be back on Sunday. I'll meet you.'

'All right. It won't be until quite late, I imagine. Thank you, dear.'

She realized his good manners wouldn't allow him to go into the station until she'd gone. She blew him a kiss and drove off.

She woke in the pre-dawn of Saturday. She looked at the clock. Half past four. I've broken my all-time record. Too early to get up. Sleep. I'll go back to sleep.

But I might dream, if I do. *She's* been threatening, since Rafe came, more insistent than she's been for years. Because I've been thinking about her, of course. Talking to Rafe about her. She's on my mind, so it's logical I'd dream of her.

Only she doesn't have it all her own way.

She reached for the cup on the bedside table, containing the herbal infusion she'd taken up with her last night. She sipped at it. Ugh. The taste doesn't improve with keeping. But it works. Thank heavens, it works.

She closed her eyes. That'll keep *Her* at bay.

Alienor. He said her name's Alienor.

Don't think about it. Don't give Her any invitations.

Nor him.

Think about gardens, and flowers.

She felt herself drifting. Strangely, the day-dreams gradually turning into night-dreams seemed to be accompanied by a slight smell of cloves.

She sat over a breakfast cup of tea. She had no appetite, and it was all she could manage.

I wish he'd said what time he'd be coming. He never does. Only the day. And 'Saturday' could mean anything.

What's the very earliest he'd be here? Eleven? Twelve? Hours away.

She did some washing, and some ironing. Then some desultory tidying. She had a long bath, washing her hair and then blow-drying it, brushing it till it gleamed. She took some time deciding what to wear. She made herself eat a sandwich for lunch, then prepared a beef stew and put it in the slow oven.

Then, having run out of ideas, she lit the fire in the living-room and went to sit beside it.

At four-thirty she heard a car draw up.

She leapt to the window, peering out for long enough to confirm it was his, then sat back in Sem's chair.

A paper! Where's the paper? I can't be sitting here just *waiting*. She found *The Times*, still lying unopened on the mat, and hastily picked it up.

She heard a tap on the glass. She turned.

He was wearing her cloth cap. He looked happy.

She ran through to the kitchen and flung open the back door. Without even pausing to say hello he took her in his arms, kissing her with an intensity which suggested he'd been anticipating the pleasure as much as she had.

After a minute he stopped, putting his hand on her hair and pushing her head into his neck. He smelled nice. He said, 'I've missed you.'

The moth in her stomach had started on a different sort of aerobatics, one that hit nerve-endings going straight to her knees. Via some deep central port of her whose existence she'd all but forgotten.

Not knowing what to do, at a loss as to what should happen next she said, 'I've cooked a stew.' And wondered why he burst out laughing.

She became acclimatized quite quickly. Talking to him, being with him, made his presence feel more normal and he no

131

longer threw her into confusion. They talked about ordinary things. She thought, look at this! All that mental frenzy beforehand, and her we are at the kitchen table drinking tea and discussing the least congested route out of London. Any minute now I'll be suggesting a stroll to the pub and a sherry ot two before supper.

When it came it was his suggestion. They walked up to the village arm-in-arm, and people in the pub greeted them with friendliness. She was sure some of them had been there the other night. And the landlord said to Rafe, 'Nice to see you again. Becoming quite a regular, aren't you?'

She was torn between being glad to be seen with him and being worried about the awkwardness she could foresee ahead.

When he was no longer there.

'You cook as well as Sem,' he said later when they'd eaten her stew. 'I like the dumplings. The herbs perk them up, don't they?'

'Herbs with everything,' she remarked.

'It's all right with me. And you have to be an advertisement for your own produce.'

'Coffee?' she asked, putting the last of the dishes to soak in the sink.

'Yes, please.'

'Go and sit by the fire. I'll bring it through.'

When she went in he was lying back in the corner of the sofa, staring into the fire. She was proud of the fire; she'd been nursing it all afternoon, and now it was beautifully into its stride. Just right for baking potatoes, she thought. Or mulling wine. And perfect for a cold night with the curtains drawn.

She was nervous about looking at him, not wanting to meet his eyes. She darted quick glances at him. At his profile against the firelight, the strong features, the hard line of his mouth. At his broad body and the thickly-muscled legs.

She could feel sensuality in the air. She knew what was going to happen. It had been inevitable, since that first kiss.

132

The mark had been put upon them, on him and on her, and the pattern set. Attraction, arousal, desire, consummation. You couldn't break the chain.

She crouched to put the coffee mugs down on the hearth, so aware of him sitting there just behind her that her skin felt ultra-sensitive, as if she had a fever. And then, as she had known it would, came the touch of his hand.

He ran his fingers across the skin on the back of her neck, under her hair. Response shuddered through her, right down her spine. His hand moved round so that he held her jaw, and he turned her head so that he could look into her face. Nerving herself, she met his stare.

Oh, he has that look of happiness. It's in his eyes. They go sort of half-closed from underneath, like cartoon characters' eyes do when they're laughing. It's as if he's laughing too, but inside, and it's only showing in his eyes.

And below the laughter and the happiness was something else. His expression straightened. Not speaking, he leaned closer. And she shut her eyes as he began to kiss her.

He was arousing such feelings in her, kissing first her lips, then moving his mouth down her neck, his tongue against her flesh as if he were tasting her. He unbuttoned her shirt with a firm hand that didn't fumble, and his lips travelled over her chest, her stomach. He moved off the sofa to kneel with her in front of the fire, and she felt him reach behind him to get cushions, throwing them down on top of the hearthrug. He put his hands on her shoulders and pushed her back, down into the softness and the warmth. Kneeling above her, he ripped off his sweater and his shirt, pausing to stare down at her as she lay beneath him. Then he said softly, 'Take off your clothes.'

She felt shy, momentarily hit by the thought that it was crazy to be lying on the floor in front of her fire, at his whim about to be naked in her own living-room.

But it's not just his whim. It's mine too.

She looked up at him, feeling almost that she was dreaming.

His chest was broad and deep, and he wore a thick gold chain round his neck on which hung a Byzantine cross, its triangular arms glistening as they caught the light from the fire. His shoulders and upper arms were heavy with muscle, and she thought how strong he must be. Her eyes went back to look into his face; he was half in shadow, and she could only see the cheek that bore the scar.

She reached up to touch it with her fingertips, and he turned his head towards her hand. He seemed so tender, for all his strength, and she was moved again at the thought of him being drawn here, of him being hurt, involved in something he didn't understand. She wanted him, she wanted to give herself to him, to have him give himself to her. Wrestling with the fastenings, she hurriedly undressed.

As soon as she was done he was down on her, his body heavy and hard against her, his mouth once more on hers and his tongue inside her mouth, searching for her, sucking on her as if he were drawing her into him. With a part of her mind she thought, this is like the first time, by the meadow. And he's inexorable, there's no way that he won't achieve his desire. My desire. Swept up with his, no more opinion of my own. His hand was on her stomach, a warm area of heat on her skin that caressed and delved deeper, his fingers touching the very edge of her sensitive area of body hair, pausing, slowly sliding down between her legs so that she wanted to scream aloud for him to go on, go on, go further in, come to the heart of me.

He seemed to sense her need, responding to her tension under him by renewed fervour in his kissing. Then he moved his mouth to her breast, taking her nipple between his lips, touching it with his teeth, his tongue, until she thrust her body up towards him in desire. He lifted himself from her, and she lamented the loss of his weight on her, ached to have him back. Something hard hit her, his belt-buckle. With smooth, unhurried movements he undressed.

Then his naked body fell on to her.

134

His legs lay along hers, his hand working on her, in her, making space between her thighs. Eyes closed, drowning in sensation, she could feel his penis against her, feel the hot hardness of him pressing into her stomach. She wanted to touch, to feel, and she reached down to enclose him in her hand. She felt him leap inside her palm, felt the throb of him in the nerves of her fingers. He pushed down with his knees and forced her legs apart. Then he was there right against her, nudging into her, but so gently, oh, so slowly, that even while her body yearned for all of him she was aware of gratitude that he should not hurry.

And then he stopped.

Why? Oh God, oh dear God, why?

She lifted her hips to him, tried to position herself so that he would feel her ready to take him in, feel her crying out for him.

After an endless moment she opened her eyes.

His face was right above her. The left side glowed in the firelight. And the scar was a great white worm that slithered down his flesh.

His left eye was shut. From the black right side of his face his eye gleamed dully red.

His expression was stern, angry, and full of passion. But it was violent passion.

He started to smile. But it wasn't Rafe's smile.

He didn't really look like Rafe at all.

He breathed in deeply and she saw the muscles bunch in his shoulders and his arms.

Then the tight-curbed power was released.

With a great thrust of his pelvis he pushed himself deep inside her. She felt as if she were being impaled. It was invasion, hot and impatient; her body tightened in alarm at the onslaught in a desperate attempt at self-preservation, but he paid her no heed. Now it was all for him, and she knew she counted for nothing in his headlong race for gratification. With a long smooth stroke he pulled out of her, only to drive

135

straight back in, over and over again in a faultless, urgent rhythm that stretched her to her limits until she felt her flesh bruise and break. She opened her mouth, wailing in her anguish. But he was there, his hot breath against her lips, his jaws working and his tongue forcing her mouth further open, gagging the agonized protest. So big, so overpowering, he was. She couldn't move, could scarcely breathe, could only lie and suffer him as passion gave way to the heartbreak of anguish and pain.

His left side was scorched by fire. The skin of his arm and his thigh felt tight and itched in its heat. The smell of woodsmoke was in his nostrils, and a sickly-sweet stench of ordure, of farmyard dung. Woven in, like a strand of silver thread dropped in the mud, was the scent of cloves.

His eye ached as if a red-hot needle were in it. And it wouldn't open.

He turned his head slightly trying to see with his good eye, but the room was dark. The fire was dying, and its glowing red-hot heart gave out little light. His right side, away from the hearth, shivered with cold.

As he stared out into the darkness his eye adjusted. He thought he saw a flimsy wall, riddled with gaps through which shone the light of the moon. His knees were on bare earth, his elbows scratched and pricked as they dug into straw.

Where is this? What happened to me?

The woman beneath him stared up at him. She was moving her lips, shaping over and over again the same words. Gradually their sound came to him.

'You'll always be mine!'

AT LAST! Oh, God, at last.

The hunger rose in him, and his breath came fast. He fixed his good eye on her, trying to focus. A pale face framed by two long, long braids, silver ribbon threaded through white-fair hair. *Touch me!* he thought she said. *Feel me!* His desperate hands tore into some smooth fabric, ripping it aside to get

136

to her, scrabbling down across her belly and into the soft
hair of her groin, pushing with his fingers, two, three fingers
together, forcing his way into her, sliding into the hot, wet,
wide-open-mouthed vortex that was the essence of her, that
yearned for him and drew him in with the power of her desire.

Yes! Yes! More, hurry!

His hand moved to guide himself into her, into the waiting
flesh that reared up towards him. Without pausing to be
gentle, without waiting for her to adjust to him before screwing his great size into her, he obeyed her summons and pushed
with all his strength.

His mouth was on hers, her jaws wide apart so that she
seemed to suck him into her. His good eye tight up against
the skin of her cheek, he could see nothing. But an image of
her face exploded inside his head, sea-green eyes broiling with
lust, long braids twitching and coiling against the beaten earth
floor. And he saw her white legs, naked, her skirts bunched
up anyhow around her waist, pushed out of the way as her
legs strained to part ever further. Around his waist he felt the
soft flesh of her inner thighs crushing against him as suddenly
she clasped her ankles fiercely together behind him. Moving
his hands to her buttocks he lifted her hips, tilting her off the
ground, shoving deeper and impossibly deeper into her so
that she screamed out in her abandoned ecstasy . . .

And the scream became a sob, as the voice of someone
who had reached the end of endurance said brokenly, 'Rafe,
oh, please, Rafe, no more.'

He looked down at her, sick and shocked, a terrible feeling
of guilt rising in him.

He couldn't meet her eyes. His hands were still under her,
the vicious clenching of his fingers into her flesh only now
beginning to relax.

And he was still deep inside her. As he slowly withdrew,
with a tenderness that came far too late, he saw blood on her
thighs.

He sat back on his heels, hunching into himself. He closed his eyes. He felt her move, heard her gasping, sobbing breath. And a moan of sheer agony.

The draught of movement wafted against him as she scrambled to her feet, gathering up her clothes. The door on to the staircase opened, and then banged shut.

She shut the bathroom door behind her, bolted it and sagged to the floor, leaning her weight against it.

From below she heard violent activity, and she stiffened in terror. It sounded like some animal, beating itself against the bars of a cage.

All went quiet.

Then in the silence came a great roar of anguish, and the slamming of a door.

Which door?

She gasped, tensing, waiting for the lunge, the attack.

But the footsteps were running away.

And a normal twentieth-century sound amid the horror as a car started up and drove quickly off up the road.

She sat for a long time, shivering, clutching her knees tight up to her chest.

Then, slowly because moving hurt, she ran a deep bath and clambered into it.

Her mind began to return from its defensive numbness. Against her will, scenes were replaying before her eyes. The tenderness of the early evening. The happy companionship. The slow build-up of a mood of intimacy. But irrevocably the light gave way to the dark: the vision that dominated all the rest was his face, full of desire that looked more like hatred.

What had happened? Why had he changed like that? It was if he'd become someone else. Someone who looked like Rafe but who wasn't.

Something had been abroad in the night.

A tremor of absolute horror shook through her.

Naked in the bath, under one feeble electric light, only a thin wooden door between her and whatever was out there, she was vulnerable. Her movements made awkward by panic, she hastily got out of the water and dried herself, dragging on a nightshirt over her clammy skin and wrapping herself in her warm dressing-gown.

Then she pulled from the corners of her mind a courage she hadn't known she possessed.

And went downstairs.

The door into the living-room was still shut from when she'd banged it as she flew upstairs. She put her hand to the latch, and her fingers were trembling.

She flung the door open.

The living-room was empty.

And it was as tranquil and welcoming as it always was.

With a quiet prayer of thankfulnes, she went through to the kitchen and put the kettle on to boil.

She made the drink quickly, and she made it strong. So what if it knocked her out for a few hours. It mightn't be such a bad thing.

The telephone rang.

It made her jump so violently that she dropped her cup.

It rang on and on. But she turned her back on it, willing all her concentration into clearing up the spilled liquid and the broken china. By the time she was once more filling a fresh cup, the ringing had stopped.

She went over to the fire. It was dying, and tonight more than ever before she needed a bright blaze. She put on logs, more and more, banking up the fire so that it wouldn't fail her. The great hot heart slowly got a hold on the new fuel, and soon the lively flames were throwing the shadows right back into the furthest corners of the room.

Reassured by the light, calmed by the herbal drink, she sat back on the sofa.

And she started to remember.

The cushions were still on the floor. On the hearthrug,

139

where they had lain together. Where his heavy body had crushed hers and she had felt the overwhelming power of him.

No, not of him, she thought. Of IT. For whatever it was in the room with me at the end it wasn't Rafe.

Fear returned. She looked all round her, every sense alert, holding herself perfectly still like an animal suspecting danger.

But it was all right. There was nothing there.

She moved closer to the fire, taking a long drink of her brew.

How did it know? How did it light with such deadly accuracy on the thing I've been afraid of all my life? Was it so obvious to it, that, even before I understood what it was that so terrified me, my one big fear has always been of the doppelgänger? That some half-remembered fairy tale, even some deep racial memory that I never even absorbed from living reality into my own brain, took root in me and has returned to haunt me all my life?

She was feeling slightly muzzy. The stiletto point of her fear was slowly being dulled by the stalwart strength that the old room poured out. As if a subconscious and sensible part of her was saying quietly, now what can harm you in this place of love and security?

Her mind wandered away from the present. She remembered a night of early childhood. In her parents' Cambridge house she had woken screaming from nightmare, terrified of Sem, of all people, because in her dream he'd turned from the loving father she adored into something that looked just like him but which she knew to be evil. It had worn a red hat, and its face, Sem's own dear face, had peered at her through a strangely-shaped window. And she'd run to it, putting her arm out to be picked up and hugged. Then stopped, horrified, because when she got close enough to see properly, it wasn't really Sem's face but subtly different. Her childish vocabulary hadn't had sufficient scope to describe *how* different; she'd wailed to her mother, reluctantly roped into midnight child-tending duty only because Nell wouldn't let poor bewildered Sem anywhere near, 'Daddy bad! Daddy bad!'

She'd never dreamed that way about Sem again. Although the nightmare remained in her head in all its original vividness, her immature mind had been realistic even if simple. She had recognized very soon afterwards that the instinctive reaction to her father, of wholehearted love for the one person in her small world who was totally devoted to her, was the right one.

But in other respects, the damage had been done.

She huddled into the corner of the sofa, nerving herself for a roller-coaster ride through the worst of her memories. How she'd always loathed men dressed up as Father Christmas, because she was terrified that behind the beards and the jollity heaven knew what was lurking. How Sem had apologetically had to remove her from a pantomime audience because she'd started screaming at the Ugly Sisters. 'They've got deep voices and big feet!' she'd howled. 'They're not women at all!'

Then, as she'd grown towards maturity, how the fear had changed. From being a blunt instrument to bludgeon a little girl down to the depths of dread, it became an insidious, subtle poison. She would be happy in a new friendship with a girl, or later with a boy, and then on the very edges of her mind would come the doubt. Is she as nice as she seems? Or does she go to other girls behind my back and whisper nasty things about me?

And, most damaging of all, the fear corrupted her as a lover.

Ironically, she had sometimes been quite right in her suspicions. But not always.

'No.' She spoke out loud. 'I will not think about that. God, there's quite enough to worry about without going into renewed lamentation over my past mistakes.'

The phone rang again.

She waited, cowering down with her hands over her ears,

for it to stop. Then she took the receiver off its rests and laid it down on the table.

The drink was taking effect. The fear was receding; she knew now she would sleep dreamlessly. But she was reluctant to leave the fire. She put on some more logs, then fetched blankets from the cedarwood chest and lay down.

Her final thought, sliding in when her defences were beginning to crumble, was that the last person who'd slept here was Rafe.

The cold weather eased the next day, and she was able to get out into the garden. She worked as hard as she knew how, using all her will-power to hold her mind tightly in the present. So thoroughly did she succeed that it wasn't till mid-morning that she remembered the phone was off the hook. And that Sem was meant to be calling.

'Ring soon, Sem,' she said as she replaced it. 'Then I can take it off again.'

The phone rang at half past twelve.

The urgent sound ripped into her. But she made herself be calm. She had worked out her plan of action; the first words from the caller would tell her who it was, and she was going to throw the receiver back immediately if it were . . . if it wasn't Sem.

She picked up the receiver and put it to her ear, not speaking.

But it was all right. It *was* Sem.

'Nell? Is everything all right?' he asked worriedly. 'I've been trying to contact you all morning. The operator said the phone was off the hook.'

'Yes, Sem, I'm sorry.' It was marvellous to hear him. 'I took it off last night, when I went to have a bath, and I forgot to put it back.'

'Ah!' He sounded very relieved. 'I hoped there would be some simple explanation. I'm at the station.'

'Fine. What time do you arrive?'

'I have arrived. I meant I'm at our station.'

'You're early! I though you were going to stay for lunch, and maybe even tea?'

There was a pause. Then he said, 'I wanted to come back.'

She was instantly anxious. 'What's the matter? You're not ill, or anything?'

'No, no, good Lord, no. I'm – I just wanted to be back with you.'

She had an instant of absolute certainty.

He knows. He knows all about it.

Then as quickly it passed, leaving behind just a great thankfulness that Sem was home. That she need no longer be alone.

'I'll set out right away. We'll have a pub lunch together, shall we?'

And Sem said cheerfully, 'Nothing I'd like better.'

Looking back, she didn't know what she'd have done without him, the rest of that day. At the station he looked at her intently, his face lined with worry. But, bless him, he asked her no questions. They had lunch, and quite a lot to drink, and when they got home and she said, 'If anyone rings for me, I'm out, please, Sem,' he merely nodded.

The phone rang at tea-time. She said, 'Don't answer it. Please.' and he hadn't. After it had happened twice more, he resorted to her trick and took it off the hook.

They watched an old film together in the evening. It was sentimental and silly, and she found herself weeping silently. Sem came to sit beside her, patting her hand and giving her his spotless linen handkerchief to wipe her eyes. Which made her cry the more.

He put his arms round her, as if she'd been seven again.

'There, there,' he muttered. 'There, there.'

She woke in the morning to find that it was light; she'd overslept. She thought, I must wean myself off the high-strength brew, as soon as I can.

Then she heard voices. Sem's, and a deeper one which set up in her a tearing mixture of horror and delight.

No! NO!

The voices mumbled on. They must be standing at the front of the house. Perhaps they were talking through the open living-room window.

She couldn't make out the words. Didn't want to. She wanted to run, to hide.

I can't see him. Can't think about him.

She pulled the pillow over her head, and on top of that the duvet.

After a while Sem called up the stairs to her.

'He's gone.'

That was all.

The days passed. She couldn't sleep, didn't want to eat. She worked all day until the light failed, then would stumble into the house exhausted. Her mind was engaged in a fierce battle with the thoughts that besieged her, and she went in constant fear of the first breach of her defences.

Through all of the awful week Sem watched her, love and concern in his worried face. Many times she wanted to say, Sem, help me. But it was too gross and too personal a matter, and she couldn't bring herself to tell him.

She suspected he had a fair idea of what had happened. That somehow he knew there was something evil in the air, outside their control. But what if she were wrong?

She couldn't take the risk. She might pour out to him that Rafe had suddenly turned from the nice man he had seemed to be into someone – something – bestial. Something wholly cruel, that had used her and abandoned her. But then if she'd misjudged and Sem *didn't* know they must not hold Rafe responsible, she knew without a doubt that he would blame Rafe so absolutely that there would be no possible reconciliation if ever . . .

Her thoughts screeched to an abrupt stop.

If ever what? What is it that I want?

In a flash, she knew what she'd been hoping for.

And in the same instant she realized how impossible was that hope.

The realization was like a hard slap across her face.

On Thursday she was working on the Land-Rover's interior, for want of anything better to do, removing several years' accumulated mud and rubbish. Hearing the back door close, she turned to see Sem coming up the path. He had a letter in his hand.

He said, 'It's from America. From Rafe.' He held it out, pointing to where the sender's name and address were written in the top left-hand corner of the envelope.

She made no move to take it.

After a moment he said, 'It's not like the phone, or actually talking face to face, Nell. It wouldn't hurt to read it.'

'No!'

'Oh, dear.' He paused. Then he said slightly reproachfully, 'Innocent until proven guilty. That's the just way.'

She thought, if only you knew!

He was still holding out the letter. She glanced at it. Airmail envelope. Black ink. Forward-sloping writing. Forceful, like him.

Rafe.

She put out her hand to take it.

Sem smiled. He turned to walk back to the house.

She got into the Land-Rover's cab and shut the door. Then she slit open the envelope and unfolded the pages inside.

There was no greeting.

> *I am eight miles above the Atlantic, on my way to New York. Having failed to reach you by phone and rejecting the option of forcing Sem aside to storm your house – which would be far too reminiscent, wouldn't it? – this is the only way left. I just hope you won't throw it straight on the fire.*

I have got to tell you things I'd much rather have kept from you, at least for the time being. Primarily, that although you are already aware of Alienor, what I haven't said is that in my dreams she looks exactly like you. I have no idea why – or rather I had no idea, until the night before last. Now I think I know.

She calls me Richard. I think she has me confused with someone else, someone who was her lover but who deserted her. She says, "You'll always be mine". I think she reclaims her lost Richard in me. And you are right, she is evil. And she's debauched. Perverted, perhaps. I think it's because of what happened to her, that what I' (She noticed that 'I' had been roughly crossed out) 'Richard did to her corrupted her.

And you, poor you who look so like her, have got tangled up in whatever it is. You may have stopped reading by now, thinking that in the absence as yet of any remote sign of contrition, any apology, however halting, you don't want to know. I hope not, because here it comes. I'm sorry. I'm a thousand times sorry. I can't explain, other than to say that it wasn't me and you weren't you. If ever we meet again and by some miracle we are once more in that position, perhaps I'll be able to make you see that.

I'll be in America for several weeks. Then back to London briefly, and to Italy for Christmas. After that, I don't know. I'll give you an address in New York where you can contact me, and a phone number. Reverse the charges, because if I start talking to you I won't want to stop.'

It ended as starkly as it had begun; he'd simply signed, 'Rafe'.

She sat for a long time. It wasn't me, and you weren't you. She might have said it was unbelievable, except that it wasn't.

Eventually she got out of the cab and went slowly back to the house. Instead of an ending, it seemed this was just the beginning.

III

Ten

He was hot, and it was hard to breathe. His field of vision was restricted – he had to turn his head in order to see to right and left. He strained to control the grey, uneasy in the midst of the great army moving forward with tightly-controlled power that must not be released before the order. His body poured sweat. The helmet was so heavy, and he felt panic born of claustrophobia rise in him.

Then they were racing, seeming to leap straight into the gallop, flying down the hill with unbelievable speed. The muscles of the grey bunching, thrusting onwards, head level with the leaders. In his ears nothing but a colossal, chaotic roar, and as he gasped for air the acrid dust bit into his throat.

He was hemmed in by men wielding heavy swords, knee to knee with other mounted knights whose thunderous, terrifying onslaught rode down the dark men on small horses running to intercept them, maiming and decapitating with an efficiency that made him feel it was so easy it was cheating. Then like a revelation he felt contempt, bitter contempt, and his own voice sounded in the tumult, shouting his hatred in a furious howl of aggression. His sword arm filled with warrior strength, and the light flashed on his blade until it was dulled with blood.

Ahead of him soared ancient walls, white-gold in the brilliance. A standard: three lions on scarlet. Whoops of triumph, screams of agony, the grey's great feet sliding on flesh that had become like pulped fruit. And then a sudden feeling of choking. Deadly pressure under his chin, which as quickly ceased. With his helmet dislodged, air cooled the sweat on his face. Swiftly turning his head, he saw on his left hand a dark-skinned man mounted on a bay. The black eyes screwed up in the harsh face, slits of malice that glittered jet. And as the bay wheeled under its rider, dainty as a dancer, a curved sword whistled through the air.

Something cold and hard bit down the length of his cheek. With a howl of rage he pushed his helmet back into place and raised his arm. His sword fell, and a white-grey mess of brains flew out as the brown man's skull dropped in two halves as neat as a cut apple.

He was in the press of knights, backing, trampling, triumph already in the air. His helmet felt loose, slipping around on his head as if it had become too big. He felt for a fastening, and his fingers drowned in a warm slick of his own blood . . .

He was lying down, a figure in a filthy bloodstained tunic bending over him. The sick smell of butchery filled his head, and from very near sounds of men in agony. The figure leaned closer, the reek from him wafting out in moist damp waves as he scoured and scraped, setting off such pain, such unbeliev-able pain.

His face was on fire, the blade was cutting deeper. But it was no longer one clean cut. It sawed, biting first here and then there, a continuous onslaught of torture up and down his cheek. Then through a mist the reeking figure, reaching down to remove a padded dressing that dripped yellow infection and that *moved*, seething with the maggots that had been eating out the pus.

A hand like cool water on his forehead. A clean smell, like herbs. And a new figure, robed, lined brown face against a white headdress bound with a rich cord. Someone speaking quietly an unknown language that merged into a different voice . . . 'He says this one will live. But the infection had gone too deep before he tended him. He cannot save the eye.'

He cannot save the eye.

Save his eye.

His eye.

The pain woke him. For a moment, hung on the frontier between sleep and wakefulness, the whole left side of his face felt as if someone had driven spikes into it.

And he could only see out of his right eye.

He spent five weeks in New York, a time filled with depression and worry during the day and whose anxieties spilled at night into dreams so vivid he feared to go to sleep.

He thought constantly of Nell, of what he had done to her, of how she'd be feeling now. He dreamt of her, lying in a wide bed in a strange room whose walls were slabs of yellowish stone, and watched aghast as a shuffling, dirty old crone ministered to her, lifting the rough sheet that covered her to push apart her legs and inspect the wounds he had inflicted. He saw blood, heard her scream, woke in horror with the realization that she was not Nell but Alienor.

Asleep, awake, he was never free of her. Had she read his letter? Had he gone any way to explaining? Did she understand, if understanding were possible?

Would she contact him?

At first he was confident she would. Two days for mail to get here from England? Three? But then she mightn't have written by return, she might have had to think about it for a few days.

If she's not going to write, perhaps she'll phone.

He took to making excuses for not going out in the evenings and at weekends, reasoning that those would be the times she'd call because they were when she'd expect to find him in.

When she failed either to write or call, he didn't even want to go out any more.

He wrote her letters but tore them up because, in the absence of any word from her, he could only write variations on his first brief communication. He dialled her number once, but replaced the receiver before the ringing was answered. He couldn't bear the thought of Sem saying again, as he had done on that awful morning with a stiff politeness that didn't quite mask the kindly worry in his eyes, 'I'm afraid she can't talk to anyone. I'm so sorry.'

His work suffered. For the first time in years, his output wasn't met with interested approval. 'It's trite,' someone said about his piece on Easter in the Cretan mountains. 'Tell me something I haven't been told a hundred times and maybe I'll be able to get over the clichés.'

His American agent told him to go home and take a vacation.

Dining with old friends, his concerned hostess asked him did he have a headache? He realized he'd been sitting with his fist in his left eye. and that it hurt like hell. The friend offered to make an appointment for him with an eye specialist, to which he agreed simply because it was easier to say yes than to explain to her why there was no point. And when the specialist said he couldn't find anything organically wrong, Rafe thought, I could have told you that. And saved myself a couple of hundred dollars.

In the eye vision came and went. But it gave him some degree of pain all the time.

When the day came to depart, he left New York with relief. Home mightn't be much better, but he didn't think anything could be worse. Flying back to London, his eyes closed, tired and in pain, he wondered what he was going to do next.

He phoned Stephen.

'Nice to hear from you,' Stephen said. 'Been away again?'

'I just got back from New York.'

'The jetsetting life! I envy you, London in December's awful. You can't get a taxi anywhere within ten miles of the West End. And why do Arabs of all people have to do Christmas shopping?'

He seemed to be expecting Rafe to join in his laughter.

'How about meeting for a drink?' Rafe said. He didn't feel like laughing.

'Come to dinner. Can you manage tomorrow night?'

He could. But he didn't intend to if there was going to be company.

'Er – I'm going to Italy for Christmas. I'll be a bit busy. Will it – who else is going?'

Stephen laughed again. 'Nobody. No Carolines or Malcolms or Suzannas, if that's what you're asking. Too busy respectively decorating the spare room and buying her trousseau, if women still do that. Did you know Suzanna's engaged?'

'No.' Suzanna. She seemed a lifetime away.

'It'd just be us,' Stephen said. 'Okay?'

'Yes, okay. Thanks. I'll come.'

Opening the door to him Stephen said, 'Good Christ! Whatever happened to your face?'

Rafe had been expecting it. He said, 'It's a long story. It's why I'm here.'

Stephen stood watching him warily. He nodded slowly.

'Then you'd better come in.'

He led the way into his elegant living-room. 'Sit down,' he said, going into the kitchen. He came back with ice and tonic water, and went to the sideboard to pour them both large gins. Then he came and sat opposite Rafe. For a few moments he resumed his scrutiny. Then he said, 'You bloody fool.'

Rafe drew breath for a retort. But he thought, why? He's absolutely right.

He smiled apologetically at Stephen. 'You warned me. Didn't you.'

'Yes, I damned well did. You'd better put me in the picture, if as I presume you've come to me for help. No séances, mind!'

No need, Rafe thought. He said, 'All right.'

It was relatively easy, once he'd got started. He'd thought out beforehand what he was going to say, and proceeded from step to step giving Stephen as full a picture as he could manage.

But when he'd finished, he found he was sweating. He drained his glass, and Stephen got up to get him a refill. A strong one.

'It's a sort of possession,' Stephen said eventually. 'This

153

Alienor – and incidentally I entirely agree with your Nell, that she's evil – seems to be settling for you as a substitute for her long-lost Richard. And in order to get you, somehow using Nell as a channel.'

Rafe didn't want to think about just how Nell had been used; he hadn't been able to tell Stephen that part of the story. He'd simply said, talking about the two of them, him and Nell, together in her cottage, 'Alienor sort of superimposed herself, and she became Nell. They're alike, facially.' And in those soft and generous breasts, he thought before he could stop himself, and the way the belly curves down into the groin . . . He said, hurriedly stamping down that line of thought, 'Why pick on me?'

Stephen frowned. 'For one of two reasons. Either because in some way you're like him – you look like him, perhaps, or there's something in your character – '

'God forbid! I don't like what I know of him at all.'

'I was afraid you might say that. It makes the other possibility even less likely to meet with your approval.'

'You'd better let me have it, all the same.'

Stephen got up, walking over to look out at London in the dark several floors below. 'From the way that you say you seem to *become* Richard, I wonder if it's just possible he also is possessing you.'

Every part of Rafe rejected the thought. No. Not him, not that bastard who could treat a woman like that. Make me treat her like that too.

His fierce reaction abated slightly. He looked up to see that Stephen had turned from the window and was watching him. Stephen said quietly, 'What else, Rafe? How would *you* explain it?'

And he had no answer.

'Well, it may not be that,' Stephen said. 'We needn't conclude finally that Richard himself is involved. If Alienor's desire is strong enough, I suppose it could simply be that she's projecting Richard's identity on to you. Turning you into her image of him, so that you look and act as he did. Do you experience any sensation of being inside a different character?'

Do I? He didn't know how he was meant to judge.

'No, I don't think so. Although I'm in unfamiliar places and I do things I've never done, it still feels like me doing them. Not someone else.' He frowned in frustration. 'But how the hell do I know? How you define "me", or "self"?'

'We won't go into that,' Stephen said, sounding amused, 'or we'll be here all night.'

He came back and sat down again. His face was serious, but Rafe noticed that his eyes were alight with interest.

'Fascinating intellectual problem, isn't it?' he said caustically. 'Right up your street, too.'

'Ah no!' Stephen looked quite hurt. 'I mean, yes, it is. But it's not only that. I do want to help. What do you want me to do?'

Rafe regretted his remark. 'Sorry. Thanks.' He paused. He had been half-hoping that Stephen would say it was all in his imagination. Tell him not to be so gullible and so open to suggestive atmospheres. But he hadn't. He'd taken it more seriously than Rafe had thought possible. And in the face of that, of Stephen looking so worried, the one flimsy lifeline Rafe had managed to think up seemed less than useless. What good could it do? Where was he hoping it would lead?

He didn't know. But all the same, it still seemed a good idea.

'Well?' Stephen asked.

Rafe breathed in deeply. Then he said, 'I wondered if you'd go and see Nell.'

Sem said, the receiver in his hand, 'It's someone for you.'

'No!'

Her response was instinctive, out of her before she could think. I *can't* speak to him! I couldn't make myself phone him, I didn't write, how can he think I'd want to . . .

155

'It isn't Rafe.' Sem's voice was gentle. 'It's someone called Stephen.'

Stephen? Stephen who?

Then she remembered. Saw again Rafe's face in the Magic Meadow, his eyes returning to the present from the contemplation of God knew where. Or, more likely, somewhere that God didn't know. In answer to her frantic voice screaming, '*Come back!*' he said, 'Stephen.'

This was Stephen?

Almost against her will, as if something inside her knew better and was forcing her, she went to take the phone from Sem's hand.

'Hello?' Her voice was inaudible. She tried again.

'Is that Nell?' A light voice. Well-educated accent.

'Yes.'

'I'm Stephen. Rafe asked me to phone you. I'd very much like to talk to you.'

She was nodding, then realized, feeling stupid, that he couldn't see.

'All right.'

'Oh!' He sounded surprised. Then smoothly went on, 'Where do you suggest? Perhaps a pub, in your nearest town? Rafe said you're right out in the back of beyond.'

'A bit beyond that.' She wondered why she should suddenly feel light-headed, as if she'd just been told she need no longer keep trying to do something that was beyond her strength. 'We could meet in Sevenoaks. Do you know the Queen's Head? It's on the main road, near the cinema.'

'No. But I'll find it. When?'

What was today? Wednesday. It was Christmas at the end of the week. She felt the familiar nose-dive of spirits, thinking of how Christmas would have been, with Rafe. And how it was going to be.

'Tonight or tomorrow,' she said. 'Either's okay for me.'

'Tonight, then. About eight. I'm tall, skinny and I'll be wearing a camel coat.'

156

'And I'm short and . . .'

He interrupted her. 'I know what you look like. See you tonight.'

She got to Sevenoaks early. At home she'd been too aware of Sem, making such an effort not to ask questions. It had been a relief to set off.

She parked the Land-Rover at a spot from where she could see the pub's comings and goings. Ten to eight – of course he might already be inside. She sat biting at her thumbnail, trying to overcome her reluctance to go into the pub on her own. They'll wonder what I'm after, eyeing up the men and approaching all the tall, skinny ones.

At two minutes to eight she saw a tall man in a camel coat walking down the pavement from the other direction. He paused outside the pub, then, after looking quickly around him, went in through the door marked Saloon Bar.

She was quite certain it was Stephen. She jumped down, locked the cab and ran across the road to following him inside.

He was standing at the bar, jingling change.

She crossed the room to stand beside him. 'I'm Nell,' she said.

He turned, staring at her. His light-coloured eyes were unblinking; she felt he was looking straight into her mind. His thin face was unsmiling. Then, relaxing, he said, 'I'm Stephen. I'm glad you came.'

There was no introductory small talk, with him. She hadn't thought there would be, if his manner on the phone was anything to go by. He asked her what she would have, and without further consultation took their drinks to a table away from the bar. As they sat down he leaned towards her and said, 'Something very serious is wrong with Rafe. I'm involved because he's my friend, but more so because I feel partly responsible. I organized the séance that allowed this spirit to get her hooks into him. I realized very quickly that it was dangerous for him, and I warned him. But it was too late.'

157

She was amazed.

And very indignant. She'd been thinking Stephen was an emissary, that he would come bearing Rafe's abject apologies. That that was the whole purpose of this meeting. But here he was telling her it was Rafe who was in danger, Rafe they must feel sorry for.

She thought, what about *me*? What about what he did to *me*?

With her anger rising she said icily, 'It's dangerous for other people, too. People who get too close to him in darkened rooms late at night. People like me, for example.'

'Ah.' He looked awkward. 'Yes. Of course. I was tactless. He hinted at what had happened, and I can imagine it was shocking for you.' He paused, his eyes holding hers so that she could not look away. 'But for him, too,' he went on softly. 'And what haunts him most of all is that he hurt you.' She felt he was probing her, his mind seeking entry into thoughts and memories she wasn't sure she wanted him to share. 'Don't put up barriers against me,' he said. 'Please. I want to help, but I can't if you treat me as an enemy.'

Again, she had the feeling that he was seeing right into her.

'Are you a sensitive?' she asked.

He nodded. 'Yes. But you're not. Where exactly do your skills lie? White witchcraft?'

'No!' She felt embarrassed that he should assign to her such distinction. 'I haven't got any skills. I simply learn, by trial and a great deal of error, which herbs can help you deal with which difficulties. It's ancient lore – anyone could pick it up, given access to the right books. But I've added to what I've learned, worked out some of my own variations.' She stopped, finding with surprise that it was quite an effort, that her inclination was to gabble on unchecked.

But she'd been about to permit him on to very secret territory.

'Go on.'

She fought the compulsion to do as he bid. For some moments there was silence between them. Then she seemed to hear again his words. 'He's my friend. I want to help.'

So do I, she thought. Oh, so do I.

'I know Rafe's dream-woman,' she began. 'He's not the only person she's tried to reach. Although I was never daft enough to hold a séance.' She shot him a malicious glance, gratified to notice he had the grace to look slightly ashamed. 'She did the same dream-invasion trick with me, for a long time. I hated it, but I was too frightened to try to fight back. But I got over that.' She felt a surge of triumph. See, *She* doesn't always have it all her own way. 'I experimented,' she went on, 'and I tried various herbal concoctions, looking for one that would make me sleep so deeply that even if I did dream, I wouldn't remember. By chance, I discovered an infusion that doesn't actually affect sleep-patterns. But it totally banishes the dreams.'

'The spirit can't have liked that.'

She was surprised. 'You think she really does have human reactions, then? That she'd be piqued that I've overcome her?'

'You haven't. You've merely diverted her elsewhere. But yes, of course she has human reactions. She *is* human. Or she was.'

In a flash she realized he saw Her in a different light. Saw Her as a real danger. An enemy worth the name. Her own smug triumph was insolent and worthless; she hadn't even scratched the surface. She'd been like a child believing that hiding under the bedclothes will be protection enough from the terrors that stalk in the dark.

She felt very afraid.

'I'm sorry.' His voice was quiet. He put a warm hand over hers. 'I didn't mean to frighten you so much. Well, perhaps I did. But I'm still sorry.'

After some time she asked, 'What are we going to do?'

'That depends entirely on you. If, as Rafe fears, you don't

want anything further to do with him, then you go on your way now and forget all about him.'

She said in a small voice, 'What would happen to him?'

'He'd get deeper under her power as his resistance weakened. In the end – I don't know. Probably his fate would rest on whether or not he gave in to her.'

'Not a nice prospect.' She laughed nervously.

'A dreadful prospect.' He sounded stern, as if he were chiding her for laughing.

'And what if I don't want to forget about him?'

'Then you and I together have to get him away from her.'

'How?'

He was silent for some time, frowning deeply. Eventually he said, 'First we make him well again – we can't expose him to any traumas while he's in his present state. And that's where you can help – you can give him some of your antidream brew.'

'Yes. I can do that tonight.'

'Good. Then Rafe can depart on his travels, get right away from here, from you, from the spirit, and with the aid of your brew, can be restored as near as possible to an ordinary human being.'

The memory hit her, overpoweringly poignant. Rafe saying, 'I'd like to pretend for a while that we're just two people.' Rafe's face, damaged by something he didn't understand. And for the first time since that dreadful evening she knew that she accepted, right down to her depths, that it wasn't his fault.

After that it was easy.

'Then what?' she asked. 'I'll do anything, whatever you say.'

The intensity in her voice seemed to amuse him slightly.

'Right. Good. Ah – I can't tell you what we'll have to do. I'm not sure myself yet. We'll have to wait and see.'

See what? It all sounded very nebulous. He was reaching in his pocket for his keys, preparing to go. Apparently the meeting was over.

And he'd nowhere near provided her with the information

she most wanted. Hadn't even hinted at it. Oh well, she thought. I'll just have to ask him, won't I?

'When will I see him?'

He sat down again. 'You want to see him? Really?'

She nodded.

'You can't. Not at the moment – he won't risk it. He doesn't know what would happen.' She dropped her head. 'But he'll be very glad you asked,' he added. She smiled slightly – he had a way of awarding invisible demerit points and gold stars, depending on whether you'd performed badly or well. He was an exacting companion.

'Is he in London?'

'Yes. Till Friday, then he's off to spend Christmas with a million Italian relations. His work's gone to pot, so he'll be away some time. Says he might go on to Crete, because of all places he finds it the most inspirational.'

The poignancy was back, with reinforcements, and she was finding it hard to keep her equilibrium. 'I – perhaps I could write to him.'

'You'll have to write care of his office. I can give you their address.' He got out a piece of card, and wrote quickly. 'They usually know where he is, and they'll forward mail.'

It was so impersonal. Her letters would be just like bills, or junk mail, forwarded by some indifferent hand in amongst the rest. But there didn't seem to be any alternative.

She took the card and put it in her pocket. Then she stood up.

'Are you coming for the stuff, then?'

He sat watching her, a slight smile on his face. Then he too got up. 'Yes. All right.'

She kept his headlights in her rear-view mirror throughout the twists and the double-back turns of the road out to Wellstone. She wondered if Sem would still be up. She hoped not – how was she going to explain this stranger to whom she was proposing to give a large amount of one of her more powerful patent remedies?

Lights were on in the cottage, and her heart sank. She jumped out of the cab and ran back to Stephen, pulling up behind her.

'My father's at home,' she said. 'I don't want to tell him. I'll just say you're a friend of a friend, okay? If I pack the stuff up quickly, you can be in and out again before he has a chance to ask you any awkward questions.'

He laughed. 'I quite understand. Come on, let's get on with it.'

She took him round to the back door, ushering him into the kitchen. 'In here,' she said.

She opened the door into the living-room.

Sem was watching television, and fortunately he appeared to be intent on the programme. She went up to kiss him. 'I'm back,' she said. 'I've got someone with me – I'm just going to get him something from the scullery. For a friend of his. But we won't disturb you.'

Sem was getting up out of his armchair. 'How do you do?' he called out. 'Do come in, sit down . . .'

Stephen said masterfully from the doorway. 'Good evening. No, I won't come in, thanks. I'm in a bit of a hurry. Nice meeting you. Come on, Nell.'

She noticed Sem's slightly confused look. 'Don't mind us,' she said, pushing him back into his chair. You get back to your programme. I'll explain later.'

'Very well, dear, if you're sure. It *is* really most interesting . . .'

She shut the door behind her.

'All right?' Stephen asked. 'Not too abrupt?'

She smiled. 'No. And thanks. Sit down,' she pointed to the most comfortable chair, at the end of the table, 'I won't be long.'

She went through into the scullery, getting out her key and opening the locked door into the pantry where she kept her medicinal herbs. Some of them were safer, locked away. Not that Sem ever came investigating. But if someone broke in and helped themselves out of curiosity, it might be awkward, to say the least; she had often wondered how one would stand under the law if an intruder sampled something from one's larder which subsequently killed him. And probably very uncomfortably.

She walked into the small room breathing in deeply its unique smell. More than anywhere in the house, this was her domain. The very familiarity of everything brought her peace, but also a sense of power. She glanced at her own neat handiwork on the charts pinned to the walls: illustrated lists of herbs and their uses; the season, time of day and condition of the soil when a plant should be picked for optimum potency; a painting she had copied from a library book of a medieval monk tending his herb garden. The apothecary's scales stood on the workbench, clean and shining as she always left them, the precise weights assembled neatly on their little wooden stand and not a scruple out of place. The light caught a glint of yellow from a glass pot of oil of evening primrose; she'd been making Sem some more of the preparation that eased his arthritis. She'd left it to the front of the shelf, but now she put it back in its rightful spot.

Her hands ran along the shelves. Seeds, dried leaves, oil from berries and flowers, in little glass jars and earthenware pots. Labels that she had made and illustrated; together in the far corner, here a drawing of a foxglove, there the purple-black, deathly berries of belladonna. Hemlock. Henbane. Mandragora. Monkshood. Poppy. And in a display which she kept always fresh, small branches of bay laurel, holly, juniper and mistletoe.

The protective plants.

She opened a drawer in the old pine dresser. She'd made up fifty sachets of the infusion only a few days ago, the dried herbs carefully weighed and mixed in exactly the right proportion in little muslin bags. Stephen could take them all –

163

she had one for tonight, and tomorrow she'd make herself some more. She packed them neatly in thick brown paper, folding in the ends and tying the little parcel with string.

For you, Rafe, she thought. With my blessing.

She locked the pantry door behind her and went back to Stephen.

'Here you are,' she said, handing him the parcel. 'You put one sachet in a cup and pour on boiling water, just as if you're making tea with a tea-bag. Let it infuse for five minutes. Tell – ' She hesitated. 'Tell him it's to be drunk as hot as he can,' she hurried on briskly, 'because inhaling the steam seems to be important. The drink's never so effective cold.'

He took the parcel, sniffing at it. 'Smells horrible.'

'The taste entirely lives up to the smell. But it works. At least, it does for me.' She felt anxious suddenly.

'And there's no reason why it shouldn't for Rafe,' he said reassuringly. 'Is there?'

'No. No, there isn't. Do you think – can you let me know? If it works, I mean?'

He was tucking the parcel into an inside pocket, preparing to go. He paused, catching her eye. He said, 'I don't suppose I shall have to. Cheerio.'

She went with him round to the front of the house, watching as he started his car and drove off. Part of her was hoping he'd manage to remember the way.

But most of her was going over and over his final words, till at last she convinced herself that that *was* what he'd meant.

And then, with that prospect ahead, the thought of her quiet Christmas alone with Sem wasn't so bad after all.

Eleven

Stephen came down again without any warning five weeks after Christmas.

She was in her potting shed, making the most of the failing daylight, when he put his head round the door and said, 'Sem says to tell you the kettle's boiling and he's making cinnamon toast. Happy New Year.'

'Goodness, you made me jump! What on earth are you doing here?'

'I was passing.' He caught her eye and smiled with her at the unlikelihood of anyone *passing* her out-of-the-way house. 'No. I wanted to see you.' He had dropped his nonchalant tone. 'How is everything?'

'With me, fine.' She hesitated. 'And with Rafe, I think.'

'Ah. You heard from him, then.'

She didn't want to go into details. But, oh yes, she'd heard. A registered parcel had arrived from Italy, just after Christmas, and in it had been a cashmere pullover, so soft it demanded to be stroked. Green. In a shade that echoed the colour of her eyes. And wrapped up inside it a string of jade beads.

'Oh, Nell, these are valuable,' Sem said reverently. 'The most expensive jade is almost transparent. And look!' He held the beads up to the light. 'You can see through them.'

Rafe had written on a card, 'This will be late, but happy Christmas just the same. I wish I were there, or you were here.' Then, as if as an afterthought he'd almost been too embarrassed to add, 'Thank you for your wonderful tea-bags. I had forgotten what it was like to sleep peacefully and wake up cool and calm. Bless you.' And he'd signed it as before, simply 'Rafe'.

She recalled Stephen, standing beside her. 'Yes, I've heard,' she said shortly. Before he could ask any more, she took hold of his arm, ushering him out of the shed. 'Let's go and have Sem's toast while it's hot.'

'Right. It smells good – I was standing in the kitchen while he was making it.'

She was about to set out for the house, but his words brought her up short.

'You were talking to him?' He nodded. 'But you don't know each other. What . . .'

'I said I was the Stephen who'd telephoned, and who came to the house before Christmas. And he said, "So you are. And how is that poor friend of yours who is suffering so much?" '

'Oh, God.' She sank down on to the low wall that ran along the top of the rockery, completely shocked. 'How did he know you knew Rafe? I didn't say. Did you?'

'No. But your father doesn't strike me as stupid. Far from it. He watched you being miserable when Rafe stopped appearing, then I turn up, and you dish out to me a load of mysterious goodies from your secret pantry. Soon after that, Rafe writes to you and you begin to cheer up. It wouldn't take Einstein to work out there might just be a connection.'

'Yes.' She nodded slowly. 'When you put it like that, it's obvious. And Sem's very sensitive to other people. Just because he doesn't actually talk about something openly, one shouldn't assume he hasn't noticed it.'

'There you are, then.'

'What did you tell him?' She stood up again and they went down the steps on to the patio. 'About Rafe?'

'I said he'd left England for the time being, but that he'd departed in a spirit of optimism that I hadn't seen him in for a long time.'

'And what did he say to that?'

'He nodded, and gave me a singularly sweet smile. Then he said, "Nell knows what she's doing, you know. You came to the right person." '

Sem, dearest Sem. Why don't I yield to temptation and tell you the whole story?

Because, probably, I have no need.

She felt good, suddenly, a strength growing in her because of Sem's silent, unwavering support. Smiling at Stephen, she opened the back door. Floating out together to greet them came Sem's cheerful 'Come on in!' and the appetizing aroma of cinnamon toast.

She watched Stephen make himself comfortable on the sofa, stretching out his long legs in front of the fire, chatting with Sem. Just like Rafe had done. He's nice, she thought, this Stephen. Intelligent and sharp, but clearly a good friend. With a sense of responsibility. Although she had the suspicion sometimes that what was a matter of such deep importance to her and to Rafe was to Stephen merely a diversion. An experiment, sort of, but with real live people. Perhaps – the idea amused her – he'll ask me to start making notes.

He was sitting in exactly the place Rafe had sat.

I wish he were Rafe.

The thought took her by surprise.

What am I saying? That I want him to be here again? *Here*, where it all went so wrong and I started to hate him?

No. I never hated him, not for one moment. I may have told myself I did, because of what he did. But perhaps that was the reaction I expected of myself. The response I knew I should have, to such a violation.

Rafe, I do wish you were here.

'Nell!' Sem's amused voice broke across her thoughts. 'Where were you?'

She looked up. Sem and Stephen were both staring at her, laughing.

'Sorry. What did you say?'

'Stephen was asking about your remedies, and I was telling him about my Evening Primrose stuff, and My Lord's indigestion jollop. You're missing a good chance – you could have a new recruit here!' He beamed at her.

167

'I'm very interested,' Stephen confirmed. 'How did you come by your knowledge?'

Sem got up and went over to the bookcase. She smiled; she knew what he was going to do. He drew a huge, leather-bound tome from the bottom shelf, leaning over the fireplace to blow off the dust.

'See?' he said to Stephen. 'It's been in the bookcase untouched for months. She doesn't have to refer to it any more, it's all in her head.'

'It isn't!' She felt slightly awkward at his effusion. 'I still look things up in there, sometimes. If it's something I haven't made for a while, or when I'm trying something new.'

Sem had dumped the book in Stephen's lap.

'This is amazing,' Stephen said, opening it. *The Nature of Herbs*. When was it published? 1768. Good God, it must be worth a fortune!'

Sem was leaning over his shoulder pointing to the flyleaf, his long, graceful fingers stroking down the thick parchment.

'Look. Elianor Gournay, 23 February 1769. Anne Gournay, Easter 1800. Marjorie Gurney, October 12 1836. Eleanor Gurney, 1881. My grandmother. And Rose Gurney. October 1910. My mother. Her mother gave it to her the month after I was born. And now it belongs to Nell.'

'Six generations,' Stephen said. 'What a story it could tell.'

'It does.' Nell went to sit beside him. 'Some of the pages are marked with notes, where the women added their own variations. Excuse me – ' She reached across him, turning the heavy pages until she found what she was looking for. It was a description of different rashes in children, with illustrations, diagnoses and suggested treatments. In the wide margin, a careful, decorative hand had written something, although it was too faint now to be legible. As if the writer had held the book in such respect that she hadn't wanted to deface it.

'How accurate is it? Not very, I should think.' Stephen was peering at the drawings. 'Not to be relied on, nowadays.'

'You'd be surprised.' She didn't like hearing her precious

book run down. It had been her starting-point, subtly introducing the ancient wisdom into her young mind as she sat for long nights poring over it, she and Sem together in the peaceful silence of the old cottage. 'Not all of it's of any value, of course. But . . .'

She had almost mentioned that it was something she'd found in the book that had led to her discovery of the antidream brew. She'd only just pulled herself up in time. No. She didn't want to talk about that.

'. . . but a lot of it is,' she finished lamely.

Stephen was staring at her. He's astute, she thought, he knows exactly what I was going to say. He'll be demanding a page reference in a minute. She leaned across him again, and turned to the chapter on remedies for toothache. There was a graphic picture of a tooth extraction, the anguished-looking patient strapped to his chair and two burly men holding him down into the bargain while a determined dentist groped about in his mouth with a huge pair of pliers. To emphasize the agony, the patient's bound hands were twisted into rigid claws. And blood dripped down on to his chest.

'That looks fun, doesn't it?' she said. 'And wait, I'll find you the page where it says how they operated to remove gallstones. When the herbal remedies failed, you know. That's very interesting.'

'Ugh!' Stephen groaned. 'No, thanks, I've just had my tea. I'll take your word for it.'

She closed the book, and took it from his lap.

'Another time,' she said, glancing over her shoulder as she returned her tome to its shelf. She was vindictively pleased to see he looked quite sick. Not to be relied on nowadays, indeed. That'll teach him.

The clock on the wall struck six. Sem got out his halfhunter, consulting it in verification. She thought, I've watched him do that a thousand times. He ought to know by now that the clock and his watch are close enough to synchronization as makes no odds.

'I must be making a move,' he announced. 'My Lord and I are playing bridge tonight, with the Evanses. Friends in the village,' he explained to Stephen.

'Can I give you a lift?' Stephen got to his feet, reaching for his coat. 'I ought to be going, I have an engagement this evening too.'

'Very well, then, Thank you. I was going to walk, but since you're going my way, I'll accept a ride.'

Nell listened to their muttering voices as they went through to the scullery to put on their coats. She got up to see them off.

Stephen said, casually, 'I'll be in touch.'

Sem said he'd see her later, probably, but not to wait up. He'd get a lift home.

'Goodbye,' she said absently. Her mind was on something else.

She closed the back door and then the scullery door, shutting out the night. The house felt warm and comfortable, filled with happiness.

She went back to the fire, curling up and gazing into the flames.

After a while she thought, yes. That's what I'll do.

She wondered what had prompted the thought. Stephen being here, and the natural association of ideas? Watching him earlier and wishing he were Rafe?

That's probably it.

But I don't know. I don't really care.

Whatever, it doesn't matter.

I'm going to write to Rafe.

The letter reached him in Crete towards the end of March, having taken almost two months to find him.

He had all but given up hope of hearing from her. Now, discovering suddenly that not only had she written but had done so some time ago, all the conclusions that he'd so painfully arrived at were having to be chucked away.

He stared at the various postmarks, reluctant to open the envelope. Her name and address were written on the back; it was lucky, he thought, the postal services hadn't given up and returned it to sender. It had gone to Rome, missing him there and then waiting for over a fortnight in someone's 'pending' tray till the Rome bureau woke up to the fact he'd gone back to London. So they'd sent this letter after him, only by the time it was back in England he wasn't. And no one in London seemed to have accorded it any urgency either.

He walked slowly away from the bank of post office boxes, the letter still in his hand. Outside he made his way to a bar, and sat down in the mid-morning sunshine to order a beer. Then at last he opened the envelope.

She began almost formally, as if she didn't quite know how to address him and was erring on the reserved side.

> 'Thank you very much for the sweater and the jade beads. I was so pleased with them both. The shade is perfect – Sem says you must carry colours well in your head. It was a most generous Christmas present, and so thoughtful of you.'

His heart sank. So far it read much like a thank-you letter from one of his cousins' children, written under duress and the stern eye of some correct Mama.

So far, it was totally impersonal.

He read on.

> 'Sem and I had a quiet Christmas. We went for drinks at My Lord's with quite a lot of people from the village, and on Christmas Eve we went to a candlelit carol service. But in the main it was just the two of us either side of the fire, with just our pretty Christmas tree, with its lights and decorations, and the boughs of holly over the pictures to remind us of the season. Your parcel arrived after the holiday, and hearing from you turned it all into something special – everything got

better after that, and it wasn't just because you sent me some-
thing so expensive and so nice.'

He stopped to read the last sentence again, and it sounded
equally good. She appeared to be getting into her stride, and
what she was winding up to say promised to be what he
wanted to hear; for the first time since he'd found her letter
waiting for him, he began to relax.

> *'Before I received your present I had been thinking of you*
> *constantly, wondering how you were and worrying about you.*
> *I wish that you hadn't gone away so hastily, and I wish too*
> *that I'd had the courage to phone you in New York, where I*
> *had that telephone number for you. I nearly did, lots of times.*
> *But the idea of hearing your voice answering scared me off –*
> *I just couldn't imagine what I'd say to you after you'd said*
> *hello. You said in your first letter – the one written above the*
> *Atlantic – that you were sorry, and to begin with that was all I*
> *wanted to hear. But that didn't last. I know that what happened*
> *wasn't at your own will. And even if it had been, I have had*
> *to come to terms with the fact that up to a point, it was what*
> *I wanted too. Not how it developed – of course not that. I'm*
> *sorry, I can't write about this well, but it would have been*
> *even worse trying to say it to you.'*

He put the letter down. It must have cost her, he thought,
writing that. She's too honest not to say what she's thinking,
so she had to have a try at putting it into words. Maybe that
was why she didn't write before. Until she could make herself
say what she really felt, she preferred not to write at all.

He picked up the last page.

> *'I'm so glad the brew has helped. You will be needing some*
> *more, as there was only enough for seven weeks. Let me know*
> *where to send it to. It's best if I dispatch it a little at a time*
> *as it loses its strength if kept too long.'*

She's right, he thought, I have almost run out. But it's lasted much longer than she calculated – she wasn't to know I'd find I don't need it every night. Would she think I was sensible, to start trying to sleep without it? Probably not. But I've proved to myself I can do without it. I'm in control again.

He went back to the letter.

> *'I don't know where you are now. When Stephen came down the first time, just before Christmas, he said you were going to Italy and then to Crete. He gave me your address in London – well, it was your office address, I suppose. Anyway, he said they'd forward mail to you. He's been down again, today – he left about an hour ago. I think he is a good friend to you, other than his irresponsibility in holding that séance. And he wasn't to know, I suppose, what a can of worms he was opening. But he does make me feel as if I'm something being dissected on a slab, or at the very least psychoanalysed on a couch. Is he by any chance a psychiatrist as well as a medium? You get the feeling your thoughts no longer belong to you, don't you, and that he can see right into your mind? A bit like being under attack.'*

Yes, he thought. That's exactly how you feel. The realization that Stephen had the same effect on them both made her feel very close.

He read her final words.

> *'I hope this letter finds you. Take care. I think of you. I miss you.*
> *Love from Nell.'*

He sat for a long time. Part of his mind was occupied with watching the comings and goings in the street in front of him, but they were small enough to leave plenty of room for his deeper thoughts.

He didn't need to go over her words again; he had retained

173

the letter in his head at first reading. It wasn't so much what she said as how she said it – she wrote exactly as she spoke, and he could hear her voice saying the phrases. And he could picture her now, something he'd failed to do with any accuracy since he'd so abruptly left her. He saw her standing by the Aga in her kitchen making coffee, smiling to herself at some private thought that was amusing her. Saw her scraping away the ice on his windscreen, a frown of intense concentration on her face. Saw her in the Magic Meadow, crying out to him as if from a great way off.

Saw her as she lay beneath him, her expression full of passion, smiling her welcome.

He shut off the images before they could proceed any further and begin to tarnish.

I miss you, she said. I miss her too. Have done all the time. I want her with me.

How would it be between us now? If she were to join me here? It wouldn't be like going back to Wellstone, we're a long way away from Alienor out here.

Then he thought, but here was where Alienor first reached me. At Stephen's séance.

We wouldn't have any séances. Wouldn't even have any Stephen.

And if I went back to dreaming about her like I always used to, there would be Nell's infusion to keep her at bay.

Wouldn't all that amount to a sufficient safeguard?

He couldn't convince himself that it would. He was aware that he was trying to, very hard; her company seemed suddenly so desirable that he was manufacturing arguments for having her with him when he had an unpleasant suspicion that really he should be warning her to keep away.

Because there was no guarantee at all that what had happened before wouldn't happen again.

He got up, impatient for movement. He left some money on the table for his beer, and walked quickly away.

He thought, I'll sleep on it. Then if I still feel the same

174

tomorrow I'll suggest it to her and see what she thinks. Let her decide.

A voice in his head suggested nastily that now was no time to go passing bucks. But he didn't listen.

Twelve

'I'm trying to trace Raphael Westover,' Nell said for the third time. She had obtained the phone number of Rafe's office address in London from Directory Enquiries, but it was proving useless; nobody seemed to know who he was. People kept asking her, 'Who's he *with*?', which was making her feel stupid because she had no idea.

'If you can't give me more information I'm afraid I can't help you,' this latest woman said. She doesn't sound afraid, Nell thought. She sounds as if she had two-inch red fingernails and lacquered hair and isn't scared of anything in shoe-leather.

'Sorry,' she said. 'I only have his name. I don't know who he works for. But I sent a letter to him care of your address, and I was wondering if you could tell me if it had been forwarded to him.'

There was a resigned sigh, then the woman said, 'If I'd *heard* of him, I might be able to. But as it is, of course I can't.' Her tone said quite clearly, any half-wit can see that.

Nell felt cross. You could only cringe so far, and she didn't think it had been that unreasonable a request. 'Don't you have some sort of office directory?' she persisted.

'No.'

'Well you bloody well ought to! I call this gross inefficiency. Goodbye!' And she slammed down the receiver with the sort of vigour that Sem reserved for people trying to sell him windows.

Great, she thought. That has got me precisely nowhere. Damn.

'What's the matter, dear?' Sem asked, coming in a little later and finding her still glowering at the telephone.

She looked up at him.

His face wore its habitual expression when with her, of

176

happiness and pleasure in her company. He's a lovely person to live with, she thought. So easy. I take his sunny nature for granted. And his old-fashioned courtesy.

'I – ' she began. She sat down on the edge of the sofa, and he came to sit beside her. She didn't know how to go on. He was watching her, staring eagerly into her face as if waiting for her to say something more important than just some everyday remark. She thought, so why don't I?

'I wrote to Rafe,' she said, 'after Christmas. To thank him for the present. And to – ' She hesitated. 'Things went a bit wrong, you know, the last time he was here. A misunderstanding, sort of. He felt very bad about it, and that's why he's kept away. It's all to do with him being hurt, I think. You know, his face. Because it's not just a scratch that went septic – there's much more involved. And it's frightening. I wanted to write back to him, to say I understood, because until I tell him that he won't come near me. I wrote, but he hasn't replied, and I don't know if it's because he doesn't want to write to me or because he hasn't got the letter. I was trying to phone his London office to see if the letter had been sent on to him and this *bitch* of a woman wouldn't help, and I want . . . I want . . .'

She found she was crying, her head against Sem's tweedy shoulder. His gentle hand stroked her hair, and his calm voice said things that soothed. 'I know, my dearest,' he muttered, 'I know. Not his fault. Poor young man. Not his fault. Dangerous things, here. Mustn't blame him.'

The meaning of his words began to filter through to her. He *does* know, she thought. And then she couldn't imagine how she'd ever thought he didn't.

'Sem?' She went on leaning against him. It might be easier to talk to him if he wasn't actually looking her in the face. And it was nice, sitting like this.

'Yes?'

Still she couldn't come right out with it. She said vaguely, 'Will it always be like this, here?'

177

He didn't answer for some time. But she needn't have worried that he wouldn't understand what she was asking. His voice sounding tired; eventually he said, 'I wish I could say no. But the truth is, Nell, I don't know. There is a history to the house, and to the land in the immediate vicinity. All of us who live here discover it for ourselves, in time. A degree of what is commonly called sixth sense seems to run in the Gurney family. Whether it manifested itself here because there was such a strong presence, or whether it would have happened wherever we were, I have no idea. Somehow we're linked to this place.' He stopped, and although she felt he was about to say more, he didn't.

Her mind was racing, trying to catch the meaning of what he was telling her. Linked to this place. All of us who live here. What was he saying? 'But we lived in Cambridge!' she exclaimed. 'You lived there. That's where you met Mother. You and I only came here after – afterwards. Didn't we?' She felt disorientated, as if the solid security of things she'd known all her life to be incontestably true was now proving to be less secure than she'd thought, crumbling and no longer firm around her. '*Didn't* we?'

She could feel him shaking his head. She sat up, pulling away from him. 'What are you saying?' she shouted. He flinched, and she realized her voice was too loud, too aggressive.

'This was my home, until I went to Cambridge,' he said quietly. 'The home of my forebears. I spent all my boyhood here. My parents still lived here when I married your mother, although by then they were very old. When they died, the thought of losing this precious house was quite intolerable. Your Aunt Dorothy didn't want to live here, my work was in Cambridge, so for the time being I let it. Then when your mother went, I waited until the current tenants' lease ran out and I moved us back. Back home, really.'

She felt utterly amazed. She had never even suspected –
But then she thought, yes I did.

The shock was abating, and she realized that was all it had

been. A shock to be told so abruptly that this was her family's ancient home. Not a surprise, because the information had already been there within her, in her blood. Probably for as long as she and Sem had been here.

Almost instantly, something else shot to the front of her mind, clamouring for recognition.

'The book,' she said wonderingly. 'All the Gurney women, who wrote their names in my herb book. Reading it, poring over it, here in this house. Making their remedies in the little scullery, just like I do. I'm just another bead strung on to the thread. Aren't I?' She looked at him anxiously for verification. He nodded. 'That's why it seems so right. Why I picked up all that lore so easily. I have the advantage of all their experience, seeped into these walls, and of their wish that I succeed them. And their love is here, isn't it? Keeping us safe.'

He said quietly, 'Yes, dearest.'

She sank back in the corner of the sofa. It was a lot to take in, all at once.

After a moment Sem spoke. 'I often wondered if I should have told you before. There is so much to tell, about this house and the Gurneys' long tenancy of it. But I thought, you being my daughter, that there would be no need, because you would find out for yourself. And I was always afraid that I might introduce fears into your mind, when already there was so much for you to contend with.' He coughed awkwardly. 'Your mother, you know. And you were such a sensitive child.' He looked down at his hands, folded in his lap.

She was overcome with love for him. What a burden, she thought. Poor Sem, compelled to come back because here was home, and the only place he could find comfort. And he had to bring me, with my nightmares and my fancies. The last place for me, really, in some ways. And yet it wasn't, because I belong here, too.

'You did right,' she said, reaching out to take his hand. 'You always have done.'

She didn't think she could say any more. He turned to look

at her, very quickly, and his eyes were very bright. For a second he squeezed her hand, then he coughed again and stood up.

'Tea, I think,' he said, his back to her. 'Then I must see to that fire!'

Late in the evening the telephone rang. She was wakeful, restless for some reason, and was sitting up watching a film. Sem had gone to bed with his library book.

She reached for the receiver. 'Hello?'

'Nell.'

It isn't. It can't be. I'm mistaking someone else for him, because I want it to be him so much.

'Nell? Are you there? I'm sorry to call so late. It's taken me all day to get up the courage.'

It was him. Oh, it was.

'It's all right, I wasn't in bed. I was watching a film.' She was tripping over the words in her eagerness. 'And it's not late, it's only ten fifteen.'

'It's after midnight here. We're two hours ahead.'

'Where are you?'

'Crete.'

So far away.

'How are you? Are you all right?' she said, just at the same moment he started saying something. 'Sorry. After you.'

'I said, I got your letter, just this morning. It kept missing me. I didn't want you to think that I hadn't answered.'

'No. Yes. I didn't think that, I thought perhaps you hadn't received it.'

'That's right, I hadn't.'

She couldn't get used to the sound of his voice. Almost she wanted to say, stop, wait a minute. Let me get over it being you, then we can go on.

She realized he wasn't speaking.

'RAFE!' she shouted. 'Are you still there?'

He laughed. Such a sound, she thought. More than his speaking voice, it epitomizes him. And if he can laugh he must be all right. 'Yes, I'm still here,' she said. 'Nell, I've missed you.'

'Me, too. I've missed you. Are you coming home?'

'No.'

'Oh.' Such a feeble response.

'Nell? It's okay. It's just that I'm working. For the first time in ages it's going really well, and I don't want to leave here till I've finished. I – er, I thought perhaps you'd like to come out here and join me. I only work a few hours a day,' he added.

Go out to Crete? Fly out on her own?

Be with him again?

Her hand on the receiver was trembling. She felt slightly sick.

'It's a bit short notice,' he was saying, 'and of course it must be your busy time at the moment. Perhaps you'd like to . . .'

'Yes. I'll come.'

There was silence. Then he said, 'You will?'

'Yes.'

'Oh. Oh. that's great! Book a flight, let me know when you arrive, and I'll meet you. We'll – never mind. Just come, and we'll take it from there.'

'All right. Bye, then.'

She was putting the phone down, but she heard him shouting.

'Nell! NELL!'

'Yes?'

He said very clearly, 'Have you got pencil and paper?'

'Yes. Why?'

'You'd better have my address, hadn't you? And it might be an idea if I gave you my phone number too.'

He was laughing again, laughing at her, and her hands were shaking so much she could hardly write.

But it didn't matter.

She sat in the Departure Lounge at Gatwick, on a seat from

181

which she could watch the airplanes landing and taking off on the vast runways outside. Although it was April, and early in the holiday season, the lounge was crowded. Mainly with families with pre-school children; she studied a large, disgruntled mother collapsed on the seat opposite eating an enormous bag of crisps. now and again making a grudging effort to control an excited toddler.

I hope, Nell thought, she's not flying to Heraklion. Not sitting next to me, anyway.

Her shoulder bag was clutched tight on her lap. She kept saying to herself, over and over, passport, ticket, Eurocheques, cheque card, until it became a meaningless litany.

Anyway, I'm here now. She tried to reassure herself. They've seen my passport and torn the relevant piece out of my ticket. I've been issued with my boarding pass. I am *not* going to check yet again that I've got everything.

She peeped into her bag.

When she'd inspected each of the travel documents, she touched the paper parcel of anti-dream sachets. They should be safe in my hand-luggage. I'm glad nobody rifled through my bag and demanded to know what they were – it wouldn't have been easy to explain. Not that they contain any illegal substances. At least I don't think they do.

She gazed idly around. How long till the flight? An hour and a half. I knew we'd get here too soon, but Sem's not really happy driving these days and it's better for him to get home in daylight.

Hope he's all right. Dear old Sem.

She thought back over the past ten days. Having told Rafe she'd go, she'd then been thrown into a total panic. As if I'd never been away on my own before! Stupid. There was a time when I was away more often than I was at home, when I was at college. And on my garden design course. And it's not that different, travelling a couple of thousand miles further. Not as if flying bothers me, either – I didn't mind it, that time Sem and I went to Spain.

When she had all the flight details she had dialled Rafe's number. Several times, because she kept getting no reply. But at last he'd been there, his voice on the phone accompanied by a background of people singing.

'Sounds like a good party,' she said, when the business of the call had at last been concluded. It had taken some time; hearing his voice had affected her so much that she'd found it hard to concentrate.

'Yes.' He sounded amused. 'I wish they'd all go home, but you know what these continentals are like when they get going..'

'Oh. Yes, of course.' She felt vaguely deflated, that he was clearly having such a tremendous time. Then got angry with herself for her selfishness.'You go back to them,' she urged, 'don't miss the fun!'

And he said gently, 'It's a tape. Best-loved bits of Mozart.'

Sem had stayed with her until she went through to Departures. Then as they stood together in the queue, he said he thought he'd go. For a moment he put his arms round her, hugging her very tightly, and she heard him mutter, 'Dearest Nell. God bless.'

She felt dangerously emotional. Part of her wanted to say, I'm not going, I want to stay here with you. I don't want to leave you all alone. She hugged him back, clinging to him as if she were a little girl again and he her whole world.

He pushed her gently away. He smiled at her, his face cheerful.

'Go on, off you go,' he said. 'Give my regards to Rafe.'

'Yes.' She frowned. He was going, and she had a strong feeling that there were things they hadn't said, things they ought to say. Clutching at his hand, which immediately clasped hers in its warm, familiar grip, she said quietly, 'Will it be all right, Sem?'

He paused. Then he said, 'I think so.' He stood for a moment, a look of intense concentration on his face as if he were working out the solution to some baffling problem. Then his eyes turned back to her, and his expression cleared. 'Yes, my Nell, I believe it will.' As he bent to kiss her forehead the queue moved forward, and she was swept up to the passport check desk. She turned to watch him, standing there in his old tweed jacket, and he raised his hand to wave.

'Passport, please.'

When she looked again, he had gone.

The aircraft curved away over south-east England. She thought, that's my house, somewhere down there, and a stab of emotion knifed into her. Love of home, of garden, of familiar ways. Of Sem. Departing, she was still too near home for it not to dominate her thoughts.

Then they were over the Channel, and the pilot's voice rang pleasantly out over the loudspeakers, chatting to them about the route and the in-flight services. Suddenly a large gin and tonic seemed an excellent idea.

In the pocket in front of her were head-phones, and turning the switch on the arm of her seat she located a programme of classical music. I ought to get in the mood for Rafe, she thought, settling back with her gin and a small packet of peanuts. He seems to like listening to music. I can hum along, if he plays something I recognize. Get in the mood for Rafe. She realized what she'd just been thinking. For Rafe! Oh, God!

I don't think I can go through with it.

But what else can I do? Her meal was brought, and she recovered sufficiently from the agony of her thoughts to say thank you. She didn't think she could eat it – she picked at the hot dish, but at the thought of receiving food her stomach started to twist itself into knots. She began to feel sick.

That's *enough*. Think about something else.

Think about the garden.

Eyes closed, concentrating as hard as she could, she pulled her mind back from the dangerous precipice into which she had been tumbling. Images of Rafe gradually dimmed and dispersed, and in her mind's eye she saw her potting-shed and her glasshouses.

That's better.

She opened her eyes.

I hope the garden'll be all right. I shouldn't really leave it in April, it's a daft time to go away. But it's only for a week. Jack's going to keep things ticking over for me, and I've relied on him before. He's a lazy sod, but if Sem keeps an eye on him, it ought to be okay. And I did all I could before I left. Probably why my back's aching so much.

That meal looked nice. Pity I couldn't eat any of it. But the coffee was good, very strong. It'll keep me alert, so that when we arrive I'll . . .

Don't think about arriving. It's better to travel than to arrive, never mind if you're hopeful or not.

Oh, God, what am I *doing*?

She felt like a cornered fighter whose enemy, knowing that he had won, savours a slow victory with a sadistic smile on his face.

They were landing, lights of a town appearing after the long blackness of the night sea, a criss-cross of runway beacons shining out as if in welcome. She felt sick again, rigid with nerves, unable to contemplate getting out of her seat and leaving the aircraft. I can't.

I've got to.

She leaned back, closing her eyes. The nausea increased, and she put her hands to her face. The woman next to her asked if she was all right; Nell opened her eyes to say yes, she was, and noticed the woman had a sick bag held at the ready.

She wanted to laugh. It's absurd, surreal almost. No, it's not. It's just apprehension, making everything distorted.

They had come to a standstill. Out of the window she could

185

see the airport buildings. Cars moving along a road. People, everywhere people.

And one of them was Rafe.

She dragged her bag out from under the seat in front, her mind in turmoil. She wanted to hurry; now that she was here, and it was all horribly inevitable, she wanted to get it over with. She reached the steps leading down to the tarmac, and the stewardess wished her a happy holiday.

'Oh – er, yes, thank you. You too,' she replied. And felt about an inch high.

She hurried down the steps, joining on to the great snake of people slowly going across the tarmac and up into the arrivals hall. So much for wanting to hurry! It'll take *hours*. He'll have given up and gone home.

He. Rafe.

They were queuing for passport control now, waiting to go through the double doors into the building. She turned her face to the night air, trying to relax. It's warm here, so warm! And the air smells different – a bit flowery. The breeze feels like a fan-heater, on a low setting. It's very nice, after England.

Here's the building, we're going in now. The queue's moving quite fast, it won't take as long as I thought. But then we'll have to wait for our baggage. That'll take a while.

Passport control. A friendly, dark face, smiling at her, saying welcome. The luggage on a slow-turning carousel. People pushing, jostling, someone knocking her legs with a spiky rucksack. Too soon, her own small holdall.

Then nothing to do but walk between two desks under the indifferent eyes of a couple of lounging customs officers and into the night outside.

She stood on the pavement, looking all around her.

He's not here. Oh, God, he's not here!

It's all right. Don't panic, it'll be all right. I can take a taxi, ask the driver to find me a cheap hotel. They'll be used to people turning up in the middle of the night, it must often happen.

186

How long should I wait?

There's a car parked there, right in front of the building – no, it looks like a taxi. It's an old Mercedes. But it doesn't say 'Taxi'. And there's nobody in it. No, but it must be a taxi, it's parked right on the painted writing on the road. Over the 'T'.

She could see a knot of men by the taxi rank, talking together. One of them detached himself and went to look through the glass into the baggage claim area.

He was taller than the others. Wearing a white shirt and dark trousers, like them. But he was bearded.

She shouted, 'Rafe!'

In some weird state of altered consciousness, dream-like, she watched as he turned. Saw her, and started to run to her.

Then he was here, warm, real, sweeping her off her feet in a bear-hug, kissing her soundly on both cheeks, saying her name and laughing.

She stared at him. He looked so well!

Against her will, for she had fought the memory, a picture materialized in her head of how he'd looked the last time she'd seen him. Bending over her on the floor of her living-room, his face lit diabolic red in the firelight.

Then it was gone. Thank God, that image was gone. Standing before her, his hands on her shoulders, he was Rafe again.

He said, 'You don't know how good it is to see you.'

'Yes, I do.' It was good, oh so much more than good, to see him, too. 'I mean, it is for me as well. I've been having conversations with you in my head. Oh!' She broke off, confused, embarrassed at what he would make of her remark. But it didn't matter, he looked so happy that she couldn't stop smiling. 'I thought you were a taxi-driver!' she said.

'I am. I'm parked on their rank. Come on, before they turn nasty. Or someone demands that I take them to Chania.'

She stared at the mark on his face, faded now so that it was nothing more than a duelling-scar in an old swashbuckling movie. He must have realized what she was looking at: he said quietly, 'It healed, while I was in Italy. The dreams stopped, thanks to you. It doesn't hurt any more.'

He took her arm, picking up her holdall in his other hand. He walked up to the old Mercedes and opened the passenger door for her. When he had got in beside her, she said, 'Where are we going? Are you – are we in a hotel? Or an apartment?' It's funny, she thought, that I should only think of that now. Why wasn't I agonizing over that on the airplane, along with all the other panics? Perhaps in that respect I allowed my good sense to prevail, knowing quite well that Rafe would take care of it. Honourably.

He was busy avoiding people and taxis, and didn't answer straight away. She looked at him. Looked at his profile, at the strong features, his hair and his beard black in the dim light. Looked at his powerful body, his broad chest and the muscles in his legs. And felt, like a blast of warmth from the sun, his overpowering masculinity.

Shaken, she turned from him to look out in front of her.

When they were safely out of the airport he said, 'No. We're not in an apartment or a hotel. I've got a house here – it belonged to my grandparents.'

Out of the corner of her eye she saw him glance briefly across at her. Then, his eyes once more on the road, he added 'We're going home.'

Thirteen

He wanted to look at her, to try to read from her face what she was thinking. How it felt for her, being with him again. He thought, remembering how his scrutiny used to embarrass her before, perhaps it's as well I've got to drive the damned car.

'This is Heraklion,' he said, waving to his right. Possibly small talk would help her to relax. 'Or the edge of it. Our road takes us south, we don't actually drive through the middle. But we could come for a day's visit, if you like. There's an archaeological museum. And Knossos, just outside the town. Everybody goes to Knossos.'

'That might be nice.' He thought she sounded guarded; perhaps she wasn't interested in archaeology. Her father's preoccupation with the far-distant past might well have served to put her off for life.

'I read about the Minoans,' she said, surprising him.

'Did you? Oh, good. You'll know what you're looking at, if we go to any sites.'

She laughed. 'Don't bank on it. It was just three pages, in my *Wonder Book of History*. I had it for Christmas when I was six. It said coyly under one of the pictures, "Minoan ladies liked to chatter and gossip. They wore make-up and their clothes were quite different from ours."'

He smiled, imagining what the picture would have shown. 'I don't suppose much more has happened in the Minoan world since you were six.'

He guessed she was feeling more at home with him. She'd looked nervous, standing outside the airport building, and he'd wondered if it had helped or not, having him hug her so violently. She hadn't seemed to mind. He thought, I've got to forget about what happened. She's here, so obviously *she's* prepared to.

189

She asked, 'Is it far to your house?'

'Forty-five, fifty miles. About an hour and a half. The road runs along a river valley here, so it's straight. But when we get further south it's mountainous. Are you tired?'

'A bit.'

Perhaps she'd rather not talk. He pushed a tape into the cassette player. Glancing across at her, he saw her smile.

'What is it?'

She said, 'Nothing. Nice music.'

They were almost home. He looked at the clock on the dashboard: half past three. He wondered if he should offer her anything when they got in or if she'd want to go straight to bed.

He accelerated up the slope into the village, the roar of the hard-working engine rebounding off white-walled buildings and shattering the peace. A dog began to bark. The houses, shuttered for the night, showed not a glimmer. In the headlights bursts of colour leapt out of the shadow-land of grey. Geraniums. And the rich green of abundant springtime.

He drew up outside his house, parking the car in its usual spot beneath the wall of the terrace. She was leaning forward, looking out into the darkness.

'It's so quiet!' she exclaimed. 'I thought – I don't know what I expected.'

'It's much more lively usually. It's the middle of the night; everyone's asleep.'

'Oh, I don't mind,' she said hastily. 'I don't like big noisy places.'

He got her holdall from the back, then took her hand.

'Just as well,' he muttered. 'Up these steps,' he said to her. 'I should have remembered to leave the light on.'

'It's okay, I see quite well in the dark. And all the white-wash helps. It sort of glows, doesn't it? Ouch!'

'Watch out for the climbing roses,' he warned belatedly.

He opened the door, reaching inside to switch on the lights.

He was aware of her, standing quite still beside him, looking everywhere. How did it seem, to her? He tried to see it through her eyes. It was tidy – he'd made an effort for her. And Agathi, who lived in the village and had cleaned for him and for his grandparents before him, had entered into the spirit of the occasion and given the whole place a thorough going-over. He thought Agathi was pleased for him, that he was going to have company. And she'd apparently approved of his instruction to prepare the best room – his room – for Nell while he moved into the small spare room, because on the solid, old-fashioned dressing-table she'd put a huge welcoming vase of flowers.

But he and Nell hadn't reached the bedrooms yet. That was still to come.

'It's an old house,' he said, taking her arm and ushering her into the room. 'This is the living-room, and through there's the kitchen with the bathroom beyond. Through that door,' he pointed the other way, 'is the study. The house is built in a square, around a central courtyard. Steps over there,' he pointed again, 'at the side of the courtyards, lead up to the bedrooms. And behind us, where we came in, the terrace. The view's lovely, when you can see it.'

She went back outside, walking over to stand by the low balcony wall.

'I can imagine. We're quite high here, aren't we? You get the impression of a great plain, stretching away as far as those mountains over there.' She was looking south-eastwards.

'The Asterousia Mountains. From the Greek "astron", star. Because the skies are so clear down here that you can always see the stars.'

She leaned backwards, staring up into the sky. 'Can't you just. It's wonderful.'

'I'll show you your room.' He picked up her bag from where he'd dumped it on the floor and walked across the living-room and out through the courtyard to the stairs. He heard her footsteps coming up behind him.

There was no way to lessen the awkwardness of the moment. He could only hope that she would approve of the arrangements as much as Agathi had done. Of the master bedroom given over to the honoured guest while the master slept elsewhere.

'Here.' He opened the door of the main bedroom. 'I thought you'd like the biggest room. And it has the best view.' He put her holdall down, then moved back to the door. Having installed her, he wanted to get away. Quickly. 'Do you want anything? A drink? Something to eat?' She was shaking her head. 'Then I'll leave you to go to bed. Bathroom's down the steps and on your left. See you tomorrow.'

He paused in the doorway. She had her back turned to him. She said, 'Not too early!'

He was about to shut the door when she called, 'Rafe!'

'Yes?'

She was delving into her handbag, getting out a brown-paper parcel like the one she'd sent to him. 'Could you boil a kettle, do you think?'

He wished she hadn't had to do that. For a moment he felt angry with her. He'd been prepared to risk it, why couldn't she? He'd been sleeping undrugged for several nights in a row, he hadn't needed her to go reminding him of things he didn't want to think about.

But half-obliterated pictures were flying into his mind. Of a chinz-curtained, warm and comfortable cottage room which turned into a dirty, straw-strewn hotel. Of a woman who changed identity as he lay on her.

Of a man who lost himself and became someone else.

No. Of course she wouldn't risk it. I have been supremely tactful and ushered her politely to her chaste and solitary bed, but still she has far too much to lose. He looked at her, meeting her eyes. She seemed a little wary. But even more, she looked sad.

'Of course.' Don't make anything of it. Don't admit the

192

fears, keep them at bay. 'Give me the sachets, I'll make us both a drink.'

From the kitchen he heard her descend briefly to the bathroom. When the kettle boiled he took the drinks back upstairs. She was sitting up in bed wearing a striped nightshirt, a sort of short-sleeved rugby shirt, and the bedclothes were neatly turned down across her stomach. He had a sudden memory of Suzanna lying in that same bed, her naked body twining in seductive invitation. He thought how perverse it was that whilst he'd been more than able to resist her beckonings, Nell in her boyish nightshirt was almost more than he could handle. He put the cup down on the bedside table.

'Thank you,' she said.

He was already leaving the room. 'You're welcome.'

He began to shut the door. Just before it was quite closed, he heard her say, 'I never did believe chivalry was dead.'

It was nice to be appreciated.

He had thought she might be up before him in the morning, as her body-clock would still be on English time. He went down to the kitchen, but there was no sign of her.

There was still no sign of her at midday. He decided to take her up some tea.

He laid a tray with two cups and saucers, adding a plate of biscuits. As an afterthought he went outside and picked a dark-pink rosebud.

He tapped on her door. There was no reply. Balancing the tray on one hand he turned the handle.

Sunshine was streaming across the room, bouncing off the white walls so that it was as bright as being outside. She must have opened the shutters before she went to sleep. Putting the tray down, he went to close them a little; he didn't feel up to quite such dazzling light.

He went over to the bed. She lay curled on her side, one arm thrown over her face. He put her tea down beside her, rattling the spoon in the saucer. She stirred.

He said, 'I don't know if you take sugar.'

Her muffled voice said, 'Yes, please.'

She lifted her head, then struggled into a sitting position. She looked tousled and slightly flushed. And incredibly appealing. He had been going to perch companionably on the bed, but he changed his mind.

'Have a biscuit.'

'Thanks.' She took two. 'I'm so hungry. Shall we make some breakfast?'

'It's more a case of where shall we have lunch. It's almost half past twelve.'

'Goodness!' She drank her tea quickly, wolfing the biscuits.

'There's no hurry,' he said, amused. 'We don't have set times for meals here. Restaurants go on serving till there aren't any more customers.'

'It's not that. I'm only here with you for a week, and I've just slept away a whole morning.' Instantly she looked as if she regretted her remark. 'I mean, there must be so many interesting things to see, and . . .'

He took her hand. 'I know what you mean.' He wanted to say, I love the way you say exactly what you're thinking. If you only knew how different you are from the last woman who slept in my bed. From any woman who's ever slept in my bed. 'We're going to have to pack a day's worth of interesting things into what's left of today,' he said instead. 'So you'd better get up, and I'll take you out to lunch.'

He took her to a small taverna in the next village, where the proprietor's mother had a special way with red mullet. Sitting at a table under a vine-covered trellis, the sun making spots of heat where it reached them through the leaves, he introduced her to ouzo.

'It's nice,' she said.

With the fish he ordered a very mild retzina, and she took to it as if she'd never known anything different.

'Just right with the food,' she commented.

194

He wondered, recalling the night of the boeuf bourguignon and its accompanying mulled wine, red wine, white wine and brandy, if she'd inherited her drinker's head from Sem.

The waiter approached to clear the plates and asked if they'd like anything else. Rafe looked at her expectantly. She didn't answer. He realized muzzily that she hadn't heard the question. Idiot, he thought. She doesn't understand Greek.

'Shall we have some fruit? Coffee?'

'Yes, please.'

He told the waiter what they'd like. He noticed her watching, a slight smile on her face.

'Is that Greek?' she asked as the waiter went back inside. He looked at her resignedly. She giggled. 'Sorry, I suppose it would be. It sounds as if you're angry with each other.'

'Does it? I'm not angry with the waiter – I thought the meal was quite good. But I can't speak for him.'

She moved her chair closer to him, and he put his arm round her. They were alone, the only other diners having just departed. He had enjoyed watching her observe them; there had been four in the party, all men, and, apart from a tiny dish of food, their lunch had consisted of nineteen large bottles of beer. 'A liquid lunch, with a vengeance!' she'd whispered, smiling across at him and trying not to laugh each time one of the quartet shouted out 'POPI!' to the waitress and she scurried to bring them a few more bottles.

'That's nice,' she sighed, nestling into him. 'You've got a lovely body for leaning against. Torso, I should say. I'm only referring to the bit above the belt.'

'I'm relieved to hear it. This is a public place. And any minute now the priest will be coming down the street on his afternoon calls.'

'That's all right, he'd probably agree with me. I expect he'd like people leaning against *his* body.' She sighed again. 'I don't think I could cope with lifelong celibacy.'

He wanted to laugh. 'Nor me. But Orthodox priests aren't

celibate. They're free to marry if they want to, and most of them do, unless they're ambitious for high office.'

'I wish Sem were here.'

He couldn't follow her thoughts. 'Why, especially?'

'It's another of his . . .' she paused, apparently searching for a word, then gave up, '. . . things. Whether men make better priests if they've been subjected to the rough and tumble of marriage. And children. You know, getting your hands dirty with the greasy old nuts and bolts of life. He'd talk to you all day about it, given the chance.'

He could think of a great many things he'd prefer to talk all day about.

'Our fruit's coming,' he murmured against her hair. 'Are you going back to your own place?'

'Is it difficult?'

'Is what difficult?'

'The fruit. Is it something you have to attack, like melon, or something that fights back, like oranges?'

'Ah. I see. No, it's grapes and apples.'

'In that case I'm not. I'm staying with you.'

'Oh, good.' He moved her chair a little closer to him. 'We'll share a plate. Save the washing-up. And you can help me finish the retzina.'

'We could always have another bottle,' she said wistfully.

'What about our list of interesting things? We're only on Item One.'

'Lunch in a Typical Taverna?'

'Yes.'

She turned to smile bewitchingly into his face. 'Bugger the list.'

And, her body warm against his, the beauty of the springtime countryside stretching away before them to the distant sea, and a waiter hovering about eager to grant their least gustatory desire, he entirely agreed with her.

Eventually they left the taverna, walking arm in arm back to the car with no clear idea what to do next.

'Can we go to the seaside?' she asked. 'Is it far?'

'No. It never is. This is a long, thin island.'

'I know!'

'Of course you do. I was forgetting the *Wonder Book of History*.' No doubt it had included a map or two.

'Let's, then. Go to the sea.'

'Okay.'

Since the car was parked pointing in the direction of Matala, he took her there. He had forgotten what a nice little place it was, out of season. In the summer you couldn't even find space to park the car.

They went down on to the beach, and he pointed out to her the dark mouths of the caves that riddled the rocky, golden cliffs. She seemed to be making heavy weather of walking on the sand, leaning against him and dragging her feet. He wondered if the drink and the late night were catching up with her.

'Tired?' he asked.

'Knackered. Let's sit down.'

They were nearly at the cliffs. She flopped down, her hands behind her head, and closed her eyes.

'Aren't you going to swim?'

'I haven't brought my bikini. I mean, I've brought it, but I haven't got it with me now.'

'Just as well. The water's cold.'

'Thin blood,' she muttered. 'I always said you had thin blood. Bet it's lovely in the sea. Warm as a bath.'

He didn't like to disillusion her. She stopped talking, and her breathing became regular and deep. He reckoned she was probably asleep.

He settled down beside her to wait till she woke up.

On the way home he stopped at a small shop calling itself, with pompous inaccuracy, SUPERMARKET, to buy some provisions. She came inside with him, and while he was selecting what he wanted he was aware of her pottering about behind him, investigating the shelves.

'I'm going to cook tonight,' he said, pocketing his change and picking up the plastic bags. She opened the car door for him. 'Unless you'd like to go out again?'

'No, I'm not bothered. What are you going to cook?'

'Guess.'

'Pasta.'

He started the engine. 'Quite right.'

He heard her laugh softly. He glanced at her, but she was looking away from him, out of the window.

He couldn't judge the mood between them. She seemed happy, but since she'd woken up from her after-lunch sleep she'd been untalkative. He'd noticed that she would glance at him when she didn't think he was looking, with an expression in her eyes he was unable to read.

'I would like to sit on your terrace and watch the sun go down,' she announced as they pulled up under his wall.

'You'll find that difficult. It faces south-east.'

'Oh. Well, in that case you'll have to come and sit with me and talk to me.'

'Nothing I'd like more.' He was trying to carry all three carrier bags up the steps, and he felt her hand wriggling against his as she relieved him of one of them. Again he thought briefly of Suzanna, who whenever there were bags or cases or anything else to carry managed to lose the use of her arms. As if the rest of the world were her unpaid bearers. 'Give me half an hour to make the sauce,' he turned to smile at her in gratitude as they reached the kitchen, 'then I'll be with you.'

She hovered behind him, trying to dance out of his way as he distributed the shopping into the fridge and the cupboards.

'Shall I make us a cup of tea?' she asked.

'What a nice idea. One sugar for me.'

From force of habit he turned on the cassette player, then

immediately turned if off again. She said, 'Don't switch it off on my account. I want to know more about classical music – I once said to Sem that it all sounded the same, and he's never forgiven me.'

'I'm not surprised.' He had started peeling and chopping onions, hurriedly because he wanted to give her his whole attention. 'What a dreadful thing to say.'

'Well, I was only seven.'

'This is Verdi,' he said, pushing the tape back in again.

'Oh.' She listened for a few moments, then said in a whisper, as if she felt she shouldn't interrupt, 'Is it one of your favourites?'

He hesitated. The question really demanded a fuller answer than he wanted to give just then. 'I like a lot of opera,' he said, compromising. 'I once heard a great violinist say, when asked why he had chosen the violin as his instrument, that it was because it was the closest thing to the human voice.'

She didn't respond, and he wondered if she'd heard. He turned round to look at her, and she was standing with her eyes closed. 'What's the matter? Onions getting to you?'

'No.' Her voice was dreamy. 'I'm listening.'

He said quietly, 'Beautiful, isn't it?'

She didn't answer, and he went back to his onions, putting them in a pan of oil to fry. He thought she'd forgotten about the tea, but when the aria had finished she quietly went back to her task. Pouring him a cup, she came to put it down on the worktop beside him. She reached up to kiss him very lightly on the cheek, then disappeared out on to the terrace.

I think, he decided, we can take that as a yes.

He was pleased with the end result of his cooking. The sauce had turned out well, considering he'd given it less of his mind than he should have. They'd opened a bottle of red wine to accompany the meal, but had drunk half of it before they'd started eating. She had been fascinated by the view from the terrace, and her enthusiasm had made him appreciate it all over again. He'd fetched a map for her, so that he could show her what she was looking at.

She sat with the map open on her lap.

'I don't know how you ever tear yourself away,' she said.

He smiled. 'It's not always easy. But there aren't many jobs for itinerant journalists here.'

'There aren't anywhere.'

'What's that?'

' "Itinerant" and "here" contradict each other. You can't have a "here" if you're itinerant.'

'No.'

She glanced at him, managing for a moment to look away from the scene before her. 'Sorry. I'm a bit of a pedant.'

He stood up; it was time to go inside again to see if the food was ready. 'No, you're not.' He ruffled her hair, its texture a smooth, remembered sensation. She caught hold of his wrist, turning his hand so that his palm was to her lips. The feel of her kiss made him catch his breath.

'Thank you for inviting me,' she said.

He was at a loss to know how to reply. He said, 'You're welcome,' and hurried into the house.

They had finished the meal and the wine, and taken their coffee out on to the terrace. It should have been a calm time, restful and relaxed, but he was aware of tension. He caught her eyes on him, and this time when he met her stare she didn't look away.

What is it? he wondered.

She came to sit close to me at lunch. She gave me a kiss, she took my hand. She's not exactly driving me away.

But she's here, in my house. It would be so easy for me to assume too much, and that would put her in an awful position.

She was still watching him.

He got up and went to crouch in front of her, putting his

hands on her legs. After a moment she leaned forwards to him. Tentatively she touched his lips with hers, backing away immediately.

He looked up into her face. She looked slightly anxious. Her eyes shone in the faint light, their pupils wide.

The moment stretched on, endlessly. Then, making up his mind, he took her face in his hands and kissed her as lightly as she had kissed him.

She dropped her head against his chest, and he heard her whisper, 'Oh, Rafe.' Then her hands twined around his neck as if she would never let him go.

He stood up, pulling her up with him, wrapping his arms round her and closing her body against his. In silence he bent to kiss her, a proper kiss this time, and she responded instantly, her mouth opening under his. And in the wild mixture of emotions that was hitting him there was a deep and unexpected streak of compassion, of tenderness for her, that this was what she had wanted but yet hadn't the means to ask for. So cautious, she'd been, so uncertain.

'I want you so much,' he said, kissing her neck, his hands under her sweater rubbing her skin. 'I want to make love to you.'

'Yes. Oh, yes.'

She turned his head with her hands, her mouth to his again, her soft, warm tongue searching for his. She tasted sweet, so sweet. He had the sensation that she was reading his mind, perceiving what he wanted and doing it in the same moment. Her thighs were pressed against his, her body against him rousing him, her hands moving smoothly all over him.

'Come on,' he gasped, 'let's go to bed,' and taking her hand he led her inside, up the steps and into her bedroom. His bedroom. She sat on the bed and he took off her clothes, slowly, for the pleasure of watching her body appear beneath his gaze. The soft shaded light from the bedside lamp made her look like some magical creature, her hair white-fair against her pale skin. She was reaching for him, and he undressed, throwing his clothes on to the floor. He stretched out alongside her, one hand around her holding her tightly against him, the other running down over her body. Finding her breast, so perfect in his hand, the nipple hard between his fingers. He broke off from kissing her mouth to caress her breast with his lips, holding it so that it stood up to greet him as he tasted her with his tongue. Her body was sweet like her mouth, and the texture of her skin was like a peach in the sunshine, warm, dry, slightly downy. His mouth slid to her stomach, and she seemed to rise up towards him.

Her hand was reaching for him, stroking and gently pulling at him, and he no longer had any doubts. She wanted him, as much as he wanted her. His hand delved down, over her stomach and between her thighs, and she was warm and wet in welcome so that his fingers slid into her. She moaned slightly as he began once more to kiss her lips, her mouth closing to his. He moved over on top of her, and her legs parted under his, softly yielding to him, letting him approach her, blindly search for her for an instant before, without either of their guidance, finding her.

He waited, knowing what was ahead, for this moment was unique.

Then, so slowly that at first he could hardly feel that he was moving, he started to enter her. She moaned again, her mouth kissing his with renewed intensity as she felt his advance into her. Despite her moisture she was tight around him and he held back, afraid to hurt her.

She slid her mouth from his, whispering, 'Go on! Oh, go on!'

And he said, 'Nell, I don't want to hurt you.'

'You're not. You're so gentle. It's all right.'

He increased his pressure. As if an invisible barrier had given way, suddenly it was easier. He heard her gasp, and it seemed she was torn between joy and pain. He was deep inside her, yet she didn't pull away; her hips lifted towards him, allowing him still further into her, and she gave a great shuddering cry.

He began to move faster, his body in time with hers, thrusting downwards as she came up to meet him, sweat on his body, on her body, making them slide against each other, smoothly, sinuously. He was near, and nearer – any minute, any second. He found her again, rubbing her with fingers and thumb, and she clutched convulsively at him. She seemed to hold her breath, her body suddenly quite still, then a great pulse in her slowly began to beat, closing around him as she cried out his name, her arms and legs wrapping tightly around him so that he was fused with her. A couple of seconds later, the spasms of her body a new and irresistible stimulus, he exploded into her.

He was filled with profound peace. The joy of her, the enormous sexual pleasure she had just given him, was a part of it. He glanced down at her, curled up in his arms, her body still pressed against him. A very considerable part. He felt himself stir slightly in memory.

But the peace was more than the afterglow of their lovemaking. It was a peace of the soul as well as of the body, and it was priceless because he had despaired of achieving it.

It had been Nell in his arms, every split-second of the time. No intrusions, no dream images pushed in between them. Just two people, desiring each other, giving themselves to each other. And achieving between them something so precious that the desire, and the will to go on giving, instantly multiplied.

Just Nell. Just him, making love to her the way he had wanted to before. And by some miracle that earlier occasion seemed to have been wiped out, so that it felt as if this had been their first time together.

He imagined it had been so for her, too.

Immediately afterwards, before they had separated from

their union to become two people again, she had said quietly, her voice breaking, 'Now we're there. I knew. I knew that was how it was meant to be.'

And had looked at him with such an expression in her eyes that at last he had no more doubts.

Fourteen

She was on the very edge of sleep. Her head on his chest, she could hear his heartbeat, strong and slow. Back to normal. She smiled in her happiness. I did know, she repeated to herself. It was all there, that first time, before . . . The tenderness, that wonderful way of sweeping me up and taking me along with him. Like Superman. Flying off into the night.

I've never known it like that. And never before felt that what I was giving was absolutely right, neither too eager nor too reluctant. I didn't even think. I just *did*. Perhaps that was why it was so marvellous.

Perhaps that's what's been happening all along, from the moment he asked me to come here and without knowing why, I just said, yes. Perhaps some better judgement inside me that I'm not aware of has been guiding me. Making sure I came back to him.

No regrets, now. No doubts. I'm glad, so glad. At this moment I wouldn't be anywhere else in the world.

She snuggled in closer to his warmth, and his arms tightened around her.

He said, 'Are you cold?'

'A bit.'

He reached down for the edge of the chaotic bedclothes, pulling sheet, blankets and bedcover anyhow over them. It was like being in a nest.

'Nell?'

'Yes?'

'It was all right, wasn't it?'

All right! She wanted to laugh at the understatement. Then she saw what he was saying. And was touched, in some deep part of her, that he'd needed to ask.

'Yes. Yes, it was,' she said fervently. But she couldn't resist adding. 'The all-rightest thing I've ever known,' and enjoyed the slight shaking as he laughed.

'Me too.' She felt him kiss the top of her head. 'Roll over, I can't sleep lying on my back.'

She did so, and he curved his body round behind her. She thought, falling asleep, it's like having a guardian angel. And, echoing through her head like a distant call of joy, this is where I belong.

She woke to find herself alone in the big bed, with the sun making tiger stripes through the shutters. She stretched, totally relaxed; the room no longer seemed strange, and she felt quite at home. It's because he's sharing it with me now, she thought. I no longer feel bad because I've turfed him out of his own bed.

It had been awful, the first night. It was so obviously his room that he'd shown her into, and as he stood there in the doorway she'd felt too embarrassed even to look at him. And on top of that she'd had to ask him to boil a kettle, for the anti-dream brew.

She turned over, rolling across to lie in his half of the bed, pressing her face into his pillow. It smelt slightly of his aftershave, and also very faintly of lavender. The linen was white and rather coarse, and over the sheets was a bright tan and honey-coloured blanket, too hot now that the night was over. She pushed it back, folding it over the end of the wooden bedstead.

She looked around the room. The walls were painted white, decorated with colourful hanging rugs. Above the bed hung an ornate cross, the same triangular-armed shape as the one Rafe wore around his neck. The furniture was of dark wood, and looked incredibly heavy. There was a large wardrobe in the corner, and she was just about to go over and have a look inside to see whether there was room for her own clothes she hadn't yet unpacked when she heard footsteps outside. Then the door was pushed open and Rafe came in carrying a loaded tray.

She sat up. The sheet fell away, revealing her naked breasts, and she hurriedly pulled it up again to cover herself. Funny, she thought, how even after last night, it doesn't seem quite right to sit like that. Perhaps it's because he's up and dressed – it wouldn't matter if he were bare too.

He was smiling – he must have noticed. He passed over her nightshirt.

'Hello,' she said.

'Good morning.' He bent to kiss her. He smelt nice – sort of soapy. He had on jeans and an open-necked white shirt, the sleeves rolled up. She realized he must have been up for some time.

'Have I overslept again?' she asked.

'Yes. I've never known anyone sleep as much as you.'

'I'm on holiday. I'm meant to sleep a lot.'

'I'm being lenient with you, as it's only your second day. Tomorrow it's your turn to get up and make breakfast.'

She looked over to the tray. 'What have we got?'

'Fresh bread, butter and honey. Yoghurt. Grapes. And coffee.'

He was filling a plate for her as he spoke. The smell of warm bread was wonderful, and she began to eat immediately. 'I'm hungry,' she said with her mouth full.

'Apparently.'

She watched him preparing the same for himself. He was humming gently. She thought he looked happy. She remembered the feel of him, last night. His body hard against hers. His arms around her, holding her so tightly. His voice, husky, saying her name. A deep thrill went right through her, as if something inside her had slowly turned over. She put her plate down; for the time being eating was beyond her.

'You haven't finished already, have you?' He was bringing her a cup of coffee. She shook her head. He took a grape from her plate, and put it to her lips. The touch of his fingers on her skin brought its own memories, and she felt herself begin to tremble slightly. He watched her, his face slightly quizzical. Then he smiled again.

He sat down on the bed, taking her hand and gently playing with her fingers.

'Are you all right?' he asked quietly. He raised his eyes to look at her. Dark eyes, she thought irrelevantly. So full of feeling, if you stop to look. And he *is* browner than he was at home.

'Yes, I'm all right,' she said. She was glad, more than glad, that he had said that. Last night had to be referred to, however obliquely, and he had touched exactly the right note. As if there were other people in the room, and he didn't want them to know what he was talking about. He leaned forward, hugging her quickly, then he stood up.

'Would you like a day out? I've got to interview an extremely old man who apparently remembers the 1896 rebellion against the Turks. He's probably lying through his teeth, if he has any. But he'll be interesting.'

'Yes. Lovely.' She thought, I'd like any sort of day, provided it was with you. 'Does he live near here?'

'Fairly. In a village on the lower slopes of the mountains. The Idha Mountains, where Zeus lived as a lad.'

'Perhaps he'll remember that, too.'

'Possibly. No doubt he'll tell us if so. On the way back we'll call and see my cousin in Míres.'

A whole day stretching ahead. With him. She crammed the last of her bread and honey into her mouth, reaching for her coffee cup. 'I'd better get up,' she said as soon as she could. 'You take the tray down, I'll tidy up in here.'

She was torn between wearing something suitable for scrambling up mountains and something smart for calling on cousins. In the end she decided she'd copy Rafe and put on jeans. But with a pretty shirt, she thought, and selected the new one that she'd bought to go with her green pullover, which she put round her shoulders. She hadn't brought the jade beads; they were too precious to bring on holiday.

She found him down by the car, topping up the water in the radiator. He looked up as she clattered down the steps.

'You were quick. I thought I'd have time to do a five thousand mile service.'

'I'll go back and slap on a bit more make-up if you like.'

'Please don't.' He wiped his hands. 'You look more than lovely already.' He studied her. 'I knew green was your colour.'

'Oh!' She felt stupidly embarrassed. 'Of course it's much too nice for wearing up mountains, but I thought . . .'

He put his arm round her, hugging her. 'No, it isn't. It's just right. Come on.'

She spent the journey gazing out at successive wildly different types of scenery.

'This is Míres,' he said as they joined on to the end of a traffic jam in a small market town. Cars and trucks were double-parked on both sides of the road, and they had to wait, with about fifty other far less patient motorists, for an enormous lorry to negotiate the narrow gap left in the middle of the road.

'Where your cousin lives.'

Some time after that they left the main road, turning westwards and on to a very minor road that was in places little more than a track. Rafe drove the big car with skill, easing it over the worst of the potholes. Once he said, with reference apparently to nothing in particular, 'I hope you don't mind.'

She didn't. Didn't object to disappearing roads, and potholes, didn't mind the dust in her face. She didn't think she'd ever mind anything again.

The road had been climbing steadily – she could tell, apart

from anything else, because her ears kept popping. Now the villages were few and far between, and consisted of little more than a few houses around a church, a bar and a shop.

'This is the old boy's village,' he said eventually. She looked around, wondering how he could possibly tell since it looked exactly the same as the last three they'd passed through. It didn't take more than a few seconds to drive from end to end; she would hardly have thought it merited the title 'village'.

'Do you know where he lives?'

'No. But I know where he'll be.' He pointed to a group of rickety chairs and tables spilling out of a small shop. Beneath the shade of trees, a dozen or more old men were sitting over minute cups of coffee. 'The kafenío. Where every self-respecting old boy spends his days.'

She craned round to look as he drove on a little to park the car.

'But they're all men.'

'Naturally. It's a male preserve. Don't worry – they won't mind you.'

'I might mind them!' She felt awkward at the thought of walking in with Rafe under the gaze of twenty-four rheumy old eyes. 'Could I – would you mind if I went for a walk while you talk to him? There's a track up there, look, behind that long water-trough thing, leading up into the hills. I bet the views would be terrific.'

'I don't mind at all. He won't speak any English anyway, so you won't be missing anything.'

He held her hand as they walked back to the café. Her presence seemed to arouse quite a lot of interest. But she found she didn't mind – the chorus of '*Kalimera*' from the patrons was cheerful, and a man appeared from inside the shop to pull out two chairs for them.

Rafe spoke to him in Greek. The man was frowning, saying, '*Né, né*, and pointing to the chairs. She wondered if he were offended.

Rafe said, 'He wants you to sit down and have a drink. I explained that I'm here to see the old man – that's him in the corner, he's this man's great-grand uncle – and he says you must stay too. But only for a minute – I'll tell him you want to have a look around.'

'Okay.'

He turned back to the man, talking for what seemed ages. It was always the way, she reflected, when you hadn't a clue what people were talking about – their conversations were interminable. The café proprietor smiled widely, shouted to the old boy in the corner, and hurried back inside his bar. Nell sat down, and Rafe went to greet his interviewee.

She watched him look up at Rafe, his frown clearing as understanding dawned. She could well believe he was old enough to remember whatever it was that had happened in 1896. He looked old enough to remember the Flood. His face seemed to have imploded around the central point of his mouth, where once presumably his teeth had been. Between bursts of speech he mumbled his jaws around as if he were chewing very stringy meat. She didn't like to imagine him eating or drinking. He stood up, and she saw that he wore the old mountain costume of breeches and knee-length leather boots. Coming to sit beside her, he took her hand in one that was as twisted and brown as an ancient piece of wood. He stared into her face, and she saw kindness and welcome behind the curiosity. She said nervously, 'Kalimera' and the old man lifted her hand to his lips and kissed it.

The proprietor reappeared with cups of coffee and tiny glasses of a clear liquid. She watched as Rafe and the two men clinked their glasses and downed the contents, wondering if she should do the same to the one put down in front of her. Rafe said quietly. 'It's neat ouzo. Can you manage it?'

She drained the glass with a quick flick of her wrist. It felt slightly like a grenade going off inside her mouth, but the sensation wasn't unpleasant.

Rafe smiled at her. 'We should be thankful it wasn't raki.

211

The way they make it up here, we wouldn't have any soft palate left.'

She wanted to laugh. She drank her coffee, which was hot and very strong, and sort of chewy, when you got down to the dregs. Then she thought it was probably time to go, before there was any question of having to drink another bolter and becoming incapable of movement. She looked at Rafe, and he nodded, rattling off something to the two men. The proprietor stood up, bowed to her and went back inside. Rafe said, 'See you later,' and kissed her. She picked up her camera and bag, and without turning round set off up the street to take the path up into the hillside.

The climb at first was steep. Very soon she was sweating, and she stopped to remove her pullover from her shoulders and roll up her shirt sleeves. She went on upwards, following a clearly-defined path of beaten earth, until she was gasping for breath.

I'm really unfit! I'm wheezing like a fat old woman!

She sank down on the grass to get her breath back. Already the view down the hillside was wonderful. She told herself consolingly that the panting wasn't anything to do with *her*; the village was so high up in the mountains that no doubt the air had thinned.

Relieved, she resumed the climb.

There was some sort of ruined building on the summit of the nearest hill, and she thought she'd make that her objective. Making herself ignore the temptation to keep turning round to see how much better was the panorama for each few feet of extra height, she went on doggedly climbing. The track was rougher here, as if these heights were less well frequented by – who, or what, was it that had made the path? She noticed a pile of goat-droppings in the short grass, which seemed to answer that question.

Reaching the flattened top of the hill, she saw the remains of walls, made of large stones. Only two or three courses high, at the most. In a corner was what looked like an ancient archway, except that its top was missing. On a plaque set into the wall beside it was carved an animal. Its outline was worn, but she thought it looked like a lion. With wings. Beyond the arch she could see tangled undergrowth blanketing another, smaller building.

The grass was long up here, and in amongst it were flowers. Cyclamen, orchids, rock roses. And other beautiful wild blooms – pomegranate, feathery pink, prickly poppy – which she'd never seen growing before and whose identity she knew only through her books. She knelt down to look closer. Such profligacy, such a show, and nobody to see except herself. Filled with a sense of happiness and quiet pleasure, she wandered through the broken arch to look at what lay beyond.

It had been rectangular, not very big. She paced out the two sides that were less densely entangled with vegetation: twelve paces by six. She stepped over one of the walls. The construction seemed to have been built into the hillside, and half of its interior was obscured by the fallen earth of slow decades. Centuries, probably. She prodded about in the dirt, but there was nothing to see. It was cool here, after her climb, and she sat down on a section of wall that was higher than the rest and made quite a comfortable seat.

She looked out through the ruined arch to the scene beyond. She went to reach for her camera, but stopped. I'm just going to look, she thought. You find you've made less than perfect memories, if you concentrate too much on photographing everything. It's better just to look, to begin with.

She leaned back, her hands resting on the stones of the wall. Busy with imprinting the view in her mind, she didn't at first register that her fingers were playing over something that was a strange shape for a building stone. Feels like a leg, she thought vaguely.

Then she turned to look, and jumped off the wall in surprise.

No. It can't be! It's just the way the old stones have worn.

She looked more closely. It's not. It's too regular. It *is* what I thought. But what on earth is it doing here?

It wasn't a piece of the wall that she'd been sitting on. It was a very worn, almost unidentifiable effigy, reclining on top of a sarcophagus of pitted stone.

A man, lying on his back. Head a vague oval, arms held over his chest and hands piously together in an attitude of prayer. A hollow where his stomach and loins would have been – that was where she had been sitting – and crossed legs ending in truncated, upward-pointing feet.

On the front of the sarcophagus letters were incised. They were almost indistinguishable. She traced them with her finger, but they made no sense.

Of course. Nit! They're Greek letters.

She got a pencil and notebook out of her bag and carefully copied out what she could of the inscription, clearing away small tendrils of some tiny-leaved climbing plant. Then she stepped back a pace or two and took a couple of photographs.

She heard the clonking of a bell. Like a cow-bell. Then the strange, yellow-eyed face of a goat appeared over the wall, with a dramatic suddenness that made her cry out.

'Is okay, is okay!' said a voice from near at hand. She spun round to see behind her, standing framed in the old arch, a young boy. He was small and wiry, bare-footed, black-haired. About thirteen. Or maybe a little older.

'Hello,' she said, feeling silly at having shrieked at the goat. 'You made me jump. I didn't hear you approach.'

The boy just grinned. She thought it was perhaps demanding rather a lot to expect him to understand her. But then surprisingly he said, 'Very preetty, *né*? Nice place, preetty flowers.'

'Yes, lovely. Is that your goat?'

'*Né*. Yes. All are my goats.' He waved his hand in a lordly gesture, and she saw seven or eight more goats distributed around the ruins of the larger building. One was straying further off than her companions. The boy picked up a stone,

214

lobbing it with perfect accuracy so that it landed on the far side of the wanderer, who with a leap returned towards her fellows.

He turned back to her for her approval. 'That's clever,' she said.

'I very smart,' he said modestly. 'You like old chapel?' He started to snigger. 'Come, you come. I show.'

He jumped over into the space within the low walls, stopping right beside her. He pointed at the effigy, saying something in Greek.

'Sorry, I don't understand.'

He repeated himself, his voice rising. She thought, we English aren't the only ones, then, who try to cope with non-comprehension by simply shouting a bit louder. He was running his finger underneath the writing she'd copied down.

'Oh, I see! That's his name!'

'Né, né!' He laughed with pleasure. 'His name! Come, see.' He grabbed her hand, leading her into the furthest corner where the chapel walls had collapsed into the hillside. He picked out an object from a collection of things on a rough shelf, holding it out to her and covering his laughing face with his other hand.

She took the object, then immediately gave it back to him. It was one of the figures she'd seen in the tourist shops, in the form of cheap little statues and bottle-openers, and on postcards. A leering old man, one hand in the air, one on his hip. A foot daintily pointed in front of him, and an enormous erect penis. One of the old gods, presumably. Randy old sod.

The boy was chortling. He replaced the figure on its shelf, among little pots of flowers and candles decorated with coloured ribbons. Then he put the palm of his hand in the crook of his opposite elbow, lifting the forearm and clenched fist in the universal symbol of male potency.

He repeated the Greek name of the effigy on the sarcophagus. 'He very man,' he said, 'very, very man!' He made the gesture again. 'Five hundred women, one thousand children!'

She was beginning to get the picture. Some ancient folk-hero, obviously, whose reputation lived on as an inspiration. A character worthy of adulation. Especially from young boys on the verge of manhood. 'You want your man be very man, give you baby, you bring gift to chapel, he give you baby,' the boy went on, indicating the effigy with a nod of his head. His face was serious now. 'He good, he very man.'

She sat down on the wall again. It was fascinating – in a very religious country, with churches every few miles and priests to be found in the smallest of villages, here was a throw-back to antiquity which, judging by the fresh flowers in the pots, was still very much in use.

'You want baby?' the boy asked cheekily.

'No! I don't!' She was beginning to wish he would go away; he was becoming over-familiar. Get back to your bloody goats, boy.

He came to sit beside her, rubbing at the crotch of his trousers. He smelled of his profession, with an overlay of sweat. She stood up.

'I'm going now. Thank you for showing me the chapel.'

He immediately stood up too, as if her polite words had reminded him of the courtesy owed to strangers. He bowed from the waist, inclining his head gracefully in a gesture she had often noticed among Greeks. 'You go back in big car?'

'Yes. That's right.'

'You sit in *kafenío*. With the brother of my father.'

'Your uncle. Your uncle's café.'

'Né. My uncle.'

She turned to go while the opportunity presented itself.

'Goodbye,' she said over her shoulder.

'*Chérete*.'

She hurried off down the hillside, her feet sliding on loose soil. After a few minutes she turned, and saw the boy and his goats moving slowly upwards, away from her. Relieved, she went on a little further down the path, then stopped to sit on the grass. The village was just visible below her; if she craned to the left she could see Rafe's car. That way, to the right, was the big tree that shaded the café.

Nearly back. But he won't have finished yet, I've only been gone about twenty minutes. I'll sit here in the sun, it's so warm. And the grass smells lovely, and the flowers. A herby smell. And something that smells like cloves, like my gilly-flowers at home. The ones I transplanted from the little patch just outside the magic meadow.

She leaned back, supported by the warm, solid earth of the bank. Closing her eyes, she felt the sunshine heating her face. She seemed to watch red images swimming across behind her eyelids. She felt very relaxed. She was drifting into a doze. Her last thought was, I mustn't go to sleep.

She could see Rafe. Or she thought it was Rafe. He was walking through a barley field, along a grassy path that led to distant woodlands. The scene was vaguely familiar. Above him was a pale blue English sky, fuzzy with drifting cloud. He wore strange clothes. His scar was grossly prominent, a thick, knotty cord down his cheek. And his left eye was closed.

As he came closer she knew it wasn't Rafe. Just someone that looked rather like him. But this man had anger in him, impatience, frustration. Instinctively she feared him, and she had reason to: she had seen him before. His image faded, then suddenly was right before her eyes.

He lay in the long grass of the woodland's margins, copulating with a girl whose arms and legs splayed widely open in enormity of her abandon. She had her eyes shut, and her teeth were biting at her lower lip, half-muffled sounds coming from her. The man above her was thrusting into her violently, watching her all the time with his one eye, an expression of malice on his face. She thrashed about, limbs bruising the rustling grass, long plaits writhing as if they were alive.

The two of them, man and woman, were the incarnation of lust.

Then, shutting his eye for an instant and screwing up his

217

face, he was done. With total dispassion he pulled himself out of her and sat back on his heels, straightening his clothing. After a second or two of surprised silence, the girl let out a great wail of anguish.

'No, Richard, oh, please, no! Come back to me!' She spread her legs, wriggling her buttocks around in suggestive circles. He took no notice. She started to cry, in short, hysterical bursts, reaching out imploring hands which he brushed away.

He stared down at her. 'You must learn to be more swift, my lady,' he said coldly. With a dismissive, insulting gesture, he ran his hand over her displayed genitals, then stood up. She threw herself after him, her long skirt and her thick petticoat caught up around her waist, the offering of her unwanted naked flesh the more humiliating now that he was once more fully clothed. She wrapped her arms round his leg, crying brokenly, 'Richard! Oh, Richard! I would not want you so had you not taught me to love!'

A spasm crossed his face. Brutally he kicked out with his imprisoned foot, and the girl collapsed in the grass. Before she could make another lunge at him, he walked quickly away.

The sound of the girl's heartbroken sobs gradually faded and died.

Nell opened her eyes. She felt sick and dizzy, for a moment disorientated. Where am I?

She looked around her, the edges of panic rising. She saw the car. And the big shady tree. And remembered.

Rafe. Oh, Rafe! I need you, Rafe, I've got to tell you, we've got to get *away* from here.

She jumped up, racing off down the hillside with leaps and bounds that got longer and longer, out of her control in the steep descent. She flailed her arms in an attempt to keep her balance, the camera bouncing painfully against her chest. The path turned a right-angle corner, and, grabbing hold of a stumpy tree, she fell down on one knee in the dust and slithered to a halt. Hurriedly picking herself up, she ran down the rough steps on to the road.

She looked down at herself.

Oh, God.

The path emerged right beside the long stone trough she'd noticed earlier, into which several pipes spouted water. Bending over it, she got a handkerchief out of her bag and wet it, washing her face and wiping down inside her shirt and around her neck. The water was icy, making her gasp, but the intense cold on her hot skin brought her swiftly to her senses. She sponged at her jeans, and managed to remove most of the stains. Apart from being damp, she thought she probably didn't look too remarkable. She got a comb and mirror out of her bag and tidied her hair. Her face staring back at her looked pale.

There, now I'll go and find Rafe. I've got to tell him, those people in the dream were . . .

She stopped.

No. I won't tell him anything.

I don't think it would be very fair. He's happy. He's escaped from Her. Not for ever, I'm quite sure. But for now he's having a respite. And God, if that dream was anything like the nightmares he's been experiencing, he bloody well needs one.

She saw again the man and the woman. Felt, like an assault, his cruelty. She looked over her shoulder at the mountainside, peaceful now, deceptive. She found she was trembling, as if she'd just had an awful shock.

Suddenly she was afraid, so afraid that she no longer cared if she looked funny. So what if all the old men in the café laughed at her for falling over. At least they were flesh and blood.

She started off down the road, trying to hurry without making it too obvious. When, very soon, the café came into view, with Rafe still sitting at the same table, it was the most welcome sight in the world.

Fifteen

He was relieved when she came back. He had been looking out for her; she'd been gone over an hour and he was finding he could no longer concentrate on his old boy. They seemed to have been through the most interesting of his reminiscences, anyway, and the pauses between the old man's increasingly more repetitive utterances were getting longer. Rafe's mouth tasted dry from too much coffee, and he wanted to be with her again.

He waved to her. She lifted her hand in answer. As she came up to him he stood up and went to greet her. He thought she looked pale, and the legs of her jeans were damp.

'Are you all right?'

She nodded. 'Yes. I had a sleep, in the sun.' She laughed nervously. 'Silly thing to do. I felt a bit dizzy when I stood up.'

'That's strange. The sun's not very strong. Still, I suppose it is after England. You'd better have a long drink.' He turned to call the waiter, but she caught hold of his arm.

'Rafe, could we go, please? If you've finished, that is.'

He stared at her. Her eyes were full of urgent appeal, and there was sweat on her upper lip. He wondered why she looked so worried. 'Yes, of course,' he said. Whatever the reason, the last thing she'd want was a long discussion here in front of so many interested witnesses. 'I'll get a bottle of mineral water; you can drink it as we drive along. Go and sit in the car, I won't be a minute.'

He went inside the shop to settle his bill, buying a large blue plastic bottle of water. The proprietor gave him a paper cup.

'Isn't she well, your pretty lady?' he asked solicitously.

'She's fine. Just a bit hot. That fair English skin, you know. She's very sensitive to the sun.'

'Yes, yes, you should . . .' Rafe interrupted him by shaking his hand and making his farewells; he was impatient to get back to Nell. On the way out of the café he passed the old fellow, who, now that the excitement of being interviewed was over, had gone back to dozing in the corner. Rafe put a fold of thousand-drachma notes by his empty coffee cup, then followed Nell up the road to the car.

'Are you hungry?' he asked. They were back on the main road, driving with the setting sun on their right, and he had just realized that she'd missed lunch. He'd had a plate of moussaka with his old boy – an experience he wasn't in a hurry to repeat – but Nell had been up her mountain at the time.

She was leaning back, her hand over her forehead. 'I will be soon. This water's perking me up – I think I was just a bit hot and sweaty, back there. I'm feeling much better now.'

'Good.' He had been going to ask her again what had been the matter, but decided against it. Maybe she'd rather he left it. 'I phoned my cousin, while you were exploring,' he went on. 'He says instead of just calling in, he'll take us out to dinner with him. Would you like to go?'

'Oh! Yes, all right.'

'That's what I told him.'

She laughed shortly. 'Just as well I didn't say, not bloody likely. Does he live right in that town, whatever its name was, on that awful main street?'

'Mirés. And it's not always as bad as that, sometimes you can drive straight through in fifteen minutes.' He heard her laugh again, a more relaxed sound this time. 'No, he's got a nice house outside the town. But we won't be going to his house, he'll meet us in his favourite restaurant. He sells agricultural machinery,' he added as an afterthought.

He didn't tell her about the large family who would all without a doubt find some excuse during the evening to come by and have a chat. He didn't think now was the moment.

He watched her, later, across the table from him trying to communicate with his cousin's wife, his cousin's wife's friend and her eldest daughter. She was holding her own very well, not in the least intimidated by their volubility. His cousin nudged him.

'I like this one,' he declared. 'It's a pity everyone came out to join us, but at least I had the two of you to myself over dinner.' They had moved after the meal to a café, where, just as Rafe had expected, one after another of his relations had happened along. Nell's only awkward moment had been when he'd introduced his cousin. 'This is Adonis,' he'd said, forgetting how incongruous the name sounded to English ears. She had managed it beautifully, though; after a quick, intense glance at him to see if he were pulling her leg, she'd held out her hand to Adonis and said, 'I'm so glad to meet you. It's very kind of you to ask us to dinner.'

'I like her, too,' Rafe said.

'Better than the one who ordered me off your property,' Adonis said with a laugh.

'What was she like?' He couldn't remember any of them doing that.

'Tall girl, good figure. Dark hair.' Not Suzanna, then. And he didn't think Adonis had come visiting when she was in residence. 'You know! She worked in Italy with you, and you brought her on here for a holiday.'

'Oh. Felicity.' He'd forgotten all about Felicity. Adonis had dropped in when she was sunbathing topless on the terrace, and, apparently thinking he was some sort of tradesman, she had shouted out at him to get off the terrace steps and go round the back. Quite embarrassing.

He couldn't imagine Nell ordering anyone off his terrace. Nor sunbathing topless, come to that. He had a sudden picture of her covering her breasts with the sheet, this morning. He smiled at the memory.

'Here's to your thoughts.' Adonis filled up their glasses and clinked his against Rafe's. He had a very knowing expression in his eyes. Rafe thought, I have to remember he's a lot more aware than he looks.

'Good health,' he said. 'How's the tractor business?'

They arrived home very late; Nell had been sleepy in the car, resting her head on his shoulder and singing gently along with *Highlights from French Opera*. He put his arm round her as they went up the steps to the terrace and into the kitchen.

'Do you want anything?' he asked.

'I think I'll have a brew,' she said carelessly. She caught his eye, and quickly looked away. He wondered why she should want to drug herself, after such a happy evening. Then he remembered how she'd looked earlier. Coming down from her mountain.

I don't want to ask her, he thought. I might not like the answer. Better if we don't talk about it. If I just quietly get on and make the drinks, we can pretend it's just like having a cup of tea, or coffee.

'Okay,' he said easily, filling the kettle. 'Go on up, I'll bring it when it's ready.'

'I'm going to have a wash,' she said. 'See you in a minute.' She disappeared into the bathroom, and a short while later went upstairs.

He took the drinks up, then got undressed and into bed. She was standing by the window brushing her hair. She turned to him, smiling, then took off her nightshirt and climbed in beside him. He wished she hadn't been so quick about it; her body was lovely, and he enjoyed looking at her. It was a characteristic he hadn't known in a woman for a long time, this mixture of almost prim modesty in normal, day-to-day affairs alongside a glorious exhibitionism when he had her to himself in bed. The best of both worlds. He thought again of Felicity and her toplessness – funny how she'd completely slipped from his memory till Adonis reminded him – and how much he'd disliked the way she'd had of flaunting her undeniable charms at almost anything in trousers.

Nell beside him was sipping her drink. She had almost finished. He hurried to do the same. As he put his empty cup down on the floor, he felt her arms go round him. Already excited merely by her closeness, he turned to her.

It was dark. He had no idea what time it was – nowhere near dawn. Nell was sitting on the edge of the bed, weeping.

Still half asleep, he moved rapidly across to her.

'Nell, what is it? Were you dreaming?' No, don't say that. Don't say our marvellous preventive medicine no longer works.

But she was shaking her head. 'No. I don't think so. It's just so sad, so terribly sad.' Her words trailed off into sobs.

'What is?' He sat up beside her, enfolding her in his arms, and she turned to bury her face in his chest.

'I don't know! Something. Something so sad, it's breaking my heart.'

He was filled with pity for her. He rocked her gently to and fro, stroking her back with one hand. 'Can't you say what it is? You can tell me, whatever it is.'

'Oh, I know that,' she said distantly. 'I know I can. But I've no idea what it is. Only that it's horrible. So, so sad.'

He had no idea how to help her. He went on holding her, and gradually she stopped crying. He got up, lifting her back into bed and pulling the covers up over her. Then he got in beside her, cuddling her close.

'Can you sleep again?' he asked softly. He wasn't sure she'd even woken up fully.

'I think so. Rafe, don't leave me. Will you?'

His heart turned over. It was so unlike her, to appeal to him that way. So directly.

'No,' he said. 'I'll always be here.'

He wasn't sure if he'd intended to say that. But anyway he didn't think she'd taken it in. She murmured something, and soon he felt her relax back into sleep.

He lay awake for some time, thinking about her.

Wonder what it was? Dream, probably, only she couldn't recall it.

Not one of *those* dreams, then. And everyone has the other sort. A nice, normal, everyday occurrence. Nothing to get alarmed about.

His thoughts drifted on.

I'll always be here, I said to her. That was a remark that came from nowhere – a Freudian slip, Stephen would call it. He frowned in the darkness, imagining not having Nell with him.

I like having her with me.

He admitted to himself that it was an understatement. But he didn't want to think about that, and turned his mind away.

I can work with her around – she doesn't demand all my attention. That interview went well. I'll write it up tomorrow, when I've decided how to present it. And she won't mind. I know that, without even putting it to the test. She'll find something to do, and when I'm ready for company again I expect I'll find she's still happily occupied. Perhaps, even, not ready to be distracted.

He smiled in the darkness. Full of contradictions, aren't you, little Nell?

Carefully extracting his numb arm from under her waist, he turned over and settled down to sleep.

She lay in the sun, her body glowing, listening to the sound of Rafe's typewriter. She thought, I've got to fix this moment in my memory, because it's perfect happiness.

She had managed to shut out of her mind yesterday afternoon's dream experience. Almost. Her resolve not to let Rafe know about it had been so strong that it had helped her to block it out of her own consciousness. She had a vague recollection of waking up crying in the night about some awful sadness that she couldn't identify, but this morning whatever it was had lost most of its power to distress her.

Nothing was wrong.

Nothing she could put her finger on.

I'm going to enjoy today, she told herself firmly.

Over breakfast Rafe had announced that he was going to write up his interview, if it was all the same to her. She'd been quite pleased at the idea of a tranquil day lounging about on the terrace, especially as she'd discovered Rafe had a wonderful library. Everything from science fiction to philosophy. So she had volunteered to tidy up after breakfast, leaving him free to get straight down to work, and when she had finished she collected a couple of books and went out on to the terrace. Rafe had said to make herself at home, and she did so, creating a corner in the sunshine with lounger, cushions, low table for her books and her bag, and a cold can of soft drink from the fridge.

Round about mid-morning she had become aware of being too hot in a t-shirt and skirt, and had crept upstairs to put on her bikini. She wondered if he'd mind. No. Of course he wouldn't. Nobody can see me, up here. And I'll have my clothes handy, if anyone comes to call.

It's strangely quiet, apart from the typewriter, and that's the sort of noise you learn to ignore if it's steady and not too close. Usually there's music playing in the kitchen, people singing, him joining in. I think it must be a very fundamental part of him, his music. He seems to be able to sing anything – bass, tenor, and sometimes when he's really carried away he has a go at soprano. But I like it best of all when he accompanies the baritone arias. Probably I don't know what I'm talking about, but to me his voice is as rich and powerful as anything on cassette.

She had said as much to him, 'You sound as good as that bloke who got paid for recording this.' And he had modestly replied, 'That's because the heads on the tape player need a clean.'

It was fun, dining with the cousin last night. *And* meeting that great posse of relations. They were sweet. Nosey, but you couldn't hold it against them because they did it so nicely.

How old are you? What do you do? Why are you not married? Heaven knows what we'd have got on to, if they'd spoken better English.

I love listening to Rafe speaking Greek with them all. And he's so considerate, after a while he turns to me to tell me what they've been saying. So then I make a comment, and he goes back into Greek again for another burst. And I think of something else to add, and I wait for a gap in the conversation – and *they're* few and far between – and when one comes I hesitate to say what I've thought of in case the chat has flowed right away from that topic and I'll look silly.

I like the cadences in his voice, which sound different when he's speaking a foreign tongue. But some of the syllables he pronounces the same. I wonder if he sounds foreign to his Greek relations? Does he speak Greek like an Englishman? He doesn't speak English like a foreigner.

I still haven't asked about his parents. I must, he wouldn't mind. It was his grandfather who was Italian, wasn't it? Rafe was talking in Italian on the phone the other day. Now *that's* a lovely language, if ever there was one. Like music. Like singing. He was probably saying something quite mundane, but it could just have easily have been, I want to make love to you.

She was surprised at her thought. Then it occurred to her that it was fairly predictable, under the circumstances. Good old body, turning up trumps just when I need you. I'm quite amazed at myself!

She thought it wise not to pursue that line. Reaching for her book, she went back to reading about Crete under the Venetians.

He took the last piece of paper out of his typewriter, clipping it to the others with a sigh of satisfaction. That, he thought, is more like it. Tell me *that's* cliché-ridden if you dare!

He stood up, stretching, feeling the well-being that came from a good morning's work. He wondered what Nell was doing, realizing that he hadn't heard a sound from her all morning.

He walked through the house and on to the terrace. She wasn't in sight.

'Nell!'

'Here. In the shade.'

He turned to see her lying on a chair, a t-shirt over her bikini. Her skin looked very slightly flushed.

He went over to her, sitting down on the foot of her lounger. 'Too much sun?'

'Not too much. But I think I've had enough.'

'Very wise. What are you reading?' He picked up the book, glancing at the chapter heading. ' "Redistribution of the Byzantine Empire following the Fall of Constantinople." Heavy stuff, for an April morning.'

'No, it's fascinating,' she replied earnestly. 'I didn't even know what exactly constituted the Byzantine Empire till today. And wasn't that awful, how the Fourth Crusade sacked the city and did all those terrible things to the inhabitants? And then they just allocated bits of the Empire to the victorious powers willy nilly, and if you didn't want to become Venetian, or Genoese, or whatever, it was just too bad! Do you know, they just *gave* Crete away to this chap who was one of the Crusade leaders, and he decided he wasn't bothered and sold it to Venice!'

He smiled at her indignation. 'Boniface of Montferrat,' he said. 'And before the Venetians could start enjoying their new acquisition, the Genoese nipped in and took it, and they had to fight for it. The Venetian rule didn't really begin till 1212.'

'I was going to tell *you* that. Smart arse.'

'Sorry. I live here. Now if you were going to tell me about the history of Australia, or Denmark, it would be a different matter.'

She laughed. 'You're in luck. I'm not. How did your work go?'

'Marvellously. Now I'm going to take you out to lunch, and later on we'll go to Phaestos.'

'Where the Palace is?'

'Was. It's in ruins. But the position is spectacular.'

'All right. I'd like that. Wait while I get dressed, then I'll be with you.'

Over lunch she said tentatively, 'Rafe? Can I ask you something?'

He was amused at the question. And at her serious face.

'No.'

She looked startled. 'Oh!'

He laughed. 'Of course you can. What?'

'Er – did any Crusaders come here?'

He felt as if she'd hit him. Crusader. The word brought racing to the edge of his mind all the things that haunted him, if he let them in. But no, he thought. It's only that she's just been reading about the Fourth Crusade. And I left her in no doubt that I know all about it. Smart arse.

'Probably,' he said after a moment. 'It's roughly on the sea route from Northern Europe to the Holy Land. And as you were reading this morning, it's certain that many former Crusaders did, after 1204. The Fall of Constantinople,' he added obligingly.

'Yes. I remember.'

She was silent, frowning in thought. He waited.

'And some of them might have settled here? Built themselves houses, castles, whatever?'

'Oh, yes. We could find out for certain if you like – I've got a friend who works in the Historical Museum, he's always willing to supply information.'

'No, no, thank you,' she said hurriedly. 'It doesn't matter.' He thought she had finished with the subject. But then she said, 'Their effigies showed them with crossed legs, didn't they? If the Crusader had made it to the Holy Land.'

He stared at her. Whatever had brought that on? 'Yes. Why?'

'Oh, I saw one once. In a church in Winchelsea,' she jabbered. 'Shall we have some more wine?'

When the afternoon was well advanced, he drove her up to Phaestos. There were few visitors left, and the late sun turned the golden stones to glowing orange. He resisted the temptation to tell her all about it, and instead sat down on a stone wall and let her get on with it.

Eventually she came back to him.

'The views!' she said. 'Weren't the Minoans wise, building here? And doesn't it make you feel close to them, that what seemed a prime site to them seems exactly that to us?'

'Absolutely.' He was pleased at her enthusiasm.

'Why didn't the archaeologists restore this palace too, like they did Knossos?'

'Different archaeologists. The English under Arthur Evans worked on Knossos, but the Italians excavated Phaestos.'

She nodded. 'It doesn't matter that it's in ruins. You can imagine, can't you?'

'Yes. I prefer to do that.' He hesitated. Then he said, 'My grandfather was here. With the Italian Archaeological School. I've got his notes, and his diary for 1918. And 1919, when he married my grandmother.'

'I was going to ask you about your family.' He felt vindicated. 'Was your grandmother a local woman? Only you said it's her house, where you live.'

'Yes. Her father worked on the excavations as well, although in a more lowly capacity.'

'What sort of things did your grandfather's diaries say? Were they very exciting?'

'Not really. Interesting, more than exciting. He had a pretty turgid prose style.'

'Does it say anything about meeting your grandmother, and asking her to marry him?'

230

He laughed. 'No. Sorry to disappoint you. I think "diary" may be misleading – the books were more a record of daily observations. You're welcome to look at them, but they're all in Italian.'

'Not a lot of point, then. So then they had children, one of whom was your mother?'

'Yes. And in time she went away to Athens to study, and shortly before the war met my father, who was a journalist.'

She said, as he'd known she would. 'What happened to them?'

He took a breath, holding it for a moment. 'After twenty years of what I understood to be great happiness, they were killed in a car-crash. In Italy, on the way to visit my mother's family.'

'And you escaped?'

'I wasn't with them. I was sixteen, at school in England.'

She fell silent, staring out at the scene before them. He put his arm round her and she leaned against his shoulder, reaching out to take his hand in both of hers.

His thoughts roamed away. Back to England, at the start of his lower sixth year. He'd known his parents were in Italy – he always knew where they were, for they made sure that he did. They both wrote regularly, once a week, and, foreign postal services permitting, the letters were always waiting in the 'W' pigeon hole on Monday mornings. His mother often sent him an additional letter later in the week, a sort of coda, as if her love for him and her desire for contact with him couldn't wait. Wherever she was, whatever she was doing, she would find pen and paper, dashing off a few pages full of little that was really news but very much that was pure love. Her writing was made for the expression of affection, full of dash and élan, difficult perhaps for a stranger to decipher but, from long familiarity, as easy for her son as a printed page.

And his father, the journalist in him showing vividly in the economical style and the neat, forward-sloping writing that could cram double the amount of lines to the page as could his wife's extravagant hand. From his father Rafe learned the itineraries, the plans, all the information that he considered his distant son should know. And the abstract thoughts – in the close continuity of their correspondence, father and son covered the sort of detailed ground normally only possible in one-to-one conversation.

But the news of their deaths had not, of course, come by letter.

It had been cold for early October. Rafe and Stephen had been allowed to light a fire in their sixth-form study, and they were enjoying the novel privilege of entertaining friends; they were toasting muffins for tea. They had an hour's free time before going to their new duties as dinner prefects. They had been disturbed by the school secretary.

'Raphael Westover?' Her iron-grey head remained framed in the just-open doorway, as if she were reluctant to enter their young male preserve.

'Here.' He got to his feet.

'Would you go to the Headmaster, please?'

In retrospect, he'd seen it in her face. In her reluctance to answer his mute question.

And, far more clearly written, in Stephen's eyes. Because Stephen looked as if he were torn between satisfaction at having a hunch prove accurate and distress at what the hunch was revealing itself to be.

The Headmaster had a telegram open on his desk. With two and a half lines of writing that devastated Rafe's life and temporarily blew his world clean apart.

He left the Head's room quite numb. He found himself walking out over the playing fields, his soft leather house shoes soaking from the wet grass and squelching in the mud so that a detached part of his mind, which at the moment seemed to be the only functioning piece, nudged out the thought: fine example I'm setting.

Behind the cricket pavilion was a small clearing, cut from the enclosing woodland. In it were two ancient rustic benches, originally put there presumably by someone who preferred the peace of the trees to the spectacle of white-clad figures expending their energy. And on one of the benches, quite alone, the numbness had lifted at the corners to allow him the first glimpse of the grief into which he was poised to tumble.

A time later – a long time, a short time – he felt a hand on his shoulder. His housemaster stood there, his habitual mask of reserved tactiturnity askew so that Rafe could see the warm, good heart of the man who hid behind it.

He cleared his throat. 'There are times, Westover,' he said, in a voice gruff with compassion, 'when it may not be considered unmanly to cry.'

Rafe, his wet face pressed into his icy hands, could not reply. He felt another pat on his shoulder.

'You are excused dinner duties for this evening.' The voice had been mastered. 'If you feel equal to it, I shall expect you at House Assembly in the morning.'

His English blood combined with the public school tradition in which he had grown up, and began to do battle against the southern emotion that was threatening to annihilate him. And Rafe felt a slight turning of the tide.

He knew, in the end, that it was a wise suggestion.

And that when House Assembly began tomorrow, he would be there.

He sat letting the memories wash over him. That day, he saw in a moment of insight, provided the key to his enduring yet strangely distant friendship with Stephen. He had needed someone to absorb his grief: Stephen gave him the lesser, chillier comfort of ignoring it.

Nell stirred beside him. He leaned his head against hers, grateful for her warm, silent presence. He was glad she had made no comment. There wasn't one.

They sat for some time, watching as the twilight deepened.

'They say,' he whispered to her, as the benign shades of his parents slowly retreated into the corner of his mind which was theirs for as long as he lived, 'that at sunset the gods walk.'

She shivered slightly. It was, he realized, a tactless thing to have said. But she asked gamely, 'Are they nice gods?'

'Yes. Only very ancient evils, here. Long gone.'

'Good.' She put a lot of fervour into the one word. She shivered slightly; he thought perhaps it was time to go back.

'Come on,' he said, hauling her to her feet, 'home.'

Parking the car, he heard the telephone ringing. He hurried up the steps and inside to answer it.

There was a slight pause, then a female English voice said, 'May I speak to Nell Gurney?'

'Yes. Hold on.' He went to the door. 'Nell? It's for you. A woman.'

She was at the top of the steps. Her face fell. Perhaps when he said it was for her she'd expected it to be Sem, and was disappointed. She walked past him and picked up the phone.

'Hello? Oh, Rosemary, Hello. Yes.' There was a long stream of talk from the other end. She had her back to him. Then she said, her voice quite changed, 'I see. No, you were quite right to call me. I'm sorry you've had to try so many times. We were out.' More from the caller. Nell said, 'I'll come. Of course, I couldn't not.' A pause. Then, with irritation, 'I *know*, but there's no question of staying now. I'll call you when I get home. Thanks. Thank you for calling.'

She replaced the receiver carefully on its rests.

Then she turned round.

Her face was quite stiff.

'It was Rosemary,' she said.

'Who?'

'Rosemary,' she repeated, slightly impatiently. As if he should have known. 'The doctor who gave you your tetanus shot.' In the midst of this new worry, the old, ever-present one didn't pass up the opportunity to leap out of hiding for a quick attack.

234

He waited with a deep sense of foreboding for her to go on. He already knew what she was going to say.

Her face crumpled even as he watched. As he moved forward involuntarily to hold her, she said, 'Sem's had a stroke.'

IV

Sixteen

He's not dead, she said to herself. I've got to keep remembering, he's not dead.

She was sitting in an aircraft, flying home. It was the middle of the night, and the flight was full to capacity. Parents were trying to settle small tired children, and there were babies crying.

She tried very hard not to think of Sem's dear face, pale against a starched white hospital pillow.

He's not dead!

The hours since Rosemary's call had been a nightmare. Rafe had phoned a dozen different places, trying to get her a seat on a flight as soon as possible. 'Tomorrow evening,' they kept telling him, or, 'Nothing till the day after tomorrow,' and this time she thought that what had sounded like a flow of furiously angry Greek probably was just that.

Finally he called a friend who'd been able to help. Rafe turned triumphantly from the phone.

'Tonight,' he said, 'but we'll have to hurry. One seat, charter flight to Gatwick, leaving at half past eleven.'

'How did your friend manage that, when everyone else said the flights were full?' She found that concentrating on the details moved the reason for all the frantic activity slightly into the background, so that it became less heartbreaking.

'Apparently it's a last resort they have, in emergencies. If people have booked a seat for a small child, they offer them a reduction in their fare to have the kid on their lap, so releasing a seat.'

'Oh.'

He was looking at her. 'I'm sorry I couldn't get two seats.'

She was surprised. She hadn't thought of him coming with her. 'Oh! It's all right. I'll be okay.'

After all, he's not dead.

They'd driven so fast to get to the airport. No music this time. Not even much conversation. But now and then he reached out for her hand, and his warm touch was welcome; for some unaccountable reason she was freezing cold. Around Heraklion the traffic became thick and slow-moving, despite the late hour, and she sat in desperate anxiety, seeing herself missing the flight, unable to wangle her way on to another . . . Rafe must have felt it, too. He drove the length of one main thoroughfare with two wheels on the central reservation, blasting the horn and creating a highly illegal extra lane. And she loved him for it.

The check-in desk for the flight had closed; she had a moment's panic, but he sorted it out for her. She had become incapable of looking after herself, and he had to get her passport and ticket out of her bag.

'You have to go through now,' he said gently, turning from the check-in desk with her boarding pass in his hand. 'They'll be calling the flight in a minute.'

Silently she put her arms round him, pressing herself to him, hiding her face against his chest. She couldn't bear to let him go. The prospect of finding enough courage to go on alone was hopelessly daunting. She felt him hug her, and his lips touched her hair. He let her stay like that, quite still, for some moments, as if he understood her need and was allowing her to draw some of his strength into herself.

Then he pushed her away.

'Give him my love,' he said.

She straightened up. The courage seemed to have come to the fore after all. 'I will.'

'Call me?' he said. She nodded. Then she went through passport control into the crowded departure lounge.

Two hours to go. They'd taken off a bit late, just after midnight. They'd be landing around four in the morning. What an awful time. And, oh God, it wouldn't really be four o'clock, it'd be two, because Greece was two hours ahead of England. For some reason the thought appalled her, as if having to live through another two hours of this dreadful night would be more than she could bear.

I'll get a taxi, she thought. Home, or straight to the hospital? Home. Rosemary said he was stable, whatever that means. Not in any immediate danger, I suppose, so perhaps the staff in the hospital wouldn't let me go in to see him in the middle of the night. I'll phone, though, as soon as I get in.

A meal was served, but she didn't touch it, instead drinking hot, sweet coffee. Just like when I flew out, she remembered. And that thought hurt, because now her state of anxiety was for such a dreadfully different reason. Her head ached; she found she was straining forward, urging the aircraft on to greater speed. She made herself sit back and close her eyes.

It took her a long time to organize a taxi. And then the drive to Wellstone seemed interminable, so that, opening the door into a cold, unwelcoming house, she felt she had been travelling for days. It didn't feel like coming home; the house was dead.

She went through into the living-room, switching on lights as she went. The clock on the wall said it was nearly a quarter to five. I'll have to wind it, she thought. She stood on the little footstool beneath it and reached up to open the glass and turn the key.

What am I *doing*?

She jumped down and reached for the telephone. What's the number? God, which hospital is it?

She remembered Rosemary's voice, heard again the calm, clear words. She got out the directory and found the number, then asked to be put through to the ward.

A quiet voice said, 'Night Sister. Can I help you?'

She explained who she was, that her father Spencer Gurney had been admitted with a stroke.

There was a slight pause. Then the sister said, 'I think you'd better come straight here, Miss Gurney.'

The Land-Rover was reluctant to start; the pre-dawn air was cold and damp. She raced through the lanes, her nerves taut, her reactions speeding up to meet her extreme need. The town was still asleep, but the lights of the hospital shone out to meet her, as if searching for her to hurry her on inside.

She couldn't find the ward. It was nightmare, every corridor looked the same, she could find no one to ask. A tired-looking man in a white coat demanded crossly what she thought she was doing there; when she explained he turned into a friend, walking with her to show her where to go.

It was a small ward, four beds surrounded by equipment, lights incongruously bright when surely everyone should still have been asleep. A woman in a navy uniform got up from a desk.

'Miss Gurney?' she asked softly.

Nell nodded. Her mouth was quite dry. The sister took hold of her hand.

'I'm sorry to have to tell you your father had another stroke, a couple of hours ago. A more serious one, I'm afraid.'

Nell felt a dreadful fear begin deep inside.

'Is it – is he going to be all right?'

The sister looked at her. She hesitated for a second, then said, 'No dear. We think it's only a matter of time now.'

Nell felt her eyes smart. No. Don't cry. She blinked hard. 'Can I see him?'

'Yes. I think he knew you'd come. He's been looking out for you.'

She led Nell along the ward, still holding her hand. She stopped by the further bed.

Sem was lying quite still, as if he were fast asleep. His face was pale, but otherwise he looked much like himself. His hands were loosely clasped on top of the sheet.

No, she thought. It's not true. They don't know what spirit he has, how healthy he's always been. He's going to be all right.

She went closer, taking his hands in hers. They felt deathly cold, and automatically she began to rub them.

She whispered, 'Sem?'

He opened his eyes and saw her.

There was something wrong; his eyes were smiling, just as they always did. Full of love. But his mouth wasn't right. It was sort of lopsided.

She began to realize that it might be true after all.

Don't start to cry. Don't upset him.

She prayed to any power that might come to her aid for the courage to go on smiling.

'My dearest girl,' he said, his voice a mere breath that she strained to hear. 'Knew.'

'Don't talk, it's okay. I understand.'

He smiled his strange smile again. 'Always do. Bless.'

She didn't want to look at him. He didn't look like her beloved Sem. She put her head down on his hands, stroking her cheek against his dry old skin.

'Nell?' One hand was moving. She thought perhaps he wanted her to look up.

She met his eyes. In their loving depths, Sem was still Sem. 'Yes?'

'Holiday?'

Holiday. It seemed something she'd experienced in another lifetime. Why on earth does he . . . Then she realized what it was he wanted to know.

'It *was* all right, Sem. Just as you said it would be. And Rafe sent you his love.'

He started to smile his different smile again, and she dropped her head back down so that she should not see it. She kissed the backs of his hands. He smelt slightly antiseptic. Not Sem's smell.

He whispered, 'Love my girl.'

And in the way that she had been replying all her life she answered, 'Love my Sem.'

An incalculable time later, she felt a hand on her shoulder. A quiet voice said, 'Come on, Nell.'

She turned. It was Rosemary.

'Oh, hello. I'll be with you in a minute, Rosemary. I want to be with Sem now.'

But the hand didn't go away.

'Time to leave him, Nell, I'm afraid.'

And, looking at him, his face in death once more peaceful and entirely his own, she realized that it was.

Cups of tea. Sweet. Rich tea biscuits. And paper hankies for the tears that didn't want to stop. Rosemary by her side, talking to her, the same words over and over finally penetrating.

'It's kinder, this way. The first stroke wasn't too bad, but this second one . . . Nell, he would have been an invalid. An old man in a chair with a blanket on his knees. Think how he'd have felt, dear old Sem, if he couldn't go out, couldn't go walking, see his friends, go for a pint. And what about you! Think how it would have upset him so, being a burden on you.'

She's quite right, Nell thought. And it's nice of her to say all this.

But just now I wish she wouldn't.

Later, it'll be a comfort. But now it isn't.

He's dead. And I'm going to miss him so very much.

Rosemary drove her to her own home. She said, you shouldn't be on your own. You should have someone with you.

But Nell thought, I *want* to be on my own. I want to go home and capture what's left of Sem there, in the cottage. Our cottage. I don't want to sit here in Rosemary's rather clinical living-room, having to remember to be polite.

Rosemary was on the phone. When she came back Nell said, the normality of her voice surprising her, 'Could you take me home, please, Rosemary?'

244

'Oh!' Rosemary looked startled. 'No, Nell, I think you should stay here. For lunch, at least. I bet you haven't eaten for ages.'

'I'm not hungry.'

Then she seemed to hear Sem's courteous voice. He was always so considerate of others, so graceful in his acceptance of the smallest service performed for him. And here she was, his daughter, being brusque, to say the least, to someone offering her kindness.

'Sorry,' she said. 'I didn't mean to sound rude. Yes, I will have some lunch, please. Just a little.'

Home. I want to go home.

She opened her eyes.

Oh, God, where *am* I? I want to go *home!*

She was lying on Rosemary's little sofa, and it was dark outside. She sat up violently, her head swimming.

Rosemary sat in a chair opposite, reading a book. Nell said, 'What's the time?'

Rosemary looked up, getting to her feet and coming to perch beside her on the sofa. She smoothed Nell's forehead with a cool hand. She said, 'It's all right. You've had a long sleep. It's the shock. Don't worry, it'll do you good.'

'But Sem – there must be things to do –' She was struggling to get up.

'No, nothing.' Rosemary smiled at her. 'I've seen to what was necessary. GP's job!'

Nell tried to smile back. But it was awful, waking up and remembering.

'Could I go home now?' She wanted more than ever to be back in the cottage, warm and secure in front of the fire. She didn't understand why, but if there was any place she could tolerate being, it was there.

Rosemary said something about staying the night.

'No,' she said firmly. 'It's very kind of you, but no. If it's an inconvenience to drive me, I'll phone for a taxi.'

Rosemary looked slightly hurt. 'Of course it isn't. I'll get the car keys.'

They drove to the cottage in silence. Nell was trying to recall whether there was any dry firewood inside.

Rosemary said would she be okay, and she said, yes, yes, yes.

She watched as the car turned round and drove away.

It was still and cold, a beautiful starlit night. Nell felt a sense of peace come upon her, as if Sem had lifted his gentle old hand and smoothed her hair from her face. The grief was there, quite undiminished, but it was easier to bear here.

She walked round to the back door and let herself in.

Heat. Fires.

That's what we need.

She re-lit the Aga, then went through into the living-room. A fire was laid in the grate, just as it always was. She took the matches from their place on the shelf and put flame to the spills of paper amongst the kindling. In no time, the fire took hold.

Good old Sem. You always did know how to lay a good fire.

She sat for a long time staring into the flames.

The clock struck the hour.

Which hour?

She looked up. Midnight.

I must have been dozing. The fire needs some more wood.

I'm glad I came home. You're still here, darling Sem. This is your place, your family's place. Perhaps a bit of all of you is still here.

Thank you for staying by me.

The fire was well-banked; it would last several hours. She pulled cushions from the sofa and fetched blankets from the chest, making herself a shake-down bed by the hearth.

She lay down.

I'm a primitive, she thought drowsily. I've just lost someone I've loved all my life, and the best comfort is to be here, where he used to be. By the eternal reassurance of a kindly fire.

She closed her eyes. Good night, Sem.

Arms were round her; someone had tended the fire, and its bright flames right in front of her had disturbed her. There was a feeling of love in the room.

She turned, and saw him.

Reached out to touch his marked face, because she was sure he must be a dream.

But he was warm. Solid and warm, full of strength for her to draw on.

Questions flew to her lips. But she seemed to hear someone say, don't ask. Just accept.

Gently he laid her down again, turning her so that she faced the fire. He pulled the blankets up over them both and she snuggled against him, her back protected by the curve of his body.

It was just like having a guardian angel.

He was on the deck of a ship, standing off a coastline he didn't recognize. A stiff breeze blowing on-shore was making the ship run fast before it. Danger crackled in the air; turning his head around so as to see with his one good eye, he saw with horror that a fleet of other vessels in tight formation hemmed his ship in. Incredibly, she was tied to the one on her port bow – he could actually see the cables lashing them together, slackening then pulling taut with a sickening snap as the two ships took each wave.

With terrifying speed the shore loomed down on them. A massive sea wall, a defence tower bristling with armed men. He wanted to run, to find a safe place to shelter from the inevitable catastrophe when they ran against those adamantine walls. Where? On deck, so he could jump when they foundered? Or under cover, somewhere he wouldn't be struck and killed by falling masts and rigging?

Men were shouting, drawing swords. Elbowing him out of the way, running in obedience to some plan whose logic he didn't understand. Standards flew, brilliant in the sunshine. From below came the shrill whinnies of nervous horses.

The ships ran up either side of the tower. The enormous jolt of impact threw him to the deck, stunning him.

His head stopped reeling. The ships' masters had known what they were doing, after all; they had berthed, and now a ramp led down from the lower deck to a long paved quay. Already men swarmed all along it, pushing, pushing for the walls.

Knights were hurrying ashore, leading their mounts, and he was of their number, intoxicated by their contagious excitement. The great war horses jostled against each other, their feet uncertain upon the sloping ramps. On the solid stone of the quay they were suddenly confident, eager to be in the fray, wheeling and stamping as the knights settled in the high saddles. As one, they moved towards an archway, the opening to a tunnel that ran through the wall. Brilliance gave way to a dank darkness, and he felt fear come down on him like a suffocating weight as men and horses heaved blindly together in the ever-narrower space.

Then they were through.

And in front of him a wide view of buildings, graceful and beautiful in the golden light. A great metropolis, lying like a topaz jewel bathed by the sapphire of the sea.

With roars of triumph, the knights put their horses to the gallop and fell upon the town.

The advance was riotous, uncontrolled, a great press of violent men pushing into a city that seemed defenceless against them. Scenes of horror rolled in slow-motion before his eyes. An elderly man stabbed to death by one thrust of a sword, surprise the final expression in his eyes. Two youngsters, their purloined helmets and shields far too big and heavy for their strength, mangled to bloody meat in the dust, ridden down by a quartet of laughing horsemen. Women overpowered by groups of attackers, held down, clothing ripped away, beaten and raped before the horror-rounded eyes of their little children. A grey-haired priest, stripped of his robes but not of his dignity, murmuring prayers until the last merciful moment of decapitation that ended his torments. Knights riding their horses into churches, urinating over altars heavy with sacred ornaments, stabbing with their swords at precious icons and hangings.

Blood, molten and sour-sweet smelling, running down the streets.

A frenzy of looting, everywhere men forcing anything they could find into sacks, saddle bags, into folds in their garments. He watched his own hands prise a huge ruby from its setting in a gold church ornament too unwieldy for him to carry. Watched himself ladle a mountain of coins inside the breast of his surcoat so that they clinked against the chain mail he wore beneath. Watched himself twist a rich gold diamond-encrusted collar from a woman so newly dead that the gaping wound between her breasts still dribbled red. Jewels, treasures, objects of such beauty that their worth was incalculable. What couldn't be carried away was despoiled beyond recognition.

His sword arm ached with cramp. He looked down, and both blade and hand were stiff with dried blood. He flexed the wrist, and a sharp pain ran up his arm.

Too much work. By my hand today, too many dead.

It pains me.

It prickles with the onset of numbness.

I have to move it, massage the life back into it . . .

He opened his eyes. He was lying by the fire, holding Nell; his arm beneath her neck was tingling with pins-and-needles.

He drew himself free, moving away from her slightly. He could feel sweat running down his body. His heart was beating

249

so hard that it hurt. As if he were in the aftermath to some great, adrenalin-surging excitement.

Slowly his pulse slowed down. And the terrible pictures faded.

He felt a huge relief that the dream visited on him hadn't involved Alienor. Nell. Confused, he didn't know which he meant.

This is Nell, lying asleep in front of me. Bereaved. That kind, gentle old man, her father, is dead. Soon she'll wake up, and he won't be here. And I wish I could help her carry her grief.

He rested his head on his hands, watching her. The fire still threw out some warmth, and he began to feel sleep returning. Drowsy, he saw Nell turn towards him, smiling at him in a way that made his heart start to pound again. He reached out his hand to touch her revealed white breasts falling soft against the rough blanket. Her hair tangled loose on the beaten earth floor, long, and so fair, and on her head a coronet of flowers that smelled like cloves . . .

He threw himself away from her, rolling over, scrabbling up on to hands and knees.

Nell, undisturbed, slept on, her back to him, her face towards the fire.

'Oh, Jesus,' he muttered. He clambered up on to the sofa, burying his face in his hands.

It's not safe for me to be here with her. God, if it happened again, after the joy we shared together in Crete. And *now*, with her father dead barely a day.

In despair, he thought, is there no way to fight the darkness?

An old, wise voice was speaking to him from his far memory. 'Accept,' she said. 'Keep your faith in Our Lord's protection, so that the powers of the dark may not overcome you.'

So long ago, she'd said that. Putting a gold cross into the

hand of a scared little boy who took comfort in her presence more than in her words or her beliefs.

But still . . .

He reached inside his shirt, unfastening the chain's catch. Then he leaned down over Nell and, gently so that he didn't disturb her, put his cross around her neck.

Then he went out into the kitchen, closing the door behind him.

The stove was warm, and the kettle on top wouldn't take long to boil. He put instant coffee in a cup. A lot of it. He looked at his watch: half past five. He thought, when I've drunk the coffee I'd better go for a walk.

Cruel woman, Alienor. She couldn't let us stay in our paradise. She had to find a way to bring me back here, where her power is strongest. To get her sharp claws into me again. But like this! Poor Sem. Poor Nell.

And she couldn't even leave us in peace for this night.

He finished the coffee. It had made him feel alert, but he was cold. He searched among the coats on the back of the door for something suitable, finding an old tweed coat that must have been Sem's. Then he went out into the thin light of the new day.

It's cold, Nell thought, trying to curl into her own warmth. I can't sleep if I'm cold. More blankets in the chest. 'I should have had the sense to look,' he'd said. But you don't want to get up in case you get even colder. She smiled, remembering him.

Rafe! She shot up. He'd been here! Where was he? Had she dreamt it? No, oh no, and Sem . . .

She was caught up somehow in the blanket. A button, was it? She looked down.

Rafe's gold cross.

'Rafe!' she cried.

'Here. It's okay.' He came through from the kitchen, kneel-

251

ing down beside her on the blankets. She held on to him, waiting for the turmoil of her thoughts to settle.

'I've made some tea,' he said. 'I'll get you some.'

'In a minute.' She clutched him, her fingers tightening on his sweater. 'Don't go yet.'

Once again, she drew strength from him. She began to feel a little better.

But she realized she was dreading going into the kitchen. Sem had always been there in the mornings, unless she got up especially early. Now he wasn't going to be there ever again. The kitchen wouldn't be the same, without the mild irritation of his pottering.

Rafe didn't speak. He just went on holding her, and after a while she disentangled herself. He got up to fetch the tea.

'How did you get in?' she asked later, when they'd prepared a scratch breakfast and had returned to sit in front of the renewed fire. He was sitting in Sem's old leather chair. She was glad; the rawness of Sem's absence was easier to bear with someone occupying his accustomed place.

'You left the door open.'

'Oh, dear. Did I?'

'Not wide open. Just not locked.'

'Oh. And how did you get *here*?'

'I bullied myself a place on a scheduled flight. To Athens, then on to London.'

'I'm so glad you did.' She couldn't express how much it had helped this first lonely night, having him come to her. She smiled at him, and he smiled back. She thought, it doesn't matter. He already knows.

'Was it another stroke?' he asked.

She'd been thinking about it – could think of little else – and didn't mind him asking. 'Yes. Early yesterday.'

'The hospital would only tell me he had died. They didn't want to give me any details. Were you in time?'

'Yes. The sister said he was waiting for me.'

'Come here,' he said, and she went to sit on his lap. 'This isn't the sort of conversation you should be having with half a room separating you from loving arms. Poor old Sem.'

'I don't understand!' she cried, tears and an unaccepting anger breaking out of her simultaneously. 'Rosemary said a motorist found him, slumped against the gate that leads to the footpath. The one through the barley field. And the sister said that immediately after the second stroke he said quite clearly, "Tell them I tried".'

He was frowning, his lips moving. She said, 'What did you say?'

He shook his head. 'Nothing.' After a moment he said very sadly, 'Nell, I can't stay with you. In this house. I don't think it's safe.'

She felt totally shattered. 'Why? Oh, God, Rafe, why can't you? – ' She stopped abruptly. Never admit your need.

But his arms around her were warm, and his caressing hand on her was very tender. 'Think, darling.' He had never called her that before. 'Think what might happen.'

And she did. Remembered what had happened before, in this very room. Saw again that dream on the mountainside, where the man who was Rafe but yet wasn't him had used that poor girl.

Is it *that* he's afraid of – that he'll change again into the same man, and that he and I will once more be forced to reenact the roles of that carnal pair?

Pictures flashed through her mind.

Yes. It is.

She said, 'All right. I don't understand, but I know why you won't stay.'

'I thought you would.'

She leaned her cheek against his chest. She thought, such a mixture of emotions. Equal portions of joy because we're so close, so completely in sympathy, and sorrow because he can't stay. She said, 'Don't go far, will you?'

'No. I won't.' She felt him kiss her hair. 'I won't leave you to endure this time alone. You're much too close to my heart for me to do that.'

Like the first whistle of birdsong after the devastation of storm, his words sounded in her head.

Close to my heart.

She found she couldn't reply. After some time he gave her a little shake and dislodged her from his lap.

He stayed with her until late evening, leaving just before she went to bed. Exhausted as she was, it was a struggle to keep awake long enough to finish her bedtime drink. And in the morning, only a little while after she'd got up, he was back.

The pattern continued. He didn't always manage morning till night, but for a few hours of every day he'd be there, not saying much, not even doing all that much. He was just someone to say to her, come on, we'll go for a walk, we need to get out of the house for a while. And, eat this, you've got to keep your strength up. Sem would feel awful if you fell ill on his account.

Someone to hold her when the awfulness overwhelmed her and the tears wouldn't stop.

It was he who drafted the wording of the announcement in the papers, when she was overcome with distress at the idea of telling Sem's affectionate friends that he was dead. It was he who drove her over to see the vicar, grieving almost as deeply as Nell at the loss of his old friend, and he whose strong warm hand holding hers permitted her to say what she had to say without the embarrassment of breaking down. And when she stood holding the sheaf of sad, commiserating letters that so soon began to arrive, desperately wondering what to do about them, it was he who said, 'Don't worry now. They won't expect an answer yet. They just want you to know they're sharing it with you.'

The funeral was on a Wednesday. Sunshine on the daffodils

and, incongruous on the bright day, black clothing that strangely was the very thing she felt like wearing.

The undertaker's big solemn cars, driving slowly. The coffin, surrounded in flowers like a bridal bower. Arriving at the church, where she had gone with Sem at least once every year, for the carols, and where Sem had gone a great deal more frequently. 'I like Ted's sermons,' he used to say. 'And I love the words of the prayers.' A moment of anguish standing in the doorway – all those people! I *can't* – and then Rafe appearing at her side, his hand under her elbow absorbing her trembling.

Rafe. All the way through, Rafe.

And when the time came for her to throw earth on the coffin, to initiate the abandoning of Sem down there in the ground for ever beyond her reach, Rafe's hand alongside hers so that they did it together.

They sat either side of the fire. A jug of mulled wine stood on the hearth, half of it already consumed in a long draught that they had dedicated to Sem.

He studied her: she'd changed out of the black jacket and skirt that made her so distant and formal. In jeans and an old sweater, she looked like Nell again.

He reached forward to top up her tankard.

'I'm so glad it's over,' she said. 'So many people. I had no idea.'

'They all wanted to be here.' He'd wondered how they were all going to be fed and watered; the caterers organizing the reception in the upstairs room at the pub had been told, about twenty. And he'd counted seventy-three people. He reckoned they must have had half a sausage roll apiece. But the advantage of holding the thing in a pub meant that at least the drink hadn't run out.

'I didn't know most of them.' He looked up at the sound of her voice. She was frowning. 'Did it matter?'

'Not in the least. They all knew you.'

255

'Yes.' She smiled slightly. 'They all seemed determined to remember embarrassing things like me riding my tricycle in the quad, and picking crocuses where I shouldn't.'

Silence fell between them. She was gazing into the fire; the evening was really too warm to warrant it, but he'd lit it anyway. It was comforting.

He thought, I don't want to leave her. He got up and went to sit on the floor at her feet, leaning back against her. Her hand stroked his hair, her fingers running down his temple to find the scar on his cheek.

She said, 'I couldn't have got through without you. You know that, don't you?'

'Yes, you could.'

She laughed softly. 'You're entitled to your opinion. Even if you *are* wrong.'

He turned, kneeling up to rest his elbows on her thighs.

She leaned forward to kiss him. 'I wish you could stay.'

'So do I.' He hesitated. 'I – that's the next thing. Isn't it?'

Her eyes stared back into his. Slowly she nodded. 'Yes. But I have absolutely no idea how.'

He didn't answer. He'd found time for a lot of thinking. There was, he reflected, nothing like sleepless nights of wishing you were somewhere else for making your mind work efficiently.

'Have you? Any idea?' She was watching him, her face alert as if she knew his thoughts.

Not yet, darling. I'm not going to tell you yet.

'No.' He got up in preparation for departure. 'You finish the wine, it'll do you good. And I've got to drive to London.'

She came with him to the door. He put his arms round her, beginning to kiss her, and for the first time in days felt a response in her that wasn't just the need of a grieving person for someone to hold on to.

A stab of light flashed through his vision. A woman in scarlet clung to him, pressing her breasts to his chest, grinding her hips against his groin, small hand moving, searching, down

256

across his belly. Her soft, moist lips turned outwards like some fleshy sea-creature sucking in vital sustenance.

Heartsick, he gently pushed Nell away.

He stared down into her eyes, willing her to understand. 'I'm sorry,' he said. 'I have to go.'

As he hurried away round the side of the house he heard her close and bolt the door.

Seventeen

In the morning he tried to call Stephen. His office said he was taking a few days' holiday, but there was no reply from his home number other than his recorded voice on the answering machine. Rafe tried again, several times, finally giving up and leaving a message. He thought, bet it's the first time anyone's said anything like *that* on your machine. He wondered if he'd been too dramatic. No. It'll intrigue him. Make him contact me all the sooner.

He faced chaos at work, the result of having put Nell's need before everything else since he'd returned from Crete. But he was glad to have so much to do; it was a distraction.

He hated being away from her. He couldn't get rid of the nasty feeling that he had run out on her. She'd been so brave, keeping her grief in check. Except for the morning of the funeral, when she'd lain in his arms and cried so desperately that she could hardly get her breath. Then, looking at her red, puffy eyes in the mirror, she'd started to cry all over again because she couldn't stand the thought of people seeing her like that. Rafe, saying the first thing that came into his head and by happy chance lighting on the right thing, told her gently, 'There aren't many men like Sem. He's worth a few tears. And you won't be the only person with red eyes.'

He worried about her constantly.

But I couldn't have stayed, he told himself. It's not safe. Even more so now than before, it's not safe.

He had fought accepting it, but the suspicion had strengthened until it was now almost a certainty.

Alienor's power was growing.

And he was increasingly apprehensive about going back to the cottage.

He phoned Nell in the middle of the afternoon.

'How are you?'

'Oh, not too bad.'

She sounds okay, he thought. Well, if not exactly okay, then at least not like someone who's been crying her eyes out all day. 'What are you doing?'

'Working. Spring digging and planting,' she said brusquely. 'This is actually quite a good time of year to lose someone, if you're a gardener, because you're up to your eyes in rebirth and greenness. It seems to help a bit.'

He wondered if she were still trying to convince herself. 'I'm glad you're finding it a consolation,' he said. He thought rapidly, wanting to say something to support her brave attempts to sound cheerful. 'Since you've got to do it anyway, it's convenient that it's also doing you good.'

'A virtue out of necessity.'

'Yes. But don't work too hard, will you?' He was struck with the thought that there would be no Sem to call her in to tea.

'No. Rosemary's coming round later. We're going up to the pub for a drink and something to eat.'

'Oh, good.'

'Then I'm going to have an early night.'

He suspected she was giving him a way out. As if she knew already that he was unwilling to come down to see her.

'Okay. Shall I call you tomorrow, then?'

'Yes. Oh – I'm seeing the solicitor in the afternoon. I'll phone you in the evening.'

Solicitor? He was about to ask why, then cursed himself for not realizing. I can't get used to it he thought. I keep forgetting that he's gone.

'Fine,' he said, his voice echoing in his head, the false cheerfulness jarring. 'Have a nice time tonight.'

'You too, whatever you're doing. 'Bye.'

He sat for a long time staring into space.

He wondered if Stephen had played back his message yet.

When he returned home the following evening his telephone was ringing.

'Hello?'

'Oh, Rafe! I've been phoning you for *ages*. Can you come down, straight away?' She sounded overwrought.

'I don't know.' Yes, I can, he thought. But I'm not sure it's a good idea. 'What is it?'

'I can't talk about it over the phone!' she snapped. 'I wouldn't ask you if it wasn't necessary, would I?'

He felt irritated by her crossness. Then, remembering where she'd been that afternoon, he realized that probably the anger was covering up another, more tender emotion not far below the surface.

'No, you wouldn't,' he said calmly. 'Okay. I'll leave as soon as I've changed. I'll be with you in about an hour and a half.'

She said after a moment, 'Thanks. Sorry.'

'All right. See you later.'

The traffic was thicker than usual. Friday, he thought. Wouldn't it just be Friday, when I'm in a hurry? She was peering anxiously out of the living-room window when he pulled up, as if she doubted he'd ever arrive.

As he walked round the house to the back door, she came dashing out to meet him.

'Nell, what is it?'

She didn't answer, just threw herself against him and buried her face in his chest. Then, straightening up, she said, 'I can't tell you. You'll have to read it yourself. All the papers are inside, on top of the desk. I'm going up to the pub – come and find me when you've finished.'

She pushed past him, and he heard her footsteps running away up the road towards the village.

He felt apprehensive. He had no idea what to expect. The back door was open, and he went through into the kitchen. She had left a pot of coffee on top of the stove and sandwiches for him on a plate. He smiled slightly, taking his supper through to the living-room.

On the desk was a pile of papers.

The top one was typewritten, with a solicitor's letterhead. It seemed to be about Sem's Will. Underneath were more typewritten pages, then several sheets of vellum notepaper covered with neat handwriting in black ink, clipped to an inch-thick file of papers and documents.

Nell had put a brief note on top of the pile:

'This is what I collected from the solicitor. Read everything, nothing's secret from you. It can't be – it concerns you as much as it does me.'

She had written underneath in big letters, READ ME.

So he did.

The Will was straightforward. Everything to Nell, as Sem's only child. The cottage, an unexciting but solid portfolio of investments, and a surprisingly large sum from her Grand-father Gurney. He felt an interloper, reading it; he tried to banish the temptation to speculate on what this meant for Nell. For her future. He glanced again at her note, held tightly in his hand. READ ME. It's okay, I'm *meant* to be doing this.

Added to the last page of the Will was a postscript, type-written and signed by the solicitor, to the effect that Spencer Algernon Gurney had that day left in his keeping the attached letter, addressed to his daughter Elinor Rose Gurney and to be given to her in the event of the death of Spencer Gurney.

The date on the postscript was three days before Sem died.

Rafe picked up the letter. He walked over to sit in Sem's old chair.

For several moments he could read no further than the opening words. My dearest Nell. A private letter, from a loving father to his daughter. Again and far more strongly, he felt like an interloper.

READ ME.

He made himself go on.

261

'My dearest Nell,

'I write this letter to you purely as a precautionary measure. I am quite sure that it will prove unnecessary, and that I shall be removing it from the safety of Arthur's custodianship in the very near future. However, I cannot be absolutely certain of the outcome of my proposed actions, and, as you well know, I am cautious by nature!

'My dear, I have thought long and hard about you and your Rafe, and about the troubles you have encountered through no fault of your own. You have had the air of one bearing a heavy burden, my Nell, and often seemed about to confide in me. Often, indeed, I almost invited your confidences. But we never quite made it, did we? Perhaps, knowing one another so well, each of us felt in our hearts that we had no need of confidences, because the other already knew. Before you went to Crete, I hinted at what was on my mind. Now, when it is just possible that it's too late, I wish that I'd had the courage to do more than hint. You are far away from me and I cannot talk to you, so I must write my thoughts instead. And that, my love, is the reason for this communication.

'If I mention the name of Alienor of Gournai to you, I am certain you will know of whom I speak. For that is what tradition says she was called, she whose spirit has troubled our otherwise happy hamlet of Wellstone for centuries. Probably since the poor lass died. (I already hear you exclaim indignantly, "Poor lass, indeed!" But wait, Nell. Curb your impatience. As I always used to say whilst reading to you your favourite "Beauty and the Beast" and you clamoured to know why, when the Beast was so kind to her, Beauty didn't love him straight away, "wait until I've finished the story.")

'I know a great deal about Alienor de Gournai; I have studied exhaustively the tragedy of her short life and its traumatic legacy. Recorded history goes back a very long way in this part of the world; a researcher's dream, one might say except that in this case it has turned out rather to be his nightmare.

'The starting-point is the Gurney family. My family, yours too. You have only had me to grow up with, but I as a child was better-furnished, with both parents and grandparents, plus such a vast host of great-aunts and uncles as only the Victorian age could provide. And of the Gurneys who lived in the vicinity of Wellstone, many had a tale to tell, of a presence felt, of an unaccountable fear of the enclosed meadow. Only the smallest snippets of tales, but, nevertheless, quite enough clues to set a determined young ghost-hunter on his way.

'One of the first clues was in your own precious herb book; on thin, cracked paper tucked away between its pages, I found a recipe for a sleeping-draught so potent, I imagined from the list of its ingredients, that the patient would be fortunate to awaken at all. Who had put it there, I wondered? Which of my ancestors had so neatly written it down and so carefully hidden it away? And, in Heaven's name, why had it been required?

'Because of the dreams, Nell. In our family we all dream, and we always have done. The wise women of our family each in their turn found ways to overcome this frightening thing we bore, so as to allow us to live with it. Or perhaps I should say, to live with HER, for it is, as I am sure you know, Alienor de Gournai who invades our dreams. The name, Nell! It is a French name, the name of a Norman knight who came over to England with the Conqueror and settled in Wellstone, a place that suited his descendants happily enough for them to stay there. The Anglicized version of the name is Gurney. Alienor is our own distant ancestor.

'You will remember my aerial photograph showing the site of the old manor. It was the home of the de Gournais. Knowing as we do that the manor was deserted and derelict by 1400, we conclude that Alienor pre-dates that time. (Incidentally, our own house, built in its original form around 1350, was I think a dower-house, an annexe to the main manor house, constructed perhaps for some elderly relation. I imagine it became the family's main dwelling after some unfortunate *circumstances, whatever they may have been, occasioned them to quit the big house. Our cottage, even in its original form without the later sixteenth and eighteenth century extensions, is too big to have been a workman's cottage. Also, too well-built. And it is the wrong shape to have been a farmhouse. But I digress.)*

'Back to Alienor. I know her well, for she haunts my dreams too. Or, I should say, she used to, until quite suddenly, ten or twelve years ago, the dreams stopped. I believe she confused me with her father, as I conclude from my research she did other Gurney men before me. (Should you wish to pursue such details and follow my lines of reasoning, you will find all my papers in the file which you will be given with this letter. They are all yours, Nell, to do with as you think fit. And should you wish someone to guide you through them, go and see Ted. How such a conscientious clergyman managed to find time for my obsession, I don't know, but in addition to being a grand friend and a dashing yet reliable bridge partner, Ted has been an invaluable help in my delvings into our past.)

'Alienor, poor child, seemed at once to threaten me and to fear me; in my dreams she said, "Find my Richard! You sent him away, and I want him back! He's mine!" Then she would sob, and it was heartbreaking for me because she looked so like you. And once, in a dream so sad and so shocking in its uncaring brutality that I shall never forget it, I saw her lying pale and unloved in her bed, with a baby in her arms.'

A baby. Alienor had borne Richard a child. Rafe closed his eyes, rubbing at the left one, which had started aching again. He was having difficulty focusing it.

A child. Which one of those brutal matings impregnated her?

He made himself read on, his hand covering his left eye.

'Look at the papers, Nell, if you wish. Then see if you agree with me about Alienor de Gournai, judge if my conclusion

valid. What I believe happened is that she fell pregnant to this Richard of hers, that he seduced her and deserted her, never to return. Who was he, Alienor's Richard? Where did he go? And what manner of man was he? Alienor was the daughter of a nobleman, but that of course is no reason to assume her lover was not some handsome peasant boy who had taken her fancy. However, I doubt very much that he was; daughters of the nobility were rarely in situations where peasant boys could take their fancy. I think Alienor's lover was a knight like her father, someone who had accepted the hospitality of the de Gournais only to abuse it subsequently by his violation of the daughter of the house. And by his disappearance, his absolute denial of the responsibility he owed to the young girl he had seduced. As a knight, there were many places to which he could flee, distant places where there was no possibility that he would be found. Perhaps, even, he took oath as a Crusader, and made his escape far beyond the shores of England.

'What can the family have thought, when Alienor's condition became apparent? In dreams Alienor is always young, no more than a girl, and although she lived in an age when young motherhood was common, only married young motherhood was acceptable. But if we are correct in assuming that Alienor bore her child in her teens, it would have been possible for him to be passed off as her mother's youngest child. Her "Benjamin", a name often given to sons born at a time in a woman's life when further fecundity was unlikely. Thus Alienor's son would have been brought up a legitimate de Gournai, a full member of the family.

'Then, I believe, very soon after his birth Alienor died. For she cannot have lived to resolve her unhappiness, or else she would not haunt as she does. Not for her the blunting of pain and the forgetting of shame in a new love, in a marriage which if it could not bring joy then at least might have given contentment. No. Alienor died in the full flood of her despair, her Richard lost to her for good, his disappearance so effective that she was unable even to tell him that he had a child.

Perhaps, under the circumstances, she welcomed death. She had, it would seem, very little to live for. Imagine her unhappiness, Nell. And she was only a child. Is it not right that we should spare her some compassion?'

He makes a convincing case, Rafe thought, pausing again to rub his eye. And to wait while he reassembled his hatred of Alienor and drove out the unaccustomed sympathy for her which Sem's words had brought about.

He picked up the letter again.

'But let us not become carried away with pity for the dead. For Alienor is dead, and no amount of compassion will not alter that. My concern is for the living, for you, Nell, and for your Rafe. He is a good man, a man with whom to share your life. I want to help you, and so I intend to visit the enclosed meadow to confront Alienor's spirit. She will be there – she is always there. I do believe it quite possible that all she needs, all she has ever needed, is a kindly word, and an explanation that she has lost her way. A valediction perhaps, to see her safely over to the other side where she belongs. She is not so evil that she should be refused such a blessing. She was human once, and fallible, as are we all.

'I am old, Nell, and what might be foolhardiness in a younger man is to me a carefully-calculated risk. I feel compelled to do this, and I must say that I do not honestly believe the danger to be great. However, whatever the risk, to me it is worth taking, for it is possible that my action may relieve you and your descendants of a burden borne by my family for far too long.

'Wish me luck, my beloved, and always know that you were the one love of my life that was constant and true. Marriage and parenthood came to me late and unexpectedly; whilst marriage proved a disappointment, fatherhood was, in a long life of many minor joys, the greatest joy of all.

266

'Bless you, my darling Nell,
your adoring father,
Sem.'

Rafe sat quite still, holding the letter in a tight grip. After a few minutes he made himself relax and put it down.

Sem had known. God, why hadn't one of the three of them had the sense to bring it all out into the open?

He felt anger rising, mainly against Sem. Then as quickly it had gone. Just how, exactly, would Sem have broached the subject? 'We're a peculiar family, Rafe. We all dream about an ancestor of ours who was a violent nymphomaniac. And it's strange, but Nell looks just like her'.

He wanted to smile, except it wasn't funny. Because he'd remembered what Sem had had to say about him. Remembered too that Sem's noble wish to provide them all with a happy ending had resulted in his death.

He picked up Sem's file, turning the pages. Extracts from parish records. Photocopies of old deeds. Births, marriages, deaths, through hundreds of years of Gurneys, each entry annotated by a note of its source. What labour had gone into it. How Sem had worked.

And the very early history, the only part that really mattered. Vague. A sketchy family tree full of names and dates that had question marks beside them, where diligent Sem had wanted to make it quite clear where fact ended and speculation began.

But he's right, Rafe thought, he's absolutely right.

Without knowing why, he accepted totally that Sem had discovered the truth.

Nell is Alienor's direct descendant, down through the line of the child she bore Richard. That accounts for the incredible likeness.

He went on sitting in Sem's chair. As the impact of all that he had just read became gradually less fierce, he became aware of an uncomfortable feeling that the revelation was still gravely incomplete.

We know, he thought, why Nell is involved, why Alienor will not leave the Gurneys alone.

But what about me? How do I come into it?

And who the hell was Richard?

Nell sat by herself at the corner of the bar, fidgeting with an unopened pack of peanuts. She was on her second half of lager, but, having downed the first one so rapidly that it made her head swim, was trying to make it last until Rafe came.

How much longer? It's been over an hour. What's he doing? It wouldn't take this long to read the letter – he must be going through that file. Referring to the facts. He didn't know Sem like I did, so there's no way he could appreciate that if ever Sem says, read it and see if my conclusions are valid, you can bet your boots they are and there's no need to.

What's he thinking?

She almost regretted the impulse that had made her run out of the house. But then she felt an echo of the emotions that had torn at her as she read Sem's words. No, she thought. I was right to come away. I couldn't have sat there watching Rafe's face as he went through it all too. Once was more than enough.

She wished she could make herself think about something else.

She had her hand in her coat pocket, and realized she'd been holding the big envelope of photographs that had arrived the day before. Her Crete pictures. She'd deliberately brought them up to the pub with her. It had seemed – disrespectful, almost, sending off the reel to be developed when she was in the throes of coping with Sem's death. But she'd felt compelled to do it, although she hadn't been entirely sure why.

Until what she had read in Sem's letter had verified her suspicions and turned an innocuous holiday photo into the final proof of something she shrank from believing.

She sat stiff with tension, frowning fiercely across the empty bar. She kept repeating the same words in her head, over and over, as if by concentrating exclusively on them she could make them effective. Hurry, Rafe. Oh, God, hurry.

She heard a car draw up. The door of the bar opened, and Rafe came in. He looked at her from the doorway. His face was pale and unsmiling, his left eye almost closed. For an instant he looked like the man in the dream. And that split-second was enough to start up in her the beginnings of reaction, the fear and the repugnance scratching over her skin . . .

But then he smiled, and was Rafe again.

He came to stand beside her, wordlessly hugging her very tightly. The landlord was busy in the other bar; they were alone.

She didn't know what to say.

The landlord came through to ask Rafe what he'd have.

'Brandy, please. And one for Nell too.'

He'd forgotten she didn't like brandy. It wasn't the moment to remind him.

The landlord served them, an expression of commiseration on his face. He was fond of Sem, Nell thought. And Sem of him. One of the pleasures of living in a small village, Sem used to say, was that the pub landlord becomes a friend.

'Have those on me,' the landlord said. He poured himself a measure as well. 'To Sem, God bless him.'

They drank the toast. Then the landlord tactfully returned to the other bar.

'To Sem,' Rafe repeated. His head was bent and she couldn't see his face.

'What did you think of the letter?' she asked tentatively.

'The same as you, I imagine. Irritation with myself, for not realizing that he was bound to have known about Alienor. Admiration for his courage. Regret, because he under-estimated his adversary and it led him into something he should never had contemplated.' He sighed. 'And above all sadness, because he's gone.'

She swallowed a couple of times. ' "Tell them I tried",' she said. 'That's what he said, according to the Sister. He meant, tried to tackle Her.' Knowing Her name, she was still reluctant to use it. 'He must have gone out into the Meadow, and She . . .' No. It was too awful to think about. 'The exertion and the excitement must have proved too much for him. Mustn't they?'

'Yes.'

He stood leaning against the bar, the brandy glass in one hand. She waited for him to go on, but he seemed to have said all he had to say.

She knew she must tell him. But she was scared, for she didn't know what the result would be.

Only that probably it would be awful.

With the feeling that anything would be better than dragging it out any longer, she got her photographs out of her pocket. She coughed nervously, and said, 'Rafe, I want to show you something.'

He glanced at the envelope. 'Oh.'

He hardly seemed to be paying her any attention. Not surprising, she thought. This isn't exactly the time to go showing someone your holiday snaps.

'Please listen,' she said urgently, leaning towards him. 'This could all be moonshine, and I expect you'll think I'm stupid. But I don't care, I've got to show you.' Her voice sounded intense even in her own ears, and the effect on him was startling. He turned to her, and the sudden look of sharp concentration in his eyes made her pull back.

'Go on.'

Her hands trembled as she took out the prints. Fumbling through for the right one, she dropped half of them on the floor. Neither she nor Rafe made any move to pick them up.

'The village we went to, where you talked to the old man and I went for a walk,' she said, tripping over her words in her haste. 'You remember, I went up the hillside. And I know I didn't tell you, but I found a ruined building. With the remains of a chapel. And in it this effigy, lying on a sarcophagus –' *DAMN!* Where is the bloody thing? Here. Yes, this is it. The tumbled walls, that strange, unlikely figure . . .

She didn't want to look at it, and she pushed it at him. He took it between his fingers. '– I took a photo,' she hurried on, 'this one. There was writing on the sarcophagus, in Greek. I didn't know what it said, so I wrote it down, in case it didn't come out clearly enough in the picture. I've got it here, in my notebook – I'll show you . . .'

'No need.'

He didn't sound like Rafe. She stared up at him in alarm.

His face was ashen now, and he stood with his eyes closed, swaying slightly. As she watched, he put his hand to the left side of his face. He rubbed his fingers over his scar, then, leaning his elbows on the bar, dropped his head to rest his left eye in his palm.

He said, 'Richardos o monófthalmos.'

She didn't understand.

'Oh, no. You don't speak Greek, do you?' He turned his head briefly to look at her. His expression was detached, as if he couldn't remember who she was. 'Richard One-Eye. Your crusader here.'

He threw the print down in front of her on the bar.

Then he straightened up, silently staring at her.

It seemed to her that there in the dim light he was changing, his scar growing like a live thing, turning from the real man whom she needed and trusted to a man of nightmare whom she dreaded.

Richard. Alienor's lover. Richard, whose mortal remains she had stood over – sat on! – on his own mountainside. Whose presence there had sparked off that dreadful dream in which she had seen him in an English woodland. Treating Alienor as if she were nothing more than the dumb, unfeeling instrument of his pleasure.

So cruel to her.

So harsh and heartless. Poor Alienor.

In a flash she realized that some of Sem's compassion had rubbed off. Because of Sem's loving-kindness, pointing out to her and making her appreciate aspects she hadn't previously stopped to consider, Alienor had changed subtly. And Nell found she could no longer look on her as simply evil.

She could think of her by her name. Alienor.

And that man, that terrifying man whom Rafe so resembled, had taken Alienor, used her, and deserted her. Left her pregnant, broken her heart and brought about her death.

Unable to prevent herself, she shrank from him.

He started at her sudden movement. His eyes met hers, and she saw they were full of sadness. Rafe's eyes, for sadness was not an emotion that could ever have shown itself in the eyes of that other one.

And, for all that he bore Richard's wound, Rafe's face.

She put out her hand, but he backed away.

He tried to laugh. 'Richard,' he said. 'The other partner. Buried on a hillside in the Idha Mountains. So that's where he finished up.'

He was walking towards the door.

Oh, God, he's going!

She jumped up, scrabbling for her photographs, and ran after him. 'Rafe, no! Where are you going? Please, stay!'

He caught her by the wrists as she tried to grab hold of him. 'Now I really do think you're being stupid,' he said harshly. 'I can't stay. Can I? When your precious bloody ancestress out there is determined to turn me into her blasted crusader?' He looked away from her, his face twisted with disgust. 'If you knew the half of what I do about Richardos o monófthalmos – and you ought to, for God's sake, you of all people – you wouldn't even want me to stay.'

Abruptly he let go of her wrists, pushing her away so violently that she almost fell. The door banged behind him, and she heard his footsteps hurrying away.

For a moment she stood still, feeling the reverberations of shock thump against her.

Then something in her awoke.

No. Not this time. You ran out on me before, and I thought I'd lost you.

NOT THIS TIME!

Without stopping to think, she wrested the door open and leapt outside, flying down the stone steps and half-falling into the road. But he was already moving, the engine racing, the rear wheels spinning and squealing on the wet tarmac, his headlights flashing out and blinding her as she threw herself into his path.

And the street was narrow. No room, no time, for him to swerve.

Something hard hit her thigh, and she felt herself bounce on metal. Tyres screamed, and she fell on to the road.

She closed her eyes.

I tried to stop him, she thought abstractedly. I tried. Something drifted into her mind, some words said by someone else . . . Tell them I tried.

But now I want to give up. To rest my head in this nice cool puddle and just give up.

Then heavy, running footsteps pounding on the road. People coming out of the pub, anxious, avid voices asking, what's happened? Anybody hurt?

Rafe's arms around her.

So he hasn't gone after all. How funny, I thought I heard him accelerating away.

'It's okay, I'm all right,' she said in her normal voice. She tried to sit up, and he pulled her roughly to him, crushing her against his chest. 'You'll have to try a bit harder if you really want to get rid of me. I'm quite hardy.'

His face pressed to hers, and a sound coming from him. In her bemused state she couldn't tell if it was laughter or crying.

It didn't seem to matter much which.

She felt him pick her up. He carried her to the car, parked

in the middle of the road with its lights on full beam and its engine smoothly ticking over. Someone said, 'Here, I'll open the door for you. Is she hurt?'

'No, I'm not,' she said airily to the world in general. 'It was my fault, I slipped, right into his path.'

'That's the way to treat them,' some humorist added, 'knock 'em about a bit, show them who's boss!'

Somebody whispered something; she heard the end of it. '. . . just lost her father.'

'Sorry,' the humorist muttered.

'Good night, everybody,' she called. She almost said, thank you for having me, but somehow it didn't seem quite right.

Rafe was driving them away.

She asked, 'Where are you taking me?'

'Home,' he said briefly. He turned round in someone's gateway, then drove slowly back through the village. She could see people still standing outside the pub, glasses in their hands, silly mouths open.

'Home,' she echoed.

He glanced at her, smiling slightly. 'Home. Where I shall put you to bed with a hot-water bottle and a soothing drink.' Now he sounded as if he were laughing. He reached out and took her hand. 'It looks as if I'm staying, after all. For better or worse.'

'Better or worse. Richer or poorer. Sickness and health.' Her mumblings seemed to be outside her control. She felt as if she were slightly drunk. I'm rambling, she thought. The ramblings of a drunken woman. And why did the words roll out so easily? 'Oh!' She remembered. 'That's in the marriage ceremony, isn't it?'

'Exactly.'

Exactly what? She wondered. Her brain seemed to be malfunctioning, and she kept forgetting what was happening.

Never mind. Rafe's here, it'll be okay.

She closed her eyes. By the time they had covered the short distance back to the cottage, she was almost asleep. The car stopped, and he came to open the passenger door and help her out. With his supporting arm round her waist, together they made their stumbling way into the cottage.

Up in her bedroom it was warm, for the wide chimney-breast formed a part of the wall and the fire in the living-room below was still hot. He sat down on her bed, undressed her and pulled her nightshirt over her head.

'Stand up,' he said, steadying her as she did so, and he pulled the hem down to her knees. Then he turned back the duvet and she lay down. He covered her up, then went out of the room. She heard him go downstairs.

She was drowsy, her eyes amost closing. She gazed round the room and the familiar things were a comfort. Her chest of drawers, with the big old mirror that she and Sem had bought in a church bring-and-buy sale. Her collection of Wedgwood pieces. Her books. Her photographs. All still there. *They* hadn't changed, even if everything else had. Her thoughts started to take off, into a life of their own; she was falling asleep.

'Nell?'

He was back, pushing a lovely hot-water bottle into the bed beside her, his arm under her lifting her shoulders while his other hand held a mug to her lips.

'Too hot!' she protested.

He blew on it. 'Try again. I'm not letting you go to sleep till it's all gone.'

Obediently she sipped, taking larger mouthfuls as the drink cooled. When the mug was empty he allowed her to lie down again.

'Come on,' she said drowsily, moving over, 'let's go to sleep.'

Nothing happened. With a last effort she opened her eyes again.

He was just standing there, looking down at her. And he looked so defeated that she wanted to cry.

Slowly he shook his head. 'No,' he said, so softly she could hardly hear. 'Oh, no.'

Then he went out and closed the door behind him.

Eighteen

Some time during the long night he had come to the conclusion that if there was any hope at all, it lay in seeing Stephen. And in asking, begging, forcing him to help.

It was the final impetus I needed, he thought, that awful moment when I felt the dull thump of her hitting the bonnet and saw her fall in front of the car. When I was quite sure I'd killed her, and realized in the same instant how it'd be without her.

After that it was the logical conclusion, and only a matter of time before I arrived at it.

Instead of trying to phone Stephen again, he decided he'd go to his house. Phoning hadn't done any good. He stamped down the fear that Stephen was turning his back on them: no. He'd have called, if he received that appeal. Answering machines are all very well, but it's possible for tapes to snarl up. For messages never to get through.

Saturday morning, he thought. If there's any time he's going to be in, it's now. He looked at the clock on the living-room wall. Nearly seven. Good – early still. He won't go out before mid-morning. Will he? And I can be there by nine, easily.

He didn't welcome the idea of driving. Not this morning. For one thing, he was dog-tired. After leaving Nell in her bed he'd sat downstairs on the sofa for hours, drinking coffee and going through book after book from Sem's meticulously-organized shelves. The history section was set out logically in date order, and he'd easily found all he wanted. He'd noticed that there were no works covering the years from 1600. He felt a warm glow of affection for Sem, who seemed to have considered that the end of the Tudors was also the end of anything sufficiently ancient to bother about.

But the period he had to investigate was a long time before the Tudors.

Even if he'd felt sleepy when he started, he didn't by the time he was through. He could live with the suspicions – on a good day, he'd been able to convince himself it was all moonshine, as Nell would say. But now suspicion had been replaced by certainty, and that was no longer possible. When he'd finished he passed what remained of the small hours miserably, his fear of falling asleep so acute that his subconscious kept jerking him awake whenever he slipped into a doze.

His head aching with fatigue, he stood in the kitchen drinking tea. As the cold, lonely light of early morning took over from the secret night, he reflected that a lengthy drive through thick traffic would have been the last thing he wanted anyway.

Even without the other problem.

There was no sound from upstairs, but, not wanting Nell to think he'd left without checking to see if she was all right, he took her up a cup of tea. She was lying curled in her duvet, sound asleep. He wrote a quick note, bent down to kiss her lightly on her cheek, and left.

Then, driving slowly, his head held awkwardly and his body tense with the effort of concentrating, he returned to London.

Stephen answered the door in a colourful silk dressing-gown. An aroma of fresh coffee drifted out of the flat.

'I've been trying to phone you!' he said accusingly by way of greeting. 'I've been away all week, got back last night. Found that highly alarming message you left me. What on earth do you mean – what do I know about exorcisms?'

'May I come in?' Rafe didn't feel comfortable on the doorstep. He resisted the temptation to look over his shoulder.

'Sorry. Yes, you'd better.' Stephen stood aside. 'I'll get you some coffee.'

Rafe followed him through into the kitchen, then watched as he filled a large mug with coffee from a percolator. Laid biscuits on a plate, put milk in a jug. Rafe got the distinct impression he was winding up for something.

Eventually, having run out of things to do, Stephen turned to face him.

'Trouble with the eye?' he asked unsympathetically. 'You're rubbing at it. Scar's there to stay, too. Isn't it?'

Rafe nodded.

Stephen took two paces towards him, putting his face right up close.

'You're mad,' he said with quiet intensity. 'You're in right above your head. I *told* you, I've kept on telling you, leave it alone!' His voice grew louder and he banged his fist down on to a worktop for emphasis, making some expensive-looking glassware tinkle in its rack. 'You people, you think the spirit world's all darkened front rooms and blobs of ectoplasm. Little old ladies after fake consoling messages from their departed husbands. It bloody well isn't. It's *death* we're talking about, and malevolent spirits who won't accept it and fucking well refuse to lie down! *Think* about that, just stop and think what you're up against!'

Rafe had never heard him so angry. Stephen was one of the few men of his acquaintance who didn't often swear. Which of course made it far more effective when he did.

He said quietly, 'I know what I'm up against.'

Instantly Stephen spat back, 'You know *now*!'

There was an awkward silence; Stephen looked slightly abashed at having lost his cool. After a few moments he said, 'Go on, then. I suppose you'd better bring me up to date.'

Rafe leaned back against a tile-topped breakfast bar.

'We were in Crete, Nell and I,' he said. 'She wrote to me, after you'd seen her. Thank you, by the way, for that.'

Stephen grunted an acknowledgement.

'I called her and suggested she came out for a week or so, and she agreed. It was great – I can't tell you.' I'm not going to, he thought. 'But one day we went to a village up in the mountains, miles from anywhere. And she went wandering off by herself and found an old chapel, with the effigy of a crusader. His name was carved on it – I suppose it was a nickname, the name by which the local people knew him. Richard One-Eye. Alienor's Richard.'

Stephen stood with his mouth open. Then he shook his head.

'No. Why should it be Alienor's Richard? That's too big a conclusion to draw. Richard has always been a very common name. I don't see how you can be so sure.'

But, as if he couldn't sustain his scepticism, slowly his disbelieving eyes on Rafe's slid away.

'Perhaps.' It was going to be difficult, explaining in such a way as to remove all Stephen's doubt. 'But you forget, I know a lot about Alienor's Richard. From the exploits he's been involved in which have found their way into my dreams. And once I had the clue to his time and his place which that effigy gave me, it wasn't hard to make it all hang together.' Again he thought briefly of his long sleepless night with Sem's books. 'Richard *was* a crusader,' he said. 'In one of my dreams, I – he – was wearing a white surcoat decorated with a red cross on the breast. Carrying a lance, and mounted on a great white horse. And we went into battle, which I think was the battle of Arsuf. In the Third Crusade.'

'How can you pin it down so finely?' Stephen asked.

He's losing his incredulity, Rafe thought. Intellectual curiosity is beginning to get the upper hand. He smiled slightly. Just as I hoped it would.

'I was there,' he replied simply. 'And in the history books the description of the battle was exactly what I saw.'

'But you could have read about it, ages ago, and kept the picture in your subconscious. We all have deep memories that we're unaware of carrying about.'

'Yes. I'd already thought of that. It's possible, because I've always read a lot of history. But I've been in other places, too. That dream wasn't the only one.' He hesitated. 'There was time when we were attacking a city, and we were cut with

280

sword on . . .' He stopped. His mind was back-pedalling furiously. He didn't want to think about it, because he'd discovered that re-living the dream made his scarred cheek hurt as badly as it had done when he received the wound.

'Cut where?'

'Oh – ' He thought quickly. 'On the plain before the city. Acre, perhaps, or Jaffa. The Crusaders were perpetually besieging Jaffa, or, when they'd taken it, being besieged in it by the Infidel.'

Stephen was looking at him warily. ' "We",' he muttered.

'What did you say?'

'Nothing.' But he continued to look wary. 'When was the Third Crusade?'

'1191.'

'And does that make Richard coincide with Alienor? As regards timing, I mean? Assuming, of course, that as well as battling his way round the Holy Land and ending his days in Crete he managed to spend some of his life bonking in England.'

'Yes.' Rafe decided to ignore the sarcasm. 'Sem calculated that Alienor lived in the late twelfth or early thirteenth century.'

'Oh, you've talked to Sem, then? Good idea, I'd . . .'

'Sem's dead.'

'Oh, God.' Stephen slowly sank down on to a kitchen stool. 'How?'

'Stroke. After he'd been out to commune with Alienor. To get Nell and me off the hook.'

Stephen said, very softly, 'Stroke. Less dramatic than saying Alienor murdered him.' He ran his hand over his face. 'You believe me now, don't you?'

'Yes.'

'Go on, then.' Stephen's voice was sad. He must have met Sem, Rafe thought. He probably liked him as much as I did. 'Finish telling me about Richard.'

'I think he went back to England after the Third Crusade,

and that's when he seduced Alienor. Then when he'd got her pregnant, he disappeared. I think he was involved in the Fourth Crusade as well. A good place to run from a discarded mistress and her angry father, wouldn't it be?'

'Now hold on,' Stephen protested. 'I don't know much about the Crusades, but I do know that the English weren't involved in the Fourth Crusade. It was the French and the Flemish.'

'Maybe Richard was French, then. Or partly French – many noble households did have French blood, and since the Normans there were all sorts of connections between England and France. He could have crossed the Channel to join some kinsmen in France or Flanders and gone to Outremer with them.'

'Where?'

'Outremer. The French name for the Crusader States.'

'Yes. I suppose he could,' Stephen conceded.

'Thank you. Stop interrupting and listen, will you?'

'Okay. So you think Richard went on the Fourth Crusade.'

'I know he did. I dreamt about the sack of Constantinople. We ran ashore against a defensive tower, two ships roped together.' He paused. 'Then we took the town.' He saw again the tortured priest, saw the sword-cuts lopping off his limbs, the teeth clamped down in agony against the lower lip, the poor man's bite only easing, Christ-like, to emit prayers for the souls of those who were so slowly killing him.

His sword-arm felt heavy suddenly.

He concluded quickly, aware of Stephen's concerned expression, 'We got our hands very bloody, and I don't imagine it was through any philanthropic attempts to administer first aid.'

'The attack on Constantinople,' Stephen repeated. 'Yes. From what I recall, that would be a suitably barbarous event for your Richard to have participated in.' His voice dropped. ' "We" ', he muttered again. But before Rafe could comment he said, 'Where did he go from there?' How do you make him end his days in a Cretan mountainside?'

'Crete was awarded to the Venetians, after the fall of Byzantium. What's more likely than that Richard threw in his lot with them? He was as wily an opportunist as the best Venetian.'

'And there he built his castle.' Stephen nodded. 'Created his own little kingdom, perhaps, with his share of what came out of the coffers of Constantinople.' Not only the coffers, Rafe wanted to say, remembering. 'Yes,' Stephen was saying. 'I agree it makes sense. And it gives us the Cretan connection. Doesn't it? Gives us a clue as to how you come to be involved.'

Rafe felt something within him go quite cold. 'No,' he said quietly.

'What?' Stephen leaned forward, staring hard at him. 'Of course it does, it . . .' He broke off. Then, slowly, over his face crept the same expression of superiority which, long ago, had once almost made Rafe hit him. It had the same effect now; Rafe, his hands curled into hard fists, folded his arms in the hope that Stephen wouldn't notice.

'I see,' Stephen said. 'I see. It's you who's trying to say it's far too much of a long shot now, isn't it? That it's all coincidence?'

Rafe, struggling with himself, didn't answer.

'Well, perhaps it is,' Stephen said charitably. 'But we know your Richard had already had one child, by Alienor. It's out of the question, surely, that he wouldn't have begotten more, unless he was past it by the time he reached Crete. Which somehow I doubt. No wounds in the groin, were there?' He didn't seem to expect an answer. 'Having built his castle and carved out his kingdom, I should have thought he'd next want to people it. And you do have Cretan ancestry. Don't you?'

'Yes.' Rafe thought his voice sounded surprisingly under control. 'You know quite well I do.'

'Well, I'm afraid it's a possibility, then, that you're descended from him,' Stephen said pedantically. 'But it's not so bad, is it? He was a hell of a long time ago, and most families have one or two characters in their past who were thoroughly bad lots.'

Rafe didn't answer. Stephen's attempt to lighten the atmosphere was less than useless.

'Come on!' Stephen said. 'Don't let it get to you so much!'

Rafe turned away from him. There was a mirror on the opposite wall, at the far end of the living-room. He could just make out his reflection in it.

'It isn't that. The thought of being descended from Richard isn't what's really bothering me. You're right, it was a long time ago. Although if you'd seen him in action you wouldn't be so dismissive, I can tell you.' He paused.

'What is it, then? What's worrying you so much?'

'Remember his name? Remember what his happy band of adoring locals called their hero?'

'Of course. Richard One-Eye.'

Rafe turned back to face him.

'Richard One-Eye,' he repeated. 'Yes. Call this a coincidence if you like. I can no longer see out of my left eye.'

'I don't want to do it, Rafe.'

Stephen had the air of a man battling against the inevitable and slowly losing.

'Then tell *me* what to do!' Rafe said for the fourth time.

'No. I'm not that irresponsible. Not any more.' Stephen grinned ruefully. 'Anyway, I said I don't want to do it. Not I won't.'

Rafe saw the first glimmer of light since the phone-call that had summoned Nell home.

'You're going to help, then?'

Stephen sighed. 'Yes. God knows why.'

'Because it intrigues you,' Rafe said, rapidly thinking up a battery of reasons before Stephen could change his mind. 'Because you're my friend and you're fond of Nell and you'd like to see us happy. Because you'll be able to write the story and sell it to the gutter press for some vast sum. Because you're already involved – it's your fault, you held the séance that began it all.'

Stephen had been amused, but at Rafe's last words his expression changed and he looked stricken. For a moment Rafe regretted having reminded him of his culpability. Then he thought, it was worth it. It'll make sure he doesn't change his mind.

And after all it's the truth.

'You'll have to come and stay for a while.' Stephen sounded resigned. 'If you're going to stand a cat's chance in hell, there's a great deal I'll have to tell you.'

Rafe could have wished for a less worrying metaphor. 'Okay.'

Stephen said suddenly, 'Why can't you both go away and live somewhere else? Leave Alienor and her Magic Meadow behind? You were all right in Crete, weren't you?'

Were we? He thought back. Yes, during that incredible, beautiful idyll of coming together. But we still religiously drank our herbal tea every night, although we tried not to let it spoil our fun. And then there was the effigy on the mountain. And that dream, whatever it was, from which she woke sobbing. Not necessarily significant, but you can't help wondering. And what is there to say it wouldn't be the same wherever we went?

'No,' he said.

'No?' Stephen sounded surprised. 'I thought you said the holiday was great.'

'It was. I meant, no, we can't leave Alienor behind. I don't know but I suspect she may have an unpleasant ability to tag along with us. And what peace we did have in Crete was down to Nell's herb stuff. I don't intend to spend the rest of my life being forced to drug myself to avoid having nightmares. Anyway, Nell can't leave the cottage. Not for good. It's been in her family for generations. I can't imagine her being really happy anywhere else. Especially now Sem's dead – just after

285

he died, I suggested taking her away somewhere for a few days, and she said no, she wanted to stay in the cottage because he felt near.'

'I see. Quite understandable. One would like to think that the presence of Sem's shade there might go a long way towards ridding the place of less welcome attentions.'

Rafe said quickly, 'There are none. Not in the cottage. It's got the most wholesome atmosphere of any house I've ever been in. You feel brighter just going in through the door, even if you haven't been aware of being down.'

'Yes. Of course, I never got further than the living-room, but I do see what you mean.' Rafe didn't think it necessary to tell him that until last night he hadn't been upstairs, either. And even then he hadn't stayed there. 'Does she know what you're planning?'

'No!' Rafe said forcefully. 'And I don't want her to.'

'Hm. I think you're wrong. She could be invaluable.'

'No,' he said again.

He thought of Sem. Found by a passing motorist, slumped in a ditch. For all his wisdom, defeated. You might have thought some benevolent agency would have come to his aid, he reflected. Such gestures of loving altruism are all too rare in the world. If there is a force for good in opposition to the ranks of evil, then that would have been a nice time for it to have flexed its muscles.

'Because of the danger?' Stephen was asking.

'Yes. And because it was you and I who let Alienor get through. So it's up to us to shut off the channel again.'

Stephen laughed shortly. 'Like putting down the receiver on an unwelcome caller?' he suggested witheringly. 'Oh, dear oh dear! I'm afraid it's a great deal more complicated than that – we *have* got a lot of work ahead of us!' He got up and went off towards the bathroom. 'I'm going to shower and get dressed. Then we'll get down to it.'

'What, now?' Rafe somehow hadn't expected that things would move so quickly.

'Yes, now!' Stephen went to the bookshelf, picking out a thick volume and bringing it back to Rafe. 'While I'm in the shower, you can make a start on that. The introduction contains the most concise and well-reasoned exposition I know of on the subject of possession. But handle it carefully, I had to have it sent from Haiti and it cost me two arms and a leg.'

Rafe looked at the title. He felt an instant of pure fright.

Possession and Dispossession. The Psychology of the Undead.

Nell woke to the sound of bickering sparrows under the eaves outside her window. She was too hot; strong sunshine was pouring in.

There was a cup of tea on the bedside table. The milk had formed a creamy scum. It must have been there for ages.

She remembered Rafe, last night. Holding her so tightly in the road outside the pub. Putting her to bed – goodness, he took all my clothes off and I hardly noticed! – and snuggling her down.

Leaving me, to go and spend the night downstairs.

The happiness leaping up in her was abruptly quashed as she remembered his face.

I'm glad he stayed, though, she thought, trying to cheer herself up, even if it wasn't up here with me. He must be quite used to sleeping on the sofa. And it was nice of him to bring me the tea.

She propped herself up on an elbow, and noticed a piece of paper stuck in her mirror. She got out of bed to fetch it.

> *'I think the tea was an over-optimistic idea. You MUST have been tired – even the hunting-horn in your ear didn't wake you. I'm going back to London – I'll call you later.*
>
> *Love, Rafe.'*
>
> *'PS. You have a bruise the size of a water-melon on your thigh. I'm very sorry that I almost ran you over. Please be more careful in future.'*

PPS. I kissed it better for you.

She lifted up her nightshirt to look. He was right – on the outside of her right thigh there was a large, purplish bruise where the wing of his car had hit her. She touched it, and it felt tender. 'I kissed it better for you.' She wondered when he had done that, and wished she'd been awake to appreciate it.

She went back to bed, smiling at the thought. She read through the note again, and only this time realized that the information it contained was sketchy, to say the least. She turned it over, but the reverse side was blank.

That's it?

But he doesn't say when he's coming back. Nor a word about what we're going to do.

What *are* we going to do?

She realized she had no answer. None at all.

He phoned in the evening.

'How are you?'

'I'm fine. But I miss you.' Damn it, she couldn't stop herself saying it. But he promptly responded, 'I miss you too,' and he said it far more convincingly than she had.

'When are you coming back?'

'Soon. I don't know exactly. I'm busy with something.'

He sounded a bit vague. She felt prickles of alarm.

'What? Something to do with your work?' She didn't think so. Somehow it would be an incongruous anticlimax, after all that had happened, for him calmly to go and get embroiled in his work again. Besides, today was Saturday, although she supposed that didn't make as much difference to him as to most people.

'Not work, no. It's – I can't say. I hoped you wouldn't ask.'

'That's daft,' she said dismissively. 'Of course I would. Why are you being so mysterious?' She wondered, in passing, at her new ability to be so blunt. Perhaps it was always easy to say exactly what you were thinking to someone you really got close to.

'I'm staying with someone,' he said. 'We're working on something. It'll take a week or so. It's important, believe me.'

' "Trust me" ', she said.

'What?'

'It's what they say in films. Sorry, I'm being trite. So, is this important something going to keep you away while you're working on it?'

After a moment he said quietly, 'Yes. I can't come back until it's over.'

And then she knew.

'Nell?'

She swallowed. 'I'm still here.'

'Oh. Good.'

'Can't I help? Can't I come to be with you? And won't you tell me what you're doing?' she burst out, knowing already what he would say.

'No. Darling, no. You can't help. And don't ask me about it, please, because I find it very hard to – I'll be back, I promise.'

You find it hard to lie to me, she imagined he'd been going to say. Oh. God. And he sounded distracted. So much I want to ask, she thought. But I can't. But at least he promised to be back.

Can I cope with a week, while he gets on with whatever it is?

I don't think I've got any choice.

'All right,' she said quietly.

'All right?' he echoed.

'No, but I'll manage.'

There was a pause. Then he said, sounding for the first time like himself, 'That was easier than I thought.'

She had to laugh. 'Go away, before I change my mind.'

'Okay. See you soon.'

'Yes. Take care.' What an inappropriate thing to say. It

didn't sound as if he would be preoccupied with being *careful*. But it was the sort of thing you always said when someone was going away. Or about to do something with an element of danger in it.

And, his warm voice precious in her ear, he said, 'I will.'

She went to put the receiver back. Just as the connection was breaking she thought she heard him say something else. She snatched it up again.

'Rafe?'

But there was just the burr of the dialling tone.

And I can't call him back, I've no idea where he is.

Pity, because what I thought he said was 'I love you'.

Rafe couldn't remember ever having a more extraordinary week. He spent his days in the office, making himself concentrate on the mundane, talking to people about run-of-the-mill things, coping with the usual crop of expiring deadlines and last-minute emergencies. Just as if the secret side of his life didn't exist. Then in the evenings he would return to Stephen, with a sense of relief, almost, because although the long nights of study were abhorrent, each session took him nearer to his goal. He came to realize, as the incredible week ran on, that it was the sheer normality of the days that prevented his nights from driving him to despair.

Or worse.

The things they spoke of horrified him. He realized on the first morning that there was a whole area of the world, of the human experience, whose existence he'd scarcely suspected. And he was horrified, because he realized with sick certainty that these dreadful things weren't just some aberration of one small group of people. The beliefs, the superstitions and the barbarous customs cropped up, in only slightly different forms, again and again in cultures all over the world.

It began to seem to him that half the human race must walk with spirits at its side. Spirits of abstract things that had to be treated like gods, offered sacrifice, placated, given the best of the land's produce. The gods themselves, in a rainbow of characters that ranged from absolute good to total black evil.

And, most frightening of all, spirits of dead humans. Things that had once been as living men, but who by some crumple in the natural order did not, as other men do, quietly disappear at their death. No. They were the reluctant ones, the ones who hooked their fingers into the living and would not detach. And, because they had the breath of the abyss upon them, they had an immeasurable power at which the living could only guess.

And they didn't shrink from using it.

Is that what they're trying to tap, Rafe wondered, trying to make sense of it all, these Black Sabbath congregations, these voodoo dancers, these people who spin themselves into trances? Is it that they know the darkness is there and that for some reason they are compelled to cast themselves into it?

Why?

That was where his understanding failed. He could, by a monumental effort of concentration, open his mind sufficiently to sense the – the what? What was it, that hummed and throbbed deep down in his awareness? He had no words to describe it. But it was there. And in some ancient part of the brain, some area of the brain-stem that possibly had never been able to put thought into word, he knew that what he sensed was the fundamental power of the earth and all that was on it.

And, God knew, that knowledge was enough.

Only it wasn't. Because, from somewhere in that dark spiral, Alienor had come.

Stephen drove him like a slave-master, bullying, persuading, making him open up so that, with his sensitive mind, Stephen could look in for himself and discover things of whose significance Rafe had been unaware. But it was strictly a one-way channel; as the days went on and Rafe felt increasingly

like something pinned on a slab, Stephen retreated further
into himself and became more enigmatic than ever.

How does he know all this? Rafe wondered tiredly, trying
to rid his mind of the violent, insistent imagery that wouldn't
let him rest. Did he just think to himself one day, hey, I think
I'll find out about the occult? Was his interest the natural
consequence of being psychic? And does he ever regret having
found out so much?

He wanted to ask. But there was something about Stephen
in his spiritual mentor role which discouraged such inquiry.
The closest he got was late one night when, both of them
sickened by what Stephen had just read out, there seemed to
be a particular sense of camaraderie between them.

'Why do you do it?' he asked abruptly.

'Hm?' Stephen looked up, his expression vague.

'I mean, I have no choice,' Rafe went on. 'But you! You
pursue the subject as a *hobby*, for Gods' sake.' Stephen, considering, seemed about to demur. 'Yes, you do! Just look
around you!' With a sweep of his arm Rafe indicated the rows
of books. 'Sorry.' Subsiding, he realized he had no right to
criticize his saviour.

'Why do I do it?' Stephen murmured. His eyes turned to
Rafe's, and Rafe found himself staring into them. Unable to
look away. He seemed to sense a great power tensing itself,
flexing its might.

But then Stephen laughed, turning away, and the moment
passed.

'I don't know,' he said pleasantly. 'I shouldn't think about
it too much, if I were you. As I've said to you before, it doesn't
do to meddle.'

It was exhausting. The week ground on, and as it came to an
end, they were both drained and badly affected by all that
they had read, and thought, and talked about.

But it had been worth it. Because Stephen, eyes scarlet

rimmed and face grey with fatigue, finally announced that he'd made up his mind.

'You know what to do?' Rafe asked.

He nodded.

'And it'll work?'

'Yes.' He hesitated. Then added, 'Probably.'

'What?'

'I'm going to break her contact with you. And bring you back to the living while she floats away to join the dead.'

'You are.' He couldn't help the note of disbelief. And Stephen seemed so supremely confident that, even after all they'd been through, it was an irritation.

But then he regretted it. For Stephen, lying back in his chair with his eyes closed, said in a tone of fervour that Rafe hadn't heard before, 'Oh, Jesus, I hope so.'

'Tomorrow,' Stephen said late on Friday. 'Tomorrow night.'

Rafe sat quite still. His mind seemed to have stopped functioning.

Tomorrow.

No more procrastination. Nothing more to do; Stephen says tomorrow.

And Stephen ought to know.

He got up and walked over to Stephen's bookshelf.

'What are you doing?' Stephen asked.

Rafe pulled out a murder mystery. Not the sort of thing he'd have expected Stephen to own; some guest must have left it behind. 'I'm going to read myself to sleep,' he said. 'Good night.'

Nell had gone to bed early, tired out by a week of hard work, her aching body soothed by a hot bath.

She was awake, wide awake, although a second ago she was sure she'd been asleep.

I was dreaming. Of Rafe.

Something threatening him. Something awful. It was dark,

coming out of the shadows like water flooding across a floor, and it was making for him, swirling round him and cutting him off. He was drowning in it, the blackness creeping up his body, going into his mouth, down into his lungs, sucking him to the ground, through it and into . . .

Oh, God!

She sat up, reaching for the light switch, scrabbling for Rafe's cross around her neck. Help me, help me!

Her violent shivering gradually stopped, and as the calm house and the familiar peace that it held within its walls soothed her terror, the image of Rafe slowly faded.

But the anxiety was still there, quite undiminished.

Sleep driven far away, she got out of bed and went down to the kitchen to make herself a very strong hot drink.

Something's in the air, she thought as she went back upstairs, What has he done? What has he stirred up by his actions? Oh, I wish I could talk to him! I wouldn't ask anything, I'd just sit and listen.

But I can't even do that, because I don't know where he is.

There's nothing I can do. Except wait.

It was not a cheerful prospect.

Nineteen

She realized on Saturday night that, this time, the increasingly less reliable sound-sleep formula of hard work and a hot bath was going to fail her absolutely. Despite having dug till she'd raised blisters on top of blisters, despite having put her entire domain in such perfect order that there wasn't much more she could do, she was only physically exhausted. There was bedlam in her mind, her anxieties warring for her attention, each successive worry driven out by the next long before she could harass it to anything like a conclusion.

Where is he? Is he all right?

He's being threatened. He has been for as long as I've known him. But, oh, it's far stronger now. Whatever has happened before is nothing to what's brewing now. I feel that he's – what's that phrase that ships use to warn one another?

Yes. Oh, God, yes. That's it exactly.

You are standing into danger.

She drew her knees up to her chest, huddling into the duvet. Danger. Danger.

But WHAT danger?

Suddenly she sat up, throwing off the covers and swinging her feet down to the floor. She caught sight of her mug of herb tea, into which she'd introduced some camomile as a mild sleep-inducer. It stood untasted on the bedside table.

Why didn't I drink it? Why don't I drink it now?

She put out her hand to pick it up, but it was as if she was trying to reach out through a fast-flowing current. With a shock of alarm, she snatched her hand back.

Something's making me stay alert. There's a purpose to his wakefulness.

She got up and went over to the window.

The moon was almost full, and the countryside lay revealed in its light. The sky was clear; soft pouches of mist lay in the land's hollows. She turned to look over towards the Magic Meadow and she felt her alarm soothed from her, bewitched away by the serenity before her. She began to feel calm, and sleepy.

It's so restful. So beautiful. Whatever could harm me, out there? Why should I ever have been afraid? No evil could dwell in that peace . . .

NO!

Adrenalin raced through her as she tried to throw off the trance, her own consciousness attempting desperately to punch and kick its way back into command. For a few seconds her body was a battle-ground, and neither of the opposing forces would yield.

Then abruptly it stopped.

She ran to the cupboard and found warm clothes, jeans, thick socks and a pullover. Then she leapt downstairs to put on her boots and coat, and let herself silently out into the night.

Rafe stopped some distance short of Wellstone, letting the car roll on to the grass verge.

'We'll walk from here,' he said, 'it's so quiet at night, some-one in one of the houses would be bound to hear the car.'

'How far is it?' Stephen asked.

'Quarter of a mile. Less, probably.'

They set off along the lane. The air was chilly, too cold still to carry any of the scents of spring blossoming in the hedge-rows. From out of the brooding darkness came the sudden distant shriek of some small victim meeting its violent end. Beside him Rafe heard Stephen cough quietly.

Neither of them spoke.

'Here,' Rafe said, stepping off the road and pausing in the gateway. He could have found the place in total darkness. But the moonlight would be a help when they got over into the rough ground of the field. 'Watch it, the gate's almost off its hinges.'

Stephen swore softly, batting something away from his head. 'Bloody brambles.'

Rafe waited while he disentangled himself. 'The footpath leads straight through the field. See?' He pointed. 'We branch off, at the top of the rise.'

'Yes, okay. Go on, I'll follow.'

Rafe set off along the path, very aware of the sounds of their passage through the young corn breaking the stillness. The land's entranced, he thought. Everything's arrested, not even breathing. Waiting for something. And the moon's keeping a watch over us, to see what we're up to.

I wish I knew.

Stephen's footsteps thumped stolidly on the firm earth behind him. It was a reassuring sound.

'Left here, towards the trees,' Rafe said quietly. It's that sort of silence, he thought. You don't want your voice to be the one to break it. 'The Magic Meadow's on the far side.'

Immediately he'd said the words he wished he'd called it something less emotive.

'God, it's dark in the shadows,' Stephen muttered, coming up level with him and staring frowningly ahead. 'We have to go through there?'

Rafe felt the same reluctance. The thicket was black against the moonlight. The tree-trunks looked stouter, and the entangling undergrowth more forbidding than ever. It was as daunting as a barbed-wire fence.

'We do,' he said shortly. 'Watch your face.'

He stood for a moment gathering his strength; his reluctance was growing. Then abruptly he pushed ahead, forearms crossed over his eyes, and he felt the horrible tangle close around him. Spikes drove into his hands, scratching long furrows down his arms as he thrust forwards. April didn't seem to have reached inside this awful hedge; the sweetness of budding spring was quite absent here. It smelt dead. Smelt

297

of old dry dust of crumbled leaves and broken twigs. Sour rottenness of putrified matter. And beneath all a black heart of malignancy, beating slowly and patiently.

Waiting.

Dead but she won't lie down.

Compelled to extricate himself, for anything was better than being in there, he heaved himself towards the glimmering moonlight on the far side.

And emerged with a crash into the Magic Meadow.

Vaguely he heard the sound of Stephen's passage behind him, heard him exclaim something as he too made his escape from the clutching barbs.

But he didn't care about Stephen; Stephen belonged to the world on the other side, and Stephen didn't matter any more.

Nothing from that world mattered. It was forgotten.

For sounds were loud in his head, a sweet humming that once had seemed like the buzzing of summer insects, once like the rustling of fallen leaves.

And now, oh, now, was the singing of a pure young voice.

He hurried forwards, mist clouding his feet and reaching up with insidious swirls to twine around his legs like possessive adoring arms grasping at him. Grasses grew tall, and thick amongst them sturdy plants with blotched stems and fern-like leaves opened themselves to the black night. He stopped, leaning his head back, wide eyes staring up high above him, caught up in this intense and silent communing of dark earth to dark sky. Yet even as he stared he perceived that the blackness was no longer so total. Although the moon was fast setting, the first hint of dawn was beginning to pale the eastern sky, and sharp fingers of grey were reaching to pluck out the stars.

He ran on, stumbling, drawn up into the meadow.

In the blink of an eye, the scene changed. A house, plain and square, with unfamiliar, semicircular-headed windows each one divided by an ornamental column. A square court yard. To one side the rich, turned earth of vegetable plot and beside it a geometrically-laid garden, with low walls. And, growing in profusion in the regular shapes of the flowerbeds, lilies. Pinks. Pervading all, the sweet, musky smell of cloves.

The mist and the tall grasses returned, and he shook his head violently. Where was the house? His sight was hazy, and he couldn't tell what he saw with his eyes and what was vision inside his mind.

He heard a powerful voice from beside him. A man's voice. Calling her, calling Alienor. Saying words like an incantation, words of summons. Words he knew he had once learned, long, long ago in that other world.

A movement in the mist before him.

What was it? *Where* was it? He strained to see, eyes searching wildly, scanning the milky whiteness.

A shape, rising. Growing out of the ground, uncurling itself like some monstrous plant. At first white, no more than a shape made out of the mist. Then darkening to shades of grey, light at the top, slaty beneath. Acquiring colour, suddenly, like the sunrise cascading exuberant orange and yellow across the dreaming silver of the night.

He stared, hardly believing what he saw.

A woman, in red silk.

Yes! *Yes!*

He began to smile, his heart full of joy and relief.

Behind him the incantation went on, although it sounded far, far away. He thought, no need to summon her. She's here.

He pushed on up the rise. The chanting broke off, replaced by urgent words. Look out. Remember what you must do.

What must I do?

He shrugged. He'd forgotten. It didn't matter.

The words came again, fainter. He dismissed them. Walking faster, he broke into a run, towards her, towards that fascinating, wonderful creature materializing just for him . . .

You're mine. You'll ALWAYS be mine!

She was standing before him, staring up at him. Panting, he gazed down into her face. So beautiful! Like Nell. But –

no, not like. He looked more closely. The eyes, sea green and luxuriously lashed under dark brows, were Nell's exactly. But the nose was broader across the bridge. And the parted lips were coarser. It was Nell's face before some careful hand had finished refining it.

Hair, long, white-blonde. Free of its braids, it flowed like water with sunshine on it. His hands twitched to reach out, to touch.

She said, on the breath of a sigh, 'Richard?'

And smiled.

Images fought to race each other through his head. Her moist, soft mouth on his. Her heavy white breasts, falling out of her undergarments towards his waiting, caressing tongue. Her small round belly, curving inwards to that secret wet cleft that beckoned him so irresistibly. Her surrendered body beneath him as he made love to her, poured his being into her, clutched her until it hurt. He went to move towards her, to take her in his arms, staring into her eyes.

And stopped.

For they were not Nell's eyes after all. Nell didn't have it in her to gaze up at him in open-mouthed lust with such fierce urgency in her stare.

He stepped back, away from her. Instantly her hands shot out to him, delicate little hands, long-nailed, the cuffs of some white-sleeved garment reaching in diamond-points to her narrow knuckles. Her chest rose and fell rapidly, the large breasts straining against the fine material. She stood with legs apart, hips thrust outwards, inviting him, and again, more surely now, she said, 'Richard.'

'No,' he said. His voice sounded strange to his ears. 'Not Richard. Not your Richard.'

She hesitated, her head on one side.

'Yet *like* Richard,' she whispered. 'And so long, so very long, since I saw you that I cannot recall with exactitude.' Her face crumpled like a little girl's. 'You went from me, my Lord,' she said in reproach. 'You loved me, made me love you, and

300

then you left me. And you would say not whither you were bound. Nor when you would return.' She gathered herself for a sob, keening towards him. 'Oh, my lord! My sweet Richard!'

'No,' he said. 'Not me. I am not Richard.'

She stood uncertain. 'But, my lord, your height. And your breadth.' Her eyes ran up and down his body, making him tingle. 'Your manner. And . . .' She frowned in perplexity. 'Something that I cannot name, but that I feel. In the blood, mayhap.' She lifted her chin and stared right into his eyes. 'And your face,' she said belligerently, 'marked as was Richard's. By a curved Saracen sword as you fought the Infidel beside the king whose name you bear.'

'Marked by a bramble.' His tone was gentle. He could hardly force out the words, so reluctant was he to crush all the joy from that eager face by disillusioning her. 'And by a flying stone.'

Her expression changed. Now she looked like a mischievous child caught out in a prank. 'Yes. This I know. For I embellished you with a little handiwork of my own.' She giggled, putting her hand to her mouth.

He felt the scar on his cheek throb under her gaze. She looked as if she were admiring her skill.

'Richard is far away,' he said loudly. His words had the desired effect. Distracted, her eyes flew back to meet his and the pain in his cheek subsided. 'In his own chapel,' he hurried on, 'on a mountainside in Crete.'

'In Crete?' She looked puzzled. 'I know it not. Yet . . .' She frowned again. 'Have I heard tell of this place, that in some manner I am able to picture it?' She shook her head. 'I think not. It is far away, you say?'

'Very far.'

She drooped, and the bright hair fell round her shoulders like a veil. The scent of cloves was stronger now.

Suddenly her head shot up, and she flung back the concealing hair with both hands. Her eyes were round and hard, and stared straight into his.

Her mouth was drawn down in malice.

'Richard!' She raised her hand, pointing at his face. 'Richard!'

'No, not Richard!' He felt fear shuddering down the back of his neck. Malice poured from her, washing against him and making his heart pound with fear. He felt a heavy, creeping numbness, as if his blood were turning to lead.

'You say not.' She smiled then, a knowing smile. 'But what care I what you say! You shall be to me as Richard was!'

With a leap she was on him, snaking her arms round his neck, pressing her lips to his, writhing her body against him. Without his volition desire rose in him, and without any conscious direction from him his mouth was kissing her back while his hips ground into hers.

Her taste, her smell, her feel, hit him in a great wave.

And nausea overcame him, for she stank. She was foul, and her skin was like slime.

'NO!' he shouted, throwing her away from him in revulsion.

In slow motion he saw her float through the air, landing in a heap in the misty grass. Instanly she spun to face him, venom in her eyes like a blaze of evil. Her hatred and her power hit him with the force of lightning, and he staggered. He could feel the labouring of his heart, but, sick and dizzy, it seemed that no blood was reaching his brain. For a flashing second he remembered Sem. Was this what she did to that brave old man? Was this how it felt to him? No wonder he died. He was older, less fit, less able to withstand her assault. For she is evil, and this combat is deadly.

He stared at her, transfixed. At her right forefinger aiming like a poisoned arrow straight at his left eye. He felt a pain so severe that for a second the scene in front of him spun into blackness.

She lowered her arm slightly.

Her face fell into sorrow, and even in that moment he felt stirring in him a deep and unassuageable pity.

Desolately she shook her head, and tears splashed onto her cheek. She whispered, 'Richard. Where are you? '

He took a step towards her, forcing his unwilling legs to move. Sensing his approach, her eyes flew back to him. Up went her hand again, the curled talons straightening. In terror, he fumbled inside his shirt for the gold cross.

It wasn't there.

His arm, weary and aching as if from a day's wielding a bloody, butchering sword, fell to his side. He waited, defenceless, for the end.

She screeched, beside herself with frustration and fury, *'NOT RICHARD!'*

And pointed at his eye.

He felt a soft explosion, like a bursting of an over-ripe plum under the pressure of inquisitive fingers.

He screamed in agony.

Words were being shouted behind him, loudly, in a deep masculine voice. The words he dimly remembered having been taught, back in that other world. A woman's voice had joined in, a warm voice, full of concern. Not *her* voice. He fought to recall what the words were, for he knew instinctively that they were his only hope.

But it was no good. They were erased from his mind, gone for good, and his salvation with them. The torture in his eye was overcoming him, the small amount of sight he retained in the other eye gradually obscured with a blackness that seeped like sticky, welling tar across the scene before him. And she was going, fading, off and away from him, never more to claim him as her own. His exhausted, stuttering heart seemed to break with the sorrow and the pain.

As if she too knew that this was the end, from the ground at his feet a wail rose into the cold dawn air. Mourning all that she had lost, grieving for the wasted centuries of waiting, her lamentation steadily swelled. He could no longer distinguish her, for the scarlet of her gown and the shining gold of her hair were fading back behind a misty whiteness which his weakening sight could no longer penetrate.

But he could still hear. The noise was deafening now, strengthened into a hellish reverberating bombardment, a great chord that blasted through the air and bent the tree tops. Then, slowly, faded away and died.

And as the darkness overcame him and he sank to the warm, friendly earth, the birds began to sing.

Nell crept forwards, keeping under the shadow of the hedge. Her hands were scratched from fighting her way through the undergrowth, and she wished she had gloves. She sucked at a long tear on the back of her wrist.

She could see into the Magic Meadow. The moon shining on the mist turned it milky, and out of it the hemlock stood stark. It seemed to her that some unimaginable power hovered, on the brink of release; the air hummed.

And there, as she had known he must be, was Rafe. Taking the slope into the middle of the meadow like a hound on a trail, pausing to listen, to look – even, it appeared, to sniff – and then rushing forwards again.

Behind him, cowering at the foot of the slope, was Stephen.

Everything had contracted into this time and this place, where two of them crouched frozen in horror. And the third ran to meet his danger with his arms open in welcome.

She was shaking, her heart thumping, sweat prickling her skin. And inside her head sounded the cry of self-preservation: get away! Go back! *She* is there, I can feel Her. She's in the mist, She's come for him.

Go home, where it's safe.

She began to edge back into the undergrowth.

And in the same instant Stephen seemed to overcome his fear. As she watched, he began to move forwards. He was chanting. She didn't understand the words, but one name she recognized.

Alienor.

She whimpered in terror.

Look at Stephen! she berated herself. He's Rafe's friend. He's come with Rafe to support him – in some way they've prepared for this. And Stephen's sticking by him, even now he's going out to help. Chanting like some medieval sorcerer.

I'm Rafe's lover. Can I do less?

She stood up. Took one step into the Magic Meadow. Another. And the effort it took had her gasping for breath as if she had just run up a mountain. She was frightened, so frightened, by this manifestation of the evil power that fought to keep her out, and her legs began to bend as slowly she was driven to her knees.

But the fight in her was not all used up. From somewhere, from a store that perhaps had been intended precisely for this moment, she found the last of her courage. Standing straight, she forced herself to go on.

One step. Two steps.

Stephen was within her reach now. She stretched out her arm and grabbed hold of his sleeve.

He jumped as if he'd been shot. Whipping round, he was skull-white. For a split-second he looked as if he'd never recover, but then the mask became a human face again and he hissed furiously, 'What the *hell* are you doing here?'

Equally furious, that he should reward her stupendous effort to be brave by being *angry* with her, she hissed back, 'The same as you!'

He grabbed for her hand, holding it in a grip so tight it hurt. Briefly he leaned towards her, touching his face against hers, and he muttered, 'Sorry. But, God, you made me jump.' Then before she could reply he said, so quickly she could hardly catch it, 'Stand with me. Concentrate on Rafe. Say what I say.'

She stood shoulder to shoulder with him, her hand clasped in his. Her mind was reeling, out of her control. Concentrate on Rafe. On *Rafe*. She fixed her eyes on him, silently repeating him name. Say what I say, Stephen had ordered. He had resumed his litany, and she listened intently: the strange words he was saying sounded like the ones he'd begun on before she interrupted him. But they were totally unfamiliar, in a language she didn't think she'd ever encountered, and she couldn't be sure. After a moment she realized he was saying the same thing, time after time going over the same few phrases, like someone repeating Hail Marys. As the incantation changed from gibberish to something which had a recognizable pattern, tentatively she joined in.

This is ridiculous, she thought, uttering nonsense syllables like a child speaking double-Dutch. She almost laughed at herself.

But at that moment Rafe, half-hidden in the mist and the long grass, put his hand up to his cheek as if in renewed pain. Anguish swept through her, a bitter shame that she could have made light of his peril.

She wasn't a child, and this was no game.

She raised her voice, ferociously taking up the words.

She began to feel entranced, the endless repetition of the chant dulling her mind. And as she stared out into the meadow, her own voice joining with Stephen's into a heartening sound that rang in her ears, she seemed to see a strong chain grow in the air, looping out from her and from Stephen towards Rafe. Touching him. Fastening him to them. She blinked, and it had gone.

Only to float back as the chant went on.

Then Rafe began to move away, and his body was vague in the distance. She thought she heard voices. His voice, yes. But another, female one? Perhaps she was imagining it – she wasn't certain. And then she saw his arms go out, as if wrapping someone close in an embrace. Scarlet flashed in the mist like someone shaking out a banner, and from deep in her memory came an image of a girl in a long red dress swept up in the arms of a bearded man with a sword at his side. Confused, not knowing if she was seeing or recalling, she faltered in her chanting.

And Stephen, despair in his tone, shouted the louder, his face dark with anxiety and strain. The hand that held hers pinched cruelly, and she felt the small bones in her palm grate together. In amongst the unintelligible words of the incantation she heard his furious command: 'Don't stop *now!*'

She resumed the chant. Now Rafe was staggering, stooped like an old man. She felt as if she were being buffeted by strong gusts of wind, but it was a black wind, an evil wind straight from Hell. The air was suddenly icy and she was cold, colder than she'd ever been in her life. And the wind was coming from the direction of the meadow's centre, so that Rafe would feel its initial blast. Take the full brunt. She wanted to cry, *RAFE!* But Stephen was shouting louder and louder, his whole body tense with effort, and she couldn't abandon him.

Then above Stephen's voice a great scream sounded.

Her heart quaked.

Rafe, his legs buckling, his arms hanging limp at his sides as if he had lost both the ability and the will to protect himself, was slowly shaking his head from side to side like a tormented, dying animal.

A wail shattered the silence, unearthly, inhuman. So powerful that it was agony in her ears. Growing louder, threatening to break all asunder. Then fading, and dying away.

Her head was reeling. Like a spinning black whirlpool, the earth rushed up to meet her.

She was lying curled up on her side. As her senses gradually recovered from the numbness that had followed an overload of total terror, she began to wonder vaguely what was worrying her.

Then she realized.

Birdsong.

The dawn chorus. A lovely, normal, everyday, sound. Extra-jubilant, as for the first time in centuries in this place birds raised their song to greet the sunrise.

She was lying in the gently-waving grasses of a perfectly ordinary field.

She remembered.

She shot up, staring wildly around, her frantic eyes searching. One figure, two – thank God, they were both there.

Stephen sat only a few yards away, his elbows resting on his raised knees. His head was buried in his hands, so that she couldn't see his face. But his shoulders were shaking.

Rafe lay further up the slope, right in the centre of the meadow. He was flat on his back and he wasn't moving at all.

The scream tore from her. *'NO!'*

She was up on her feet, racing to him. She bent over him; his eyes were wide open, staring fixedly at the sky.

Or one eye was. The other would never see the sky, or anything else, again.

What had been Rafe's left eye was an unimaginably rotten pit.

She threw herself on him, crying his name again and again. She tore open his clothes, putting her ear to his chest while her fingers dug into the base of his throat searching desperately for a pulse. Nothing. She tried in a different spot, but the pounding of her own heart and her gasping breath defeated her.

A cool hand caught her shoulder, pulling her off Rafe's prostrate body. Stephen put his hand to Rafe's wrist. After a moment he said, 'No pulse. He's not breathing.'

She watched as he straightened Rafe's head, tipping it backwards, and, apparently quite able to ignore the awful eye, pinched Rafe's nose and began to breathe into his mouth.

Three quick breaths. Then the slow ones. More quick ones and soon a sound of panting. But it wasn't Rafe – it was Stephen.

He rasped out between breaths, 'Can you – take over?'

'Yes.' She tried to control her own breathing, to make herself sound capable and calm. Her flashing thoughts almost defeated her. Any minute now he'll have to stop for a rest

He'll call me and I'll have to be ready. I must! So much depending on us. On me.

Then Stephen said hoarsely, 'Now,' and there she was, kneeling in his place, her lips over Rafe's mouth, breathing, breathing . . .

Soon her lungs were burning. She wanted to cough, to choke, above all to *stop*. But she couldn't, not yet. Stephen hadn't anywhere near had time to recover.

A flutter beneath her, where her hand rested on Rafe's chest.

Was it? No. Just wishful thinking.

She breathed into him once more.

Yes! There it is again!

She whispered, 'Rafe.'

Then put her mouth back over his and blew.

Under her hand a heartbeat. And with a ripple of the muscles over his ribs, his chest opened and he sucked the air out of her.

He began to sigh, in and out, making awful sounds in his throat. Stephen beside her put his fingers once more on Rafe's wrist.

'Heartbeat's irregular, but strong.' Close beside her in the wet grass, he listened with her to Rafe's agonized breathing. 'He's trying. Look.'

She was looking. And it was horrible, horrible, kneeling there with Stephen, witnessing this ghastly struggle, not knowing what to do to help.

'Can you run fast?' Stephen's voice.

'Not very.'

'Okay. You stay, I'll go.'

He was off. She heard his crashing progress above the gentle early morning sounds.

She put her head down next to Rafe's as near to him as she could, labouring with him over every staggering breath. Her hand was still over his heart. She thought its beat might be getting steadier.

In her mind she ran alongside Stephen. Through the hedge, across the field to the footpath, down the long slope to the broken gate. Five minutes, ten, to get from here to Wellstone? Then to a house – which one? – to wake up some householder and demand to use his telephone. How long to explain to someone stupid with sleep that he *had* to let a raving stranger into his house?

And how long for the ambulance to come?

Feeling close to tears, she realized that no help could possibly arrive inside half an hour.

'Rafe,' she whispered, expecting no answer. 'Don't leave me, Rafe.'

Stay with me. Not because I'm frightened – I'm not any more. Without having to think about it, and without understanding why, I know She's gone. Whatever it was that She did to make this meadow such a sinister and evil place, She's not doing it any more.

She's gone.

Stay with me, Rafe, for a different reason. Because, now that the fear is gone, I realize that I love you.

She closed her eyes.

But she grew cold, and realized he must be, too. She stretched her body alongside his and put her arm over him, trying to close in against him to preserve what warmth he had left. Close to panic, she began to imagine things. That he was turning to ice. That he had quietly ceased breathing. She rested her head on his chest, and if she closed her other ear with her finger she found she could hear his heartbeat.

Another sound was intermingling. In the distance, a vehicle, coming fast along the lane. Lifting her head to listen she heard it slow down, then stop.

There was a pause. Then the vehicle started again, this time much more slowly.

She was torn, undecided whether she should stay with Rafe or run to look. Then, whispering to him, 'I'll be back!' sh leapt up and ran for the gap in the hedge. Scrambling up to stand panting in the field, she looked across towards the lane.

Through the young barley, widening the footpath with its careful passage, came an ambulance.

Twenty

He was dreaming. Happy scenes of Nell with a baby in her arms. A girl, called Ravenna.

The baby's mouth was inexpertly trying to smile at him, and she was waving a fist in his direction. Nell was more rounded, and she looked very happy. He felt happy, too. But now he was leaving his dream, regretfully coming up from deep sleep into wakefulness.

He opened his eyes. Opened one, for the other was bound with something. He put up his hand to investigate. A thick pad, stuck to his face with tape.

Beneath it there was no feeling. A large area of his face was quite dead.

After some time a figure appeared through the curtains around his bed and stood at its foot. A woman, in a dark-blue overall, white cap on her head.

'Oh!' she said. 'You're awake.'

He was about to confirm the fact, but she had disappeared again. He tried to push himself up a bit so that he could turn his head and widen his one-sided field of vision. But the effort was beyond him.

'Lie still,' the voice said. So she'd come back. She moved to his right side, and he looked up at her. 'Doctor's coming.'

Doctor. That smell was a hospital, then? Of course it was. The woman was a nurse.

Sem had been in hospital. But Sem was dead. Sem died in a hospital. He struggled again to sit up.

A young, fair-haired man appeared beside the nurse. He had on a white coat. He put his hand against Rafe's shoulder and gently pushed him back into a supine position. He said firmly, 'Lie down.' Medical opinion, Rafe thought, was apparently united in its view that he should remain flat and motionless. 'Mr Westover, isn't it?'

312

'That's me.'

Rafe watched them watching him. The doctor, an air of puzzlement on his face, was staring at his good eye. The sister was taking his pulse, writing something on a chart.

The doctor perched on the edge of the bed. He opened his mouth to say something, but Rafe forestalled him. First things first.

'Where's Nell?' he asked.

'Nell. The woman who came in with you yesterday morning?'

Yesterday? He wondered what time it was. How long he'd been there. 'Yes, if you say so.'

'She's outside. I think she's asleep. She must be exhausted – she's stretched out along three chairs and she doesn't look at all comfortable. She refuses to go home. She said she'd rather not leave your side, but Sister shooed her out earlier and told her to find herself something to eat.'

Rafe waited patiently for him to finish. Then he said, 'Get her in, would you?'

'Ah – in a minute.' The doctor looked awkward. Rafe realized he was quite young. 'I'm afraid I've bad news for you.'

I already know.

The doctor seemed to be expecting to be given the go-ahead. Okay, then, Rafe thought. You may as well have your say.

'Well?'

The doctor said in a rush, 'We couldn't save your eye. The infection had gone too deep.'

I've heard *that* before. Although that other time, the voice was older and infinitely more weary.

The doctor was waiting for him to reply, presumably thinking that his silence indicated shock. 'No,' Rafe said calmly.

'Oh!' He's looking disapproving now, Rafe thought, finding it funny. No doubt wondering at my cavalier attitude to my body. The doctor burst out. 'Why on earth didn't you seek attention earlier?'

313

Nothing to do with anything on earth, doctor.

'I didn't realize,' Rafe said untruthfully. Then, closer to the truth, 'It all happened so quickly.'

The doctor shook his head. He had a very strange expression.

'Would you please fetch Nell now?' Rafe said. 'And I'll go home, if she can take me.'

The sister and the doctor gasped together like a couple of nuns hearing blasphemy. In chorus they said, 'You can't go *HOME!*'

'Why not?'

'You've just had a major operation,' the sister said, full of concern, 'under general anaesthetic. And losing an eye is a traumatic experience – you have to heal. You have to adjust.'

'I can do both as well with Nell. She's a herbalist.' Mistake, he thought, to have said that. When already they think I'm next door to lunacy. It's like sacrilege, mentioning alternative medicine in here.

He noticed the doctor and the sister exchanging glances, mouthing words.

'All the same, we'd rather you stayed here,' the doctor said. He had apparently elected himself as spokesman for the world of conventional medicine in the face of this attack from the lunatic fringe. 'This was an extremely toxic infection – people don't often lose eyes nowadays, with modern antibiotics – and we can't understand why you're not . . . It's possible that you may become unwell in yourself. And I'm afraid there is just a chance that whatever it is could spread. To your other eye.' The doctor looked as if he regretted having to be so blunt.

Rafe smiled. It won't, he wanted to say. My other eye is as safe as yours. Or the sister's there. He was Richard One Eye, not Blind Richard. His smile deepened as relief surged through him – if the fear that he should lose his other eye too was the main reason for their laudable desire to keep him in their care, then it was quite safe to leave.

'Thank you, doctor. Sister.' He moved his head awkwardly

to look at them both in turn. 'I appreciate your frankness. Now, if you would?'

They took the hint. The sister drew back his curtains as she left, and he saw that he was in a small ward with three other beds in it. Two of them were occupied, and from one of them a man with his head bandaged nodded a greeting. Rafe nodded back. Then he turned to watch the doctor and the sister go out through the double doors, heads together, casting glances back at him.

The doors immediately swung violently open again.

Nell, running, skidded to a halt a few paces short of his bed. She stood quite still, eyes wide with apprehension.

He opened his arms to her.

And said, 'Come here, then.'

She stared down at him. It was such an enormous relief to find him awake, after the interminable hours she'd spent praying that he hadn't gone to sleep for ever. 'Can I?' she asked nervously. 'Won't it jog your . . . Won't I hurt you?'

'No.'

She dropped to her knees, collapsing across him. She twisted her fingers into the material of whatever it was he'd been dressed in. And he was warm. Vital. *Alive.*

'Nell.'

She lifted her head, looking into his face. He looks so odd, she thought, deeply moved, with that great pad of white obscuring his eye. No. Not his eye, because his eye's gone.

She tried not to think about what had happened to his eyes. How the ambulance men, running with her up the meadow with their stretcher, had stopped short when they saw Rafe. How one of them had said, 'Oh Jesus!' and turned away.

'Nell!' he said again.

It's gone now. That awful mess has gone, and now it's just an innocent, empty socket. She made herself stare straight at him. 'Yes?'

315

He was trying to lift his head to see her better. She leaned across him to help, puffing up the pillows for him and folding the top one double.

'Thanks.' He took advantage of her closeness, wrapping his arms round her. Then, his mouth close to her ear, he said, 'Nell, will you mind living with a Cyclops?'

She wanted to cry. To say, *I* don't care, I couldn't care less. It won't matter in the least to *me*. Because after only a couple of minutes I'm getting used to it. Getting used to the ruin of your handsome face. And to you putting all the expression that once was in both your lovely eyes into just the one.

But she couldn't possibly say all that.

She blinked rapidly several times, then sat up so that she could look at him.

'Not in the least,' she managed to say, remarkably cheerfully, she thought. 'Actually it'll be great, I shall always be able to place myself on your blind side when I'm up to something.'

But she couldn't hold out any longer. She put her head down on him again so that he wouldn't see.

He didn't speak, just held her against him and gently stroked her hair. And she thought, twice I've done this, twice I've knelt at a hospital bed praying that it's going to be all right. And I loathe hospitals!

With pain she saw again Sem's lopsided smile.

Sem couldn't stay – *She* proved too strong for my dear Sem. And She almost did for Rafe, too.

But not quite. She didn't quite get him.

Under the circumstances, having him one-eyed seemed quite a bargain.

'Your visitor really will have to go now, Mr Westover,' the sister's voice said as she swept past on her way to the end bed.

'Chucking-out time, Nell.' He shook her gently – she'd been lying on him for some time, and he'd been wondering if she'd gone back to sleep.

316

She raised her head, looking at him.

'Okay, I'll be back later.' She leaned over to kiss him, and he caught hold of her, not letting her move away. 'What is it?' she whispered.

'Bring me some clothes,' he said softly, right in her ear. 'I'm breaking out.'

She straightened up, beginning to shake her head. 'Oh, but . . .' she began. He forced as much authority as he could muster into his right eye, and she started to smile.

'If you're going to use those sort of bullying tactics, I might just leave you here,' she said.

'You wouldn't be so cruel.'

'No. I wouldn't.' She started to go slightly pink, then bent her head over her handbag as she rummaged for her key-ring. She muttered, 'Don't worry. I'll take good care of you.'

'I know you will.'

She raised her head, looking straight at him. 'I love you.'

'I know that, too.'

She stood awkwardly, and he thought she probably didn't know what to say. He blew her a kiss, and she turned and hurried away.

In the evening Stephen arrived.

'They didn't want to let me in!' he said indignantly. 'I had to tell them I was your psychiatrist.'

'They seem to think I need one.'

'So do I.' Stephen pulled up a chair and sat down. He eyed Rafe, his glance resting on the left side of his face. 'So do I,'he repeated under his breath.

'It's over now. Alienor won't come back.'

Stephen didn't answer.

'You saw, did you?' Rafe asked. 'I missed the very end. I heard that great wail as she went, but – well, I didn't see.'

Still Stephen said nothing. Rafe wondered if he found it all something of an embarrassment, now. He said, 'I'll never refer to it again, I promise. But I've got to know, and you're the only one who can tell me. What did you see?'

'But Nell was . . .' Stephen began. Then, frowning, he said, 'I saw nothing. Sweet bugger-all.'

'What do you mean?' He couldn't believe it. 'You were there, I heard you chanting. You called her, didn't you? All the other stuff you taught me went out of my head, but I swear I heard you say, "Alienor".'

'Leave it!' Stephen said angrily. 'I don't want to think about it.'

'I can't leave it!' He felt desperate. 'Surely you can see that?'

Stephen looked at him, and a flash of sympathy replaced the anger in his face.

'Yes. I suppose I can.' He hesitated. 'The thing is, I don't like thinking of myself prancing about in a field making incantations.' He laughed self-consciously. 'We got in so deep, we forgot the reaction of the ordinary man. I felt such an absolute fool, getting people out of bed and begging to use their phone, and babbling away to a couple of unimaginative ambulance men about mortal danger attacking someone in a field. In the middle of Kent!' he added indignantly, as if it made any difference.

Rafe smiled. 'I see,' he said. 'I'm sorry I caused you so much embarrassment. Only it was all real enough to me. It still is.'

Stephen sighed. 'To you, yes. But I'm afraid that can't alter the fact that all I saw was you, walking up a meadow, appearing to tangle with an invisible foe, then collapsing in the grass.'

'That's all?'

'That's all.'

'No hint of the supernatural?'

'Not one. Well, I did think it was eerie at first, yes. But that could be explained by all that you'd put in my mind. I *expected* it to feel weird.'

Rafe said very softly, pointing to the pad over his eye, 'And what about this?'

Stephen looked at him for a long moment. It seemed he wasn't going to answer. But eventually he said, 'Ever heard of psychosomatic illness? Yes, of course you have. A technical way of saying, it's all in the mind.'

'But it wasn't only me!' Rafe protested. 'What about Nell and Sem? And all the earlier Gurneys whom Sem found out about?'

'Who saw what? Nothing! Who dreamt, who felt vague apprehensions about an old field that had always been deserted. They *expected* to be scared of it, just as I did.' He paused, then went on more quietly, 'No. When you come down to it, Rafe, all this arose because you made it. It's you. All from you.'

All from me. It was a sobering thought.

He's wrong, he's got to be wrong.

All from me?

He thought rapidly back. The séance. Being drawn to Wellstone, compelled to search for Alienor. Finding Nell. Who looked so like the woman in his dreams. His childhood, lifelong dreams.

And Richard, seeing Richard's life pass in episodes before his eyes. So real, just as if he were living it himself.

'It's all in the mind. All from you.'

And now, now that Alienor had gone and would never come back, he found it difficult to recapture the compulsion she had held for him. Hard, too, to remember the moods of passion, anger, and terror that she'd inspired.

She was gone.

It was over.

Stephen had risen to his feet and was looking out of the window.

'There's a Land-Rover coming into the car-park,' he

remarked. 'Nell's, I think. Looks incongruous, amongst all those neat and tidy saloons.'

'She's coming to fetch me.'

'They're letting you out?' Stephen sounded incredulous.

'Not so loud!' He turned to look at the other occupants of the ward, but they were too far away to have heard. 'No, I'm letting myself out.

'But surely you're nowhere near ready? They'll want to treat you, fit you up with a glass eye, or whatever.'

'In time,' he said calmly. 'Not now – I want to go home.'

Stephen nodded. 'Yes. Well, you're proving my point. I've always said you were mad.'

'You have indeed. That's one of the more polite things you've always said I was.'

They exchanged affectionate smiles, and Rafe felt the long years of friendship that stretched away behind them.

'Mind you,' Stephen added, 'I have to admire your good sense in hanging on to Nell.'

'Thank you.'

'Don't sound so smug. She must be mad, too, to take you on.' He reached for his coat, which he'd slung across the bed. 'I think I'll leave you to it – I'm off. I'm not going to be a party to your irresponsible behaviour.' He took a step towards the door, then turned. 'Give Nell my love – tell her I wouldn't be in her shoes.'

'I will.'

He watched as the doors slowly stopped swinging after Stephen's departure. He imagined him running down the stairs and out to the car-park, and wondered if he would pass Nell. She'll be here soon, he thought. Even if she bumps into Stephen and they have a quick moan to each other about my irresponsible behaviour, she won't be long.

He felt drowsy, and the prospect of getting up, dressing and going home was momentarily daunting.

Then he started to picture the cottage. Himself and Nell

in the peace of the living-room. Warm, welcoming fire, and fresh flowers in vases. Good health-restoring food and drink. A warm bed to share, without the fear of intrusion. From any source.

Above all her love and her care.

The sum total was, he considered, worth a bit of effort.

He got out of bed to test his legs, walking several times across the room and back. The man with the bandaged head asked him how it felt.

'So far, so good,' he replied.

He sat down in the chair, just as one of the swing doors opened a crack and Nell edged into the ward. She was carrying a large carrier bag, and her face was flushed with excitement.

'I just saw Stephen!' she said. Then, coming closer, she added in a whisper, 'There's nobody about. Come on!'

He felt extraordinarily happy. She was here, his beautiful girl. Coming to take him home. He stood up, putting his arms round her, and bent to kiss her hair.

For a moment a fleeting drowsiness came back. He shook his head, and the sensation cleared.

Funny, but just for a split-second he could have sworn he smelt cloves.

Fontana Paperbacks: Fiction

Fontana is a leading paperback publisher of fiction. Below are some recent titles.

- [ ] ULTIMATE PRIZES Susan Howarth £3.99
- [ ] THE CLONING OF JOANNA MAY Fay Weldon £3.50
- [ ] HOME RUN Gerald Seymour £3.99
- [ ] HOT TYPE Kristy Daniels £3.99
- [ ] BLACK RAIN Masuji Ibuse £3.99
- [ ] HOSTAGE TOWER John Denis £2.99
- [ ] PHOTO FINISH Ngaio Marsh £2.99

You can buy Fontana paperbacks at your local bookshop or newsagent. Or you can order them from Fontana Paperbacks, Cash Sales Department, Box 29, Douglas, Isle of Man. Please send a cheque, postal or money order (not currency) worth the purchase price plus 22p per book for postage (maximum postage required is £3.00 for orders within the UK).

NAME (Block letters)_____

ADDRESS_____

_____